"*Chef's Choice* is at once an enormously fun romp of romance tropes while also being incredibly important—by turns genuinely hilarious and swooningly romantic, and all the while, unabashedly, joyously trans. . . . I am so glad this book exists."

—Anita Kelly, author of *Love & Other Disasters*

"Start with two charming, lovable main characters, add a lot of laughs, and finish with a healthy pinch of spice and you've got *Chef's Choice*. I devoured every morsel of this delicious romance."

—Amanda Elliot, author of *Best Served Hot* and *Sadie on a Plate*

"A total delight, filled with queer joy and found family and so much warmth. Luna and Jean-Pierre stole my heart. Jean-Pierre is a tour de force of grumpy depressed European queer chaos and I would personally die for him."

—Cat Sebastian, author of *The Queer Principles of Kit Webb*

"Like Luna's beloved cheese plates and charcuterie spreads, this appetizing romance has something to delight a wide variety of readers. A first choice for contemporary romance collections."

—*Library Journal* (starred review)

T0036652

PRAISE FOR *CHEF'S KISS*

"It's hard to say which aspect of TJ Alexander's novel is sweeter: the slow-burn romance or the drool-worthy desserts."
—*Time*, "100 Best Books of the Year"

"Like a dish of comfort food you'll want to devour."
—*The Washington Post*

"One of the most intricate and satisfying queer romances in years. Fans of Casey McQuiston will be wowed."
—*Publishers Weekly* (starred review)

"A luscious dessert of a novel, a romantic comedy as classic as it is modern, as satisfying as it is groundbreaking."
—Camille Perri, author of *When Katie Met Cassidy*

"An utter delight, filled with sumptuous food and adorable banter. This is the first time I've read a book with a nonbinary love interest, and I was cheering for Ray and Simone the entire time. . . . The ultimate feel-good read!"
—Jesse Q. Sutanto, author of *Dial A for Aunties*

"Brimming with delectable baking and memorable characters. . . . A sweet treat that is sure to melt your heart!"
—Farah Heron, author of *Accidentally Engaged* and *Tahira in Bloom*

"Beyond the delicious recipes and the playful banter between the charming leads is a story about the sometimes difficult realities of the queer experience, and Alexander effortlessly tackles heavier topics without ever losing sight of queer joy and the happily ever after these characters deserve!"
—Alison Cochrun, author of *Kiss Her Once for Me*

"A truly delightful debut, as queer as it is sweet. . . . This tasty, modern rom-com celebrates loving fiercely, living authentically, and eating well."

—Georgia Clark, author of *Island Time*

"Alexander whips up a delectable couple with Ray and Simone; they are each on their own journeys for self-awareness and self-confidence, which they gratifyingly achieve on an individual level. Alexander's romance confronts workplace discrimination, internal biases, and issues like transphobia and misgendering with ease. Baked to perfection."

—*Kirkus Reviews*

"A cute, romantic tale . . . For fans of *The Charm Offensive* and *Red, White, and Royal Blue*."

—*LibraryReads*, "May 2022 Top Ten Picks"

PRAISE FOR *CHEF'S CHOICE*

"Addictively fun."

—*Teen Vogue*

"Generous, tender, decadent, and sparklingly funny, *Chef's Choice* is a revelation as sublime as biting into an éclair. . . . As with a perfect meal, you'll want to savor every moment and share it with everyone you love."

—Lana Harper, *New York Times* bestselling author of *Payback's A Witch*

"TJ Alexander's witty and insightful voice, complex characters, and full-throated celebration of the joy of queer community make *Chef's Choice* a treat worth savoring."

—Ava Wilder, author of *How to Fake it in Hollywood*

ALSO BY TJ ALEXANDER

Chef's Kiss
Chef's Choice

Second Chances in
NEW PORT
STEPHEN

a novel

TJ ALEXANDER

EMILY BESTLER BOOKS

ATRIA

New York   London   Toronto   Sydney   New Delhi

EMILY
BESTLER
BOOKS

ATRIA

An Imprint of Simon & Schuster, Inc.
1230 Avenue of the Americas
New York, NY 10020

First Emily Bestler Books/Atria Paperback edition December 2023

EMILY BESTLER BOOKS/ATRIA PAPERBACK and colophon are
trademarks of Simon & Schuster, Inc.

For information about special discounts for bulk purchases,
please contact Simon & Schuster Special Sales at 1-866-506-1949 or
business@simonandschuster.com.

The Simon & Schuster Speakers Bureau can bring authors to
your live event. For more information or to book an event, contact the
Simon & Schuster Speakers Bureau at 1-866-248-3049 or visit our website
at www.simonspeakers.com.

Manufactured in the United States of America

1 3 5 7 9 10 8 6 4 2

Library of Congress Cataloging-in-Publication Data is available.

ISBN 978-1-6680-2196-5
ISBN 978-1-6680-2197-2 (ebook)

For Tony: lawyer, philosopher,
architect, and colleague

AUTHOR'S NOTE

This is a funny book with a happy ending. However, it contains some heavy subject matter, including the rise of hateful transphobic legislation; the loss of a parent in an accident, which occurs before the events of the book; discussions of racism; and alcoholism. You can find a detailed list of content warnings at tjalexander.com.

CHAPTER 1

December 15

Eli Ward counted four MAGA flags on his parents' street, and those were just the ones he could see in the dark.

They were mostly in tatters, having weathered years of Florida thunderstorms, some so raggedy as to be illegible. There were yard signs, too, one bent completely backward on its coat-hanger legs. Oh, and a couple matching bumper stickers slapped on the backs of SUVs.

In a perverse way, Eli was comforted by all this. At least those households were displaying their intentions; it was the homes with empty yards that made him wonder.

The truck trundled by a house that was positively festooned with star-spangled merchandise. Eli craned his neck to take in the scene on the driver's side. Jesus, they'd decorated the signage with red Christmas lights, giving everything a decidedly demonic cast. It wasn't the first time he'd seen a fervent display of right-wing sentiment—he'd been on the road during election season, when there were pockets of it everywhere: the Midwest, the South, Up-state New York—but it felt different here in New Port Stephen, where he'd grown up.

He glanced at his cousin in the driver's seat, but Max didn't seem to register the house, eyes firmly on the road. When had the kid gotten old enough to drive? Eli's most enduring memories of Max were from Facebook photos of a toddler picking clover. It just didn't compute with the lanky beanpole in combat boots and a billion necklaces who'd picked him up from the airport. Bit of a queer vibe, but who knew what teens were like these days. He should probably make an effort to find out, at least when it came to his own flesh and blood.

Eli cleared his throat. "So, uh, how's school going?" Great opener. He only sounded about nine hundred years old.

Max gave an eye roll because that's what teens did; it wasn't because Eli was irredeemably uncool, *surely*. "It'll be better in a few months. When it's over."

That gave Eli pause. "Wait. You're graduating this year? Seriously?"

"I'm eighteen," Max drawled, guiding the truck along a snakelike bend. "I know the Florida public school system hasn't improved much since you were in it, but they did teach me simple addition."

Eli resisted the urge to fling himself from the slow-moving vehicle to hide in a ditch, where he could spend the rest of his twilight years without being sassed by young'uns. "And how is Port Stephen Prep these days?" Seemed polite to ask, like the school was some mutual acquaintance of theirs.

"Closed. Hurricane damage." Max shrugged. "No one's sure when it'll reopen; some fight about who pays for the repairs. I might have to finish the year out at Southern."

"That sucks," Eli offered.

"Not really. It's all the same," Max said.

Couldn't argue with that. Eli looked out the window, letting his breath make a circle of fog on the glass. The house he'd grown up in finally came into view. For the first time in almost twenty years, Eli was back.

The driveway was packed with cars, so Max parked on the street. Eli took his time unbuckling his seatbelt, staring at his parents' house through the passenger window. Of all the houses he'd seen so far, it was the most decorated for the holidays. Eli's dad had always gone a little overboard with the lights back in the day, but this was something else.

Eli got out of the truck to take in the full effect of the Christmas display. Strand after strand of multicolored lights flickered in a repeating pattern. The eaves were dripping in lights, as were the azalea bushes out front. And the squat cabbage palm in the flower bed. And the mailbox. And the arch of the carport. And a million other things, probably, that Eli's overwhelmed eyes hadn't yet noticed. A half dozen holiday characters sat on the lawn, including a plastic Santa wearing a Panama hat and an inflatable Rudolph with a glowing red nose. The rest of the reindeer were represented by pink flamingos with felt antlers glued to their heads.

"Dad really went all out, huh?" he said to Max, who was getting his suitcase from the bed of the truck.

"You should have seen it a couple years ago." Max slammed the tailgate shut. "It was like Disney World. Tons of people came to take photos." A shrug. "Uncle Wen said this year he wanted to scale it back. Tasteful or whatever."

Eli watched as a robotic deer outlined in bright white lights lifted its head from the front yard's grass, swiveled it around Exorcist-style, and, apparently satisfied that no Christmas predators were close by, lowered back down to fake-eat.

"Huh," Eli said. "Tasteful." He took his suitcase from Max.

As they neared the wreath-bedecked front door, Eli could hear the clamor of overlapping voices and Christmas music. He took a deep breath and held his suitcase handle in a white-knuckled grip.

Why had he flown in tonight of all nights? He should have waited one more day. He should have found another couch to crash on. He shouldn't even be here.

No. This was going to be fine. There were worse things than a family holiday party. A party was just a performance, and he was used to performing. Sure, he hadn't actually been onstage in over a year, but it was like riding a bike. Probably. He hadn't done that in decades, so he couldn't be sure.

The door was unlocked as usual, and Eli stepped inside. He had just enough time to get a vague impression of the house: Christmas kitsch on every available surface and stuffed to the gills with people, most of whom he didn't recognize. Probably his parents' friends and co-workers. A few turned to give him polite nods, clutching their red Solo cups. Bluetooth speakers scattered around the room belted out that song that went, "So this is Christmas . . ." The John Lennon version, not Céline, because life wasn't fair.

"Eli's home!" A woman with gray-streaked hair swooped out of the throng of people, caftan flapping. Her Bakelite bangles—red and green, naturally—clinked as she wrapped Eli in a fierce hug. She still wore plumeria perfume. "You made it," Cora Ward said right into his ear.

"I made it," Eli said, hugging back with one arm. She felt smaller than he remembered. Were his parents shrinking? He certainly wasn't getting any bigger. The T had done all it was going to do at this point. He closed his eyes and tried to enjoy a moment of floral-scented comfort.

"Hey, *son*." Giddy emphasis on the *son*. Eli opened his eyes to find his dad standing by with his arms held wide. What hair remained on his head was grayer than the last time Eli had seen him last year. He wore a navy sweater vest over his long-sleeved button-down, and his glasses were horn-rimmed. His mustache was neatly trimmed, but not too thin because he felt that was the mark of a pervert, which Eli still thought about every time he trimmed his own Selleck-esque 'stache.

In short, Wendall Ward looked like a librarian because he was one. Cora had been a librarian, too, until she'd retired the year prior.

"Hi, Dad." Eli released his mom to hug him.

A flurry of activity followed.

"Where's Max? Max, get in here!"

"Close the door; the cat's been trying to get out all night."

"How was the flight? Let me take that bag—no, no, I insist."

"Was traffic bad coming up from the airport? I swear, gets worse every year. Last week—"

"My god, what did you pack? Bricks? Max, do me a favor, sweetie, put this in the back bedroom for your cousin."

"—it was shut down for four days, every single lane. That's why I always take the Turnpike."

"No, the *back* bedroom. That's the front. Wen, you can't take the Turnpike to the airport. It doesn't go to the airport."

"Yes, it does. You just have to exit before the dog track."

"Wow," Eli said in a desperate bid to interrupt their double act, "look at all these old photos, huh?" It was the first thing that caught his eye, the only thing he thought might derail another hour of patter about the Florida highway system. He slipped between his mom and dad to examine the framed photographs on the wall of the sitting room. A few partygoers obligingly stepped aside to give him a better view.

His mom took the bait. She cooed at the pictures of Eli in eighties and nineties film of varying quality. There was a second little kid in many of the photos: black hair, gangly legs, oversized T-shirt. "You two were the cutest," she said, tapping a fingernail against the glass that covered the other kid's tousled head. "Do you keep in touch at all? Facebook, that kind of thing?"

6

TJ Alexander

"No," Eli said, only half-conscious of the question. "No, I don't do social media anymore." He stared at the figure in the most central photograph. Aunt Honey and Uncle Hank's wedding. Must have been ten or eleven. Wearing a poufy purple dress. He didn't bother trying to discern a familiar nose or a tilt of the mouth. There was nothing about the kid in the picture that looked like him except the haunted look in the eyes that seemed to scream *Get me out of here*.

That, Eli could sympathize with.

"His dad's here if you want to say hello." Wendall pointed over to the family room, where a dark-haired figure was standing next to a folding table covered in finger foods, chatting with Aunt Katie. "He still lives over on Papaya."

Eli could see only the back of Mr. Wu's head, and he had no plans to see much more than that. This day was stressful enough. "Yeah, maybe later," he said.

Wendall was called away to mediate a debate between his friends, but Cora stayed right where she was, like she couldn't bear to take her eyes off Eli. She was practically bubbling over with excitement. "So how is the new job going?" she asked.

Eli cracked his neck side to side. "Oh. You know . . ." There was only so much you could say when you didn't want to say anything.

Because the truth was, there was no job.

The truth was, after having a decent career in various writers' rooms for years, all that had evaporated like so much canned milk. The truth was Eli's plane ticket had been one-way because his apartment in Brooklyn was currently home to a subletter, and Eli had no idea how or when he'd be going back. The truth was Eli was possibly stuck in Florida for the foreseeable future while he got his shit together, but if he tried to explain this to his mom in the middle of her annual Christmas party, he was going to have to tell her how he was a huge disappointment, and then she would cry, which would make his dad cry, which would make Baby Jesus cry, and Eli was going to throw up just thinking about it.

"It's going," he finally choked out.

His mom beamed at him, oblivious to his internal whirlwind. "You'll have to tell me all about it later. I'm sorry I never caught that last show you worked on, but you know how your father and I don't care for raunchy humor."

"Yeah. I know." His parents subsisted on a media diet of public radio and the odd rerun of *Antiques Roadshow*, and he didn't expect them to start watching M-rated streaming dramedies simply because their only child was writing the material.

Or had been.

Cora sighed gustily. "Working in television must be so interesting. Much more interesting than anything in our sleepy little town! I hope you don't get bored while you're here."

In the dining room, someone dropped a cup. His parents' cat—a hefty ginger named Sweet Potato (the third of his name)— tried his best to lick up the sticky concoction that had spattered onto the floor before being shooed away by the guests. Eli hoped that would require his mom's attention, but Wendall stepped in to clean it up instead.

"Hey-hey!" A meaty hand landed on Eli's shoulder, making him startle. "The prodigal . . . whatever returns."

"Son," Cora said in a singsong voice.

Eli turned to face his mother's younger brother. "Hi, Uncle Hank. How've you been?"

Hank's red face stretched into a grin. "Getting by, getting by. How's life in the big city? You doing all right in that crime-riddled hellhole?"

"Ridden," Eli's mom said. "It's crime-*ridden*. And Eli lives in a nice neighborhood, not one of the bad ones."

"Mom . . ." If he cringed any harder, Eli was going to implode.

Uncle Hank leaned in like he was imparting state secrets. "You heard about the new law they're trying to pass here?"

"Yeah, Uncle Hank. I heard," Eli said. "I don't live under a rock, so . . . yeah."

The proposed law was the subject of opening monologues on the late-night circuit, a topic of conversation for internet trolls, a headline for days when there was nothing else happening. It was the brainchild of the governor—a guy who looked like undercooked pizza dough and with a haircut to match. The poorly written law prohibited "cross-dressing" on the campuses of state-funded schools and universities, making it illegal for "biological" men to wear skirts or dresses and "biological" women to wear . . . pants. This last part, naturally, had caused so much confusion and uproar that the real issue—the fact that some douchebag in Tallahassee wanted to terrorize transgender people to the ends of the earth—was usurped by round-table discussions about women's lib that had all the relevance of moldy cave cheese. It was so depressing and predictable, it made Eli want to crawl into said cave, wrap himself around a cheese wheel, and sleep for a month.

"Ridiculous." Eli's mom clicked her tongue. "They wouldn't even be able to enforce that law."

Not its biggest flaw in Eli's opinion, but okay.

Hank pointed at her with the hand that was holding his plastic cup. "I told Honey, I said to her, I said, 'No way are they going to make my nephew wear a dress.' Not even if it's, like, a really nice dress. I'll fight 'em. Sock 'em in the mouth if they try."

"Amazing allyship, Uncle Hank, thank you. I don't plan on visiting any school campuses while I'm here, though." Eli eyed the sloshing cup in Hank's hand. Smelled like rum. "How many of those have you had, by the way?"

"Why, do you want one? I can get you one."

Cora sighed. "You know Eli is sober."

"You can't even have *one*?" Hank's eyes went wide with disbelief.

"Oh, I can," Eli said. "I'll just have nine or ten more in quick succession, and I'd rather not spend Christmas getting my stomach pumped."

It was an old punchline that Eli usually pulled out at parties. It was easier than explaining how bad his drinking had been when he first moved to New York, back in his early days on the stand-up circuit. How he'd woken up in an MRI after getting blackout drunk on two separate occasions. How his closest friend, Margo, had not-so-gently pointed out that once might be classified as a funny story to tell in greenrooms, but twice was a pattern, and he should probably talk to someone about it. How therapy had pulled off his alcoholism's Scooby-Doo mask to reveal—surprise!—repression! Gender stuff! All the things he'd been trying to avoid his entire life!

How he'd gotten sober and transitioned and pulled himself together just so he could go on Christmas vacation in a state where the leading government body was actively trying to make his life a living hell.

Yeah. Much better to tell a joke.

Eli smiled tightly. "I'm going to get some water." He gave his uncle a manful pat on his arm. "*Incredible* seeing you again, Hank," he said, putting every sense of the definition into the word.

The kitchen was crowded since that was where all the booze was. Eli squeezed between bodies and snagged a Zephyrhills bottled water from the fridge, then headed for the screened-in back patio for some fresh, albeit humid, air.

He closed the sliding glass door behind him. The sounds of

the party were muffled instantly, and the noises of the night bugs took over. Eli listened to them trill and buzz while twisting the cap off his water bottle, then gulped it down in a long series of swallows. He just needed a second to regroup, then he could continue pretending to be fine and normal.

He could feel a headache coming on.

Is it possible your guilt is manifesting physically? said a voice inside Eli's head that sounded suspiciously like the therapist he had stopped seeing when he'd lost his health insurance. *Very helpful observation, doc. Thanks for that.* He paced around the porch, finishing off his water and leaving the bottle on the table.

The sliding glass door opened, and Aunt Honey stuck her head out. The sounds of various wails floated onto the porch. "Can I borrow you?" Her soft voice held a note of resignation. "Sweet Potato got outside. We're organizing a search party."

Eli felt deeply for the cat. He also wanted to escape this party, even if it meant running into the scrub pine wilderness.

He left the porch via the screen door that led into the side yard, his aunt right behind him. Christmas lights and cell phone flashlights provided pools of illumination. Eli sensed movement on the edges of his parents' property, but he could make out only vague shapes while his eyes adjusted. The voices of the partygoers called out in different directions: "Sweet Potato! Come here, boy. Come on, Tater!"

"He's a cat, not a dog," Aunt Honey informed the person closest to her in the back flower bed. "He won't come when you call." Her tone made it clear she found this a huge defect.

"I think I found him!" someone shouted. Then: "Nope, never mind, it's a plastic bag."

"Oh, dear god." Eli rubbed his forehead with the heel of his palm. Clearly he'd picked the wrong decade to stop drinking.

A figure appeared from behind the crepe myrtles and jogged

up to him. It turned out to be Eli's dad, his glasses fogged from his exertion. "Can you give me a hand? Hank fell into the swale."

"What?" Eli couldn't hide his surprise. The swale, the gutter-like ditch that ran along the front of the properties all throughout the neighborhood to collect excess rainwater, could only be half a foot deep at the most. "Can't he just . . . stand back up?"

"Muddy patch. His foot's stuck." He grimaced. "I think he's had a few."

"You have *got* to be kidding me." Eli was tempted to suggest they leave him there for the rest of the evening, but he knew that would probably not go over well. The Ward family was famously polite in that buttoned-up, mainstream-liberal kind of way. Eli's parents had no doubt watched a PBS docuseries on the dangers of leaving uncles stuck in swales.

Several yards away, somewhere close to the street, Eli heard a collection of grunts followed by a wet pop. "Got 'im!" Max hollered into the shadows. Cries of relief came from all corners, so Max amended: "My dad, not the cat!" Huffs of disappointment from the Greek chorus. Eli's head throbbed.

Aunt Katie sauntered by with a margarita glass in hand. "It wouldn't be Christmas without Hank making an ass of himself," she muttered to no one in particular.

"Sis, can you please at least pretend to be looking for the cat?" Wendall called after her.

Eli was about to suggest opening a can of tuna when a Creamsicle burst of color rocketed out of the underbrush. Eli's dad yodeled in triumph. "There he is!" He took off running after Sweet Potato with more verve than Eli would have given him credit for. Eli stood where he was and let everyone barrel past him as they pursued the escaped cat. Too many cooks, he decided.

Eli's mother trotted up then. "Oh, there you are, sweetie."

"Here I am," Eli said, like he couldn't believe it either.

His mom smiled at him, a hint of anxiety clouding her face. "You know what? Could you do me a favor and go to the store to get more drinks? We're running low somehow."

Eli looked over at the scene still unfolding by the swale, standing on tiptoe to see over some bushes. Aunt Honey was trying to swipe the mud off Uncle Hank's pants leg and was only succeeding in spreading it along the length of his khakis. "Yeah. Somehow."

Cora followed his gaze, shaking her head. "I'd ask someone else, but everyone's either had one too many or is underage. Please?" She held out her keys, a confused jangle of novelty key rings and supermarket savings cards.

"No problem." Eli swiped the keys from her hand. Living in New York for so long meant his driving skills were likely rusty, but honestly? A fender bender sounded like heaven compared to staying at this party.

Cora bobbed her head in thanks. "There's a Wine Barn down on Route 1 where the Circuit City used to be. You know, the one they burned down for the insurance money?"

"That was never proven in court," Eli said automatically. Why was this town so goddamn weird?

His mom dug her Mastercard out of a pocket in her caftan. "Beer, wine, some of the hard stuff, mixers. Oh, and some more limes. They have everything there, so you won't need to make more than one stop. Drive safe, okay?"

"I'll be back as soon as I can." Lies. He was going to dawdle like he'd never dawdled before.

From deep in the woods out back, Eli heard the yowl of a cat who presumably had been captured by many sets of hands.

CHAPTER 2

Nick Wu stood in front of the chardonnay section of the Wine Barn with his brow furrowed and his cart empty. He'd assumed that his Christmas shopping was complete, but then his beloved restaurant staff—those fuckers—had surprised their favorite general manager with a truly dizzying array of gifts consisting of shit he did not need. What would he even do with an air fryer? Who needed to fry with air when there were three serviceable deep fat fryers down at the Thirsty Manatee that could cook high-calorie food as nature intended?

Now he was obligated to buy last-minute holiday presents for all the people who had gotten *him* a present, which was a stressful fulfillment of the social contract and yet another reason for him to consider Christmastime to be the absolute worst. Nick had intended to get this chore done earlier, but he'd been delayed at the intersection where Magnolia met Route 1 because a gopher tortoise was crossing the road. Nick had risked salmonella by carrying the reptile to the other side to save it from being flattened into a pancake by oncoming traffic.

Because he was a good guy, he reminded himself. Good guys

saved tortoises from certain death. They reciprocated gifts. They didn't have meltdowns in the chardonnay aisle seventeen minutes before closing time because they couldn't decide which bottle of wine best said *thank you for the air fryer I'll never use!*

Nick rubbed a hand over his tired face. He needed to pull himself together. The season was ramping up, with snowbirds starting to trickle down south, filling the tables at the Manatee. More business meant more work, longer hours. Though if Nick were being honest with himself, Sandra and the rest of the staff had their shifts pretty much under control. Even packed weekend dinner services were running like clockwork. The owner of the place seemed happy with the results, which was what really mattered.

But it wasn't just work that was leaving him exhausted. Juggling schedules with Laurie—Zoe's soccer practices and day care and all the stuff that came with trying to make Christmas fun for a four-year-old—was also draining. Nick couldn't even remember being four. Was Zoe really going to be emotionally stunted if her parents didn't get the requisite pictures of her on a mall Santa's lap before December 25th? Maybe she'd like an air fryer instead. Two birds with one stone.

This was getting him nowhere. Nick pushed his cart toward the sparkling section. Everyone liked bubbles, he was pretty sure. He'd grab a case of whatever mid-range bottle had the prettiest label.

His shopping cart collided with something that made a metallic clang and glassy rattle. Nick whipped his head up, realizing belatedly that he'd T-boned a fellow shopper. The guy blinked at him, his own cart filled to the brim with more wine and hard liquor than Nick had ever seen outside of the Manatee's storeroom.

"Sorry," Nick blurted out. "I was—sorry." He backed his cart up a few feet so he could maneuver around his victim, keeping his gaze down out of embarrassment. "Wasn't paying attention."

"Nick?" said the guy. "Nick Wu?"

Nick lifted his head and took a better look at him. His eyes were wide and his mouth was open in surprise. He was short, had brown hair, a mustache, about Nick's own age, maybe a little younger. He didn't look all that familiar. "Sorry, do we know each other?"

"Yeah." The guy stared at him for a long beat. "We do. We did? We do. It's—me." He pointed at his own face. "You really don't recognize this mug?" Far from being offended, he seemed delighted by the prospect. His hazel eyes were shining, a grin stretching across his lips.

"I'm really sorry, I can't place you," Nick said. He was still using his polite business voice in case the stranger was someone from the county health inspector's office. "It's been a long day. Refresh my memory?"

"Nick Not-Short-for-Nicholas-No-Middle-Name Wu," he said in an admonishing tone. The strange man's voice dropped into a register reserved for whispered secrets. "And they say you never forget your first."

Nick's brain clicked into gear. A flood of memory surged through his body. Sharing a back seat in Mrs. Cora's minivan during preschool carpools. Tramping through the woods that had surrounded his house with his best friend at his side. Laughing until he puked in a Taco Bell parking lot the weekend after he got his driver's license. Sitting in the back row of the dollar movie theater, a place that didn't exist anymore, and screwing up enough courage to hold someone's hand for the first time since they were little kids using the buddy system.

His first kiss. His first—everything.

"Oh my god. K—?" He stopped himself before he blurted

out a name that he was pretty sure wasn't currently in use. The
floor felt like it was dissolving under his feet. "Sorry! I mean . . .
Who do I mean?"

"Eli!" Eli threw his head back and laughed long and loud.
"It's Eli now. Holy shit, your face. You really went on a journey,
huh? That was wild."

"Eli." The name was new in his mouth, but it also felt strangely
fitting there. He stared at what had once been the most familiar
face in his life, now made different. Was there a trace of the old
Eli in the way he squinched up his nose? In the laugh lines around
his mouth? Nick could feel his neck getting prickly and hot; only
Eli had ever gotten that kind of reaction out of him. "I knew that.
I mean, I'd heard that. I'm not on Facebook, but Penny— You remember Penny? From middle school? We're co-workers. She said
she'd seen your posts about it. Not that you were some hot topic
of gossip or anything! And this was years ago, I think, so—"

"Yeah, I know. I was living it." Eli's smile did not abate. Now
that Nick knew who he was, he couldn't believe he hadn't realized
it before. That smile was as unique as a fingerprint with its little
curl downward at the corner. Lopsided. That's how Nick used to
think of it back when they were—

When they were kids.

Friends.

Dating.

When they were other people. People who knew each other
by the shape of their smiles.

"Wow, what's it been?" Eli said. "Like, two decades? You look
good, man."

"Thanks," Nick said in an automatic daze. "You look—" He
struggled for something to say. "Different." He shook his head.
He was messing this up. "I'm sorry I didn't realize who you were,
it's just—very different."

"Hey, no sweat. It's actually a big ego boost, you know?" Eli leaned over his stuffed cart, using that secret whisper again. "I want to look different. That's kind of the goal."

"Right. Exactly." Nick nodded a bit, then lapsed into silence. He was still having a hard time believing that this was really happening. That after all these years, he was in a wine store talking to his first—girlfriend? No, that seemed disrespectful. . . . Boyfriend? Except Nick had never dated boys. Except that he had, apparently. Retroactively.

Eli waved a hand in front of his eyes. "You okay there, bud?"

Nick blinked back to himself. "Yeah! Like I said, long day." He groped for anything normal to say and focused on Eli's jam-packed cart. "You throwing a party?"

Eli looked down at his selection of wine and booze like he'd forgotten the bottles were there. "Oh. No. I mean, *I'm* not. My mom is. I'm just doing a liquor run for her."

"Right, your parents' Christmas thing." Nick snapped his fingers. "My dad mentioned it."

"Yeah, I saw him. Well, literally saw him, period. I didn't have a chance to say hi or anything." He looked suitably embarrassed. "The cat made a break for it—long story—and then I got sent on this mission." He rattled his cart, bottles clinking. "Anything for the party people."

"Sounds like a fun time," Nick offered.

"Yeah, I guess, if you're a drinker." Eli's nose squinched tellingly.

Nick couldn't recall either of them ever drinking much during their teenage years. "Never got the taste for it?"

"Uh, no. I did. Got too many tastes, actually." Eli's smile went brittle. "Had to give it up."

"Ah." Nick gave a worried glance at the shelves that surrounded them. Bottles of premixed margaritas and piña coladas sat in rows of neon-painted labels. *Not exactly the most comfortable place in the world for a person trying to stay sober*, he thought.

Eli must have noticed his wary look. "I can be around it. It's not going to kill me to watch other people drink. It's just kind of boring."

A weak laugh left Nick. "Yeah, I was going to say—"

"That would be bad," Eli finished for him.

They stood in awkward silence for another moment. Nick wondered if now was a good time to say their goodbyes, but Eli spoke before he could broach the tried and tested *Well, I'll let you go. . . .*

"I heard about your mom," he said, gnawing on his lower lip. "I'm really sorry."

Nick's breath caught. When his mom had died six years ago, before Zoe was even born, most people didn't know what to say. She'd been walking along a newly opened stretch of road that bordered the wildlife preserve, always wanting to get her exercise in. It had been early morning, and a car hit her. The driver kept going. A year or so of stilted condolences, worthless thoughts and prayers, and then no one seemed to mention her. Even Nick's dad didn't go out of his way to talk about her or the accident anymore. The hit-and-run had been a nightmare, but the ensuing erasure of his mom was the thing that hurt the most.

Nick swallowed. "Yeah, I—thank you for those flowers." Even with the haze of funeral planning, he remembered the wreath of white mums from the Ward family and the accompanying card that contained all their names, including Eli's old one.

"Least I could do," Eli said. "Your mom was such a nice lady. Always had the best snacks."

That made Nick feel less heavy. "Remember the cake she used to make?"

"Yes! My mom called it air cake because it was so light and

fluffy," Eli said with a laugh. "Your mom would give us a slice for breakfast on the way to preschool. Fuck, she was awesome." He looked at Nick warmly. "I think about her all the time. Hope that's not weird to say."

"It's not weird. I'm—I'm glad." Nick realized that if his mom were there, she'd be chiding him to remember his manners. "You must be in town to see your folks for Christmas, right?"

Eli opened his mouth to respond, but he was cut off by the sudden appearance of a Wine Barn employee in the requisite orange vest, looking harried.

"Excuse me, gentlemen, but the store is closing."

"Oh." Nick looked around and saw that the sprawling warehouse of alcohol was completely empty except for them. He'd forgotten he was working against a ticking clock when he ran into Eli. His shopping cart didn't even have anything in it yet. "Uh—"

"I should get going," Eli said, pushing his cart carefully around Nick's. "It was good seeing you, though."

"Yeah, good seeing you." Nick turned to watch Eli and his overloaded cart trundle toward the registers, escorted by the beleaguered Wine Barn employee. Something about the line of Eli's shoulders reminded him of another time Nick had watched him walk away. Without thinking too hard about it, he called out, "We should catch up while you're in town."

Eli paused somewhere around the malbecs, the orange-vested staff member stopping alongside him with a huff. He turned to look over his shoulder, curiosity pinching his face. "Totally," he said. "We should."

"I'm running the Thirsty Manatee now," Nick said. "If you ever want to swing by."

"Wow, that place is still open?" Eli leaned one elbow on the handle of his shopping cart. "I'm impressed. Waterfront property and all, I was sure some horrible condo developer would have bought it by now."

"Nope, we're still there." Nick tried to inject some pride into this statement, but it sounded more weary. Like he wasn't talking about the bar and grill anymore. "Still . . . sticking around."

"Gentlemen, I really hate to break this up—" the Wine Barn employee said.

"Right! See you, Nick." With a wave, Eli departed, shoving his squeaky cart the final dozen yards.

Nick watched him for a moment, seeing Eli's mouth moving without hearing what he was saying to the staffer. Probably a self-deprecating apology disguised as a joke if the cashier's half smile was anything to go by. *The more things change*, Nick thought, *the more they stay the same.*

It was impossible not to notice that they hadn't actually made any solid plans to meet up. Not that Eli was obligated to. Maybe he thought it was weird for high school exes to hang out. For all Nick knew, it probably was.

Yep, Nick thought as he rushed to get all his shopping done before he was thrown out of the store. In all likelihood, he would never see Eli again.

CHAPTER 3

December 16

Eli saw Nick again the very next day.

It wasn't his fault. His parents surprised him by taking him to the Thirsty Manatee for dinner. "You always liked this place!" his mom tittered as they made the turn off the causeway, with Eli dreading every moment in the back seat. Maybe he should have mentioned running into Nick at the wine store, explained that going to the Manatee would likely make things awkward. But that would have opened up whole pallets of worms, and Eli didn't really want to get into it with his parents.

Maybe they'd get lucky. Maybe it would be so busy, Nick wouldn't even notice him.

As they walked toward the entrance, Eli's mom leaned in to stage-whisper to him, "How's it feel, being back at the old stomping grounds?"

Eli shrugged. He wasn't really sure what to say. It felt weird. Everything felt weird.

The Thirsty Manatee had always been Eli's pick for dinner if there was something to celebrate, like a straight-A report card or the end of a school year. Once they had their drivers' licenses, it was where he and Nick would go after swim practice to chow down on cheesy loaded potato skins and do their homework. It was where they'd gone for their first date after seeing *Fellowship* at the movie theater, both of them splurging on the surf and turf and making a terrible mess when it came time to crack open the lobsters. It was one of those rare places that was casual enough to hang out if you wanted to, but with a nice enough view of the waterway that it felt like a special occasion.

The restaurant itself was low and flat-roofed, surrounded by skinny palms and bushes of bougainvillea. The pink-and-yellow neon sign with the restaurant's namesake manatee was lit, and as Eli watched, the sea cow's martini glass flickered up to its mouth, then back down, over and over again. He'd always wondered how a manatee was supposed to hold a glass with its flipper. There were new touches, too, for the holidays. Thick garlands of silver tinsel outlined the glass double doors with the standard OPEN sign covered in shiny gift bows. Eli could smell the sharp tang of seaweed, not too bad, but it dug up his memory of how the waterfront stunk during low tide.

"Come on." Eli's mom threaded her arm in his and bustled toward the front doors. "I want to make sure we get a good table."

"It's six o'clock."

"Exactly!" Wendall said. "Dinner rush for this town."

They weren't wrong, as it turned out. When they pushed their way into the restaurant, Eli could see that all the tables and booths inside were occupied, with the outdoor deck beyond packed to the gills. Behind the long wooden bar that lined the far wall, he spotted a bartender with a high pony slinging margaritas onto a serving tray. The gleaming espresso machine must have been a new addition. A group of older teens in Saint Stephen County High varsity tracksuits sat in a booth, splitting an order of mozzarella sticks. Everywhere he looked, tables were loaded down with burgers, broiled fillets of mahi-mahi, baskets of crispy

conch fritters, and Eli's longtime favorite, the fried grouper sandwich on a Cuban roll. It was nice to know that, even after the
soulless national restaurant chains had swooped in to take over
the town, the Manatee was still doing a brisk business.

The sweet-faced greeter informed them that there was a high-
top available outside on the patio if they "didn't mind the chill."
Eli bit his tongue; seventy degrees was chilly here, he reminded
himself. As his parents murmured between themselves about
whether or not they should wait for an indoor table to open up,
Eli scanned the dining room for Nick. He finally spotted him in
the farthest booth in the corner, where Nick was bent over what
looked like a bunch of paperwork.

Eli's parents decided the patio would be fine. If anyone got
cold, there was a sweater in the car, Cora pointed out. As the
greeter collected some menus, Cora followed Eli's line of sight,
landing on Nick as well.

Cora squinted. She had glasses but rarely wore them when
she wasn't driving. "Honey, am I being racist or is that Nick Wu?"

Eli tried not to roll his eyes too hard. "Both can be true."

Cora ignored the potshot. "We were just talking about him
at the party. Shouldn't you go over and say hi?"

"He looks really busy," he improvised. "He probably doesn't
need me interrupting."

As the words left his mouth, Nick picked up his head and spotted Eli from across the dining room. He smiled, lifted his hand, and
made the universal signal for *come on over; your mom is about to become insufferable because she is, once again, correct.* Eli stifled a groan.

Eli's mom nudged him toward the back booth. "Looks like
he doesn't mind being interrupted at all," she said. Insufferably.
"Don't be rude, go on."

"You can meet us on the patio," Wendall said, already following the greeter toward the door that led outside.

Nick was still beckoning. Eli couldn't ignore him unless he wanted to snub him like some period-drama villain. He moved toward Nick's booth, awkwardly dodging servers and customers who pushed their chairs back without looking.

"Hey, you made it," Nick called to Eli when he was within hearing range. "For a minute there, I thought you were going to blow me off like some New York big shot."

Eli hoped his cringe was not too obvious. "No, definitely not a big shot. Not even a—" As he approached, a small, dark head peeked around the side of the booth. "Little. Shot," he mumbled as he stared at the tiny figure sitting across from Nick.

It was a kid. Wearing a cartoon dog T-shirt and itty-bitty sneakers. Feet kicking way above the floor. Staring back at Eli with a distinctly unimpressed air.

"This is my daughter, Zoe," Nick said.

"I'm going to be five in February," Zoe said. "Who are you?"

"Eli is a . . . friend, honey. An old friend of Daddy's." Nick gathered up his paperwork in a neat stack and pushed it to the side. "We grew up together."

"I'm going to be forty in July," Eli offered.

Zoe considered this with a hum. "That's old."

"You're telling me."

"Daddy is going to be forty in July too," Zoe said.

"I know. Our birthdays are only ten days apart." Their moms used to throw them a shared party to save money.

"Really?" She seemed pleased. "You're both old."

"Sweetheart," Nick said in a put-upon voice. Both Zoe and Eli turned their heads, and it was only after an embarrassing two seconds that Eli realized the appellation was not meant for him. That was another lifetime. "Can you please scoot over so Eli can sit down with us?"

Zoe groaned and flopped closer to the wall with a dramatic

flail of her arms. Eli sat down next to Nick's mini-me, still shocked at the unexpected reveal. A server arrived with a glass of ice water for Eli and a top-off from a pitcher for Nick. Eli picked up the paper-wrapped straw that the server had left without even asking—that never happened in New York these days—grateful for something to fiddle with.

"So . . ." He looked over at Zoe, who was now shredding her paper napkin into little bits, then looked back at Nick. "This is new."

Nick's lips parted. "Did I not mention I have a daughter?" He sounded honestly surprised at himself. "I could have sworn I did."

"I think I would have remembered that." Then, because even to Eli's ears, that had sounded bitchy, he added, "Then again, we were being corralled out of the Wine Barn by a disgruntled employee, so I wasn't exactly listening too closely."

"What's disgruntled?" Zoe asked, reaching as best as she could across the table, her fingertips mere inches away from Nick's red pen.

"It means grumpy." Nick plucked the pen from atop the pile of papers and handed it over along with his own intact napkin. "It sounds like a grumpy word, doesn't it?"

"Yeah, I guess so." Zoe smiled so that her nose scrunched up, then accepted the pen and paper like it was her due. "Thank you, Dad," she singsonged, then uncapped the pen and began doodling on the napkin. It looked like nothing more than a ball of squiggles to Eli's eyes, but what did he know about fine art?

"You're welcome, sweetie." It was impossible to miss the easy warmth in Nick's eyes.

Wow, he was really good with kids. This kid. His kid. Nick was good with his kid. Eli had never pictured him as a dad, let alone a good one. Probably because his most vivid memories of Nick involved making him laugh so hard he lost his lunch in a Taco Bell parking lot. Hard to take someone like that as a serious candidate for fatherhood, but now that the evidence was right in front of him, Eli couldn't deny it: Nick had grown up. Way more than Eli had, apparently.

"I'm here because someone got sick!" Zoe said.

Nick caught Eli's confused look and said, "Tonight's supposed to be my night off, but the assistant manager called out. Zoe's mom is shopping for"—he mouthed the words *Christmas gifts*—"so the munchkin is hanging out here with me."

"Oh." Eli couldn't help the instinctual glance at Nick's hands, where they rested on the tabletop. No wedding band, but maybe he just didn't like wearing one. But then why say *Zoe's mom* when you could be saying *my wife*? Was he overthinking this? He was probably overthinking this.

"Mom and Dad are divorced," Zoe said, not looking up from her tornado drawings. "That means they still love each other, but it's in a different way, so they live in different houses now. But they love me the same because that doesn't ever change."

"Thank you for that . . . backstory," Eli said.

Nick gave him a look that said, *Kids. What can you do?* "She really likes repeating things. Unfortunately." He leaned in. "So what's new with you?"

"Nothing big." Eli watched as Zoe began stabbing the red pen at her napkin to make a shower of tiny dots around the whorls. When he looked up, he saw that Nick was staring at him with the disbelief that only a cis person could have when told by a post-transition trans guy that there was nothing new in his life. He decided to stick with the basics. "I mean, no kids, no husband. Just me." That got a polite nod of interest from Nick; Eli felt the need to elaborate for some reason. "My last serious relationship only went so far as sharing an apartment. And a gym membership. Oh, and a very mean cat. The other guy kept it after we broke up." He took a big gulp of his water.

"And what do you do for work these days?" Nick asked.

Great change of subject, only marginally more embarrassing than his lack of a love life. "Started doing stand-up comedy, got a few writing gigs. Now I'm mostly working in television. Good, solid projects." Eli was glad Nick couldn't see the back of his neck. He tended to go all red and splotchy there when he was forced to bend the truth.

"Oh? Anything I would recognize?" Nick asked.

No way was Eli going to mention his last real job. "Right now I'm helping out a friend who's developing a new show. It's good. It's about a queer commune, like an ensemble thing? If it ever gets made, it's going to kill." That part wasn't a lie, at least. He had been filling the time looking over Margo's stellar pilot script.

"Wow, exciting. And you helped write it?"

Eli shifted on the squeaky faux leather of the booth. "I mostly punched up some dialogue, came up with some character sketches. Nothing major." Before Nick could ask any more probing questions, he turned it around with an interrogation of his own. "And you? You're the boss of this whole place, huh?"

"Yeah." Nick scratched at the back of his neck. "Came home for a bit after college and sort of . . ." He gestured to the kitschy manatee-themed junk that lined the walls. "Fell into this. My dad knows the new owner from back when they worked together at the power plant; heard he needed someone, liked that I was a local kid." He gave that self-deprecating shrug that Eli could pick out of a lineup. "I just stuck with it, I guess. Not nearly as impressive as working in TV."

Eli blinked. Apparently Nick was having the same reaction over the career question that Eli had had about the family-slash-relationships one. "Trust me," he said, "it's not that impressive."

Nick leaned back in the booth and folded his arms across his chest. "So how are your holidays going?"

Eli was well-practiced at hiding winces. He shoved his instinctual reaction down. "Oh, you know how it is. Christmas is always kind of a letdown when you're an adult. Nothing can compare to getting your first Huffy when you're seven." He took a sip of water. "Mom will have the whole family over for dinner, I'm sure. I'm not too up to speed on the details; this is my first time visiting for the holidays in ages. Or at all, actually."

"Wow, really?" Nick's eyes widened. "I just assumed you, uh, were still close with your family."

"We are. But they usually come to New York to visit me." Eli leaned back in the booth. "Yep. First time in a long time, being back in good ol' Neeps. Does anyone still call NPS that?"

"Not since we were young," Nick said. "You must be bored; it's not like this place compares to New York."

Eli made a face. "Now that you mention it, I am going a little stir-crazy. It's only been a day and I'm, like, climbing the walls." He paused. "No offense."

A smile lingered at the edge of Nick's mouth. He picked up his water glass and huffed a laugh into it before taking a sip.

Eli felt a thrill he hadn't experienced in a while—the rush of making Nick laugh. His specific laugh was so satisfying. It felt like slipping into an old sweater that still fit somehow, all warm and cozy. Eli used to go on for hours back when they were teens, goofing off, joking around, anything to make Nick snort. They played off each other so well in those moments. Eli the clown and Nick his straight man.

Eli dropped his gaze to the table. Nick was still very much the straight man, he reminded himself. This was not a double act. And frankly, it was weird to even entertain a passing thought that, after all this time, there was anything between them. They shared a past, not a future.

"I'm bored," Zoe declared. During the adults' conversation, she had turned boneless and was sliding under the table, only her head and shoulders remaining on the lip of the bench seat. "Can we go out on the dock? Please?"

"Honey, Daddy is still talking with Eli, okay?"

"You can talk with Eli out on the dock," Zoe said with a pout that was sadly underutilized, given that only Eli could see it from where he was sitting. He imagined, as its usual target, Nick would be unaffected anyway.

"I wouldn't mind getting some fresh air," Eli said. The dining room *was* pretty loud and crowded. "My folks got a table outside, so I need to get out there at some point."

Zoe popped back onto her seat. "See, Daddy? Eli wouldn't mind."

Nick gave Eli a look that probably meant he should have kept his big mouth shut, but Eli wouldn't apologize for teaming up with a fidgeting four-year-old. He could relate to her restlessness more than he cared to admit.

"Fine," Nick said in that long-suffering way of his. "Let's go."

Zoe cheered and clambered over Eli's lap without waiting for him to move, kneeing him in the bladder as she went. Eli stifled a loud *woof* as all the air was punched out of him. Nick gave him a bland look that said *serves you right* before following his cannonball of a daughter out onto the back patio.

One of the defining traits of the Thirsty Manatee was its dock, which stuck out into the brown water of the lagoon. Pleasure boaters and fishermen would tie up so they could enjoy a leisurely lunch before heading back out. Tonight the dock was devoid of boats, but it was still a welcoming spot for any restaurant guests who wanted to take in the scenery after their dinner.

The sun had already set—a sign of winter, even here where the air was warm and humid—but the rays of gold and pink were still painting a twilight picture of the sky. Night was creeping up in purples and blues oceanward, the first stars winking against the dark. Eli craned his head back to take it all in. You didn't get nights like this in New York. Then again, you did get decent bagels, so it all balanced out.

Zoe ran to the end of the dock at full speed, her tiny sneakers pounding against the wooden slats, lights on the heels flashing.

"Don't lean out too far, please!" Nick hollered after her. To Eli, he said in a quieter tone, "She likes to look at the fish."

"Who doesn't?" Eli smiled to himself. His eyes tracked along Nick's face. His features had sharpened in places, softened in others, but he was still recognizable as the Nick Wu he'd known. "You seem like a good dad," he said, because it was true and apparently needed to be blurted out.

Nick blinked rapidly in that way he used to when he was pleasantly surprised. "Maybe reserve judgment. You haven't seen one of Zoe's epic meltdowns yet. I'm the worst father in the world when that happens."

They meandered along the old dock, hands in their pockets. Zoe was a pink-and-blue dot in the distance. The wind picked up her hair and made it dance around her head.

"Does it feel weird to you?" Eli tipped his chin toward the end of the dock, where Zoe was sitting on the edge with her legs kicking out over the water. "Like, being a grown-up. Having a kid depend on you. Being mature."

"Well, I am pushing forty." Nick gave him an appraising glance. "You are too."

"Yeah, but I'm pushing a queer forty, which is like a straight twenty-six," Eli quipped. "I didn't come into my own until, like, five years ago. And even then, I still feel like I'm just pretending to know what I'm doing all the time."

"Oh, I promise you, I feel like I'm faking it pretty much every day." Nick dragged a hand through his thick black hair. "All adults are, even us straight ones. I bet our parents were just pretending like they knew what they were doing when we were kids."

"Really?" Eli snorted. "That's comforting." He turned to look over his shoulder. His parents were seated at their table with all of their attention on a huge platter of the Manatee's iconic pineapple pulled-pork nachos. As he watched, his mom fussed with a speck of salsa that had landed on Wendall's shirt collar, swiping at it with her napkin. They were too far away for their conversation to be heard, but Eli could fill in the blanks: Cora complaining about Wendall being a messy eater, Wendall protesting. He loved his folks, he did, but they sure were a certain way.

His gaze must have said something that Nick picked up on, because he said, "If you're ever feeling trapped at your parents' place, I can give you a ride somewhere, get you out of the house."

Eli turned back to him. "Really? You'd do that?"

"Yeah." Nick scratched his ear. "It's not a big deal. I like to go down to the beach in the mornings sometimes. Get a quick jog in before the day starts."

"Jogging? You?" Eli couldn't help but sound incredulous. Back when they were on the high school swim team, their least-favorite thing was the coach's once-a-season foray into running laps around campus. "What happened to 'swimming is the only exercise you need'?"

"That's still true." Nick bobbed his head. "But swimming is a whole thing; you need a pool and at least two hours for the changing and the workout and the showering and the drying off. After Zoe was born, a quick run was the best I could do." His lips twisted to one side. "Though I haven't made the time lately even for that, if I'm honest."

Eli grimaced. "I can't ask you to go out of your way like that."

"No, really, you'd be doing me a favor. It'd give me a reason to get back in the habit." Nick stopped in the middle of the dock and turned to face him, so of course Eli had to stop too. "I'm not offering to be polite, okay? I wouldn't say it if I didn't mean it." A glimmer of good humor reached his eyes. "I'm not like those posers you hang around with in New York City."

They shared a laugh, and Eli ducked his head so his wide smile was directed at his shoes and not his very straight ex-boyfriend. If he didn't know any better, he'd think this might be flirting. It had been a long time since he'd flirted with anyone.

"All right," he finally said once the giggle fit passed. "I'd really appreciate a ride to the beach. I'll even join you on that jog, if you don't mind me slowing you down." Eli's workout schedule had been sporadic at best lately. He didn't harbor any delusions about his land speed.

"I won't mind at all," Nick said. "Pick you up tomorrow at, say, seven?"

"In the morning?" Then, because he didn't want to lose his only chance to get out of the house without his parents, he hooked his thumbs into the back pockets of his jeans and feigned a nonchalant stance. "I mean, cool. That works."

A subtle smugness worked its way into Nick's smile. "Your folks still live in the house on Pineapple Top?"

"Yep, just around the bend."

"I live out past Palmetto, near the canal. Not far at all."

Eli nodded, mentally shaking off the dusty map of his hometown. Palmetto, near the canal. Their bus had gone along that route back in elementary school. A whiplash memory: their assigned bench seat, fifth on the right. Nick at seven years old, knees scraped up from dodgeball, showing Eli the bruise on his knobby elbow. *It really hurts, but I didn't cry.*

Eli came back to the present with a slow exhale. "Good. That all sounds good."

A small smile spread across Nick's face. "Okay, then. See you at seven. Make sure to bring a bottle of—oh." His head whipped to the side as he squinted at the end of the dock. "Excuse me."

Before Eli could even blink, Nick was gone. Like, he moved so fast he could have left a Nick-shaped dust cloud in his wake à la Wile E. Coyote. He barreled toward the end of the dock, his boat shoes slapping on the old wood. In the distance, Eli could see that Zoe had somehow climbed atop one of the pilings and was executing a dizzying series of pirouettes. Then Zoe's feet tangled and she began to falter, almost in slow motion. Eli's heart was in his throat: the kid was either going to fall several feet onto the dock, or she was going to fall much farther into the water. And who knew how rocky it was beneath the surface.

As Eli watched in horror, Zoe tripped off the piling—and right into Nick's arms.

"Whee!" Zoe squealed.

Nick set her on her feet. "Please don't climb up there, all right?" he said, but she was already scampering away to examine a bug that was inching along the dock. Nick put his hands on his hips and heaved a sigh, then glanced back at Eli.

Eli stood frozen in place with a hand pressed over his mouth in the gayest stance possible. He was pretty sure he'd just had a heart attack. Maybe a series of heart attacks. He'd witnessed Nick Wu transform into some kind of Super Dad with real swooping rescue action.

"What was I saying?" Nick swept a lock of hair off his forehead, calling down the dock to Eli. "Right. Bring a bottle of water."

The hand fell away from Eli's gaping mouth. "Seriously? You snatched your daughter out of thin air and all you've got to say is *remember to stay hydrated*?"

Nick gave a self-conscious roll of his shoulders, ambling back toward him. "I guess I've developed a sort of sixth sense when

Zoe's getting into trouble." He cleared his throat, then gave Zoe another cautious glance. She was still enamored with the beetle. "Part of the job."

Eli studied Nick's face as he watched his kid play a few yards away. There was worry in that gaze, but also pride, and fondness, and a bunch of stuff that Eli couldn't even identify. It made his whole face—already handsome—soften into something wonderfully tender.

Eli straightened with a jolt.

Oh no. Nick hadn't just grown up. He wasn't just a father. He was a Hot Dad.

Competent, nurturing . . . and hot. So hot. And still so painfully straight.

"Eli?" Nick's hand waved in front of his face. "You okay?"

He snapped back to himself. No more thinking about his former childhood friend or whatever in that context. At least not in public. "Yeah, sorry. I'm fine. Totally fine."

Nick looked unconvinced, and pointed to the restaurant's deck. "I was saying, your folks are trying to get your attention."

Eli spotted his mom and dad waving at him. Cora pointed at her menu and mouthed *time to order.*

"Right, yeah. I should get going," Eli said. "And I guess you—"

"Should get back to work." Nick walked over to where Zoe was crouched on the dock and picked her up like she was a sack of potatoes. Zoe screamed with laughter. "So I'll see you tomorrow?"

"Yeah. See you tomorrow." Eli watched Nick head back inside with Zoe squirming under his arm. His shoulders looked so broad under his plain button-down. So capable.

And Eli was so thoroughly screwed.

CHAPTER 4

The back porch was a good-enough place to make a private FaceTime call with only the night insects and the dark for company. Eli held his phone out at arm's length, trying to find an angle where the camera wasn't looking up his nose or making him look like death warmed over. It was not an easy task.

Margo picked up after a half second. "E, where the hell are you?"

"Merry Christmas to you too," he said.

"Christmas isn't for another nine days, my beautiful gentile. What's going on?" Margo's concerned face filled the screen. Her henna-dyed hair was arranged on the top of her head in a lopsided bun held in place by a chicken-patterned scrunchie, of all things. She was wearing her signature heavy eyeliner and bright pink lipstick, and her skin was dotted with flecks of sweat. Eli could see a few scattered pieces of weight-lifting equipment over her shoulder.

"Are you at the gym?" he asked, because he couldn't pass up an opportunity to crack a joke with his best friend. Only remaining friend, really. "Wow, you're already a Californian. Soon you'll be putting flax on everything and telling me how shitty the four-oh-five is."

"Don't jinx me," Margo barked. "LA is already messing with my head. Everyone smiles all the time here. It's like, fuck off, what are you smiling about? The world is ending in fifteen years and we're all going to get cancer."

She was on the West Coast to pitch the mockumentary-style comedy that Eli had given her a handful of notes on. It was called *Friends of Dorothy*, with Margo herself playing the titular Dorothy. The story followed an ensemble cast of queer people as they attempted to form a commune in rural Washington state. It had all the small-town charm of *Schitt's Creek* and the bizarre goofiness of *What We Do in the Shadows* with the added bonus of characters handcrafted to be played by some of Margo's favorite queer and trans actors. Eli knew the concept was strong, but he had a hard time believing it would ever get off the ground. The really good stuff never did, in his experience. Maybe the bigwigs were taking her seriously, if they'd asked her to come all the way to Hollywood for a meeting. Or just feigning progressiveness; it was hard to say.

"But what the fuck's up with you?" she demanded.

Eli couldn't help but smile at Margo's familiar brusqueness. She was older than Eli by ten or twenty years, although Eli had never had the courage to ask for a number. Margo was old-school, a force of nature the likes of which most comedians only dreamed of becoming. She could stalk out onstage and have the whole audience eating out of the palm of her hand in ten seconds flat. As an opening act, she was legendary. As a headliner, she was fierce. And she'd been doing it since the nineties, when lesbian comedians weren't supposed to be out, let alone killing it.

Back when Eli had first moved to New York to work the stand-up circuit, she had taken him under her wing. "We gals have to stick together," she'd said, which, at the time, had not been inaccurate. Eli had been performing under a different name then, and a different gender, doing jokes about being a woman that never felt right in his mouth. But after he came out—Margo hadn't cared. She'd just stabbed her Virginia Slim into an ashtray and said, "You'll need a new act, huh? So let's start writing."

She'd been there through the whole thing: attended his first AA meeting with him, made sure he wasn't skipping his therapy appointments, helped him pick out big boy clothes that actually fit. She was like his fairy godmother and drill sergeant, all rolled into one.

Eli sighed and rubbed a hand over his face. Margo knew him too well. Well enough that he couldn't keep putting this off. Besides, she was the only friend left standing in his corner. No one else would even reply to his texts.

"I'm in Florida," he said.

Margo's eyebrows rose high enough to disappear beneath her sweaty bangs. "Why?" she said, like the very notion offended her.

"Christmas. Family. You know." Eli swept his arm around, using his phone's camera to capture all the strands of lights and tree-shaped cutouts that adorned even the back porch.

"But you never go back home. Not even for the holidays." Margo frowned on the screen. "You're not giving up or something, are you?"

Eli ignored that question. "Hey, have you ever run into an ex and thought, damn, if I had just held on to him for twenty years and if he was at all gay, I'd be sitting pretty?"

"Eli—"

"Because the wildest thing happened. Ran into my old boyfriend from high school. Well, childhood best friend. Both. He was both."

"E."

"He got hot, Margo. I mean, he was pretty cute back in the day, but it was the nineties, so no one looked *great*. Baggy clothes and wallet chains, bleh. Now he's got this whole top-tier DILF thing going on, and I'm like, maybe . . . ?" He pulled a face like he was thinking deeply about his prospects, then shook his head. "But nah. You've never met a straighter man. Nick's like a ruler in human form."

"Eli, are you lusting after your painfully unattainable ex-boyfriend instead of confronting the reality of your unemployment?" Margo's face was like a hatchet, and her eyes were twice as sharp.

He fixed his gaze on the corner of the porch ceiling, where a few spiders were hanging out in messy webs. Looked like they'd caught some gnats or something. Good for them, being productive. *Couldn't be me*, Eli thought miserably.

Ever since he'd lost his job as a story editor on the long-running comedy series *Beck's Call*, Eli had been struggling to find work. It had come to light that the star of the show, a middle-aged white comedian named Winston Beck, had been strong-arming production assistants into giving him "massages" to help with his "stress." It had apparently been going on for the entirety of the show's run, and probably would have continued forever if one of the women hadn't come forward. She'd been nineteen at the time. Nineteen!

Eli was still sick to his stomach over the whole thing. In hindsight, Beck's shitty attitude toward the women on staff and his tired jokes about heterosexual sex made a lot more sense. But working alongside the guy over so many years, Eli had never once thought he might be a straight-up abuser. Eli knew better than most just how much bullshit women in their industry had to put up with—he had put up with it, too, before he transitioned; now he put up with entirely different bullshit—so he was doubly responsible for not noticing. How could he have missed all those red flags? How could he have allowed this to happen right under his nose?

In fact, so many people were demanding to know the answer

to those questions that he'd deleted his social media accounts. There had been some really vivid descriptions about ways Eli should be murdered, too, which weren't technically death threats under the Terms of Service. So that was fun.

Didn't matter now. *Beck's Call* had been canceled in the middle of filming its eighth season, and Eli was no longer needed to write the jokes that Winston Beck would deliver as his own. Eli and the other comedians in the writers' room were not having much luck landing new gigs—one dude named Geoff managed to snag a spot on a kids' show, but as far as Eli knew, the rest of them were still shit out of luck. Blacklisted to hell and back for even being associated with Beck's monstrous behavior. Eli was all for consequences, and he didn't want to be That Guy who whined about getting caught in the line of fire, but he couldn't help but notice there didn't seem to be too many consequences for Beck himself. He was still in the news occasionally, spotted eating dinner with women who were not his wife and generally living large. Like nothing had happened.

He swallowed and pursed his lips. "Look, I thought you'd get a kick out of this story, but if you'd rather not hear it—"

"I'd rather you tell me what's really going on with you," Margo said. "Have you heard back from the dating show people?" Eli had applied to an open position writing copy for a reality show; that was how desperate he was getting.

He shook his head. "Ghosted. Just like all the others." He winced as he prepared to tell Margo something he hadn't told anyone. "I sublet my apartment for a month. Figured while I'm down here anyway, no sense in paying the rent myself."

Margo's eyes bugged out of her head. "You're staying in Florida for a whole month?"

A whippoorwill started chirping somewhere in the dark brush, loud enough to make Eli jump an inch out of his chair.

Did nature have to be so loud? And so late at night? He took a second to calm down before focusing back on Margo.

"Possibly longer. I haven't made any firm plans," Eli said. He started chewing on the tip of his thumbnail, a nervous habit he used to have as a kid that had only recently resurfaced.

"What do your folks say about all this?" Margo asked.

"I—" Eli worked his tongue around in his dry mouth, then glanced through the sliding glass doors to see if anyone was listening in, but his parents had gone to bed at ten and didn't seem to be stirring whatsoever. All the house lights were off, and nothing was moving, not even the cat. "I haven't told them about it yet."

Margo's face collapsed. "Dude."

"I mean, they know about the show getting canceled. But I kind of . . ." He went back to his thumbnail again, giving it a solid bite before saying, "I let them think I found a new gig."

"So you lied."

"I declined to correct false theories."

"Oy vey." On the tiny phone screen, Margo pinched the bridge of her nose.

"It's not a big deal. They're thrilled that I'm here. I could stay until Valentine's Day and they wouldn't bat an eye. Besides," he said with a sigh, "they think I'm some big-shot funnyman who has New York at his feet. I'm the one person in the family who *made it*."

"You mean made it out of that shithole town," Margo said with her trademark dryness.

"Same difference." Eli's shoulders slumped. What kind of loser came crawling back to his hometown like this? It felt like he was right back at square one, like nothing he'd done with his life up to that point meant anything at all. *God, Mom would be so disappointed*. "I can't tell them. Not right now. It would ruin Christmas."

"Right. Your most sacred of commercialized holidays." Margo rolled her eyes. "Yeah, wouldn't want to sully your celebration of a teen mom."

"I know. We goyim have issues," Eli said. "At this point, I would take anything. A kids' cartoon, a movie punch-up . . . hell, I'll even write speeches for the governor of Florida if it'll pay the bills."

"Isn't he the one who said women can't wear pants anymore because the devil will turn them gay or something? The women, not the pants."

"The very same."

She gave him a concerned half smile. "Well, fingers crossed I sell this pilot," she said, "then you'll at least get a writing credit out of it."

"I barely helped you with the script," Eli said. "You don't need to throw me a pity cred."

"You created, like, at least three of the main characters out of whole cloth! You stayed up late helping me break the entire arc of season one! You're not a pity cred, E," Margo said, "you're practically my coproducer."

Eli bit back a sigh. "Sure. Yeah." He was certain Margo was exaggerating his contributions just to make him feel better. She never let him wallow for long.

Margo looked like she was going to keep on him about *Dorothy*, but thankfully she moved on. "Maybe this is a good time for you to take a crack at a new act. Do you have anything cooking?"

Eli resisted the urge to fling his phone through the screen porch's mesh and into his mom's flower beds. Even before he'd lost his job, Margo had been on his ass about writing new material for himself. Truth be told, he hadn't done any stand-up in an entire year and had no real plans to get back into it. Life had been busy; he'd thought he was in a good place financially with his writing jobs; and if he was honest, he was starting to think his well had run dry. His stand-up used to be the thing that drove him, the reason he'd taken writing gigs in the first place. Now, Eli wasn't sure he had anything new to say. The thought of getting back onstage made his skin prickle.

"I've been noodling around with a couple things," he finally said. Lied. When it came to people he didn't want to disappoint, Margo was a close second behind his parents.

"Well, concentrate on that while you're banished. Oh, and check your email later. I'm going to send you some rewrites for the pilot script. Can you look it over for me?"

"Of course." Eli bobbed his head. He didn't mind giving Margo notes. He owed her way more than that, so it was the least he could do. "All right, my whining time is officially over. Tell me all about LA. How many vegans have you seduced since you arrived?"

Margo lit up, her whole face glowing. "Zero. Too busy working. Listen, I think the people at the network really like me. I've got another meeting with them on Monday, and then another with the financial team after Christmas. That's serious, right? You don't involve money people unless you're really excited about an idea. That's what Gerald keeps saying."

Eli hummed in agreement, although he silently wondered if Margo and her agent, Gerald, were only seeing the best in the situation. The pilot script was really good, but in Eli's experience, it didn't matter how wonderful the concept was, or how clear Margo's artistic vision would be: people like Margo, like him, never caught a break.

That was just how the business worked. Other comedians—thinner, straighter, less-funny comedians—got pilots greenlit all the time. Well, maybe not all the time, but way more than people like Eli and Margo did. There were probably hours-long meetings happening right now over whether or not Margo was too old to play the lead—even though she couldn't be much older than Winston Beck.

"Just don't get too comfortable out there," Eli said, trying for a light tone. "The East Coast can't function without you."

Margo blew a raspberry at him. It was her mature poise that he'd always admired. "Screw you, Ward. God forbid I actually be positive about something for once. You weren't in the room with them; they were falling over themselves for *Dorothy*."

"I just don't want you to be disappointed, is all."

Margo flipped him off. "Get your own shit together before you comment on mine. And tell your parents what's going on with you before they hear it from some dude subletting your place." She moved the phone so close to her face only one flashing eye was visible. "And for fuck's sake, don't get sidetracked by some old high school flame. Focus on your future."

"Great pep talk, coach," Eli muttered.

"What was that?" Margo cupped a hand to her ear. "'Thank you, Margo Kaufman, for making sure my head stays out of my damn ass? For taking time out of your busy star-fucking schedule to listen to me complain? Especially when you've got so much on your plate with this pitch?'" Her voice rose until it was a high, dog-whistle whine.

Eli couldn't help but laugh. Even when she was giving him shit, Margo was still one of the funniest people in the world. And she was sticking by him through thick and thin—more thin lately—which he couldn't say about anyone else.

"Okay, okay." He gave the camera a wave. "I love you too."

"Love you. Bye," she said before disconnecting the call.

Eli took out his earbuds. Margo was right. Getting all excited over reconnecting with Nick was an exercise in futility. It wasn't like his attraction would ever go anywhere. What was the point of drooling over some straight single dad? Tomorrow, he resolved, he would be a normal person. Going for a normal jog. With another normal person. While they were both being super normal.

He went inside to see if there were any more spritz cookies in the kitchen.

CHAPTER 5

December 17

Nick kicked off his sandals and left them with the other abandoned shoes at the base of the boardwalk stairs. He dug his toes into the sand, still cool this early in the morning. The two bottles of water he'd brought—because of course Eli had forgotten to bring one as instructed—got driven into the sand next to his sandals; hopefully they'd still be cold when they returned from their run. He scanned the length of the beach, noting a few pairs of old folks getting in their morning walk before it got too warm out, a couple surfers, fishermen. Gulls swarmed above them, no doubt looking for bait. It was a peaceful scene, no sound except for the birds and the regular whoosh of the waves lapping at the sand.

It was also an increasingly unfamiliar one. How long had it been since he'd made time for a morning run? He always felt good afterward, but getting himself out of bed early enough to do it—especially if his insomnia was acting up—was a massive chore. Maybe he'd make a New Year's resolution to get back into doing it daily. Or at least three times a week. Mondays and Fridays for sure, to start.

"So," Eli said as he sat on a sandy step and unlaced his own sneakers, "how far are we thinking? A mile? Two?"

If Nick tried to jog for even half a mile, he was sure he would collapse. "Let's just play it by ear," he said, neatly dancing around the question.

"Sure." Eli bounced to his now-bare feet. He scrubbed a hand through his bedhead as he surveyed the lay of the land. "It's nice out here."

"Yeah." Nick made a visor out of his hand to shield his eyes from the sun, watching a sailboat a few miles offshore. "Way nicer than the beach at the other end of the island. You know, the one where all that cocaine washed ashore about eight years ago?"

"I remember that being in the news," Eli said. "It's always something around here, huh?"

"Yeah. We don't go to that beach anymore." He braced his hands on the side of the wooden staircase and started stretching out his calves. "Let's get going soon. I need to warm up; it's so chilly."

Eli made an attempt to stretch his quads, wobbling a little in the sand. "It's seventy-eight degrees."

"Yeah." Nick switched legs. "Like I said. Chilly."

Right on schedule, Eli's nose wrinkled. He grabbed the hem of his T-shirt. "I'm already sweating. I'm going to leave this here." He lifted his shirt over his head, popping back into sight with even more bedhead than before. Even his mustache was rumpled. Nick pretended to be preoccupied with watching two older ladies speed-walking by with tiny weights in their hands. Seemed like a better place to look than at Eli. He didn't want to stare. He understood, on some level, that Eli being bare-chested wasn't scandalous now that he was—Eli. Not that anyone being bare-chested was scandalous. Was not looking weirder?

Eli's voice piped up from behind him. "You don't think anyone will steal my extremely stylish AIDS Walk 2015 T-shirt, do you?"

Nick turned and watched Eli drape the shirt over one of the handrails on the stairs. He was surprised to see no visible scars on Eli's chest. No, wait—there were some faint lines under his pectorals that Nick probably wouldn't have noticed otherwise. He'd been expecting—he wasn't sure what, actually. Something more obvious, maybe.

"I think your shirt is safe. Like the shoes," he said.

"Cool." Eli pushed a flop of hair out of his eyes, looking up and down the beach. "So. Which way?"

They started jogging north. The pace was relaxed for Eli's comfort—and because Nick hadn't exercised in weeks and needed to ease into it, not that he'd ever admit that. For a few minutes, they didn't speak, just breathed in tandem. Side by side, footprints pressing into the wet sand, freezing waves sometimes washing up to their ankles.

"Still cold?" Eli panted as they passed a fisherman. "We can move up to the dry sand. If you want."

"I'm good." It was about ten times harder to run in the powdery sand above the waterline, and Nick was already struggling. "Hey, remember—when we'd have—swim team—practice—early in the mornings? When it was—so cold out—you could see your breath?"

Eli groaned. "Coach would make us jump into the water off the blocks. No easing into it."

"You would scream."

"Well, it was torture." Eli rolled his eyes as he smiled. Another old habit that had Nick rocketing back into the past. "You tried to be so Zen. 'Imagine the Sahara. Pretend it's a hundred degrees out and all you want is cold water.' That never fucking worked."

"I was—an annoying little prick," Nick said. He looked out over the water again, scanning for swimmers and finding none. "Being on the swim team—was great exercise, though. Best shape of my life. Won't ever—have abs like that again."

Eli cast a glance in his direction, eyes flickering down to where his middle was covered by his worn T-shirt. "You didn't exactly let yourself go." Then, before Nick could even register the compliment, Eli faced forward and added, "Why don't you get back into it? You live on a peninsula surrounded by water; there's a pool in every other backyard. Can't be too hard to figure out."

"Maybe someday—I can find the time," Nick said. He jogged around a hole in the sand dug by a spirited dog. "How about you?" he asked, turning it around on Eli instead of explaining how he was too old and busy to do things like swim anymore. "You ever get a few laps in—at the gym or whatever?"

Eli made an incredulous noise in between puffs of breath. "A pool? In Brooklyn? Forget about it. And anyway—" He waited for a particularly strong wave to finish washing over their feet, splashing up toward their knees. "I'm not exactly eager to revisit my swim team days. It left me with a lot of hang-ups, you know?"

Nick whipped his head to the side to stare at Eli's profile. "Hang-ups? Really?" In his memory, Eli had been brimming with self-confidence when they were teens. He'd been—Nick tried to think of a more respectful phrase but couldn't—downright stunning.

Which he almost certainly shouldn't be thinking about.

Some of his internal realizations must have shown on his face, because Eli laughed at him. "Yeah, can't really hide much in those skimpy suits they put us in. Being on the girls' team while actually being a boy was a real trip."

Nick stopped jogging for a second, panting for breath with his hands on his hips. Honestly, he really needed a break; his knee was complaining loudly. But a serious topic like this was a good excuse to stop moving. "I had no idea," he said. "You never—there was never a conversation. About what you were going through."

Eli slowed to a stop as well. He looked winded, too, thank god. He placed his folded hands on the top of his head, an old trick they'd done at swim practices to lower their heart rates. "I didn't have words for what I was going through. I wouldn't have known what to say." He exhaled, facing the sea like he was looking for something out on the water. "I wasn't hiding it from you. I just didn't know."

"I didn't mean for that to sound accusatory. I—" Nick struggled to find the words. *I wish things could've been different.*

But before he could figure out what to say and how to say it, Eli pointed to some dunes in the distance. "Hey, isn't that where we used to make out?"

Nick blinked. "Huh?"

"Yeah, I recognize that condo down where the coastline curves. Is this—?" Eli turned to him with a wicked grin. "Wait a minute. This is *our* beach, isn't it?"

Nick could feel the heat of embarrassment crawling through his belly. Holy shit, this *was* their beach. The same beach they visited at night back when there was nowhere else to go for a few hours of kissing. Fuck, had he really brought Eli to the same place where they used to mess around as teens?

"I, um—I honestly forgot," Nick babbled. "It wasn't like—I come to this beach to run because it's so much nicer than the other one. The cocaine one. I'm not, like, reminiscing or whatever. Seriously."

Eli gave him a light punch in the arm. "I was that unmemorable, huh?"

Now that Nick was thinking about it, he couldn't believe he'd forgotten. The memories were as crisp and clear as if it had all happened yesterday. The way it felt to kiss this person he'd been in love with for years and finally, finally getting to do it as much as they wanted. Overheated skin on skin, sand in awkward places, not caring because it all seemed so important and heightened and necessary. Losing a shoe in the dark of the dunes and driving them home barefoot, holding hands atop the gearshift of his first car.

"No," Nick said, voice strangled. "I remember."

Eli's face fell. He dropped his gaze somewhere on the lapping waves. "Ignore me, okay? I didn't mean to make you uncomfortable."

"I'm not uncomfortable," Nick said, even though it wasn't strictly true. It wasn't that he didn't want to be reminded of the old days, he just wasn't sure he was allowed to think of them.

"It doesn't make you gay." Eli dragged a hand through his sweaty hair, but it just flopped back into place. "The fact that you dated me back then. It really doesn't. Just like dating you didn't make me a straight girl."

Nick hadn't even thought of that. Now that Eli mentioned it, it seemed like a strange thing not to think of in this situation. "No, I know."

"We were just kids, right? Nothing you do before the age of thirty even matters." The smile was back on his face, but in a brittle way that made Nick sad.

It mattered to him. Eli had been his first kiss. His first dance. His first date. His first love. Maybe it was just the holidays making him maudlin, maybe it was just Eli's sudden reappearance in New Port Stephen, but when Nick thought about those firsts now, his stomach swooped all over again. Was it normal to care about those things still? He wondered if Eli would want him to let all those memories go, to forget what they'd been to each other. He didn't want to ask.

Then Eli broke into a grin and started jogging backward. "Hey, remember when we were here that night, it was clearly about to rain, and you kept saying, 'It's going to rain,' and I kept saying, 'Nah, it's going to pass over us; we'll be fine' because I was so horny and didn't want to stop making out, and then that state trooper showed up with the flashlight, and I had my top off and you had your dick out—"

"You almost got me arrested." Nick laughed to himself, hoping the scandalous story wasn't being carried on the sea breeze to anyone's ears.

"—and then it started fucking pouring and we all ran to our cars?" Eli let Nick catch up to him before facing forward so they were running side by side once more. "Good times."

"My first brush with the law was a good time?" His voice went all arch and high at the end.

"Oh, Nicholas." The old nickname Eli used to tease him with, because Nick wasn't short for anything. "You haven't changed a bit."

Nick couldn't decide whether to take that as an insult or not. "I've changed some," he muttered.

Eli got quiet then, gazing ahead at the empty stretch of beach ahead of them. "I mean, yeah, some. You've got a kid, you're older—we all are. I just meant the stuff that makes you *you* hasn't changed."

That piqued Nick's curiosity. "Like what?"

Eli shrugged. "I don't know. Being hilarious. Getting grumpy about the times you were right." He turned and gave Nick a knowing look. "Giving an old friend from way back a ride out to the beach because you can tell how much his family is driving him up the wall. That stuff."

An old friend. Nick rolled the phrase over in his mind. It wasn't inaccurate—they'd been friends before they'd been a couple, and for way longer—but still. Something about it felt off. Like Eli was giving him an out he hadn't asked for.

"Well," he said as they jogged, "it's nice to see you haven't changed that much either. You're still trying to be funny."

"*Trying?*" Eli sounded mock-hurt.

"It's comforting," Nick said pleasantly.

Eli rammed his shoulder into Nick's, nearly upending him into the surf. Their laughter echoed as it hit the dunes.

When they eventually turned back to the stairs where they'd left their shoes, Nick was struck by the realization that he didn't want their morning together to end. He was having fun. For the first time in a long time, he was enjoying himself.

Guilt immediately swamped him. He had fun with Zoe, he really did. She was the best thing in his life. Everything else should be a distant second. Right?

"This was nice," Eli said as they crossed the last few yards of sand. He sounded sincere, even wistful. "I'm glad I came."

Nick looked at him, taking in his mustache and freckles at the corners of his eyes, and the way he squinted as he cast his gaze over the now-busier beach. He looked so good. Better than Nick had ever known him to be. Almost like the person Nick had grown up with had finally grown into himself.

He pushed down the guilt and went with his first impulse.

"Do you need to go home right away?" he asked.

Eli turned to him. The wind lifted the hair at the back of his head, making a mess of it. He looked intrigued. "No. Why?"

"I have plans with Zoe later this morning. Kayaking. Why don't you come with us? It'll keep you out of the house for a few more hours." He could feel his heart rate picking up. *Please say yes.*

Eli's face went through a series of thoughtful scrunches. "I wouldn't want to horn in on daddy-daughter time." Even as he said it, Nick could hear that he was just being polite.

That riled him up. Here they were, two people who'd grown

up together, who knew each other better than anyone else in the world, and they were pretending that etiquette mattered?

"It would be fine. Seriously. Zoe's been asking a thousand questions about you ever since you showed up at the restaurant last night. She'd be thrilled to see you again."

Eli shook the sand out of his shoes before slipping them back on. "You're sure?"

"Absolutely." Nick plucked his shirt off the rail and handed it to him.

"Then yeah. Let's go kayaking." Eli stuck his head through the tee, popping back into view with a smile on his face. "This is the most active day I've had in my adult life. Exciting!"

Nick grinned at his enthusiasm, shaking his sandals out before putting them on. He was about to put a light hand on Eli's back to guide him up the wooden steps—something he'd done a thousand times when they were younger—but then he realized that it wasn't a normal gesture for two guys, and he dropped his arm with a quickness.

He cleared his throat and headed up the steps first, listening to Eli clattering up behind him.

CHAPTER 6

The river contained a lot less wildlife and a lot more trash than Eli remembered.

He stood where the cement boat launch met the murky brown water and watched as a Doritos bag floated by, just missing a flotilla of bobbing soda bottles. What had happened to all those childhood lessons they'd been quizzed on at school? Reduce, reuse, etc.? Maybe society really was going to hell in a handbasket. Or maybe the local river had always been kind of trashy, and it was Eli's memory that was faulty.

"Excuse me a second." Nick squeezed past him, then stooped to fish the trash out of the water with his bare hands.

"Whoa! Don't touch that stuff." Eli shrank back, fearing river water splatter. "You could get some weird garbage disease." He could see the headline now: *Florida Man Discovers, Dies from Rare Bacterium*.

Nick looked over his shoulder with the same air as someone who meant to tidy up a house before guests came over, chagrined but determined to fix the misstep. "I'll be fine. There are wet wipes in the car. I've got a four-year-old, remember?" He held the various pieces of dripping refuse away from himself and walked off toward a trash barrel.

Zoe, who had been poking a stick into the dirt in the gravel parking lot, gave up on that and skipped over to Eli. Her shoes had purple flowers on the toes, and the backs lit up in bright fuchsia every time she took a step.

"Cool shoes," Eli said.

"Thanks." She pushed her hair out of her face and peered up at him expectantly.

How were you supposed to make conversation with a little kid? Eli had no experience in this arena. "Did, uh, your dad buy them for you?"

Zoe nodded gravely.

"Yeah. That makes sense. I mean, it was either your mom or your dad. Unless you, like, found them. Or stole them." Eli winced. "Not that you would steal anything! I'm sure you're a good kid."

She stared at him some more, her eyebrows knitting together in bewilderment. Eli started to wonder if this was a good idea after all. He knew basically nothing about children. And it had been ages since he'd been in the great outdoors. This outing would have him dealing with both, possibly for hours. Why had he ever agreed to this?

Oh, right. Because he was a loser who couldn't say no when Nick offered to spend more time together.

That morning at the beach—it had felt so familiar, whiling the time away with Nick. He could still make Eli laugh better than anyone else in the world, even Margo. Nick had always been a magnet for Eli; when they were kids, all he wanted to do was spend time with him. He could remember inhaling his dinner so he and Nick would have more time to play in the woods before sundown.

Nostalgia was a hell of a drug. That was all this was. Memories gone mad. Reminiscing gone rampant. The past gone—

"Or my grandma," Zoe said out of nowhere, breaking Eli from his thoughts.

He blinked down at her. "Huh?"

"Grammy Kay. I have two grandmas. Ah Ma is gone, but Dad says she loves me no matter where she is. Grammy Kay is still here. She could have bought these for me."

"Oh." Right. They were discussing Zoe's footwear. "I didn't think about that."

"That's okay. Grammy is kind of—" Zoe looked back at where Nick was scrubbing his hands with a wet wipe. She turned back to Eli and dropped her voice to a whisper. "A pill."

Eli's eyes almost bugged out of his skull. Yaaaas, drama. More of this, please. "She is?"

Zoe nodded some more. "Mommy says not to say so out loud, though. You won't tell on me, will you?"

"I would never." It wasn't a lie. Eli loved to gossip, but he also knew the importance of keeping a secret. "What makes her a pill?"

"She hates fun. When she saw these"—she marched in place to set off another light show—"she said I looked like I was from the red-light district."

Eli choked on his own spit. He bent at the waist, trying to catch his breath. "Uh, you know what a red-light district is?" he struggled to say once his pipes were clear.

Zoe shrugged. "Someplace where they keep lights on all the time, I guess."

"Right. That's—yep, that is exactly correct."

"I don't know why that's such a bad thing. Do you?"

"Well." Eli thought fast. "I live in a city where they keep the lights on all the time. Some people don't like it. They think we're all hoity-toity types."

"What's hoity-toity?"

"Like when someone is fancy and kind of a"—*don't fucking curse in front of the small child*—"silly Billy about it?"

Zoe chewed on her lip in thought as she gave Eli another once-over. "Yeah," she finally said, "Grammy probably would call you hoity-toity."

Eli couldn't help it. He threw his head back and laughed. This kid was funnier than most of the professional comedians he had worked with, no contest. "How am I hoity-toity?"

"Your hair," she said matter-of-factly. "It's fancy. Like, too fancy."

Eli gasped, his hand flying to the back of his head. "I'll have you know—okay, yes, I did pay way too much for this haircut." His barber was on the Lower East Side and charged about four times the going rate, but the staff went out of their way to never misgender him. Eli had been willing to spend the money for that alone.

"My mom cuts mine," Zoe said reasonably.

Eli examined the careful line of her bangs with a critical eye. "It looks good."

"Do you want her to cut yours?"

He propped his hands on his hips, delighted with her moxie. "How did we get onto this topic?"

"My shoes." Zoe stomped one tiny foot. Her heel flashed.

"Good memory."

Nick finally returned, waving his hands like fans through the air to dry them. He lit up just like his kid's shoes. "I bought her those," he said with naked pride.

Zoe huffed. "I already said that, Daddy. You were over by the trash, so you didn't hear."

"Well, thank you for bringing me up to speed." Nick turned. Eli could see himself reflected in Nick's mirrored sunglasses. "Want to give me a hand?"

Right. They were here to kayak, not banter with a four-year-old with better comedic timing than most. He helped Nick unlash the bungee cords that held the kayak to the roof of his van, and together they carted it and the oars to the water.

It was a three-person kayak—an artifact from his marriage, Eli guessed—with two deep seats molded in blue plastic and a smaller space up front for Zoe. As Nick got her settled, Eli fumbled his way into his own seat, consoling himself with the idea that surely no one looked cool trying to get into or out of a tiny boat. Eli took up the middle position and put his feet in the footwells ahead of him. As he did so, it became clear to him that he would essentially be sitting in the V of Nick's legs. So that was happening.

Zoe turned around and waved frantically at him. He waved back weakly. In addition to being in closer quarters with Nick than he'd initially expected, it dawned on Eli that if Zoe tried to lean out of the kayak, he was the closest adult. Mental drills went through his head as he pictured just how fast he'd need to grab the back of her life jacket. Holy shit, how did parents handle this on a daily basis? They hadn't even left the dock and Eli was already sweating with the responsibility.

"Okay, Zoe, stay low," Nick said as he stepped smoothly into the kayak. Eli twisted his head around to watch in consternation. Apparently, there *was* a way to do it like a suave motherfucker, and Nick had perfected it. Annoying.

Eli faced forward again and tried to ignore Nick's sandals coming into view as his feet settled on either side of Eli's thighs. He swallowed hard. If his mind would heft itself out of the gutter, that would be ideal. It wasn't like they were squished together or anything; there were several inches of space between them. But it was still hard to ignore the fact that, if Eli leaned back just a little, his head would be resting against Nick's chest.

Nick tapped Eli on the shoulder, making him almost jump out of his skin. "Ready to get going?"

"Y—" Eli cleared his throat. "Yep!" He took the dual-lightsaber-style paddle that Nick handed to him. "Zoe, you ready to be our lookout up there?" he said.

Zoe turned around and gave him a very serious salute. Dear Lord, this kid was the funniest person on the planet. Eli saluted her back.

Nick gave a gentle push with his own oar on the side of the dock, and off they went. It took Eli a few minutes of Nick's patient coaching to understand paddling in tandem, but he soon got the hang of it. He just hoped his arms held out; his lats were already burning. Not to mention the heat of Nick's legs snug against his hips was driving him to distraction.

The river was a brackish vein that snaked its way through black mud, lined with tangles of mangroves and bunched clusters of cabbage palms. Here and there a scraggly pine or a stately cypress poked out from the tree line. The huge blue of the sky and its puffy white clouds were reflected almost perfectly in the river water, disrupted only by the occasional flop of a fish or skim of a white egret.

They paddled along quietly, the silence thickening as they got farther away from the park and the traffic on the bridge.

Zoe twisted around to face Eli. "Have you ever seen an alligator?"

"Sure. Tons." It was hard not to when they got into every canal, lake, and deepish ditch.

"Have you ever seen one eat someone?"

"Uh. No." Eli twisted around to give Nick a look. He hoped Nick could interpret the *what the fuck?* raise of his brows.

Nick rolled his eyes. "Zoe wanted to swim in the river last year, so we had to explain to her why that's dangerous. She's been kind of obsessed with the idea ever since."

Eli stared straight ahead and paddled faster. "Hey, speaking of deadly local wildlife, remember when we were taught to do the stingray shuffle?" he said in a loud voice. Anything to get them off the topic of alligator attacks.

"I know about the stingray shuffle!" Zoe turned almost completely around, abandoning her post as lookout. "I learned it at the nature center. 'Keep your feet on the sand,'" she recited, "'and rays will swim away as planned.'" She shuffled her shoes against the bottom of the kayak.

Eli shot Zoe a smile. "Your dad and I would get yelled at when we ran through the shallows with our knees up. Man, we got in so much trouble at summer camp."

Zoe's mouth fell open. "Daddy got in trouble?"

"Only because Eli tossed hermit crabs in my hair," Nick muttered.

Eli laughed at the memory. "The camp counselors ended up dividing our group into boys and girls just to keep us from horsing around."

Zoe's face scrunched. "But you're both boys."

Eli nearly lost his grip on his paddle. He rowed faster to cover it, mind racing. How was he supposed to explain so a little kid would understand? He turned around to face Nick. "Uh, do you want to take this one?"

Nick spoke to Zoe over Eli's head, his steady, smooth voice filling the quiet of the river. "When we were younger, people thought Eli was a girl. When he got older, he realized he's actually a boy. We call that being transgender. It's a medical condition, like Grandma's diabetes. Some transgender people need medicine to manage it, just like Grammy does. Make sense?"

"Mm-hmm." Zoe sounded bored, or maybe just unimpressed. "Can I have a fruit snack?"

Eli turned around to boggle at Nick, who just gave him a

what? shrug of his shoulders. Like he didn't know how amazing he was. An age-appropriate discussion of gender *and* fruit snacks? Was Nick even *real*?

"Yes, you can have a fruit snack." Nick produced a tiny purple packet from his pocket like a magician and handed it to her over Eli's shoulder.

Zoe ripped open her packet and chewed on a brightly colored cherry. "Will any of my friends be transgender when they get older?" she asked.

"They could. It's pretty rare, but it happens." Nick paddled along placidly. Eli faced forward and got back to work too. "If it does, your mom and I will help you learn any new names they pick out."

Zoe stared open-mouthed at Eli. "You got to pick a new name?" Then, not waiting for the answer, she pummeled him with follow-up questions. "Did you know right away which one to pick? Why'd you pick Eli? Is it short for something?"

"Yes, actually," he said, deciding to focus on the last question. "It's short for Elijah. My best friend, Margo, she just calls me E."

He could feel Nick perk up behind him. "Wait, seriously? *Elijah?*" An edge of amusement was already in his voice. He must have made the connection. "You gigantic nerd."

Eli closed his eyes with a sigh. "Look, early aughts Elijah Wood was trans masc culture. When *Lord of the Rings*-colon-*The Fellowship of the Ring* came out, it was the first time a short dude with great lashes got to be the hero in something, okay?" He'd been . . . more than obsessed with the film back in the day. For reasons which only became clear later in life.

"You named yourself after a hobbit," Nick crowed. His oar faltered in the water, apparently because he couldn't handle it while laughing his ass off. "Oh my god, that's perfect."

"I would name myself after Skye if I wanted to change my

name. She's my favorite *Paw Patrol*," Zoe said. "But I like Zoe for
now." Then: "Oooooh, a bird!" She thrust her finger in the direction of a gray-and-white osprey in flight with a wriggling fish in
its talons. "It's got something!"

"Whoa, pretty cool." Nick started talking all about birds of
prey and how they caught fish, and Zoe asked a million questions,
and Eli sat motionless with his oar resting across his lap in a daze.

He wasn't sure whether he was about to laugh or cry. Were
there seriously parents like Nick out in the world, telling their
kids that being trans was fine? That was . . . so bizarre. Not that
he expected Nick to be a jerk about it, but he also hadn't expected
him to be absolutely *perfect*. He'd just explained things calmly
in a way Zoe would understand. Eli couldn't help but think of
his own coming out five years ago, when he'd taken his parents
to Central Park, sat them down on a bench near the bandshell,
and told them he was going to start going by Eli, that he'd been
taking T for months. His mom had sat in stunned silence, and
his dad had picked up his hand and said, "We'll love you no
matter what." Perfect, ten out of ten, no notes, really should have
stopped there, but then Wendall Ward had cleared his throat and
added, "After all, you'll always be our daughter."

Fumbled it right on the ten-yard line. Eli's therapist had lived
off that moment for about a year and a half, all told. His parents
were better about that stuff these days, but woof.

He watched Zoe squeal with delight as some tiny green fish
flashed by under the surface of the water. She was only four.
Would she even remember what her dad had just said? Before
coming out, Eli had scoured his own memories for any clues as
to how his parents felt about trans people and could find hardly
anything. It just wasn't a topic they'd ever discussed; it was at
most a joke. It was sitting in a theater with his parents watching
Ace Ventura and hearing everyone, himself included, act grossed

out when the villain was revealed to be a trans woman. Yeah, it was a different time, but what a shitty time to be in a body that didn't fit. Eli would have given his left arm to have heard his parents say one-tenth of what Nick had. Not that he blamed his parents. Like Eli himself, they hadn't had the words for it.

Then Zoe stood up, rocking the kayak as she pointed frantically at something in the water up ahead. "Look! Look!"

Eli fumbled to grab her, though he had no idea what the best course of action was when a four-year-old was seconds away from going headfirst into the water. He ended up catching her by the back of her kiddie life vest and gently tugging her back down. Zoe just gave him a confused look.

"Sorry, I—" He looked back at Nick for confirmation that he'd done the right thing. "Was that an overreaction? I didn't want you to fall in."

Zoe huffed. "I wasn't going to!"

"Zoe," Nick said with endless patience, "I told you to stay low, right? Good job, Eli. Now, let's keep our voices down, too, or else you might startle them."

"Them?" Eli was so preoccupied with his mini heart attack that he hadn't even noticed what Zoe was so excited about. He craned his neck and looked where she had been pointing.

Up ahead in the teak-colored water, a few gray lumps floated peacefully. One lump rose above the surface, a bristly snout revealing itself to take a puff of air.

"Whoa." Eli reminded himself not to stand and rock the boat like Zoe had just done. "Manatees."

"A whole herd of them." Nick stopped paddling and laid his oar across his lap. Eli followed suit so they could drift alongside the group of sea cows at a safe distance.

Eli couldn't remember the last time he'd seen a manatee in

person. The elementary school he and Nick had attended used to take field trips to the local power plant, where the highlight of the otherwise boring tour was a trip down to the water, where the warm reactor runoff was pumped into the estuary. The manatees, truly nature's connoisseurs of coziness, would gather in droves to enjoy the bathtub effect. As a kid, Eli had worried they'd get radiation and turn into monsters, but seven-year-old Nick had assured him that a manatee with superpowers would do nothing dangerous. "They'd just be super lazy," he'd said, which made perfect sense to Eli.

Zoe counted the gigantic bodies floating off their left side. "One . . . two . . . there's three. And—Eli, look! There's a baby!" She pointed emphatically, and Eli made a bar with his arm along the edge of the kayak just in case she forgot the rule about staying seated.

"Where?" Eli peered into the water until a small, fat shape came into view beside one of the huge ones. "Oh, I see it," he whisper-screamed.

"It's so cute," Zoe said in the same hushed squeal.

Okay, maybe all the heart attacks were worth it if having a kid meant you got to feel a sense of childish delight in something as wholesome as spotting an endangered species in its natural habitat. The baby manatee looked like a puffy gray marshmallow. It stuck its nose into the air and blew a light mist. Zoe was beside herself, and Eli was right there along with her.

"That one's me," Eli said, pointing to a sea cow who looked like he'd nodded off in the shallows. He bumped into a bundle of mangrove roots and just kept floating.

"I'm the baby," Zoe said, like it was obvious. She pointed to the biggest one at the head of the pack. "And that one's Daddy." Her grin was wide enough to split her face.

Nick's laugh was smooth as honey. "It sure is, sweetheart."

Eli watched all their manatee counterparts floating around like one big happy family, trying to concentrate on the wonders of nature and not on whatever inappropriate non-feelings he was totally not experiencing.

CHAPTER 7

Nick helped Zoe out of the back seat and onto the hot black pavement of the Checker's parking lot. Laurie was already there, waving at them from a table underneath a hard plastic umbrella. The smell of thick grease hung in the air. This particular Checker's on Route 1 had served as their traditional rendezvous point for the last year. It had been Laurie's idea. "We want Zoe to associate hand-offs with good things. Like french fries and milkshakes."

"Isn't that the plaza where the old Blockbuster was swallowed up by a sinkhole back in '98?" Nick had asked. He had associations too.

"We don't have to tell her that part, okay?"

Nick kept an eye on the remnants of the sinkhole a few hundred yards away. The gash in the earth was filled in with sand and tall grass now, but he still didn't trust it. If it were up to him, they would meet at the Wendy's up by the county line, closer to the Thirsty Manatee, but that would be more driving for Laurie. The compromise meant Nick would have to go straight to work from lunch to get ready for dinner service, but who needed little things like showers? He kept a stack of clean polos in the back office; it was fine.

Zoe ran to her mother, the black curtain of her hair swishing as she went. Nick followed more sedately with his hands in his pockets. Even at a distance, he could hear his daughter's chatter over the traffic at the nearby intersection.

"—and he lives in New York City where the lights never go out but he grew up here with Daddy and he's really funny. Do you want to hear the joke he taught me? Okay, so! How did . . . no wait, where was the cow—wait, I said it wrong." Zoe blew a giant raspberry right as Nick reached the table. "Why did the cow get an award?"

"I don't know, why?" Laurie smiled gently, her green eyes shining as she watched Zoe's antics. She tipped her head back and mouthed a hello at Nick.

"She got an award because she was outstanding in her field. Get it? Out! Standing!" Zoe jumped in place for emphasis.

Nick had already heard this joke twice, once when Eli said it in the car on the way to drop him off, and again when Zoe wanted to practice it. Still, he laughed. It was a good joke.

"That's pretty funny," Laurie offered, though she only smiled a tiny bit wider. There was a crackle of tension at the corners of her mouth, like it was a strain to keep up the cheery demeanor for Zoe's benefit. Nick recognized the sign as clear as day—it was one that had heralded their divorce, after all.

It didn't hurt as much now when he thought about the breakup with Laurie. Over a year's worth of distance made it feel less like a failure and more like a fact. He held no ill will toward Laurie herself; she'd been right when she'd told him, "I don't think this is working." Now, when he looked at her and saw her struggling with something, he felt a tinge of his former love for her, but mostly he felt camaraderie. They were a team, and he took that responsibility very seriously.

"Hey, sweetheart," he said, tugging playfully at Zoe's hair, "your mom and I are going to order lunch. Why don't you stay here and make sure no one steals our table?" The walk-up window was only a couple feet away; he could keep an eye on her and still have a semiprivate conversation with Laurie.

"Can I get a 'nana shake?" Zoe asked, already scrambling up on the plastic seat and glaring at an older couple that dared pass within a yard of the table. She took her responsibilities very seriously too.

"As long as you let me have one sip," Nick said. They pinkie-swore on it.

Laurie shot him a grateful look and joined him in the line for the order window. They stood quietly for a few minutes, studying the garish menu and listening to the teenagers at the front of the line arguing with the Checker's employee about the price of fries.

"You doing okay?" Nick finally asked.

"Yeah. Fine." Laurie dragged both hands through her long brown hair the way she always did when things were not fine. "Mom might join us in a bit."

Nick pursed his lips. His ex-mother-in-law Kay was not his biggest fan, and the feeling was mutual. His marriage had been challenging enough without Laurie's mother hovering in the background, making snide comments and judging every single one of their decisions. Nothing Nick did was ever good enough for Grammy Kay, from the shirts that he wore ("Knockoffs, are they?") to his job at the restaurant ("Waste of a college education, in my book."). Even Zoe's name had nearly set off World War III. Kay had found it "too exotic."

"Isn't she going to deal with enough?" she'd said when Laurie was eight months pregnant. "Being mixed origin, I mean." Like Zoe was a bag of coffee beans.

Nick would never actually punch an old woman, but that day? Oh, that day, he'd come really close.

So no, eating Checker's with his ex-wife's mother was not on Nick's list of preferred activities, but the woman was family, so Nick had to grit his teeth and get through it. "Should I get her a burger?" he asked, striving to be more pleasant than Kay herself would ever be to him.

"If you do, she'll say she wanted the chicken. If you get the chicken, she'll say she wanted a burger. If you don't get her anything, she'll complain that we didn't think of her. There's no winning here, so don't bother wasting six bucks. Let her order her own lunch."

Nick tried to hide his surprise, but he knew his eyebrows were probably rising over the tops of his sunglasses. "That's pretty pragmatic." It was more diplomatic than asking her why she was suddenly standing up for herself in some small way instead of bowing to Kay's domineering personality. Laurie from five years ago would have texted her mother asking for her order and would have waited for a reply that never came.

"Therapy," Laurie singsonged. She whipped out her own sunglasses from her purse and settled them on her button nose. "It's a trip. You should try it."

It was delivered like a joke, but Nick didn't laugh. They'd tried couples counseling before the divorce, but Nick hadn't gotten much out of it. Their counselor had been about a billion years old and had some old-fashioned views on how a marriage was supposed to work. His only redeeming quality was he took their insurance. Recently, though, Laurie had found a better therapist for herself.

"So the new doctor is working out?" Even if he personally didn't put much stock in therapy, he wanted to at least try to be supportive.

"It's exhausting, I guess, hashing out all this stuff, but yeah. I think it's good." They finally made it to the front of the line, and

Laurie began rattling off her order along with Zoe's and Nick's. While they waited for the food, she turned back to him and said, "But enough about me. Who's this new best friend Zoe can't stop talking about? Eli, I think she said?" She glanced back to check on her.

"Yeah. We went to high school together. He's in town for Christmas." Normally he would be honest and up-front with her about the whole story, but that would mean explaining that Eli was transgender. That seemed rude without his express permission.

Laurie examined him impassively from behind her Ray-Bans. "I don't think you've ever mentioned him. Have you two stayed in touch since high school or . . . ?"

Nick looked over to where Zoe was still sitting at the table, humming to herself. "No, we ran into each other the other day. Pure coincidence."

"Huh." Laurie gazed thoughtfully into the middle distance, in the direction of the Applebee's parking lot. "Well, I'm relieved you've found someone to hang out with. Surprised, but relieved."

Nick eyed her, not taking his gaze away even as the Checker's employee handed him their tray of food through the window. "What's that supposed to mean?"

"It means exactly that," Laurie said. She took the molded paper tray of drinks. "The closest friendship you have these days is with your dad. And don't say the restaurant's appliance repair guy counts; just because you see him twice a month doesn't mean you're friends."

Nick couldn't even argue with her, but he did roll his eyes at the old chestnut. Ever since Wu Tian-yi (or Ah Gong as Zoe called him) had retired a few years back, Nick had felt responsible for his dad's well-being. Nick's only other friendships were ones from college, and time plus distance had made it difficult to keep up with the old group from the U of M Asian Society. Ken was out in San Francisco now; Wilma was doing high-powered government work; the Li twins were globe-trotting. Nick's own life wasn't half as exciting, and he wasn't sure if he had anything left in common with them. They had a group chat to keep each other updated on major life events, but he hadn't checked it in ages.

"Sorry to make you worry about my lack of a social schedule," was his only rejoinder.

"I'm being serious," Laurie said as they made their way back to the table, where Zoe was bouncing with excitement for her incoming milkshake. "You need to take stock of your priorities."

"I have priorities," Nick protested.

"Making time for yourself should be one of them," Laurie said. Spoken like a true recipient of therapy, Nick supposed. "Maybe if you cut back your hours at the restaurant, you would have more time for your own life *and* Zoe."

Nick resisted the urge to groan. It was an old argument between them, predating the divorce. Yes, he worked long hours, but he really didn't have a choice, financially. Especially now that he relied on his single income. "I'm doing my best, all right? I even have some time off scheduled soon."

"Yeah, only because I got on your case about it," Laurie said. "I swear to god, Nick, I'm like an inch away from nominating you for *Queer Eye.*"

Nick was saved from responding to that by the pristine white SUV that pulled into the lot at that exact moment. It slotted itself directly atop the dividing line of two parking spots. Eric Clapton blared from the stereo. Kay had arrived.

Her tiny figure descended from the driver's seat, clad in head-to-toe Christmas clothing: a thick sweater with real metal jingle bells sewn along the tips of appliqued tree branches. Her leggings had reindeer printed all over them. Even her socks had little snowflakes. Nick would have found this overblown display of holiday cheer charming on literally anyone else, but seeing Kay decked out like that rubbed him the wrong way. How could someone so miserly with their affections be so devoted to the season of giving?

"Hello, all," Kay said as she whipped off her sunglasses. "You didn't order for me, did you? You really shouldn't put yourself out like that." She was clearly expecting an answer in the affirmative, already gearing up for a gleeful refusal of the item that had been bought with her in mind.

"Oh, we didn't get you anything, Mom," Laurie said as she doled out the food on the table. "I wasn't sure what you'd be in the mood for. Want to grab something for yourself?"

Kay clearly needed a moment to absorb this development, blinking in the sun. "No, that's all right," she said, readjusting her purse strap. "I probably shouldn't indulge in fast food, anyway." She turned to Zoe, who was happily munching on her fries. "It makes you very fat, you know."

"Mom," Laurie said in that tired way she had. She'd been combating her mother's fatphobia without much success for years, Nick knew. At this point, he didn't hold out much hope for her to change.

"All bodies are good bodies," Zoe chirped. At least someone was absorbing Laurie's lessons. Nick snuck his promised sip of her milkshake, giving her a wink.

"How are you, Kay?" he said as he handed the cup back, hoping to steer the conversation in another direction. One that wouldn't give his daughter body image issues for life.

She heaved a sigh and dropped to the bench next to Zoe. "Aches and pains. Pains and aches. I'm really getting too old." She turned to Zoe and said, "And what did you and your father do today, sweet pea?" She snuck a couple of Zoe's fries out of their wrapper. No one pointed out the hypocrisy.

Zoe swallowed her mouthful of milkshake. She'd been scolded about talking with her mouth full by Kay last week. "We went kayaking with Eli. We saw manatees. They were really cute!"

Kay didn't seem impressed with their manatee sighting. Instead, she asked Laurie, "Who is Eli?"

Laurie set her jaw in a way that Nick knew meant *I wasn't even there, Mom* before saying in an even tone, "An old friend of Nick's who's back in town for the holidays."

"He makes people laugh as a job, and he said my shoes were cool, and he sat in the middle so I could be lookout, and he got to pick his name because he's transgender," Zoe said, digging her fries through the creamy surface of her milkshake like Nick had taught her. "Then we ate fruit snacks."

A couple things happened in swift succession. Laurie's eyes went wide, visible even behind her Ray-Bans. Kay's mouth fell open to emit a sound like a slowly deflating tire. A few yards away, in a completely unrelated incident, a kid dropped a bag of french fries all over the pavement and started to wail. Loudly. Nick felt like joining in, but for Zoe's sake kept it together.

"Okay." He put his burger down on its wrapper. "So, Zoe, I should have explained this earlier, but it's not nice to tell people that someone's transgender without their permission. It's really personal. I only told you when we were kayaking because Eli said I could. Okay?"

Zoe, thank everything good and pure, kept on eating her fries, oblivious to the sudden tension. "Okay," she said.

"*That's* what you're concerned about? Personal privacy?" Kay rounded on Laurie. "Did you know about this?"

"Nick doesn't need my permission to see a friend, Mom," Laurie said. Her voice shook, but she got the words out. "They just went kayaking."

"And you call yourself a mother!" Kay screeched. Laurie dropped her gaze back to her chicken sandwich. Nick could practically see her curling into herself like she always did when her mom was on a tear. "A real mother would be a hell of a lot more vigilant, I can tell you that."

"Whoa." Nick held up both hands. He'd witnessed Grammy Kay berate Laurie many times, but even for her, this was extreme. "You don't get to talk to her like that, Katherine." He tried to keep the snap out of his voice, but he wasn't totally successful. Zoe looked up from her fries, chewing slowly, her gaze bouncing between all the adults at the table. Her brow crumpled in what might have been concern or even fear. Nick's heart broke.

Kay turned on him with her nose in the air. "It's none of your business how I talk to my own child."

Nick very much disagreed, but before he could say so, Laurie stood and said, "That's it. I'm taking Zoe home now. We're still doing the mall Santa thing on Wednesday, right, Nick?"

Nick stared up at her, then remembered the family photo shoot she had arranged with all of them, Kay and his dad included. Laurie had been weirdly insistent on them all being there together. "Yeah. I'll see you there." He hoped her therapist gave her a gold star during her next session; she was really self-advocating today.

"Great." She shrugged her purse strap over her shoulder and looked down at Kay, whose mouth was hanging open. Her gaze skipped right over her to Zoe, whom she gave a big smile. "C'mon, kiddo. Say goodbye. You can finish your shake in the car."

"But I just got here!" Kay said.

"And we're just leaving," Laurie replied. "We'll see you at the mall in a couple days, Mom. Hopefully you'll have calmed down by then."

Zoe flung herself at Nick, her little arms going around his neck. "Bye."

Nick squeezed her tight, then let go. "Love you, sweetheart." He'd talk to her on the phone tonight before bed, their special wind-down ritual. Maybe then he'd have a chance to explain how none of Kay's outbursts were her fault.

"Give me a hug goodbye, too, Zoe." Kay opened her arms imperiously. She looked like some dictator presiding over the Checker's table.

Zoe looked at her, then zoomed toward Laurie's car at a fast clip.

Laurie cleared her throat. "I've told Zoe she doesn't have to hug anyone she doesn't want to. It's important that she learns that."

Kay sputtered. "W-well, I've never heard of anything so ridiculous. I'm her grandmother, not some stranger." She whirled on Nick. "Did you let her hug that transgender?" Apparently, she thought the word was a noun, which was bizarre.

Nick stood as well, slipping on his sunglasses and following Laurie's lead. If Kay wanted to act foolish, she was going to be foolishly alone. "Let me get this trash out of your way, Laur." He hefted their lunch trays, congratulating himself on not staring down Kay as he did so. Being an adult—and not a petty one—was really difficult sometimes.

Nick wasn't worried about Eli having a negative impact on Zoe, but he was worried about his ex-mother-in-law. It didn't seem fair that no one questioned her presence in her granddaughter's life. Just because someone was family, did they need to be given so much leeway?

"Moooooooom." The sound of Zoe trying the car door handle over and over rang out across the cement. "Let me iiiiiiin."

Laurie swept past Kay. "Coming, sweetie."

"I won't be ignored!" Kay called after her. Laurie didn't even turn around, so Kay scowled in Nick's direction instead. "I *won't*."

There was nothing Nick could say that would be more satisfying than simply walking away and leaving that sad woman alone in the Checker's parking lot. So that was exactly what he did.

CHAPTER 8

December 18

Christmas tree trimming was a big deal at the Ward house.

There was already a tree set up in the sitting room, of course. That had been necessary for the party. But that tree, according to Eli's mom, was the "aesthetic" one: artificial, tastefully decorated in shades of red and gold. It had been moved to the dining room to make space for the "real" tree. The "family" tree. The bonkers-as-shit mess of a tree.

Cora insisted on getting a live tree for this purpose, even though Sweet Potato would probably chew on the pine needles and puke them up. This tree was destined to be covered with a mishmash of ornaments, most of which had been hoarded in the attic since Eli was a baby.

Eli struggled to get the sawed-off base of the trunk into the tree stand, his nose mashed into the scratchy needles. He was inhaling nothing but that fresh pine smell, and personally, he did not care for it. But as long as Mom was happy, he told himself, that was all that mattered. He was a good son. Ostensibly with plenty of upper body strength.

Eli's father stood between the armchairs in the sitting room and tried to direct Eli in arranging the tree. "A little more to the right. No, my right."

His mom, meanwhile, sat on the satiny sofa and had a different vantage point altogether. "I think a little more to the left, actually, dear."

"No, definitely right."

"Which way am I going?" Eli half screamed into the pine boughs.

A beat of hesitation, then Wendall said, "To the left."

"There, there, hold it right there!" Cora cried, even though, in Eli's estimation, the tree was in the exact same spot it had been for the past ten minutes. "That's perfect."

Eli stooped and tightened the screws in the base as fast as he could. He could hear his dad opening the old pickle bucket that had served as their Christmas ornament repository ever since Eli could remember. The lid crackled as it was peeled off. Eli finished securing the tree and turned to find his parents bent over the bucket of shiny baubles.

"This is the first time we've been able to do this as a family in ages," his mom said. She picked up one of the ornaments from the top of the pile, holding it up to the light. It was a cheesy plastic snowflake-shaped picture frame, and smack-dab in the center of it was Eli's baby picture. He was wearing a pink velvet dress with his hair done in two pigtails that shot up from the top of his head.

"Awww, look how cute you were," his dad said.

A familiar feeling of disappointment wove its way through Eli's stomach. It wasn't like he hated the picture itself, which was a bit embarrassing but not soul-searingly terrible. It was the fact that his parents were cooing over it, tapping their fingertips against the plastic casing like they wanted to touch the baby's chubby cheeks, treating it like it was—real. When Eli looked at that photo of himself as a baby, or one of the million other child-hood photos his mom proudly displayed around the house, he didn't see himself at all. It was like he was looking at a picture that had come with the frame from the store. That kid was a stranger. He felt no connection whatsoever.

Obviously, it was different for his parents.

"Do you want to hang this one?" His mother held out the snowflake.

"Yeah, you should have first dibs," his father chimed in. "You are the guest of honor, after all."

"I'm not a guest, I'm your son," Eli mumbled, but he took the ornament and hung it on some random branch to get it over with.

They soon fell into a rhythm of tree decoration. Wendall managed to unknot the strands of lights reserved specifically for the tree. Cora dug through the ancient ornaments, choosing each new addition with all the care in the world, even though they were mostly crumbling bits of macaroni that Eli had made in elementary school, his old name scrawled on the backs. Eli took each ornament she handed to him and applied it to the tree as quickly as possible. The faster they decorated, the sooner he could fling himself atop his childhood bed and stare at the text messages he'd received earlier that morning. The words were already ingrained in his head:

10:33 AM: **I had a really nice time at the beach with you yesterday.**

10:34 AM: **And kayaking. That was also nice.**

10:38 AM: **This is Nick, by the way. You gave me your number.**

10:47 AM: **I guess I didn't need to tell you who this is. It's not like you went kayaking with more than one family yesterday.**

A rare quadruple text. Of course Nick would be the type to blow up his phone. Eli was sure that if they'd had cell phones back when they were teens, Nick would have been texting him nonstop. As it was, their moms had had to restrict their landline usage, since they both lived in fear that there would be an emergency and the line would be busy. God, he was old. Old enough to remember lying on his stomach across his bed, feet kicking in the air while he played with the curly phone cord. What had they even talked about? Whatever it had been, Nick had laughed a lot. That, he remembered.

He'd sent Margo a screenshot of Nick's texts along with a voice note that said, "What time is it right now on the West Coast? Because here it's DILF o'clock."

Margo had replied with a series of middle-finger emojis and one single eggplant.

He grinned at the memory as he hung yet another tatty handmade ornament, this one an inoffensive reindeer made from a clothespin.

"Oh, I like that one," his mom said, breaking into his thoughts. "You were such an artistic child."

"Yeah," Eli agreed far too readily. "Thanks. Very talented at . . . reindeer." He went back to quietly putting ornaments on the tree.

"Maybe try to space them out a little nicer." His mom plucked a shiny orb that had lost almost all its red paint and moved it a foot down and to the right. "You're clumping them all up, Eli."

"He's just out of practice." His dad's booming laugh echoed through the sitting room. "I bet it's been a while since you've put up Christmas decorations, huh, kiddo?"

It was true. Eli rarely put up a string of lights on his fire escape, let alone tried to fit a tree in his tiny apartment. His Christmases in New York were nothing special. He usually treated it like any other day, got some work done, watched some TV, ordered Chinese food with Margo if she was free. His parents had expressed sorrow at what they considered his lonely and sad holidays, but Eli didn't mind a quiet Christmas.

In fact, he could really use one right about now.

"All the more reason to focus on doing a good job today," Cora said primly. "Who knows when we'll get another chance to be together for the holidays like this?"

And there it was, the patented Ward passive aggression. Eli had known it would rear its head eventually, but he'd hoped to dodge it for at least a few more days.

He tried to make a joke out of it, like he usually did. "Maybe next year we can all get together in Aspen," he said in a fakey posh accent, all *Lifestyles of the Rich and Famous*. Turning to the sofa, he picked up the afghan his mom had crocheted years ago and draped it around his neck. "The slopes are just to die for, darling. And that powder." He gave a cocaine-esque sniff and then faux-whispered behind his hand. "The snow isn't too bad either."

Wendall laughed, but Cora's mouth thinned into a tight line. Tough crowd.

"I'm sorry you think it's silly to want to be together at the most wonderful time of the year," she said, ducking down to inspect the pickle bucket of ornaments again.

Eli unwrapped the afghan from his neck with a swallow. But before he could apologize, his dad swooped in.

"He's not saying it's silly, he's just goofing around. That's his job; he's a professional goofer."

Guilt formed a heavy stone in Eli's chest. That *was* his job, past tense. Probably not the best time to update his parents on the latest, though.

"Well, *I* think," Cora said, rummaging through the bucket with more force than necessary, "that our time together is precious. It would have been nice, for example, to see you at all yesterday, Eli. But you spent all morning and most of the afternoon out with Nick Wu, and by the time you got home, all you wanted to do was nap for hours!"

Eli spread his arms wide like he wanted to show he wasn't hiding anything—which was a lie, but one he was committed to. "Mom, I went for a run and then kayaked down the river. That was more exercise than I'd gotten in, like, years. Of course I needed a nap."

"I always liked that Nick Wu," Wendall said to no one in particular as he tested bulbs along a strand of lights, trying to find the one that was causing a dead patch.

"When we were visiting you in New York," Eli's mom said, "I wouldn't sleep a wink! Certainly wouldn't nap. I wanted to spend as much time with you as possible."

That was true. Eli had hosted his parents in his one-bedroom Brooklyn apartment once a year. He loved his mom and dad, truly, but his back always hurt from sleeping on the couch, and his head always spun with the myriad of museums his mom wanted to visit, and his feet ached from the million miles his dad wanted to walk to see the city "as it was meant to be seen." Honestly, the one good thing about his trip down to Florida was the idea that he could count this as their annual get-together and skip the hosting duties in the new year.

"I want to spend time with you, too, Mom. But what was I supposed to do? Tell my childhood best friend to get lost?" He waggled a handful of deteriorating paper ornaments at her. "It's your fault that you raised me to be so polite. So when you think about it, you have no one to blame but yourself."

"Ha ha, whoa, zing! He's got you there, honey."

Eli shot a fond glance at his dad. At least he always laughed at Eli's jokes.

Cora ignored her husband entirely. She propped her fists on her hips and said, "I'm going to use my I statements." His parents were both big on I statements. I feel [fill in the blank with an emotion] when you [fill in the blank with an action]. It was the kind of thing progressive parents in the nineties learned about in magazines. "I feel hurt when you act like it's a chore to be here. Like at the party the other night—"

"I was fresh off a very long flight, Mom! I'm sorry if I wasn't in the mood to watch Uncle Hank get plastered and rant about how the governor is going to force me into a dress."

"It was a *party*. You could have tried to have fun instead of moping around. As it was, you couldn't get out of here fast enough."

"You're the one who sent me to the store!"

"Because I didn't know how else to deal with you!"

Wendall stood slowly, leaving a trailing nest of half-lit Christmas lights on the terrazzo floor. He raised his hands in his usual gesture of peace. "Hey, maybe we should all take a break. The holidays are stressful for everyone. Why don't I mix up a pitcher of sangria, and we'll just sit on the lanai and chill out?"

Eli pinched the bridge of his nose and squeezed his eyes shut. "Dad, I have been sober for years." Wendall always seemed to forget that when it suited him.

"I'll make yours a virgin."

"That's not a thing! A virgin sangria is just fruit salad!"

"I don't want sangria," Eli's mom said, pointing at Eli with verve. "I want to discuss why our only child is so hell-bent on ditching us at every opportunity."

"I'm not *ditching* you. I'm here right now, aren't I?" He could feel his pulse ratcheting up. Visions of the doughy governor danced in his aching head. "Even though this isn't the most welcoming spot in the world."

Cora's hand flew to her mouth with a gasp. "My home isn't welcoming to you?"

"Honey, he probably meant Florida in general," Wendall jumped in.

"It's not only that, Dad." Eli could see himself as if watching from a great distance, like he was in the audience at a movie theater. There he was on the big screen, about to make a huge fucking mistake. But all he could do was eat popcorn and let it happen. "This whole house creeps me out."

"What? How?" Wendall demanded at the same time Cora wailed, "But I just cleaned!"

Eli focused on his dad's somewhat more coherent questions. "The baby photos and the high school photos and—all of this stuff!" He tore the plastic snowflake ornament off the tree, waving it in the air. "This place is a shrine to my deadname. How do you think that makes me feel?"

"Use your I statements," Wendall said.

Deep breath in. Then, letting it all out, Eli said, "When you talk about how cute this picture is, I feel like you don't want me here, not really. You want this kid." He tossed the ornament on the coffee table, the sunny child in the photo grinning up at them.

"But that's you." Cora dabbed at her damp eye with the inside of her wrist. She always tried to fight off tears when they happened, unsuccessfully. "I know you've changed a lot—everyone does. But it's still you."

Eli clicked his tongue and looked away. He stared at the tree, at all the crumbling handmade ornaments and the gaudy tinsel. Why had he even bothered coming here?

Oh, right. Because he was a failure. At pretty much every aspect of being an adult.

He glanced over at his mom. She was weeping openly now, tears streaming down her face. She wiped them away with her fingertips. "You should have told us. If seeing our old photos makes you uncomfortable—" Her lip trembled. She looked around the room. From where they stood, at least a dozen child-hood pictures were visible in various frames on the walls or standing on tables. "Oh, it makes me sad to think about throwing away all these memories. Is that really what you want me to do?"

"I didn't say that." Eli was so tired. His body still ached from overdoing it with Nick, and now his head was pounding. He couldn't begin to think of a solution that would feel right to him but also keep his mother from dissolving further into tears. He wasn't out to hurt his mom or cause drama, but what could he say when it was clear her precious memories came first?

Wendall crossed the room to hug Cora to him, letting her cry against his neck. His eyes met Eli's, and for a moment, Eli wasn't sure if his dad blamed him for the sorry state of their tree-trimming afternoon or not.

He didn't really want to find out. He headed for the door, snagging his flip-flops from the shoe rack. "I need some air. See you later," he said, and pushed his way outside. The sunset was starting, the sky turning all the colors of sherbet.

Eli walked to the end of the driveway before realizing there was nowhere for him to go. There was nothing within walking distance unless he wanted to cross a busy thoroughfare. No stores, no public park, nothing to do. He was trapped in the honeycomb of his parents' suburban neighborhood, hemmed in by palm trees and jacarandas.

He needed an escape route.

He took out his cell phone to call an Uber. The app informed him that the next available ride was about forty-five minutes away. Way too long to wait. He swiped out of the app and saw Nick's text messages staring back at him.

It wasn't even a decision. Eli pressed the call button before he could think about the consequences.

It rang twice before Nick picked up.

"Eli! Hi! How are you doing?" He sounded genuinely pleased to be called by his ex. Weirdo.

"Oh, I'm spectacular," Eli said, drawing the word out into about ten syllables. "Can I ask for a favor?" He squinted into the sun. "Can you come pick me up?"

CHAPTER 9

Nick pulled into the sandy parking spot and switched off his headlights. Without the noise of the engine, he could hear the warble of crickets deep in the sea-grape bushes. Eli sat in the passenger seat, as motionless and silent as he'd been when Nick had picked him up. When he'd asked Eli, "Where to?" he'd gotten a grunted "Anywhere." So here they were. Back at the beach they'd visited the day before. Their beach. Or formerly their beach.

It wasn't the worst place to spend a night off work. Better than sitting on his couch, zoning out like Nick was wont to do when he had no other plans.

"Do you want to go someplace else instead?" Nick finally asked when it became clear Eli was not going to move on his own.

Eli blinked, his thousand-yard stare dissipating as he turned to Nick. "Huh?" His head swiveled around as he took in the thick dark of their surroundings. There wasn't much to see; they were the lone car in the otherwise empty lot. "No, no, this is fine."

They picked their way down the wooden boardwalk that led

to the beach. Eli fished his phone out of his pocket and turned on its flashlight so they could see where they were going in the dark.

"You'd think they'd have some lights out here," he grumbled.

"Turtles," Nick said, a quiet reminder.

"Oh, right." Eli's brow furrowed in the shaky light of his phone. "They get all turned around, don't they? When they hatch."

"Yeah, disoriented. I think they're supposed to aim for the moon? But if there's a bright light, they end up going that way instead." He carefully started down the stairs that led to the sand. No shoes piled up at the bottom at this hour; they had the beach to themselves.

Eli clattered down behind him. "Wait, that can't be right. The moon moves."

"Oh yeah. I forgot that part." He expected some truly epic ribbing at his expense, but Eli just kicked off his sandals and dug his toes in the sand.

He clicked off his phone's flashlight, leaving them in murky blackness for a moment until their eyes adjusted. Nick looked up at the stars overhead, then out to the condos in the distance, windows lit here and there in rows. The waves shushed back and forth down at the waterline.

Pretty peaceful.

Eli sighed out a huge gust of breath. "I made my mom cry," he said, and started walking down the beach.

Nick lost some time untying his shoes and placing them on the last stair, but soon followed. His legs were longer, so it didn't take much time for him to catch up.

"Want to tell me about it?" he asked once he was at Eli's side.

"Not really." Eli laughed to himself. "It was a really pointless argument. Embarrassing, actually."

"Okay." As they trudged across the sand, Nick thought of a million things he could say to keep the conversation going.

It must be hard being back here after all these years.

Family is tough.

I watched you bomb at the fifth-grade talent show when you tried to sing in front of a cafeteria full of ten-year-olds; there is nothing you could tell me that would be more embarrassing than that.

But he didn't say anything. He just hoped he'd appear to be a good, trustworthy listener if Eli decided to talk.

It did not take long.

They hadn't gone more than ten yards before Eli exploded. "Do you ever get the feeling like your dad misses the kid you used to be? Like, he would rather have that kid back than deal with adult-you? Or is that just me?"

Nick considered his answer. He and his father had always been close. When Nick had been plucking up the courage to ask Eli on their first date as teens—his stomach turning itself inside out at the thought of ruining his longest friendship on the off chance his feelings were returned—his dad had been the one he went to for advice. ("Be honest. Try not to faint.") His dad was the one who helped him pick out his clothes and style his hair before he and Eli went to the movies on their first real date. ("Any more gel and you're going to crackle in a stiff breeze.") And his dad had been the one to gently explain to his mom that using up an entire disposable camera to take photos of Nick and Eli was probably overkill, and she should let them get going before they missed the trailers.

"Why?" Nick asked. "Did your folks say something like that to you?"

"Not exactly. It was more like a . . . gesture. Maybe I took it the wrong way." Eli kicked at a seashell, sending it careening into the ocean.

Nick watched it go. "I get it. My dad has this image of me in his head, you know? Like, he hardly ever updates his mental

Rolodex. I'm not sixteen anymore, but I dent the bumper of his car *one time*, and to this day, he says, 'Oh, Nick, don't drive at night. That's when you had your accident.'" He mimicked his father's nasally voice, his familiar accent. It wasn't a mean impression, but it was pretty spot-on, if he did say so himself.

It got a laugh out of Eli, at least. "Oh my god, I remember that! Wait, wasn't I the one driving?" He whipped his head toward Nick with his mouth hanging open. "Holy shit, I was. I backed into that cart in the Walmart parking lot and you took the fall for me."

"Well, you were still trying to get your license." The memories came flooding back to Nick: Blink-182 on the radio, the vast emptiness of the parking lot after midnight, Eli nervous and sweaty in the driver's seat as Nick tried to talk him through the finer points of parallel parking. The sickening smack as the car backed up a tiny bit too much. "You failed that test, like, four times."

"It was a bad test! Who the fuck needs to parallel park in Florida? There's no street parking unless you go down to Miami, and even then—" Eli stopped, coming to a halt in the middle of a nest of dried seaweed. "Hold on. Your dad still thinks it was you that dinged the bumper?"

"Of course he still thinks it was me. I'm not a narc."

Eli threw his head back and laughed long and loud. A clutch of ibises took flight, startled from their perch in the bushes. Nick could see the long curve of their beaks against the starry sky.

"I can't believe you never told him! And he's still dragging you for it? Dude, I would have blown up at him years ago, like, '*I'm* not the bad driver! It was the kid down the street who couldn't fucking drive!'"

"There's still time. Think I should?" Nick said. He could feel the corner of his mouth twitching, on the verge of busting up too.

"Oh, absolutely. Maybe save it for his birthday." Eli smiled and turned his head to look out over the dark water. Nick could see his profile picked out against the sky. Now that his eyes were used to the dark, there seemed to be plenty of light to make out his expression as it softened to something more thoughtful. "Hey, thanks for bringing me out here. I needed a break."

"Anytime," Nick said, and meant it.

It gave him pause, the shock of how much he meant it. If Laurie were there, she'd be wondering aloud how funny it was that Nick was making himself so readily available to Eli when, historically, he wasn't that reliable with anyone else, himself included.

Nick was very glad Laurie wasn't there.

By unspoken agreement, they started heading back down the beach, their pace slow, almost matching the lull of the waves. Eli had his hands in the pockets of his shorts. Nick, who was wearing jeans in deference to the low-seventies evening temperatures, was shivering just looking at him.

He was content to let the conversation lie where they'd left it, but after a few minutes of silent trudging, Eli spoke again. "We were putting up the tree. There were all these ornaments with my baby pictures." The whole story spilled out: how he felt detached from the person in the old photographs, his parents' fawning, the way Eli couldn't shake the idea that the current version of him was, on some level, not living up to their expectations.

"But you're a model son," Nick protested. "Trust me, I would know. The way you left for the city? Got a big, important job?"

Eli looked paler than usual in the moonlight. "Yeah. About that." He bit his lip. "I'm not exactly employed at the moment."

"Oh?" That was a surprise. But then again, Nick didn't know much about the television industry. "So, like, you're in between projects?"

A bitter laugh huffed out of Eli. "'Between' implies there's something new coming down the pike, and if I'm honest? This might be the end of the road for the ol' writing career." He glanced at Nick and shrugged, his face an arrangement of discomfort. "The last show I worked on—the lead harassed a bunch of women on set. Totally disgusting. The show got canceled, which, fine, didn't want to write that dickhead any more jokes anyway. But I'm having a hard time getting a new gig. Or even having someone return my calls."

"Shit," Nick said with feeling. "But I thought you said you were working on your friend's new show—the queer ensemble thing?"

Eli sighed. "I mean, I gave Margo a hand with a few little things, but if she doesn't sell it, I won't see any money for that work. Honestly, I'm not going to hold my breath. *Friends of Dorothy* is a long shot."

"Didn't you say it was really good?"

"It is, absolutely. Margo's a genius. But that doesn't necessarily mean anything, not in this industry." Eli shrugged. "Now I'm not sure what's next. I might need to move back here for a while, come up with a plan. Get back to my stand-up roots somehow."

"Did you enjoy that?" he asked. "The stand-up?" He wondered if any of Eli's performances could be found online. Maybe he could look it up tonight.

Eli made a so-so gesture with his hand. "I liked parts of it. Feels like a step backward, though."

Nick knew a little bit of how Eli might be feeling. When Nick finished college and moved back home to start working at the Manatee, his parents had been . . . not unkind, but definitely confused. His mom had asked repeatedly, "Is this really what you want to do?"

"What do your folks think?" he asked.

Eli looked downright ill. "I . . . haven't told them. They think I'm still working, actually."

Nick tried not to let his surprise show, but apparently that was impossible. Eli knew him too well.

"Yep, that's me," Eli said. "Winner of the Worst Son of the Year award for not only hiding my employment status but also for making my mom cry over fucking Christmas ornaments. Also terrified of having to come back here, no offense."

"None taken. I get how it would feel like a downgrade." Nick shrugged. "I didn't have the easiest time when I decided to put down roots here, and I didn't have to worry about the governor trying to legislate what I could wear on school campuses."

A look of grateful relief took over Eli's face. "Exactly." He blew out a breath. "Wow. Did not mean to get this deep." He laughed, but it was strained. Then he turned toward the water. "Want to go swimming?"

Nick stopped in his tracks. "What?"

Eli was already stripping his shirt over his head. "Come on. Shit's too heavy; I need to do something silly to balance it out."

"Why night swimming?"

"Why not? We used to when we were younger." He flashed a smile, all teeth.

They'd done it exactly twice, by Nick's recollection: once before they started dating, right after Eli finally passed his driving test and got his license (a celebration of sorts, the tension between them palpable, Nick at sixteen averting his eyes when Eli's denim miniskirt and cropped tank top hit the sand) and again after—well, after their first time. Losing your virginity on a beach sounded romantic, but it was uncomfortably sandy in reality. They'd plunged naked into the ocean, and that time, Nick had looked as much as he liked.

He realized he had zoned out, and his gaze was currently somewhere around Eli's bare navel. He looked away with a cough.

"Well, for one thing, I didn't bring a towel." Even to Nick's ears, it sounded like a pathetic excuse. Something an old man who was more worried about his car upholstery than living life to the fullest might say.

"You can towel off with my shirt," Eli said.

Nick scanned up and down the beach. They were totally alone still. "I don't know," he said, wavering.

"Suit yourself. I'm going in, though." Eli shucked his shorts down to his ankles, revealing dark underwear—Nick averted his eyes yet again before he could make out any details—and ran down to the water, whooping the whole way.

Nick lifted his gaze once Eli was far enough away that it didn't feel too weird. He watched the pale beacon of Eli's bare back as he trudged through the waves, finally submerging where the bottom fell away. He splashed around in the gentle waves and hollered, "It feels great! Not even that cold." He scrubbed his wet hands over his face and through his hair. It stuck up in points, darker now that it was wet. "You sure you don't want to come in?" His voice echoed in the dark.

Fuck it. Nick dragged his shirt over his head and dropped it onto the sand. By the time he'd stripped down to his boxer briefs, Eli had noticed him undressing. He stuck his fingers in his mouth and gave a loud wolf whistle as he treaded water.

"Shut up," Nick called to him. He made his way down to the water with more caution than Eli had, hissing as he got wet. In the summer, this stretch of ocean was as warm as a bath. Now, though, it was chilled to freezing, at least to Nick's lifelong Floridian sensibilities. He steeled his jaw to keep his teeth from chattering as he waded up to his knees.

"This part is always the worst," he said, calling over the sound of crashing waves so Eli could hear him. "Cold water up to your waist. It's torture."

"Don't be such a baby. It's not that bad." Eli started floating on his back, his gaze riveted to the night sky.

"Promise me you won't make any jokes about shrinkage." Nick sucked in air through his teeth and took the last shuffling step that brought the water up to his chest.

"Excuse me, shrinkage hasn't been funny since 1996," Eli said. "Give me some credit. Anyway, I'm not a fan of small-dick jokes. For obvious reasons."

Nick bobbed in the water. "What? Why?"

"Uh, I'm trans?" Eli righted himself so that he was bobbing too. His tone sounded like he was very close to adding a *duh* to that statement. "People talk about cis guys having small dicks, and the joke is always that he's either not a real manly man"—he dropped his voice to a deeper register—"or that he's some aggro asshole trying to compensate." His voice went back to normal. "You can see why I might be tired of it."

"Eli," Nick said, "I'm Asian. I know all about small-dick jokes."

"Yeah, but you *know* you've got a big dick!" Eli swept his arm through the water, sending a miniature tidal wave in Nick's direction. It would have splashed him in the face if Nick hadn't twisted to the side with a shocky laugh.

"It's not *that* big," Nick said, still laughing. He couldn't remember the last time he'd had such a ridiculous conversation.

"I remember it differently. Meanwhile, I'm sitting here with my small dick with no good comeback except, like, I'm trying my best."

"You really have a distinct, enduring memory of my penis and its dimensions?"

"Don't feel too flattered," Eli muttered. He looked out over the waves. "I remember the first subway rat I ever saw too. That's just the way brains work."

"Sure." Nick smiled down at the water. He didn't know if Eli would see it in the dark, but he hoped he would.

They were treading water farther from shore now, the light of the stars and planets limning the crests of the black waves in white. One particularly strong wave came from nowhere and washed over Eli's head, leaving him sputtering and wiping salt water out of his eyes. Nick tried to school his face out of its goofy grin. There was a bubble of something frothy and buoyant in his chest, something that startled him with its intensity and unfamiliarity.

Oh, right. Fun. He was having fun.

He didn't do that much these days, did he?

Immediately the arguments rushed in, his mind filled with reasoned thoughts that would banish that too-tender one. He had lots of fun with Zoe. She was the light of his life, an endless fount of wonder. Nick could survive on one of her giggles for weeks.

But this was different, something inside him whispered. As much as he loved Zoe, he couldn't deny that parenthood was exhausting. When was the last time he'd taken a few minutes out of his day—or night, in this case—and had fun all for himself? Was it selfish to want that? A little time just for him?

"Hey, you okay?" Eli swam in front of him. "It's not too cold for you, is it?"

"No," Nick said way too quickly. "It feels nice once you get moving." Something brushed his ankle, probably seaweed, but Nick jolted, paddling closer to Eli. In the dark, in open water, everything seemed more dangerous to the lizard part of his brain.

Eli laughed at him. "You sure?"

"Yeah, just—" Nick caught the look on Eli's impish face, wavering between mirth and concern. Beads of water dotted his neck, dripped from the ends of his hair. He was really beautiful—handsome. Not that men couldn't be beautiful, but Eli might not like being thought of that way. Although, in the privacy of his thoughts, Nick didn't see the harm.

Maybe being selfish wasn't the end of the world.

He crossed the short distance between them, swimming up to Eli until they were nose to bobbing nose. Eli's eyes went wide, catching moonlight.

"Could we—?" Nick raised his hand and touched Eli's slick shoulder. He telegraphed his movements as best he could, slow and careful, drawing himself closer. The waves pushed him along so that it took hardly any effort at all.

He leaned in, still waiting to see if Eli would pull away.

He didn't.

It was barely more than a peck, Nick's mouth brushing against Eli's, the taste of salt between them. And yet the chill of the water seemed to fall away, and Nick felt enveloped instead by urgent heat. Eli's mustache tickled at his lip, a novel experience that made Nick shiver.

Then it was over, and Eli's breath was against his cheek, and Nick opened his eyes to see a very pale face staring back at him.

"Why did you do that?"

"I thought—" Nick floundered. Pretty literally, once he let his hand slip off Eli's shoulder. "Didn't you want to?"

A disbelieving huff left Eli's lips. "Jesus Christ, Nick." He turned and started swimming toward shore, arm over arm.

Nick floated there in the dark water for a moment. *Fuck.* His stomach sank to his toes, so heavy that he could have been dragged to the bottom of the sea. He forced himself to follow with a loud splash. "Wait! Eli, hold on."

Eli did not hold on. He staggered through the breakers, leaving the water with no grace at all. Nick watched the pale shape of his naked legs trudging up the sand to where their clothes were.

Nick made his own ungainly exit from the ocean and jogged to catch up. Eli was clothed in his shorts by the time Nick reached him, shaking out his shirt to find the right way to put it on. He didn't even look up at Nick's approach.

Nick reached for his arm, then thought better of it. His hand dangled uselessly at his side. "Look, I'm sorry. I thought I was getting some kind of—vibe."

"Doesn't mean you have to act on it," Eli said to his shirt.

It wasn't a denial, Nick noticed. "So there was something there? It wasn't just me?"

Eli sighed and dropped his shirt lower, tilting his head to stare at the sky. "What is your deal? You never used to be the type to go fishing for compliments."

"I'm not looking for compliments. I just want to know what I did wrong."

Eli whirled on him. "Where do I even start? Nick! You're straight."

"So?"

That was perhaps not the best response, because Eli blinked furiously, rearing back with his mouth hanging open. "So I'm not. I am, in fact, a gay man. Maybe you can conveniently forget that, but I can't."

Now Nick's mouth dropped open, this time in horror. "I didn't *forget*."

"Yes, you fucking did." Eli stooped and snatched Nick's pants from the sand, tossing them his way. Nick caught them on instinct, but the rest of him was frozen in place as Eli continued to talk. "I get it, okay? We've done a lot of reminiscing about the good ol' days, so it makes sense that all that would go to your head. But nostalgia isn't enough." Eli finally got his shirt over his head, his torso disappearing into the fabric. He tugged the hem in place. "You remember me as someone else, someone you used to kiss. I'm not that person anymore."

"That's not true," Nick said. "I don't look at you and see—" He bit his tongue, keeping it trapped between his back molars. He didn't want to lie. He was doing his best to see Eli as just a regular guy, but even that way of thinking—*regular*—didn't that prove he thought of Eli as irregular? Hadn't he had an argument with himself, mere moments ago, about thinking of Eli as beautiful?

"I didn't realize I was being disrespectful," he finally said, quiet and ashamed. "Sorry. It won't happen again."

"Yeah, it better not." Eli fished his phone out of the pocket of his shorts. The screen lit up his face, casting it in an eerie glow. "It's getting pretty late. We should get going."

"Right." Nick nodded a few times. "Of course."

Eli waited a beat. "You should probably get dressed," he added. His gaze stayed pointedly on Nick's face.

Said face went hot. "Yep. Doing that. Doing that now," Nick babbled as he stuck his wet leg into the jeans that were still in his hands. Ugh, the ride back to the Wards' place was going to be so awkward, he just knew it. Not only because of the damp denim, one of his least-favorite sensations in the world, but because he couldn't conceive of a way for them to get back to their easy camaraderie after what had happened.

Eli busied himself with retrieving Nick's button-down from the ground and shaking the sand out of it. "Hey, I don't want this to, like, explode everything," he said, his voice soft. "We've been friends since we were three years old. I'd like to stick with that, if it's all right with you."

"Absolutely." Nick took the offered shirt from Eli and shrugged it on. "Friends."

Better than he could have hoped for, given the circumstances.

For a moment there, he'd been convinced Eli would never speak to him again, and they'd go back to being nobody to each other. Nick could be happy with friends. Friends were good. Laurie was always on his case about how he didn't have enough of them, anyway.

But as they made their silent march back to the car, Nick couldn't help but feel that Eli was wrong. Nostalgia wasn't the only thing urging him to kiss Eli. If it was, surely now that it was all spelled out, he wouldn't want to anymore.

And the fact was, he did want to. Maybe a couple more times, to get the hang of it, because that last kiss had been too brief. He glanced over at Eli walking beside him. His gaze was on the ground, his cell phone lighting the way. Concentrating on where to put his feet. Nick, on the other hand, couldn't stop looking at Eli's mouth. There had been a hint of stubble when they'd kissed. That had been—new. Not bad. Kind of cool.

This is probably the part where I'm supposed to have some kind of massive gay panic, Nick thought idly. He waited for the wave of anxiety to come, hounded by questions: Was he not as straight as he'd always assumed? Was he bi? Was this really all a subconscious bid to cling to the past, relive his glory days?

The panic didn't come. Sure, the questions floated into his head, but they floated away harmlessly. He didn't feel the need to answer them right now. Why rush, especially when Eli had made it clear they were just friends?

"Want me to drive?" Eli said, breaking their long silence.

Nick blinked. "Huh?"

"I could drive if you want." They'd reached the parking lot by that point, and Eli made a big deal of looking around at the empty spots that surrounded Nick's lone car. "There's not a lot for me to back into right now, but I could probably make it happen. For old times' sake."

SECOND CHANCES IN NEW PORT STEPHEN   103

A startled laugh escaped Nick's chest. This was why, he knew. This was the reason he felt the way he did about Eli. Sure, it was complicated and confusing and perhaps not what was supposed to happen at all, but he had fun with Eli. He laughed more than he usually did, and he felt—better. Like he was more himself.

It was selfish, but Nick wanted to keep that feeling in a small fishbowl inside his chest, where he could tap on the glass from time to time and watch it swimming around. He didn't have to share it with anyone; Eli had made it clear that he didn't feel anything close to it, after all. But Nick could keep it for himself. Just to enjoy it.

He dug around in his pocket for his keys. "I think I'll do the driving, if you don't mind."

Eli put his hands up in a gesture of defeat. "All right, fine, but the offer's open. Anytime you feel like your pristine bumper needs a couple of dings, I'm your man."

Not really, Nick thought as he unlocked the car. Eli would never be his, not again.

CHAPTER 10

December 20

"Why did we have to come here?" Grammy Kay asked as the extended Wu family fought their way through the Auntie Anne's–scented hellscape that was the New Port Stephen Shopping Center in December. "We could have gone to the mall up in Pine Beach. No one was ever abducted in broad daylight from the one in Pine Beach."

"Oh, yes, I saw that one. *Unsolved Mysteries*," Tian-yi said. "Did they ever find the boyfriend?"

"No, Dad, that's why it's unsolved." Nick hefted Zoe higher on his hip and squinted up and down the length of the mall's main artery, trying to determine which way Santa's Village was. The wayfinding in this place was terrible.

"Sometimes they solve them," Kay said with unexpected optimism. "DNA. That's how you do it these days."

Tian-yi made a sound of polite interest. "So she does believe in certain types of science," he said to Nick in Hokkien, the dialect Nick had grown up speaking at home. "I suppose that's something." Nick's dad and Laurie's mom—a retired nuclear engineer and a believer in mind-altering chem trails, respectively—had had many debates about science in the past.

"Be nice, Dad. It's the holidays," Nick answered in kind. His Taiwanese wasn't as good as his dad's, but decent enough. His Mandarin would never hold a candle, though, along with the five other dialects his dad spoke that Nick had no hope of mastering. He felt a twinge of bittersweet longing in his chest. He wished his mom were here; she'd have kept Nick's dad in line with a single glance.

"Can we please table the case of the missing blond woman from the eighties? At least until after Christmas?" Laurie pointed to the left. "This way, I think." She tossed a grin over her shoulder to Zoe. "Excited to see Santa, honey?"

"Yes! I'll tell him I've been good this year, and he'll ask me what I want for Christmas, and then we get a picture taken with Santa and me and you and Daddy and Grammy and Ah Gong." She recited the day's rundown, as Nick and Laurie had been explaining it to her for weeks.

Nick herded them all in the direction Laurie had chosen, walking under the oversized Christmas ornaments that hung ponderously from the ceiling. Crowds of holiday shoppers flowed all around them. The mall's current soundtrack was a rendition of "Jingle Bells" that several country music stars had recorded a decade ago; Nick wasn't sure if the song was actually twenty minutes long or if they were playing it on repeat. Either way, he wanted to duck into the sporting goods store so he could take a baseball bat to the loudspeakers. It was almost as anxiety-inducing as his dad being in the same ten-mile radius as Laurie's mom.

Kay and Tian-yi were, to put it mildly, two very different people. They rarely interacted now that Laurie and Nick were divorced, but at least Kay was making an effort to be pleasant. Maybe it was holiday cheer. Or maybe Kay was just on her best behavior after that incident at Checker's.

"Oh, would you look at that?" Kay scoffed as they passed a shop window displaying tween fashions. "Who would want to dress their child in something so skanky?"

Or maybe not.

They finally reached Santa's Village, a collection of wooden cutouts painted to look like snow-dusted conifers and cottages situated between the food court and the Dillard's department store. The line of parents and kids waiting to see Santa snaked all the way past Spencer's Gifts, almost reaching the store where you could buy crystals and butterfly knives.

Tian-yi gave a low whistle. "Looks like a long wait."

Zoe twisted in Nick's grip and pointed to the small holiday-themed playground nearby, replete with cotton-batting snow among the slides and seesaws. "Can I go play?"

Kay turned to Nick. "Why don't you let your dad and I watch her while you two wait in line?"

Nick would have vastly preferred being the one with the fun job, but he supposed he should give the grandparents some quality time with Zoe. "Okay." He set Zoe on her feet and watched her take Grammy's hand, then Ah Gong's, before walking between them to the playground. Her little shoes flashed purple with every step.

Laurie heaved a loud sigh as she and Nick joined the end of the line. "This is going fine, right? Mom's not picking fights, at least."

"Not unless you count her criticizing your choice of mall," Nick said. Kay wasn't totally off base, though. The other one was much nicer. "Why *did* we come to this one instead of going to Pine Beach?"

Laurie rolled her eyes. "The Santas up there are white. I wanted Zoe to get her photo taken with a Santa of Color. She deserves good representation."

He craned his neck to get a look at the Santa sitting up on the dais that had been constructed for the occasion, gold throne and all. "Laur, the guy's Latino."

Laurie tossed her hands in the air. "Well, Asian Santas are mighty thin on the ground. This was the best I could do, okay?"

Deciding that this was not the hill he wanted to die on, Nick held up his hands. "Okay." He tried to imagine getting to see a non-white Santa when he was Zoe's age, but he couldn't quite picture it. Maybe it would have made a positive impact? There was probably no harm in giving it a shot, at least.

He made a mental note to try to find some more picture books about East Asian women for Zoe's growing pile of Christmas gifts. The Connie Chung board book he'd bought two years ago was falling apart at the spine.

To stave off boredom, Nick let his thoughts wander to Eli. A few days had passed since their night swim, and Nick had practiced extreme self-control in not reaching out to Eli. Eli, though, had texted him a photo of Mr. Ward napping on the sofa in their family room, mouth open and eyeglasses askew on his nose. Nick had replied with what he thought was a very friendly crying-laughing emoji that hopefully didn't indicate any one-sided feelings whatsoever.

"After this, do you want to get Chick-fil-A for lunch?" Laurie asked.

Instead of answering, Nick asked, "Hey, do you think I might be gay?"

Laurie's brows rose until they were hidden under her bangs. Her mouth opened and shut a few times before she said, "Do I think you're what now?"

"Gay. Or, like, some flavor of queer." Nick glanced around, but everyone else in line was focused on managing their fussy children or beating the next level of *Candy Crush*. No one was paying attention to their conversation. "Did that ever cross your mind? Just curious."

She dropped her gaze and furrowed her brow. That was her serious face. "No, I don't think so. Why do you ask?"

"You probably know me better than anyone." With the exception of maybe Eli, who'd known him since before they could even remember. "Wondered if you had a take on it."

Laurie nodded a few more times, then stood on tiptoe to watch Zoe climbing over a gingerbread playset, Kay and Tian-yi both taking pictures with their phones. It was good that they both had the excuse of watching her. Eye contact during a conversation like this was not easy. "Is this about Eli?" she asked. Her voice was carefully modulated, the way it had been in couples counseling. Stripped of even the barest hint of judgment.

"How'd you know?"

"Doesn't take a detective. He's the only new thing to come into your life in a while. Well, come *back* into your life, I guess. And you told me when we started dating that you only had one other serious relationship and it was in high school, so I connected the dots. He's your ex, right?"

"Got it in one." He was kind of impressed that Laurie hadn't said "ex-girlfriend."

"Have you talked to Eli about this?" Laurie asked.

"Nah. Not really. Don't know if it's a good idea," Nick said. No way was he telling her about the failed kiss. Some things you just couldn't tell your ex-wife, no matter how close you were. He felt something brush his fingers, and he looked down to find Laurie's hand slipping into his. That was a surprise. They hadn't been very touchy-feely since the divorce. Hugs hello and goodbye sometimes, but nothing else.

She squeezed his fingers, and their eyes met. "I wouldn't care if you're gay," she said.

He knew that. He wouldn't have even broached the subject with Laurie if he hadn't been sure she was cool. Hell, he would never have married her. But still, hearing her say it out loud made him feel warm inside.

"Thanks, Laur." He squeezed back. "But I don't know if I am, honestly."

Her hand slipped out of his. "How can you be so calm about this?" she asked. "Most guys in this situation would be panicking."

"Guess I'm not most guys," he said.

Laurie made a gesture Nick privately called her "what the fuck?" move, twisting at her waist with her hands palm up like she was asking some unseen audience to weigh in. "That's it? You like a guy for the first time and you're like 'oh well'?"

"I've liked him before."

"Yeah, when he was a woman. That doesn't count."

"I think it does." He frowned. "And I don't think he was ever a woman, actually. We just didn't know it at the time."

"Okay, yes, my bad. But here you are, twenty-some years later, and you're not freaking out at all about this new development where you might be kind of gay?"

Nick thought about it carefully before answering. "There is a little—I guess you'd call it an indignant feeling? Like, I'm almost forty. Why am I only now realizing that I might not be straight? Which makes me wonder, maybe it's nothing. If it were something, wouldn't I have figured it out years ago? Then again, look at Eli. He didn't come out until he was in his thirties. So maybe it's not that weird." He took another step forward as the line moved, gently guiding Laurie by the elbow so she wasn't holding anyone up. "To be honest? I'm fine with not knowing for sure for right now. Either way, nothing changes, right? I'm still the same person with the same life." And the same completely platonic relationship with Eli.

He didn't have all the words to describe what a *delight* it was to be discovering a new part of himself. At his age, he'd almost given up on uncovering anything new or noteworthy, but now that there was a chance that he wasn't done growing, he found himself kind of—excited. Not having a label for it yet wasn't a huge crisis. In a way, it was a relief.

Laurie eyed him for a second. "Well, I'm glad you seem to be taking this in stride. I'm proud of you."

"Thanks, Laur. Sorry to be dumping all this on you. I know it's kind of above the pay grade for an ex-wife."

She hip-checked him, her arms folded across her chest. "Shut up. You know I'm always there for you if you need to talk."

"Hey, goes both ways," Nick said. Then, wishing Eli were there to hear it, he joked, "Like me. Maybe."

Laurie snickered. "Dork." Then she lapsed into what seemed like a thoughtful silence, her gaze going distant. They shuffled forward another step as the line moved.

Laurie spoke up once more. "Have you ever thought that maybe you're—?" She bit her lip.

"Maybe I'm what?" Nick asked.

"Look, I'm just a straight white girl here. I'm not exactly an expert in human sexuality, so I should probably keep my damn mouth shut."

"No, please. Might be useful for me to hear it."

That seemed to make her fold pretty quickly. "Well, I was wondering, have you ever considered you might be"—she waggled her head like she did when she was trying to broach a delicate subject—"demisexual?"

"Uh, since I have no idea what that word means, no. I have not considered that," Nick said. "What is it?"

"I think it's like—again, not an expert, just read an article in *Allure* one time—but when someone is only attracted to people they have a deep emotional bond with."

Nick screwed his mouth to one side. "Isn't that how everyone operates?"

"Not really," Laurie said. "I think most people can be attracted to a stranger if they think they're hot."

"I can appreciate a hot stranger," Nick protested.

"Oh yeah?" Laurie scanned the busy mall before pointing to a woman standing about a dozen yards away next to the Sbarro. "What about her?"

Nick sighed and tried to get a look at the woman without appearing too creepy. Thankfully she was busy texting on her phone. She was objectively gorgeous: dark skin, high cheekbones, a sleek sweaterdress hugging her curves, delicate corkscrews of hair framing her face.

"She's very pretty," Nick said, facing ahead again.

"And?" Laurie prompted. "That's it?"

"What do you want me to say?" Nick balked. "Not all men are sex-crazed animals who can't stop thinking about getting laid!" That earned him a glare from the mother in front of them. Nick grimaced in apology, comforted by the fact that her baby was small enough to be resting against her shoulder; it wasn't like any of this was going to penetrate. He lowered his voice. "Do you walk around thinking about sleeping with every attractive man you cross paths with?"

"No, but I can picture it if I want. Can you?"

Nick glanced back at the woman in the sweaterdress. As he watched, she was approached by another woman about her age, and they greeted each other with jubilant hugs. He tried to imagine going up to her and maybe asking for her number—shit, did people still ask for numbers?—but all he could think about was how rude it would be to interrupt. His imagination apparently craved some kind of narrative through-line. Did she appreciate goofy action movies? Did she laugh a lot? What was her Monopoly piece? Would she get along with his dad?

"I mean, not without getting to know someone first," he said. "There's nothing weird about that. It's mature."

"Right, but my point is, lots of people have *fantasies* that are not grounded in reality. Like, I would never *actually* walk up to that woman and ask if she wanted to get busy in the Macy's changing room, but I can indulge in a fantasy, can't I?"

"That's . . . so specific. What happened to being a straight white girl?"

"Oh, please. I may be a two on the Kinsey scale, but if someone that beautiful was down?" Laurie stuck out her lips in a pout. "I would consider it."

Nick shook his head. "So sexuality is not black-and-white. Great. But I still don't think there's anything wrong with only liking people you actually *like*."

"No one's saying it's wrong! Well, some people might, but they're dicks." She flipped her hair over her shoulder. "Listen, you've only had two serious relationships in your entire life, right? Me and Eli. And in both of those instances, you knew us for years before you started dating us."

That was true; Nick had met Laurie a few years out of college. She'd worked as a server at the Manatee while going to night school to become a registered nurse, and they'd become close. Laurie had liked goofy action movies and board games, and when she wasn't around her mother, she laughed a lot. After Laurie left the Manatee to start her nursing career, Nick had stayed in touch, and that had naturally progressed to dating, then all the rest. Nick had never made the connection between that and his long friendship with Eli before they started dating in high school, but it was a pretty similar trajectory, now that he thought about it.

"Hm," he said. He pulled out his cell phone and started googling. "What's it called again? Demo—?"

"Demisexual." She peered between his phone and the playground where Zoe was throwing around fake snow. "It's a flavor of asexuality, so that'll probably pop up too."

Nick stopped typing and looked at her. "Isn't that when someone doesn't like sex? Because that is not me." It had been a while since he'd last done it, but he always enjoyed it. And he hated the stereotype that all Asian guys were sexless math-obsessed machines.

"It's not cut and dry, remember? There's, like, a complex rainbow under the asexual umbrella." Laurie outlined an invisible rainbow arch with her hands. "According to *Allure*, at least."

Nick tried to look less skeptical, but he couldn't have been doing a very good job because Laurie rolled her eyes.

"Read up on it," she said. "Maybe it'll click, maybe it won't. I only brought it up because it seemed like a likely candidate if you're looking for a label."

Nick had been labeled a lot of things in his life, not all of them flattering. He wasn't sure he was in a rush to apply a new one, but at least if he did, it would be something he picked out for himself. He'd take his time with this one, and if it turned out it didn't fit, he could always take it off again.

"I'll look into it," he promised, bookmarking a couple of articles that seemed to be from reputable organizations. The ones that promised to "fix what was broken," he skipped. Like Laurie had said, fuck them. "It does seem interesting. I didn't know my approach was so—abnormal."

"Or we could use the word 'rare.'" Laurie frowned. "Although I'm not even sure if it really is rare. Different? Unique!"

"This is all stuff I can figure out, if it comes to it," he said with a smile. "Thanks for the insight, whatever happens."

"And absolutely no pressure to prove my instincts correct, you know." She nudged his shoulder with hers. "I could be completely off base. As long as you're happy."

Happy. He had been on the verge of rediscovering how happy he could be when he'd messed things up with Eli. Finding a word that best described himself was nowhere near as important to him as figuring out a way to show Eli how he felt. If he could convince Eli he wasn't confused or affected with a case of extreme nostalgia, all the other stuff would follow. He was certain of it.

The line moved again, with only the angry woman with the baby in front of them now. Nick beckoned Zoe and the grand-parents over. "Come on, kiddo, it's almost time to meet Santa."

Zoe bounded over, her hair in disarray. Grammy Kay took a small comb from her purse and hastily tried to tame it. "I'm going to ask for a puppy," Zoe squealed as she wriggled away from the combing.

Laurie shot Nick a pained look. "Honey, I don't know if Santa can swing that. It's so cold up in the air when he's flying from the North Pole, a puppy might not be safe."

"But Alice and her brother Artie asked for one last year and Santa brought it. It's named Pickle and it's really long, like a hot dog." Zoe held out her arms to show precisely how long Pickle was.

"That's very long," Ah Gong agreed.

Nick fussed with Zoe's hair, trying to comb it back into some semblance of neatness with his fingers. He knew she hated the drag of a comb. "Well, it doesn't hurt to ask. But remember, Santa can't grant every wish."

"But it's the only thing I really want," Zoe said.

Nick's heart lurched. He could relate.

"Try to ask for some other stuff too. In case he can't fit a puppy in the sleigh," Laurie said, then made desperate eye con-tact with one of the nearby elves. She made a slashing motion across her throat, and the elf gave a firm nod.

Later, when they were paying for the (exorbitantly priced,

they all agreed) photos in their cheesy snowflake-covered frames, Nick took a good hard look at the family portrait: Zoe on Santa's lap, cute as a button; Laurie and her mom on one side, smiling stiffly; and Nick and his dad on the other, arms flung over each other's shoulders, a void next to them where Nick's mom would have stood. She'd hated having her picture taken, but she would have smiled wide anyway, her perfect, toothy "album face" as she called it. He thought about what Eli had said when they were kayaking, about Christmas being a big letdown after the high of childhood, and he wondered how many more good years he had left to make them count for Zoe.

He also wondered if there wasn't a way to try to recapture that magic for Eli.

"Hey, Dad," he said as Kay and Laurie argued about who was going to pay for all the pictures, both of them trying to shove their credit cards in the poor cashier's hand, "do you still have that bike you got from a yard sale?"

"Of course. It was a good deal," Tian-yi said. "Why?"

"I need a favor."

CHAPTER 11

eing alone in a suburban house was like being in a horror movie. After years living in New York apartments, Eli
chafed at the sprawling silence inside his parents' home.
His folks had left to run errands hours ago. They hadn't given
Eli any details, just grabbed their keys with a cursory goodbye,
which was par for the course ever since their tiff over the Christmas ornaments.

With only the cat for company, Eli was hyperaware of every
sound, like the bang of the ice maker or the creaky whoosh of
the air conditioner. The rest of the neighborhood was so quiet,
no white noise of constant traffic to cover up anything. So when
he heard a scraping sound at the front door, he immediately
assumed he was about to be attacked by some Floridian super-
criminal.

He put down the biography of Patton he'd snagged from his
dad's bookshelf, picked up the golf club his parents kept in the
corner next to the sliding glass door, and crept toward the front
of the house. If he was going down, he was going down swinging.
Florida Man Dies, Looked Cool Doing It. The doorknob rattled,

the sound like a gunshot through the hallway. Eli stopped breathing, his grip tight on the driver. Thank god he'd convinced his parents to at least lock their door if they were leaving the house.

Then he spotted a familiar head of dark hair bobbing outside the sidelight windows that flanked the door. A relieved sigh left him.

Eli lowered the club and twisted the lock on the door, flinging it open to find Nick crouched right outside. He looked up at Eli in surprise. In his hand was one of the many ceramic garden gnomes that Mrs. Ward kept scattered around the front porch.

"Oh. Sorry," Nick said. "I didn't think you were home. No car in the carport."

"What the hell are you doing?" Eli shook the driver in his hand. "I was about to bash your head in."

Nick scrambled to his feet. "I was looking for the spare." He showed Eli the hollow bottom of the gnome he still held, the one with the bright red hat. Taped inside was indeed a copy of the front door key. "Guess your parents still keep it out here, huh?"

"Seriously?" Eli boggled. "Okay, I am going to have to talk with them about basic home security. It's not 1992 anymore."

"At least they lock their door. My dad still leaves his unlatched, even when he leaves. Says there isn't anything worth stealing."

"Oh my god." Eli couldn't fathom it.

"I know. Believe me, you're not the only one worried about prowlers." Nick gestured at the golf club. "But, uh, think you could put that away now? Or are you still trying to decide whether to give me a good whack upside the head?"

Eli hastily leaned the club against the plaster statue of a heron that guarded the foyer. "So why were you trying to get in the house?"

"Well . . . ." Nick cast a nervous glance over his shoulder. "It seems kind of silly now."

Eli went up on tiptoe to catch a glimpse of Nick's car parked on the street. He could see that the trunk wasn't completely closed, fastened with bungee cords. Zoe was in the yard as well, twirling around in circles while humming to herself. She seemed to have found a friend in the fake reindeer among the Christmas lawn decor, blowing it kisses every so often.

"What's that in your trunk?" Eli asked with suspicion. He left the doorway and pushed his way past Nick, letting the door shut behind him.

"Nothing," Nick said, trying to get ahead of him and block his view.

Luckily Eli was nimble and slipped right past him. "Hey, Zoe," he said as he marched by on his way to get a closer look.

"Hi, Eli!" Zoe stopped spinning long enough to wave, then threw herself on her back in the grass, kicking her legs up at the sky. "Do you like it?"

"Maybe," he told her with perfect honesty. "I need to see what it is first." He stopped, finally getting a good look. Sticking out of the trunk of Nick's sensible Toyota was a bicycle wheel. It was slowly rotating in midair, its spokes catching the sunlight.

He stood speechless. If the sprinkler system his dad had installed years ago chose that moment to pop out of the ground and start spraying water across the yard, Eli still wouldn't have moved. He was rooted to the spot.

"So," Nick said from somewhere on his left, "we got you a bike."

"You got me a bike," Eli repeated in a daze. "Why did you get me a bike?"

Zoe rocketed past, her two pigtails flapping behind her. "Because you said the last time you had a good Christmas was when you got a bike! The best present ever, remember?" She tugged at the hooks on the bungee cords, trying to release the trunk lid. "Dad said you deserved to have a good Christmas again."

"He did, huh?" Eli looked over at Nick, who seemed to be shaking off his initial embarrassment at getting caught playing Santa Claus. His chin stuck out at a stubborn angle as he met Eli's eyes.

"I did indeed." He swept past Eli to pry Zoe's little fingers off the cords. "I'll get that, honey, don't hurt yourself." Then, over his shoulder, he said, "I was going to leave this on the back patio for you, but I guess this is better." He unhooked the bungee cords and lifted the bike out, setting its wheels on the grass. "What do you think?"

Eli approached slowly. The bike was black with neon green streaks running down the frame. It was the same color scheme he'd expect to find on bottles of three-in-one men's shampoo/conditioner/face wash. Super masc. The seat wasn't too high, just right for his smaller stature. There was a basket, which seemed practical. And the handlebars sported actual gears, unlike the bikes of Eli's childhood. He reached out and squeezed one. The bike made a happy click in response.

"It's secondhand, nothing fancy," Nick said in an apologetic tone. "My dad picked it up at a yard sale. No idea why. He hates bike riding."

"You didn't want it for yourself?" Eli asked.

"Nah. I figured you'd get some real use out of it while you're down here." He pushed the bike toward Eli. "It's not a car, but it'll get you places if you ever feel stir-crazy again." His deep brown eyes held an impossible warmth. "Merry Christmas, Eli."

Eli took hold of the handlebars in earnest, and Nick's hand slipped away. "Oh, wow." He marveled at the bike. It was in good condition, and if things got dicey again with his folks, he wouldn't have to rely on someone being available to furnish him with an escape. "I don't know what to say. I mean, I didn't know we were doing presents. I didn't get you anything!"

Nick laughed. "You don't have to. Seriously, it was just sitting around."

The thing was, when Nick said stuff like that—*you don't have to get me anything; really, it's not a big deal*—he meant it. He was honestly that nice. It was so infuriating. Eli's last serious boyfriend, Rick (the one who took the cat), hadn't been half as nice. When Eli had turned thirty-seven, Rick took him out to dinner to celebrate, but when Eli had tried to order the steak, Rick had said, "You're going to end up taking half of that slab of meat home with you, so really that's two meals. I've only budgeted to treat you to one birthday dinner. Order something else."

That had devolved into a huge argument where Eli pointed out how he had been more than generous with Rick on *his* birthday (dinner *and* tickets to a terrible off-Broadway play that they could make fun of afterward), and Rick accused him of "keeping score," and Eli said he didn't see anything wrong with that, since Rick was clearly a big fan of numbers, which made Rick throw down his napkin and storm out. Eli broke up with him immediately via text. Their two-year relationship was kaput in under two seconds.

And that dig about keeping score was still circulating in Eli's head.

He shook himself. Nick was not his boyfriend, not anymore. Just a friend. And friends did things for each other all the time. It didn't mean anything except . . . friendly stuff. He was clearly reading too much into it.

"Wait! We were gonna put this with the bike so when you found it, you'd know who'd left it for you." Zoe shoved about a metric ton of silver tinsel at Eli along with a folded piece of construction paper covered in Crayola scribbles.

Eli clutched the items against his chest and let the bicycle lean against his hip. "Oh, thank you, Zoe. It's . . ." He struggled for words.

"A card," Zoe said. She tapped the edge of the creased paper excitedly. "Come on, open it!"

Eli made a show of unfolding the construction paper with a flourish, juggling the tinsel before stuffing it in the basket that hung from the bike's handlebars. The card had a crude drawing of a Christmas tree on the face, each triangle-tip branch playing host to a brightly colored orb. Inside was a face clearly drawn with a four-year-old's skill. There was a nose and eyes and a slash of a mouth, and although they weren't exactly where they should have been, Eli recognized the swoop of his light brown hair on top of the bulbous head.

Happy Holidays, it said in red crayon—that was Nick's penmanship. Eli could still recognize the way he looped his P's and Y's into the next letter. *From: Zoe & Nick.* The signatures were done in purple. Zoe must have demanded to sign her own name; the Z looked a little wonky.

Eli loved it. He traced the drawing of his own face with a fingertip. "This is so good, Zoe. You really captured my soul. My inner turmoil."

"Mm-hmm." Zoe nodded like she knew what that meant. Hell, maybe she did; kids were so much smarter these days. "I'm a good draw-er."

"You know," Eli said, "your dad was terrible at drawing when we were kids. He made me look like a potato when he drew me." Zoe giggled, so he went for the punchline. "I didn't mind, though. I like potatoes."

That got a bigger laugh from his tiny audience. Eli looked up to catch Nick's eye, faltering when he saw what Nick's face was doing. He looked—it was hard to say, exactly. If he didn't know him like he did, Eli would say he looked uncomfortable, the lines around his mouth and eyes creasing. But when Nick was uncomfortable, he fidgeted, and at the moment his hands were relaxed, one tucked into his back pocket and the other dangling at his side. Wistful. That was the look. Like he was watching from a distance something that he wanted close.

Well. Time to do what Eli always did when faced with a serious moment: act like an unhinged clown.

"Hey, Zoe, it's been a long time since I rode a bike," he said, directing his gaze back down to the little girl. "Do you think you could help me get the hang of it?"

Zoe looked up at him, then at her dad, a silly smile growing on her lips. She was in on the joke, and probably wasn't used to that. "Um, I don't know. I have a bike, but it's got three wheels." She held up the requisite number of fingers to illustrate. "It's not the same."

"Three wheels? Oh, wow, mine only has two." Eli pouted as he looked over his new bicycle. "You must be a way better bike rider than I am since you have a whole 'nother wheel. Way more advanced."

Zoe laughed that high-pitched laugh that kids make before they get too self-conscious to make noises like that. "Eli! That's not how it works. More wheels are for kids, and I'm a kid."

"If that's true, then how come a car has four wheels, huh? Cars are only for adults."

Zoe screeched in delight. "You sit in a car, not *on* it! It's not like a bike."

"No?" Eli made a big production out of thinking that over. "Well, you obviously know more about this stuff than I do. So will you help me relearn how to ride a bike?" He picked up his leg to sit astride the bicycle seat, plunking the handmade card into the basket with the tinsel. "What's the first step?"

Zoe adopted a pose that was so cute, Eli wanted to scream. She curled her fist under her chin and eyed Eli's bike like it was a serious problem, but her eyes were twinkling like she knew it was all for fun. "First, you have to stay on the grass," she declared. "That way, when you fall, you won't break anything."

"*When* I fall?" Eli gasped and clutched at his imaginary pearls. "Zoe, have some faith in me! I'm your best student."

Zoe giggled into her hand, then composed herself. "When you figure out how to balance on the grass, you can go on the driveway."

"Oh, all right. Tough, but fair." Out of the corner of his eye, Eli saw Nick walk back to the porch, where he took a seat in one of the wicker chairs. He was smiling and relaxed, watching their antics. Eli concentrated on his bike school gag. "Okay, I'm on the grass. Now what?"

For the next several minutes, he let Zoe put him through his paces. Some of her lessons were grounded in reality, like when she directed him to hold on to the handlebars and not let go, while others only made sense in Kid World. Eli didn't mind roaring like a tiger every time he put both feet on the pedals, since it made Zoe double over with laughter. Plus, he couldn't be totally certain it wasn't helping. He started pretty wobbly, of course; decades of never getting on a bike except the stationary ones at the gym would do that to anyone. But soon he had graduated to making slow, careful donuts on the driveway while Zoe ran behind him, shrieking in delight at the progress she'd overseen.

"Now I'm the dolphin trainer," she said, "and you're the dolphin."

"Can dolphins ride bikes?"

"If they're *trained*." The "duh" went unsaid. She placed her thumb and forefinger in front of her lips and made a tweeting noise like she was blowing an imaginary whistle. "Do your tricks! Do them!"

Slapstick wasn't normally Eli's favorite form of comedy, but he didn't mind doing a pratfall onto the grass if it got Zoe laughing.

Eli had never, not once in his entire thirty-nine years, pictured himself having kids. Before his transition, he'd been a mess, drinking too much, staying out too late. He couldn't take care of himself, let alone a child. Then he started to get his life together. Got help. Came out. Even now, years later, it all seemed so fragile, like one wrong move and it would all come crashing down. Eli hated to admit to living in fear, but the idea that one shit-headed law or a single change in health care policy could upend his life was very real. Who had the time to start a family with all that looming over his head? Not to mention, he'd never found someone he'd want to start a family with. Now, careening toward the big four-oh, he'd figured he'd missed the boat long ago. If kids were supposed to happen, they'd have happened by now, he'd thought.

But here was Zoe, taking to his bit about being a terrible bicyclist like she'd been playing the straight man her whole life. Making it sillier and more bizarre than Eli ever could with his stodgy adult brain. It was like watching a master of the craft. Eli had never realized: kids were naturally hilarious.

Damn. At what point did the world try to suck all that dry? He was seized by the desire for Zoe to always be like this, laughing and joking and acting out the little melodramas that only made sense in her head. He wanted to defend that right of hers. Wanted to keep the dreary adult world at bay for as long as he could.

Ah, shit. Eli skidded to a stop at the bottom of the driveway, still astride his bike. Maybe he was dad material after all. Or step-dad material.

Not to Zoe, of course. Some other child, maybe. Though this one in particular had really good timing.

"I'm done," Zoe called from the grass. She was back to twirling in circles, now with a stick in her hand.

"Yep." Eli cleared his dry throat. "Think I've finally got the hang of bike riding. And being a dolphin. Thank you, Zoe."

"You're welcome," she said.

Eli looked over at where Nick was sitting on the porch. Nick was staring back at him, an unreadable emotion curled into his faint smile. A wave of vertigo washed over Eli, a feeling of falling through reality. In some other lifetime, this could have been an alternate path where he stayed in Florida, stayed with Nick. If he squinted, he could imagine a glass of iced tea in Nick's hand, and the house where Eli had grown up was theirs.

The mirage shattered as Nick clapped his hands to his knees and rose. "We should get going. Enjoy the bike." He ushered Zoe toward the car.

"Yeah, I will," Eli said dully. He walked the bicycle into the carport, leaning it carefully against the stucco wall.

He stood on the driveway and waved goodbye until Nick's car turned at the corner. When it was gone, he dropped his hand and whispered only to himself and the lizards on the porch, "Well, fuck."

CHAPTER 12

December 21

Eli was stretched out on the bed in the guest room, texting back and forth with Margo, when he heard his parents' car pulling up the driveway. Margo was in the middle of explaining to him that she'd had no more news from the network, and Eli was attempting to distract her as best he could with bad puns. Margo one-upped him in the pun department as the sound of car doors closing reached Eli's ears. Sweet Potato was curled up around Eli's neck like a fuzzy scarf, which might have been cute and cozy if it weren't so hot.

"Should probably go face the music," Eli told the cat, and nudged him until he finally leapt to the floor with no sympathy whatsoever for Eli's plight.

He texted Margo to let her know she'd won the pun war (for now) while he shuffled on bare feet into the kitchen. He needed a glass of juice, something to get the lump out of his throat before he spoke with his parents. The standoff over the Christmas ornaments had gone on for several days, and he figured it was time to clear the air.

The front door slammed. "Eli? Are you here?" his mom called. She didn't sound angry, just kind of anxious.

"Whose bike is that outside? Meant to ask about it yesterday," his dad's voice floated through the house.

Eli gulped down a mouthful of Minute Maid before calling back, "Mine. Thought I could get some exercise while I was here." It wasn't a lie, but he hesitated to mention that the bike was a gift from Nick. His mom was probably still sore about all the time Eli was spending with him.

Cora Ward popped her head in the kitchen, beaming at Eli. "Are you busy at the moment?"

Eli looked around the empty kitchen, then down at himself. He was obviously dressed for a lazy day with his loose basketball shorts and an old high school T-shirt with the sleeves cut off, leaving ragged edges. "Can't say I have any pressing plans."

He could hear some commotion in the sitting room, like his dad was fussing with something and muttering under his breath. Eli craned his neck to try to get a peek around the corner, but his mom stepped directly into his line of sight, just like Nick had yesterday with the bike. "Your father and I have a surprise for you. If you're up for it." She glanced at his rumpled clothing with pursed lips. "You might want to change. And fix your hair."

"Why?" Suspicion dripped from the single syllable.

Wendall appeared briefly holding a box. From the stilted way he moved, it must have been heavy. He disappeared again, his footsteps echoing down the hallway.

"I need to grab some things from the closet." Cora stepped forward and gave Eli a peck on his slack cheek. "Max is outside when you're ready."

"Wait, why is Max—? Okay, already walking away," Eli muttered to no one, now that his mom had bustled out of the kitchen.

Eli headed for the hallway bathroom to get his hair under

control. He noticed there was a blank space beside the bathroom door where a picture frame was supposed to be. Strange. He distinctly remembered seeing it there this morning. He stared at the bare nail with his hand on the bathroom doorknob. "Mom?" he called, but no one answered him. He looked over his shoulder and saw a neat row of ghostly rectangles on the wall of the hallway. Outlines of dusty gray where frames had hung against the cheerful robin's egg paint for decades.

Okay. Freaky. Maybe his parents had decided to toss all the old photos after all.

Eli quickly fixed his hair and changed into his old stand-up uniform: black jeans and a black tee. On his way out the door, he passed by barren sideboards where picture frames had once bristled, noticing the lines they left in the faint dust on the furniture.

Max was, indeed, standing outside with a huge Nikon—big enough to get some good paparazzi shots of the moon. Cora and Wendall were there, too, freeing their old family photos from the box of frames and showing them to Max. Cora looked up with a bright smile when she heard the door.

"Okay, sweetie, so first of all, if this isn't something you're interested in doing, just let us know."

"I don't even know what this is," Eli pointed out.

"Consider it an early Christmas present," Wendall said. He carefully lifted the back from another picture frame and snagged the photograph from inside. Eli recognized it even from a distance: some summer vacation, his hair in tiny pigtails, he and his parents all lined up eating ice cream cones of different colors, their faces jammed together as Wendall took the photo selfie-style.

It was a cute picture, even if Eli didn't feel any real connection to it.

"This was all your cousin's idea." Cora patted Max fondly on the cheek. "Such a brilliant photographer."

Max slouched further, eyes darting to the far corners of the yard. "Normally I take portraits of roadkill, but sure, I can handle this."

"Maybe someone could explain it to me like I'm five?" Eli asked. "A hint, even. First word sounds like . . . ?"

Wendall placed the liberated photograph in the growing pile on the corner of the cement planter in front of the porch. "Here's the story, morning glory: we're going to take some new pictures. Replacements."

"You can pose just like you did in the old ones," Cora gushed. "Look, I even brought costume changes!" She hefted a giant Beall's Outlet shopping bag, showing Eli the wads of clothing that threatened to spill out.

"And then we'll have brand-new pictures of you and us that we can put up in the house instead." His dad flipped through more of the frames in the box, then stopped at one that showed Eli proudly holding up a microscopically small fish that he'd caught on the causeway. "Look at that *smile*. Oh, we've got to do this one for sure."

"It's, like, a meme?" Max said. "Re-creating childhood photos as an adult. People post them online like before and after, but we can just focus on the after."

Eli stood there, stunned. He could barely understand what his parents and Max were saying. "You . . . really want all-new pictures? Of me?"

"I still don't want to throw the old ones in the trash," Cora said, "but I could put them away in some scrapbooks and display the new ones instead. What do you think?"

"Uh, I think—" Eli's throat went tight. "I think that's cool." It came out all squeaky, on the verge of tears. Fuck, when was the last time he'd had a good, long cry? Probably years ago, when he'd first gone on T. There was a lot of talk about testosterone making trans guys angry and aggressive, but in Eli's experience, it just made everything feel *more*. Like the intensity of everything was dialed up to eleven. This was like that, except without the huge hormonal shift. "Oh my god, I'm sorry, I just didn't expect all this," he said, wiping at his wet eyes with his T-shirt sleeve.

"Oh, my baby." Cora flew to him, not even noticing when the Beall's bag tipped over to spill old jackets and shirts on the driveway. She folded him into a hug. "I want you to expect it from now on, okay? Expect the effort."

"Did you get that from a bumper sticker?" Eli sobbed onto her thin shoulder.

"All right, Mr. Jokes." Wendall joined them, wrapping his arms around them both. "We're trying our best here. Sorry we don't get it sometimes."

"No, you guys, I don't—" He knew if he used the word *expect* his mom would have another fit. Eli pulled back out of their little hug knot to hold them both at arm's length so he could look them in the eye. "I know you've gone above and beyond. There are lots of moms and dads out there who wouldn't give a kid like me the time of day; I'm really, really lucky. What more can I ask for?"

"The world, Eli," Cora said. "We want to give you the world. I don't want to win Mom of the Year just because the bar is really low. I want to win outright, in *all* categories."

Eli sniffed and ran the blade of one hand under his damp nose. "You know there is no actual award, right? No one is grading us."

"Well, they should." Cora tossed her head. "Because I am doing very good work."

Jesus, his parents were nerds. Eli loved them very much.

The soft click of a camera went off, and they all looked up to find Max standing on one of the wicker chairs on the porch, taking a photo of them at a high angle.

"That's going to be a nice one," Max said.

"I think you're right, kiddo." Wendall squeezed Eli by the shoulder. "What do you say? Want to redo some baby pictures?"

Eli rubbed at his face, making sure to get the last of the tears. "Hold on, I need to get some ice." No way was he going to pose with puffy eyes. He darted back inside to make a quick cold compress.

A lot of the photos could be retaken in or around the house since it was the house Eli had grown up in. Many of the earliest photos showed infant Eli being held in laps or playing in the front yard. While Eli clearly couldn't rock a onesie any longer—although he guessed that somewhere in Bushwick there were adult-sized footie pajamas being made to order—Cora had a few creative workarounds.

The first picture they re-created showed an early 1980s Wendall sitting on the porch with baby Eli in his arms, Cora beside them, looking rad with her Farrah Fawcett hairdo. Instead of trying to fit in his dad's lap, which was physically impossible, not to mention weird, Eli instead draped himself over the armrests of the wicker porch chairs. A bolt of cloth printed with small birds stood in for the cutesy zoo animal onesie baby Eli had been wearing. Max draped it over his torso with an artistic eye.

"I'm feeling very Grecian, very Bacchanal," Eli said as he waited for the picture to be taken. He propped his head on his hand and affected his best serene look.

"Max, do you think we could hurry this one up a little?" Wendall asked. "Eli's surprisingly heavy."

After that, they moved on to other poses: Eli sitting inside a laundry basket on the driveway. Eli mid-cartwheel on the grass in the front yard. Eli holding out a lizard on his finger for the camera to see—that one had taken some effort to set up, as adult Eli was really out of practice as far as lizard-catching went. It took

him a good forty minutes to finally grab one of the brownish
striped anoles that were sunning themselves on the driveway.

"Remind me why we're doing this again?" he said as he struggled to keep the lizard from leaping out of his cupped hands.

Max calmly switched out lenses. "Because it's Christmas.
Now smile like you're ten."

The ornament photos were redone, too, with Wendall don-
ning a Santa hat and beard that Cora had dug out of the holiday
decor boxes. Eli mimed perching on his dad's knee for the oblig-
atory mall Santa photo.

"You don't need to hover," his dad groused.

"I'm not going to be responsible for snapping your joints.
You were just saying how heavy I am."

"It's going to look awkward."

"Dad, I am screaming my head off in the original photo. It's
supposed to look awkward."

From somewhere behind Max, Cora gave a loud sniffle.

Eli squinted at her, trying to maintain his chair pose. "Mom,
are you crying?"

"I'm just so happy we're all here together like this."

It was such a mom thing to say that Eli ended up smiling
more than he should have.

The senior prom photo caused some debate. The original
showed Eli at eighteen in a backless red gown with his long hair
held up by about four dozen mini plastic butterfly clips. Nick
had been his date, of course, looking gawky in the same black
suit he wore for jazz band performances. They were posed in the
Wards' sitting room in front of the picture window, goofy smiles
on their faces. There was a bright red corsage on Eli's wrist. He
could remember how cold it had been, fresh from the Wus' fridge
when he'd slipped it on.

"I am not wearing a dress," Eli said as he examined the old photo.

"Of course not. But maybe you could dress up? I could call Nick, see if he has a minute to swing by." Cora bit her lip. Maybe this was her way of extending an olive branch, since she'd been so sensitive about Eli and Nick hanging out lately.

Eli shook his head at her idea. "No way. We're just friends these days; asking him to re-create a couples photo we took while we were dating is beyond. Besides, I didn't bring any fancy clothes." He'd packed for mild depression and warm weather, not a prom. He had one nice dress shirt that he'd planned on wearing for Christmas, but since he hadn't removed it from his suitcase yet, it was sure to be in need of ironing.

"Well, I want to replace this with something," Cora said. She flicked the corner of the photo in Eli's hands. "It looked so cute in the hall; I'd hate for that spot to be empty."

"I've got an idea." Wendall bustled back inside the house. "Eli, pick out one of my ties! Top-left dresser drawer," he called without turning around.

"I don't have any collared shirts," Eli hollered after him.

The echoing response came through the door he'd left ajar. "Just wear a T-shirt, then! It'll look funny."

It looked ridiculous, but this whole exercise leaned into making Eli look ridiculous. And since looking ridiculous was kind of Eli's entire career up to this point, there was some comfort in it. He found a truly ugly purple-and-green paisley tie in his dad's dresser and looped it around his neck, knotting it in a single Windsor over his black tee.

He came into the sitting room to find his parents and Max unfolding something he hadn't seen in years: the cardboard cutout of Legolas he'd bought from a Sam Goody back in '01 at the height of *Lord of the Rings* mania.

Eli froze. "You have got to be kidding me."

"I kept it in the attic after you moved out. Thought it might be worth something," his dad said as he straightened the back support that kept Legolas upright.

Cora rolled her eyes. "I told him, if *Antiques Roadshow* ever comes around, we are not taking this. I will not be laughed out of the convention center."

"Hey, the elf should be dressed up too if this is a prom photo. Eli, get another tie. Or—oh! Maybe we should put one of your mother's dresses on him?"

"Wen, we are not putting a dress on this thing. You'll stretch it out!"

"Okay, okay, it was just an idea."

Max, who had been standing well off to the side with the camera, turned to Eli. "This is fucking gold, by the way."

"Glad someone's having fun." But despite his flippant demeanor, Eli realized he, too, was having fun. No wonder he'd turned out so silly if these were his parents. He felt his heart grow three sizes, Grinch-like, as he watched them fuss with the angle of the Legolas cutout, trying to position him exactly so. He let himself be tugged by his parents and arranged next to his two-dimensional date.

"You'll have to put your arm around him since he doesn't have the range." His mom put his hand on the cardboard cutout's trim waist.

Wendall stood back with Max and made a frame out of his hands like he was Cecil B. DeMille. "What do you think? Better than your real prom, huh?"

"Depends. Is he buying me dinner?"

"Say cheese," Max said, and started snapping pictures.

Eli looked over the results on Max's camera with a laugh. One had caught him in the middle of a blink. He looked ridiculous.

Margo would love it. "Can you text me that one later?" he asked Max. "That's going to be my new headshot."

Then came the picture that was taken on Eli's graduation day. In the original, he and his parents were standing out in front of his old high school, Eli in his cap and gown and clutching the black folder that held his diploma. He looked a little dazed, likely because his breakup with Nick had still been fresh. Behind them was the sign for Port Stephen Preparatory with the puma mascot slinking across the words in profile.

"Let's hop in the car and head over there," Cora said with unvarnished excitement in her eyes. "I bet we can find the exact spot we were standing."

Eli raised both brows. "Isn't the school shut down because of all the hurricane damage?"

"There's a fence," Max said, "but only around the buildings. This looks like it was taken out in the parking lot, right? That should be fine."

Wendall looked up from his self-appointed task of folding up Orlando Bloom. "We still have your cap and gown too. It's hanging in the laundry room."

"Why on earth would you keep that?" Eli asked.

"It cost fifty dollars!" Cora protested. "Plus, it's still good. Max can borrow it at the end of the year, save some cash."

Max snorted. "Yeah, if graduation ever even happens."

"Oh, honey, one way or another, you'll have a graduation. It just may not be the one you pictured." Cora patted Max on the shoulder, but her gaze was locked on Eli.

Very subtle. Eli took off his tie and followed the chaotic bustle of his parents ushering everyone into the Subaru.

They reached the school as the sun started going down, painting the sky all kinds of oranges and pinks. Max muttered some comment about losing the light, which Eli felt was a tad dramatic. They pulled into the abandoned student parking lot, now ringed with a chain-link fence that bristled with warning signs about the danger of trespassing beyond that point, by order of Saint Stephen County.

"Hurry, get this on." Cora tossed the voluminous burgundy graduation gown in Eli's face before he'd even had a chance to fully exit the car.

"Why does this smell like lavender?" he asked as he wrestled it over his head.

"Your mother's potpourri game is, as the kids say, on point." Wendall plopped the matching mortarboard on Eli's now-free head.

"No kids say that. Not since, like, 2004."

Wendall put his hands on his hips and surveyed the damage beyond the fence. Some of the metal roofs had been peeled back by the high winds like the lid of a tin can, the scraps either littering the ground or barely holding on to the roofline. "What a mess. We won't need to have this in the background, right?"

"I'll crop it out." Max jogged backward several yards, holding up the original photo to use as a guide. "A little more to the left, I think. Yeah, come closer? Perfect."

"Which side is Eli's tassel supposed to be on?" Cora called. She brought the mortarboard tassel to the front of the hat, switching it from left to right and back again. "I can't remember which way is post-ceremony."

While she and Max hashed out that small detail, Eli let his gaze wander over the high school buildings. Some of it was new construction, completely unfamiliar to him, but he could spot the old single-level classrooms he'd used, all connected by open-air walkways. He remembered how chaotic it had been when it was time for classes to switch. Those sidewalks had roiled with bodies, every student desperate to use the four or five minutes they had to high-five a friend, to kiss a girlfriend or boyfriend, to visit the dank restroom at supersonic speed. Eli could practically hear the late-nineties alt-pop, could smell the cucumber melon body spray that the pretty girls seemed to bathe in. And he could feel, in the pit of his stomach, the old sinking dread that this place had filled him with every day for four fucking years.

It had taken years of therapy for him to grasp what had happened to him in high school. It wasn't that he'd been bullied or had a hard time with his teachers; on the surface, everything was normal. He hadn't been super popular, but he wasn't disliked. He wasn't the smartest kid, but he got decent grades. His swimming career wasn't record-breaking, but he was a dependable member of the team. He had a secondhand car, parents who weren't divorced and didn't want to be, and a sweetheart of a boyfriend in Nick. It all looked ideal.

But growing up trans without knowing what it was? Without knowing that trans people even existed? That had hollowed him out, like there was a piece missing and no one would tell him what it was. He thought it was normal, that everyone must feel that way from time to time, so he ignored it right up until he couldn't anymore.

In the original graduation photo, he was smiling, but he remembered it being a smile of relief. It had felt almost manic, the way he wanted to claw his way free while sitting in that back row at graduation with the rest of the W's, Nick just a few Williamses away. Some people had weird dreams about going back to high school because they forgot to take some test or pass some class, but Eli's nightmares of Port Stephen Prep were different. When he dreamed of PSP, he saw everything exactly as it had been. No monsters, no surprise tests, no naked speeches in front of the class. Every detail was true to life, right down to the horrible feeling that something was wrong. And no one could tell him how to fix it.

"Eli? Hey, you in there?" His dad snapped his fingers in Eli's face a couple times.

Eli tore his attention away from the school and back to the present. "Yeah, sorry, I—got nostalgic, I guess." Deep breaths, he reminded himself. The worst had already happened; right now, he was taking a graduation photo twenty-five years after the fact with parents who loved him and were trying their hardest to show it. Plus he wasn't wearing an itchy floral dress under the graduation gown this time around. Maybe the rest of his life was a wreck, but in the big picture, it was a pretty great glow-up.

Max lifted the old photo, squinting into the sun and gauging the Port Stephen Preparatory sign in the background. "Okay, I think that's about right. Stay there, Eli. Aunt Cora, you're on his other side, yep, there you go. Uncle Wendall, your eyes are kind of closed in the original. Do you want to do that again now?"

"I think a little improvement is fine. I'll try not to blink."

"All right." Max tucked the photo away in a back pocket and lifted the camera into position. "Big smiles. Even bigger. There we go!" The digital shutter sound rang out as Max snapped away.

Eli had his arms around his parents' shoulders as they posed, and he hugged them closer to his sides as Max took the photos. "Thanks for this," he said.

"Our pleasure, honey." Cora sniffed against his shoulder. Eli was worried she was going to start crying again and ruin the photo, but instead she just said, "Gosh, that lavender does smell nice."

Eli ended up smiling wider for the new photo than he ever had in the originals.

After Max wrapped up the photo shoot, they piled back into the car. Eli felt like a little kid again, sitting in the back seat with his cousin. Not in a bad way, especially when Wendall said, "Who wants ice cream? We can stop by the Twistee Treat."

"The Twistee Treat is still in business?" Eli blinked. "I always thought that place was a drug front." He had probably seen a grand total of four cars in the cone-shaped ice cream stand's parking lot over the years.

"No, no, it's good. They have a yummy key lime pie flavor; I'm going to get that," Cora said.

They pulled into the drive-through and ordered: key lime for Cora, vanilla with a chocolate dip for Wendall, caramel turtle for Max, and raspberry for Eli. Wendall snapped a selfie of all four of them to replace the old ice cream one that had sat on the sideboard.

Max inhaled the last of the cone and turned back to the camera. "Some of these shots came out really good. Look."

Eli focused on the camera's preview screen that was shoved in his face. The one Max had chosen showed Eli and his parents huddled on the sofa with Eli holding an old pumpkin-shaped bucket. He had three lines drawn on either side of his nose with Cora's eyeliner as whiskers. It was an homage to a Halloween photo they'd taken when Eli was eight. He'd wanted to go as a cat very badly for some reason. In the new photo, they were all caught in the middle of a laugh, Eli's dad looking at them both fondly.

"Wow." He zoomed in on their faces. "We look so happy."

"Must be nice," said Max with patented teenage energy. Eeyore was getting a run for his money with this one, Eli thought.

He felt a twinge of guilt looking at the photo, about not just the silly argument they'd all had over the ornaments but skirting the truth about the bike and tiptoeing around the topic of Nick. After the day they'd shared taking all these pictures, Eli felt so much closer to his parents. Maybe he couldn't be honest with them about everything—broaching the subject of his puttering career was still too big a mountain to climb at the moment—but surely he could be up-front with them about what was going on with Nick.

"So, uh, that bike?" He leaned forward so that his head was between the two front seats. "Nick actually dropped it off for me yesterday. Said his dad had got it at a yard sale, figured I could borrow it while I was down here."

"Oh, how thoughtful," Cora said. Her tone seemed carefully pitched to sound excited.

"I always liked Nick," Wendall said. He turned onto their street, signaling even though no other cars were around.

"Yeah." Eli glanced over at his mom, then at his dad, who was concentrating on pulling into the carport with laser precision. "It's been pretty fun reconnecting with him. You know, talking about the good ol' days, remembering all the laughs we had as kids." He flashed to that weird, quick kiss during their night swim: the dark water, the starry sky, Nick's mouth on his.

That had been fun, too, but there was no way he was going to tell his parents about that piece of the puzzle. Hell, if he could still afford his therapist, he probably wouldn't be telling her either.

"That's the great thing about being an adult." Wendall threw the car into park and turned off the engine. In the quiet that followed once the noise cut out, he said, "You're past all the teenage drama, and you can enjoy a shared history. When you were eighteen, that breakup was the biggest deal in the world to you, and now? Water under the bridge."

Eli popped open his car door and stepped out onto the concrete. "Well, if anyone was going to hold a grudge over what happened back then, it would be Nick, right? Since I broke up with him." He shut his door, fully expecting to hear the other car doors echo right behind it, but they didn't. Complete silence had descended over the carport.

He looked up to find his parents standing beside their open doors, staring at him like he was from Mars.

"What?" Eli asked.

"Honey," Cora said slowly, "you didn't break up with Nick back in high school. He broke up with you."

Max popped up from the other side of the car with wide eyes. "Oh shit."

"Huh? No he didn't." Eli screwed up his face, waiting for the punchline that didn't come. "I told him I wanted to break up right after senior prom. We were in the cafeteria at school—I can picture exactly where we were sitting!"

"Your mom's right, kiddo," Wendall said. "You came home all in tears."

"Yeah, because it's hard to break up with your first boyfriend."

"No, because he told you he wanted to end things. That's what you said. I remember that clearly." Cora smacked the roof of the car with her palm. "I called up Ming, and we talked about it for hours. It was so heartbreaking, seeing you both like that. After all those years growing up together—poof, it was gone."

"Because *I* ended it." Eli gestured helplessly. He really did remember the whole scene. He'd been wearing a purple blouse. The cafeteria had been serving fish sticks; just the mention of fish sticks had made him nauseous for years afterward. He'd sat with Nick at their usual table and broke the news. He could still see Nick's tearful, crushed face. Every inch of his skin felt like it was on fire. "I can't be misremembering this entire thing!"

"Maybe you can," Max offered. "I'm taking Psychology as an elective this semester. They say there's all sorts of ways you can repress a memory or replace it completely."

"Exactly!" Cora pointed at Max like the word of an eighteen-year-old goth was gospel. "It's probably repressed."

"I don't know if you're aware of this, but I am not a repressed person. Remember?" Eli flapped a hand up and down next to his body in illustration. "Totally un-repressed."

"Sure, these days," Wendall said, "but back then, I imagine you were going through a lot, right? Maybe it was the only way for you to deal with it, to remember it happening differently."

"That's not what happened! Oh my god, this is so bizarre."

"There's an easy way to figure out who's right, you know." Max stuck a finger in the air. "Just ask Nick how it all went down."

"Maybe I will," Eli said. If he was being Mandela-effected, he wanted to know.

His mom shrugged. "I think you should."

"Okay. Fine." His eyes landed on the bike leaning against the house. "I'll do it right now." He grabbed the handlebars and began wrestling it out of the carport. The spokes of the front tire had somehow become stuck in the tines of a rake that was propped up next to it.

"Let me drive you," Wendall said.

"No thanks, Dad! Think I'll confront my ex-boyfriend regarding the circumstances of our breakup on my own. I could use the exercise." He tucked a handlebar under his arm and pulled out his phone to shoot Nick a text.

Hey where are u

The reply was almost immediate: **At my dad's place. Why?**

Eli weighed the pros and cons of inviting himself over to Mr. Wu's house to have this out with Nick, but in the end, he knew he'd do whatever it took to prove he wasn't losing his mind.

I'm coming over

He pocketed his phone, hopped on the bike, almost fell off, righted himself, and then made his shaky, tipsy-turvy way onto the street.

"Looking good," Max called from the driveway, where Eli's family was watching him bike away. Very slowly. "You'll probably get where you're going in, oh . . . six years."

If it had been happening to anyone but him, it would be funny. Eli made a mental note to tell Margo to add a sad biking-away scene to the pilot script.

CHAPTER 13

Nick awaited Eli's arrival on his dad's driveway with his arms folded over his chest. He'd tried sending Eli multiple follow-up texts explaining that he was about to eat dinner and maybe they could get together some other time, but the messages went unread. So much for having a relaxing meal with his dad tonight; looked like trading the assistant manager his Thursday dinner shift for two lunch shifts wasn't a good deal after all. What was the point of trying to make time for family when it hardly ever worked out the way Nick wanted?

Tian-yi was hard at work in the kitchen, putting the finishing touches on the grilled fish, and Nick figured he had about ten minutes before his dad came to chide him about dinner getting cold. As he waited, the timer for his dad's Christmas lights clicked on, illuminating the roofline. Nick had helped him hang them the day after Thanksgiving since "the Rasmussens on the corner put theirs up last week!" Tian-yi hated being behind schedule for anything, even holiday lights.

He saw Eli turn onto Papaya Place on the bike Nick had given him. It seemed like slow going. At last, Eli huffed and

puffed to the foot of the driveway, reaching his toes down to the
ground as he came to a stop. His hair was stuck to his forehead
with sweat. Two bright red circles adorned his cheeks.

Nick's heart flipped over in his chest. Like a fool.

"You okay?" Nick asked.

Eli glared at him like it was Nick's fault that he'd biked over.
"Peachy keen," Eli said, struggling with the kickstand. "Though
I've probably sweated out half my body weight on this thing."

"Our parents' houses aren't *that* far apart. We used to ride
bikes back and forth all the time." Sometimes a dozen times a
day. Those long summers of sunshine and sunburns.

Eli finally managed to get the kickstand down and levered himself off the bike with an ungainly flail of his arms. "It's not the bike
ride that's got me sweaty! Although—holy shit, I'm out of shape."
He bent forward like he meant to touch his toes. Nick winced as
he heard two audible pops from Eli's spine. "It's because—I have
to ask you something, okay?" Eli directed this at his sneakers, still
bent at the waist with his head hanging toward the ground.

"And this couldn't wait?" Nick glanced over his shoulder, but
his dad hadn't yet made an appearance. "My dad and I are about
to eat dinner."

"This won't take long. It's a simple question," Eli said, finally
standing upright and sweeping his hair back into place. "Did I
break up with you? Back in high school?"

Nick was almost certain he had misheard. He had to have.
"What? No. It was the other way around."

Eli's face went through a series of expressions before finally settling on what Nick could only describe as quizzical. He propped
his fists on his hips, opened his mouth, then shut it again. Finally,
he held up both pointer fingers and said, "So you're saying, beyond a doubt, that *you* broke up with *me*? You're sure?"

"Yes," Nick said slowly. "Very sure." It had been the most

painful day of his life up to that point, and one of the hardest decisions he'd ever made; he wasn't about to forget it anytime soon.

Eli groaned and shuffled over to the grass, where he sat down heavily. He tipped his face up to the sky, eyes shut. "I'm losing it. Officially."

Nick sat down next to Eli on the thick carpet of his dad's well-tended lawn. (He'd gotten really into gardening since retiring from the power plant.) "Why do you say that?"

"I thought I broke up with you," Eli said.

Nick waited for the rest of the gag, but Eli didn't roll out anything more. "Why would you have broken up with me?" he asked.

"I don't know!" Eli opened his eyes and tossed his hands in the air. "We were about to go off to different colleges or whatever—you had that full ride to Miami and I had one for Florida State—and I didn't want both of us miserable, trying to do long distance, driving eleven hours or however the fuck long it takes to get down there from Tallahassee—"

"Those were all the reasons I gave you when we broke up."

"So I'm told." Eli looped his arms around his knees, curling in on himself. "I feel like I'm stuck in a bad reboot of *Minority Report*. How is this possible?"

Nick lifted a hand but hesitated to place it on the plane of Eli's back. His fingers curled into a fist in the air, then unbent. Comfort was friendly. He wasn't crossing any lines. He put his palm against Eli's sweaty shirt and rubbed a few soothing circles there. "Memory is a funny thing. I'm sure there's lots of stuff that we remember differently if we compared it one to one."

"Yeah, but this is kind of a big detail to forget. I really, really thought *I* was the one who broke up with *you*," Eli said to the ground.

Nick thought for a second. His hand moved to Eli's shoulder, kneading it carefully. "Does it matter?" he asked.

"It does to me." Eli lifted his head enough to look Nick in the eye. "I thought I had a streak going. I'm always the one who ends all my relationships, starting with the *very* first one. I was never the one getting dumped; I was the dumper. Fuck, I even had a bit about it in the first hour of stand-up I ever did!"

Nick made a mental note to try to find that on YouTube. "You've dumped every boyfriend you've ever had? Except me?"

"Yeah. They all sucked." Eli dropped his head again.

"Huh." Nick couldn't lie to himself: it was kind of an ego boost to know that he was the one guy Eli hadn't ditched. Even if Eli himself didn't remember that. He realized his hand had stilled on Eli's shoulder, so he got back to rubbing. "Is being the guy who always bounces really that important to you?"

"Isn't it obvious?" Eli said. "I can't commit to anything. Not even the gender I was assigned at birth."

"Was that from an old stand-up routine too?"

"Why? Was my timing off?"

"No, it's funny—"

"You're not laughing."

"I'm trying to have a serious conversation with you," Nick said. He hesitated but figured it was better to be honest than let Eli wonder. "If it makes you feel any better, breaking up with you was the hardest thing I'd ever done."

Eli turned to him, his eyes huge. "Really?"

"Yeah, of course. It meant losing you *and* your folks, and they were like family to me. But I didn't know what else to do. You weren't happy. I could tell, even if everyone else couldn't. It felt like there was this huge thing going on that you didn't want to talk to me about, and I didn't understand why. Now it's obvious, but back then . . ." Back then it felt like he was losing his best friend and his first love, and it was all his fault.

Eli sighed. "Yeah, I was really going through it." He reached for one of Tian-yi's lush red hibiscus bushes, plucking a bloom and worrying the stem between his fingers. "Kind of amazing I'm going to make it to forty, honestly."

Nick didn't feel almost forty, sitting here with Eli. He felt like he was eighteen again, sixteen again, ten, seven, and here they were, still having their heaviest, most important conversations with each other. (At eighteen: *What do you think we'll be doing when we're older?* Sixteen: *Can I take you out on a date?* Ten: *I think it's harder to make someone laugh than it is to make them cry.* Seven: *If dinosaurs were real, what's stopping them from coming back one day?*)

Eli let the flower flutter to the ground with a short bark of laughter. "Well, it's a good thing you broke things off with me back then. Can you imagine if we'd tried to stick it out?" He looked over at Nick, then looked away just as quick.

Nick had imagined. Lately, when he was alone in his dark house with nothing to do but brush his teeth and go to bed early, he'd wondered what might have happened if they'd stayed together. Eli might have dumped him at some point in college, but maybe not. Maybe things would have fizzled out when Eli went to New York, but maybe not. Maybe the relationship would have crumbled when Eli finally realized he was trans.

But maybe not.

"I'm sorry." It was the best Nick could do. "I know I hurt you."

"Listen, it's nobody's fault," Eli said. "Teenagers fall in and out of love all the time."

"Eli." Nick swallowed. "I was still in love with you."

He wasn't sure why he said it, only that he was compelled to say what was true. The idea that Eli might think, even for a minute, that there was a time Nick hadn't loved him was—it was just wrong. And as the words left his mouth, Nick realized something that should have been obvious since the moment he ran into Eli at the Wine Barn.

He'd loved him then. He loved him still. He would never stop loving him.

Fucking shit-hell ball sack. He was *in love* with Eli.

Maybe if he sat very, very still, Eli wouldn't notice this monumental internal revelation he was currently experiencing. *Please don't notice, please don't notice*, Nick kept thinking on a loop. But also simultaneously and just as loud in his mind: *Please notice. Please say something. Please put me out of my misery.*

"Oh," Eli said. He blinked a couple of times, then looked down between his knees at the grass. For once, he was slow to speak. "Well. That's—"

The garage door opened. This was a slow process accompanied by many a creak and squeal of the mechanism. Nick's dad called out in Hokkien, "Dinner's ready! Let's hurry and eat before it gets—oh!" The garage door finished raising, and Tian-yi spotted them both on the lawn. He switched to English to address Eli: "Hello there."

Eli stood quickly, patting down his ass to get any grass off. Nick followed suit, feeling a bit tongue-tied. Reintroducing the love of his life to his father right after the conversation they'd had was not in his top ten ways to spend an evening.

"Hi, Mr. Wu," Eli said, giving a cheery wave as they met in the middle of the driveway. "It's good to see you."

"Nice to meet you." Nick's dad bobbed his head and gave him a wide smile. "Are you a friend of Nick's?"

Eli opened his mouth but said nothing, instead turning to Nick like he expected Nick to jump in and explain.

Nick switched to Hokkien for the sake of his own sanity. The last thing he wanted was for Eli to hear his dad—or Nick himself—say something embarrassing while they cleared this up. "Dad, do you remember who I dated in high school?"

"Oh, of course." His dad didn't miss a beat, switching to English. "So *this* is Eli. Hello! Merry Christmas! It's been so long." He reached for Eli's hand and shook it heartily.

Eli looked delighted by this, his grin stretching his face so that the faint lines at the corners of his eyes creased. "It really has."

Nick tried not to let his mouth hang open; that was an invitation for his dad to tease him about catching flies. "Wait, how did you—? *I* didn't even know who Eli was until last week!"

"The Wards are old friends," Tian-yi said with all the patience of a fisherman. (Fishing was another hobby he'd gotten serious about recently, going down to West Palm on weekends to meet up with other retired uncles.) "Obviously we talk about our children."

And here Nick had been racking his brain, trying to figure out a way to explain the transgender experience when he didn't know the Hokkien word for "trans" or "gender."

Tian-yi must have seen all this pass over Nick's face, because he sucked his teeth and laughed. "Ai ya, you always make things so complicated, Nick. Relax." Then, to Eli, he said, "It is good to see you again, Eli, for the first time. Would you like to stay for dinner?"

"Dad—"

"Boy, *would* I!"

Which is how Nick ended up sitting next to Eli at his dad's kitchen table while Tian-yi laid out about fourteen different dishes, from the grilled fish to scallion pancakes. He couldn't even be angry about his dad's out-of-the-blue invitation, since Eli's eyes were as wide as the serving platters. Maybe they could find some time to speak privately after the meal. Nick felt they'd left a lot unsaid. For the moment, he steeled himself to eat dinner while consumed with longing.

Conversation continued without much input from Nick, thankfully. Eli asked Nick's dad if he was still working at the power plant, and Tian-yi began telling him all about his retirement, and how long it had taken him to get the yard in the shape it was.

While they chatted, Nick examined a bowl of bite-sized xiao mantou that was sitting innocuously next to a pitcher of iced tea. They didn't look like the ones you could buy in the one Asian supermarket in the shopping plaza where the Italian bakery and the bingo hall were. Those came mass-produced in a pegboard bag. These looked like they were slightly different shapes and sizes, like they were homemade.

Nick's dad didn't bake, though. That had been wholly his mom's wheelhouse. Had he taken up yet another hobby in his retirement? Nick picked up one of the tiny pale biscuits between his thumb and forefinger. The texture totally gave it away. Definitely fresh.

"Where did you get these, Dad?" he asked.

"Oh, a friend gave them to me," Tian-yi said with uncharacteristic vagueness. "Here, here, eat these before it gets cold." He pushed a platter of fragrant run bing across the table.

Nick eyed him closely. He had so many follow-up questions. What friend? These cookies had to be super fiddly to make, and therefore indicated a depth of friendship that Nick didn't think Tian-yi had with his fishing buddies. But before he could ask, the conversation was moving on without the critical xiao mantou backstory.

"I remember these," Eli said as he reached for a run bing. "Thank you so much, Mr. Wu. I could never find ones that taste as good as yours in New York."

What a suck-up. No wonder Nick loved him.

His dad preened under the compliment, fighting the little

smile he usually got when someone praised his food. "Oh, it's nothing special. Really, I didn't even make the wrappers thin enough this time."

"Are you kidding? They're as thin as a sheet of paper. I could eat this whole plate if you let me." He finished his first one and reached for another.

This seemed to endear Eli to his father in a way that Nick should have foreseen. "Please, please. It's a good thing you came; I always make too much." Tian-yi pushed the platter toward him, almost out of reach of Nick, who gave Eli an affronted look even as he munched on another roll with a truly aggressive amount of eye contact. "So, Eli," Nick's father said, "your parents tell me you work in television? Do I have that right?"

Eli nearly choked on the run bing. Nick whacked him on the back, trying to help him breathe. "Sorry," Eli wheezed. He reached for his glass of iced tea. "Yep. That's me. Working in television."

Nick tried to keep his face schooled into something neutral, but he couldn't help the questioning look he threw Eli's way. Why would he lie about something like that? Eli, however, wouldn't meet his gaze.

Nick's dad nodded politely. "Your parents must be very proud."

The back of Eli's neck flushed pink, a telltale sign of agitation that Nick could recognize a mile away. "Yeah, sure," he said. "But what about Nick here? Being a dad and all?" He tipped his chin to point at him across the table. "Zoe is such a cool kid. You've got to be the proudest grandparent in the world."

That successfully changed the subject, with Tian-yi regaling his guest with stories about his beloved granddaughter. Nick picked fish bones from his grilled snook and watched Eli's an-imated face as he chatted with his dad. Soon even his private freakout seemed less important than seeing his two favorite people laughing over the dinner table.

At one point, his dad said to Eli, "You know, when your mother was pregnant with you, Ming told her she should expect a boy. She was very gifted at that. She knew Nick was going to be a boy weeks before her first ultrasound. She could always tell."

"Really? I didn't know that," Nick said. Even all these years later, he was still finding bits and pieces of his mom. It was kind of comforting, like he was still getting to know her even though she wasn't there. And it was nice to hear his dad talking about her, a rare thing for the past few years.

"Huh." Eli smiled, an amused quirk to his eyebrows. "That's pretty funny. Sorry I ruined her streak, I guess."

"Nonsense." Nick's dad poured them all more iced tea. "She would be very pleased, I think, to be proven right after all these years." He sipped his drink. "I am glad we had this chance to meet again."

"I'm glad too," Eli said, quiet.

Nick could see how touched Eli was at Tian-yi's words, and how softly his dad smiled when speaking about Nick's mom. He was glad his dad could talk about her with joy in his voice; that hadn't always been the case, those first hard years after the accident. He put his hand on his dad's shoulder and squeezed. His dad placed a hand over his and squeezed back.

After everyone had eaten their fill, they started the long process of cleaning up. Tian-yi excused himself to the garage with the teetering stack of leftovers in their mismatched containers—there was a bonus fridge out there with enough space for everything. Nick started washing the dishes, and without even being asked, Eli got into position next to him at the sink with a towel at the ready, drying what Nick rinsed clean.

They worked in companionable silence for the time it took

to wash two platters and a pair of chopsticks before Nick spoke up. "You could have told my dad about being unemployed, you know. He wouldn't have thought any less of you." That, he thought with wry fondness, was reserved for Nick himself.

Eli made an uncertain noise while he dried a serving spoon. "I didn't want to make it a whole thing. Sometimes it's easier to let people think what they want instead of explaining every detail."

Nick wondered if that applied to being trans, too, but he held his tongue, instead saying, "So no news on your friend's show?"

"Nothing yet. Like I said, I really don't want to pin my hopes on that." He stacked a dry plate atop the others on the counter. "I might have to go back to stand-up after all."

Nick soaped up his dad's grill pan. "That would be cool, right? I mean, you're really good at it."

"How would you know?" Eli demanded.

"I watched some clips of you." Nick tried to look as calm as possible while scrubbing a pan. "Not because—I mean, when you mentioned your old stuff, I got curious." He hoped that didn't sound too stalker-ish.

"You liked my old stuff?" Eli stared at him like he was actually Santa Claus, come to bestow Christmas cheer and traverse rooftops. "Seriously?"

"Sure. Those impressions you did of your parents?" His shoulders shook a little with laughter as he remembered. "That was great."

"Thank you," Eli said, quiet and subdued, like he wasn't sure how to take the compliment. He took the now-gleaming pan from Nick, their fingers brushing. "I—" He cleared his throat loudly. "I really need some new material, though. I'm not sure where it would even come from."

Nick hummed in thought. "I noticed you didn't do any jokes about being trans," he said in a leading sort of way.

Eli made his own feelings clear with an incredulous raise of his brows. "Not sure I want to go digging in the deep well of my trauma for laughs, to be honest."

"I get it. No one likes being pigeonholed," Nick said.

"It's not even that, really." Eli took a pair of tongs from Nick's nerveless fingers; Nick hadn't even noticed he'd washed them. "It would be different if I was performing for other trans people. But I'm supposed to be as palatable as possible to ticket buyers, right? I can't ignore who I'm talking to. And they're not people like me, for the most part."

"I'm not trans," Nick pointed out. "You don't seem to mind performing for me."

Eli didn't even protest that his antics were a performance at times; he looked at Nick again with soft eyes. "But I know you," he said. "I know you're safe."

"Oh." Nick felt a frisson of pride work through his chest. "Thanks."

Eli was not done, apparently. "But this is my art, right? This is where I'm supposed to pour out all the good stuff. The whole damn spectacle." He placed some dried utensils in the caddy on the shelf, exactly where they belonged. Like he remembered where Nick's parents kept everything. "No one expects white cishets with hour specials to share anything more traumatic than their worst blind dates. *They* get to have fun. I've got to carve my heart out and put it on a platter? Fuck that. We can't all write *Nanette*, okay?"

Nick squinted at him. "Who's Nanette?"

"Oh my god." Eli put his drying cloth down and looked as pained as if someone had told him Publix had run out of deli sandwiches. "Please, I'm begging you: seek out queer media."

Nick shrugged. "All right, all right. I'll look it up." He handed Eli a knife, handle first.

Eli took it and carefully dried the blade. "All I'm saying is there's a limit to how much I want to give of myself. It's not me being a coward; it's how I learned to get by. You'd understand if you just—ugh."

"If I just what?" Nick couldn't help the defensiveness welling inside him; he wanted to try. If Eli would let him.

"I don't know. It's hard to explain. Like, Mom and Dad took me by the old school earlier and I felt so . . . helpless." He planted both hands on the counter, his shoulders hiking up to his ears. "Like I was a scared little kid all over again. Like I wanted to scream at the whole damn place to leave me alone."

"Okay," Nick said. He thought about that for a moment. "After we finish up here, do you want to go on a drive? Confront some demons?" They could stand outside the gates and have a good, cathartic outpouring.

Eli looked him up and down as if he was considering. "You're really up for that?"

"Sure. Why not?" Any excuse to keep Eli in his orbit, even for another hour or two.

A smile spread across Eli's face. "Okay, wow. Dinner and demons. You sure know how to make a guy feel special."

It was a joke because it was always a joke, so Nick laughed along as he watched the dishwater go down the drain.

CHAPTER 14

Eli stepped out of Nick's car and onto the cracked concrete of the sidewalk outside their old high school. Even though he had been there only a few hours ago, the place felt completely different at night. Shadows buried the buildings. The school's sign stood without illumination, the dot-matrix ticker below it dead and gray. Once Nick's headlights cut out, only the weak streetlamps threw any light. The surrounding neighborhood seemed abandoned. An eerie quiet seeped through the air, making Eli shiver.

"Come on," he said, switching on his cell phone's flashlight. "Let's confront the past or whatever." He tugged at the nearest swath of chain-link fence. It gave without much effort, revealing a break near one of the fence posts. Well, that was easy. Although Eli wasn't really surprised—the county was notoriously cheap.

"Wait, we're going inside?" Nick was beside him with his own phone flashlight switched on. It cast weird shadows along his face, highlighting his cheekbones. "Why do we have to do that? You can scream from out here."

"I want to make sure it hears me." Eli slipped through the

break in the fence, letting the chain link clatter back into place behind him.

"Eli!" Nick's whisper-shout came in that frantic register that Eli had heard when they were thirteen and Eli tried to sneak one of his uncle's Natty Ices.

"It's fine," he said over his shoulder. "You can wait out here if you want. Your choice."

He wasn't even finished speaking before he heard Nick wrestling with the fence. "Absolutely no way am I staying behind. That's how people die in horror movies."

"This isn't a horror movie." Eli trained his light on the closest wall, trying to get his bearings. "Well, maybe a ghost story," he mumbled to himself. The old gym loomed on his right, with the front office on his left, which meant— "The library must be this way. Let's go."

Their flashlights bobbed along the weed-choked ground as they picked their way over brown palm fronds and pieces of broken glass.

"Why the library?" Nick asked in a hushed voice.

"Why are you whispering?" Eli whispered. "There's literally no one else around."

"It just feels like we should whisper. You're doing it too."

Couldn't really argue with that. "I want to see if it's how I remember." He couldn't quite articulate why, but the library felt like the most appropriate place to investigate if they were going to revisit the past. It was the literal center of the campus—or, at least, it had been when they were kids. Eli remembered spending study hall and lunch periods in the quiet of the stacks at one of the brown tables covered in scratchitti. The librarian, Mr. Vine, didn't mind if Eli listened to his Discman or split a bag of Sun Chips with Nick. Damn, he hadn't eaten Sun Chips in years.

He turned and watched Nick avoid a muddy patch of ground. "Do they still make Sun Chips?"

"I think so. Why?" Nick squinted at him in the dark. "Oh. Our old lunch snack, right?"

"Right." If he wasn't careful, he'd fall into a pit of remembering and never come out. Eli led the way across the empty courtyards and down the echoing paths. The walkways were supposed to be covered to protect the students from rainstorms, but Eli saw that over half of the metal shades were now stripped away, leaving the concrete walkways exposed to the elements. To distract himself from how freaky all the debris looked in the dark, he started playing tour guide.

"This was the band room, here on the left. Down there was where the chorus practiced, right? And over there—we had ninth-grade science down that way. What was that teacher's name? She called me a natural skeptic. I still don't know what the fuck she meant by that."

"Mrs. Farraduke," Nick said.

"Yes. Farraduke. The cafeteria . . . oh, they must have torn it down. Or was that basketball court always there?" Eli swung his light over the tattered hoops, the scuffed backboards. "Ours used to be back by the gym, didn't it?"

"I don't know. It's hard to tell in the dark."

Eli could only remember the worst parts of P.E. class: being forced to dress out, the locker room full of chattering teenage girls, the way he'd have already sweated through his clothes before class even started. Those girls saw every weakness in the armor. Like when sharks smelled blood miles away. Candice Skanner had called him Stinky up until junior year. Mild as far as bullying at PSP went, but still.

"Do you remember Candice Skanner?"

"That girl who was mean to you?" Nick scoffed. "We hated her. I put molasses on her windshield in junior year after she teased you in front of the seniors, remember?"

Eli stopped in the middle of the walkway, his flashlight droop-ing. "Oh my god, you did. It was lovebug season." The little black winged bugs swarmed in the spring. They mated by sticking their rear ends together until they died, still connected, in droves that choked the town's pools and gutters. Eli remembered thinking even as a child that it was kind of fucked up to call that love.

"Yep. Her car was plastered with dead bugs by the end of the day." He could hear the grin in Nick's voice, even in the dark.

"That was so—" Hot. It was hot. "Effective. Wonder what-ever happened to her."

"Last I'd heard, she'd joined some cult out in Ocala. It's, like, Christian but they also worship birds or something? The servers at the Manatee talk."

Good, Eli thought. Candice's life went nowhere, and she was still stuck in Florida, doing Floridian bullshit. Then he felt terri-ble for thinking that, because Nick was still here. And so was he, at least for the foreseeable future. Great self-own, in addition to being petty.

He kept going through the ruins of the old school until he fumbled his way to the front of the library. The metal double doors stood ajar, one of the release bars hanging by one last screw. There was a thick scent of decay in the air, like wet leaves.

"Okay, so we're really doing this," Nick muttered from right behind him. "I swear to god, if I see a ghost, I am leaving you."

"Not this time, you won't." Eli's mouth worked faster than his brain. That sounded so—forward. And bitter. He coughed in his fist to cover the awkwardness. "Because I'll be right behind you. Now let's go."

He pushed one half of the double doors all the way open and aimed his flashlight into the room. The library had not been spared from the storm—part of the roof had caved in, and a royal palm had speared right through one of the windows. Its dead fronds waved like unfurled fans in the night breeze. Eli stepped inside, his light roving over the library shelves. They were still stuffed with books, waterlogged and swollen with bits of dirt and oak leaves stuck to them.

"They didn't save the books," he whispered. "They left them all here."

"Where would they have put them?" Nick was right at his elbow, his voice lower than ever. "You evacuate people in a hurricane, Eli. Things can be replaced."

A thought occurred to Eli. "Were you and your family okay? This was a really bad storm."

"Laurie got through it all right. Dad needed a new roof. A tree fell in my backyard, but it didn't hit anything."

Eli nodded, trying to remember. "I think my folks said they lost power. I got a text from them saying they were fine after the storm passed. I didn't even try to call them. I was working on the sweeps-week episode." He shook his head. "Christ, I'm an asshole."

Nick's hand found his arm in the dark. He gave Eli's elbow a weird pat. "It's hard to know how much to worry when we're all adults."

"Yeah," he said, even though he wasn't sure he agreed.

They went deeper into the library. Except for the way that nature had forced its way inside, it was surprisingly untouched. The round tables where students had studied were still where they'd been left, boxy padded wood chairs pulled up along their edges. At the console tables in the center of the library, where the card catalog used to be, dozens of computer monitors stood silent and dark, keyboards choked with sand. Eli ran a fingertip along the edge of a shelf as he passed and felt the silt on his skin.

Nick went to a section of the stacks they used to frequent, the one low shelf containing the library's tiny collection of books on paranormal topics. Nick reached down and pulled out an ancient hardcover with a drawing of Bigfoot on the front, the protective plastic cover flashing in the lights from their phones. "Can you believe they still have this? We must have checked it out once a month when we were freshmen."

"I still say the swamp ape is real." Eli kept moving, wanting to see more. Nick stayed behind.

"Do you remember how we used to mess with Vine?" He was no longer whispering. "We'd wait until his back was turned and then straight up steal shit from the checkout desk. That time we took the stamp thing—" Eli looked over his shoulder and watched as Nick mimed making a fist and punching it down against unseen papers. "The thing he used to stamp the due dates on the cards. He was so pissed."

"We were little shits," Eli said.

Nick moved over to the place where the outdated microfiche machine used to live, behind the encyclopedias. "We really were. The way we . . ." He trailed off. The hand not holding his phone went to his hip as he looked around at the walls and the floor.

Eli wondered if he was remembering how they used to go back there, when the bulky microfiche viewer could hide them from sight, and make out until their lips went numb. He was very sad, all of a sudden. Nothing would ever feel like that again.

Grow up, he told himself. *Get over it. It's not like these were the best days of your life or anything.*

Although maybe some parts had been.

Eli ducked down an aisle in the reference section before he did something foolish and asked Nick what he was thinking about. His flashlight moved up the wall and landed on a startling framed photograph. A ghost with a round white face and a wealth of brassy red hair stared back at him, her creepy smile not reaching her eyes.

"We meet again, Principal McGoin." He could recall nothing about her except how nasal her voice sounded over the morning announcements, but Eli remembered this part of the library vividly. The long line of framed pictures hung above the windows, showcasing every principal who had served at Port Stephen Preparatory. He moved his flashlight to the right and saw the future: white woman after white woman all the way to the present day, he supposed. He tracked back to the left and went into the past. Before McGoin there had been a string of white guys, each more joyless and hatchet-faced than the last. And then, all the way back to the beginning: the Black men who had been principals in the sixties and seventies.

He remembered staring at the portrait wall as a kid and asking Mr. Vine, "What happened there?" He had pointed at the time jump between Reginald Brown, Jr. (1969–73) and Geoffery Billings (1981–88), to the gap between the last Black principal and the first white one.

"The school was shut down and then reopened as a desegregated institution," was all Vine had said, and as a fourteen-year-old, Eli hadn't thought to question it. He'd learned the truth years later from a podcast, of all things. He'd been sitting on a stalled D train on his way to Brooklyn while someone with an NPR accent informed him that his alma mater was one of hundreds of excellent schools operated by the Black community that had been turned into a majority white magnet school. Desegregation as an excuse to steal a school with a sterling reputation and a sprawling campus.

They hadn't taught that shit in history class.

Their history teacher had, in fact, been a huge dickhead who complained vocally every time he was "forced" to teach one section a year—one! Like the equivalent of a paragraph—about either a historically significant woman or a person of color. Eli didn't remember anything about the begrudging lesson he'd received on Eva Perone, but he did remember the exact words Mr. Green had said: "No woman has ever done anything worth studying."

Meanwhile, they'd spent three weeks on the JFK assassination. Green had been a total gun nut, so. Priorities.

He felt the air shift as Nick came to stand beside him, hands perched on his hips, his head tipped back as he stared up at the portraits too. "Do you ever think about what a fucked-up place this was?" he asked. "Like, from the very start, way back when."

"A rotten foundation," Eli murmured. He snuck a glance over at Nick, taking in the shadows that hid among his cheekbones.

"I don't think I ever told you—I didn't want to sound like a whiner, probably—but it was weird," Nick said, "being one of about four Asian kids in this school."

Eli considered this. "No, you never told me before." He waited, letting the empty air between them be the invitation.

Nick shook his head. "The way teachers were always mistaking me for the other two guys, even though we looked nothing alike. I remember we laughed about it at the time but—I hated that. I still hate it."

Eli reached over and put his hand on Nick's bare forearm. He squeezed lightly, wishing he could say or do more, but his voice was caught in his throat. He dropped his hand before it could be construed as overly familiar.

He walked down the long line of principals' portraits to put some distance between them, staring up at the ghostly faces in the frames. "There was only one out gay kid in the entire school, remember? Fuck, what was his name? He was a year ahead of us, and they bullied him so much he dropped out."

"Lane," Nick said quietly. "His name was Lane."

Eli whirled his light back to Nick's face. "Yeah. That was it."

He hadn't thought about that kid in ages. He gazed up at the portraits, wondering what had happened to him. "The teachers, the rules, the actual school itself—the biggest lesson this place taught us was that you had to pretend to be normal at all costs. You *had* to."

"Hey." Nick came out from behind the desk, light in his hand. "We survived, didn't we?" He reached out like he was going to touch Eli's arm.

Eli moved back a step so he was out of reach. "But it didn't have to be so hard."

Nick stared at him in the wavering light for a long moment. "I'm so sorry. I've been meaning to apologize."

"What?" Eli scoffed. "You were the one bright spot when we were here. Why would you need to apologize?"

"Because it wasn't just the teachers, or the school, or whatever. It was never just one thing. It was all of it together—and I was a part of that, whether I knew it or not." Eli made a dismissive sound, like a horse huffing, but Nick wasn't deterred. "I commented on your body *all* the time when we were dating. I treated you like—someone you aren't."

Eli remembered; of course he remembered. *No other girl on the team has an hourglass shape like you do. I love those hips of yours. Geez, look at your legs.*

He shook his head. "Sure, but I wasn't exactly the most enlightened white kid. I made those shitty jokes about your dad's accent." He still cringed when he thought about it. "God, why did you put up with me?" Eli's flashlight lowered to his feet. He looked off to the side, into the dark, and sighed through his nose. "I was a total jerk. You were just being a good boyfriend."

"Okay, so we were both products of our time," Nick said. "So what? I was trying to be normal, too, I guess. But now I'm older, so: fuck normal."

"Fuck normal," Eli repeated. It felt right, so he said it again, louder. "Fuck normal!" It echoed through the dark chamber of the school. He was shaking; his flashlight shivered along the floor with it. "I want to punch something."

"Me?" Nick asked.

"No, not—Jesus, you really are a glutton for punishment." Eli looked around the already trashed library. "I want to punch the whole thing right in the face. How do you punch society?" He spied a boxy wooden chair nearby and gave it a one-handed shove. It barely moved, it was so heavy. "Stupid fucking piece of—" Eli lifted his leg and kicked, sending it tumbling end over end into a shadowy corner. A tinkle of broken glass and the crunch of damage followed.

"There you go," Nick crowed. He swiped at a computer monitor that was already cracked, shoving it to the ground with a loud crash.

Eli stared at the remains of the monitor, bouncing on his toes. "Hell yeah. Feel good?"

Nick looked up at him, his eyes wild. "Yeah, actually. Feels right." He shook his shoulders like a boxer readying for a match.

Fueled by Nick's unexpected enthusiasm, Eli tucked his phone in his pocket and attempted something he'd always dreamed of doing: flipping a table. Unfortunately the round library table was too heavy. He couldn't get a good angle with his sneakers slipping on the tattered carpet.

Nick immediately divined his intentions. "Here, we'll do it together." He put his phone in his shirt's breast pocket so the light still shone from the top, then took his place at Eli's side. Their hands braced against the lip of the table. "On three, ready? One, two—"

They lifted in unison. The table didn't technically flip over, but it did tip upward before crashing sideways against a nearby bookcase. Eli watched in horror as the entire bookcase swayed. A headline flashed through his mind: *Florida Man Squished to Death in Abandoned School Due to His Own Hubris.*

"Back up, back up!" He thrust out an arm and corralled Nick away from the imminent collapse. Luckily, when the bookcase fell, it fell in the opposite direction, taking out the next row of stacks, and then the next, each falling like dominos.

Eli had a firm grip of Nick's arm by that point, and he could feel each wince they shared every time a bookcase toppled with a bang. The explosive noises seemed to drag on forever until, at last, they stopped. Dust and debris whirled through the air. Swollen, storm-damaged books spilled in huge mounds all along the ground.

Nick coughed hard, waving away the dust. "You okay?"

Eli took stock of himself. "Yeah. I'm good. You?"

"Not a scratch."

"That was wild." He gave a nervous laugh.

Nick looked over at him, a streak of dust on his brow. He laughed too.

Soon they were both laughing at the sheer ridiculousness of the whole thing. Real laughs, the kind that made Nick shake and had Eli's eyes watering. He realized he was holding Nick by both arms now, and Nick was holding him back, and their faces were getting closer and closer. How was that happening? Oh, it was Eli moving into Nick's space, close enough that he could see the faint stubble along Nick's upper lip, the tiny scar on the bottom of his chin. Eli had been there when Nick had earned that scar: pool deck, 1994, a slip and fall. He'd needed stitches.

He was staring. The room went quiet. Nick went still, his eyes wide.

"Eli?" he asked.

Eli had no idea how it happened. One minute, he was

standing there. The next, he'd swayed forward the barest inch until he was kissing Nick. It was like nothing he'd ever experienced and the most familiar sensation in the world all at once. Nick made a high noise of surprise, and Eli was sure he was going to pull away, but then he leaned into it, kissing Eli back with a kind of devotion that made Eli's knees weak.

He let go of Nick's arms to slide his hands up the planes of his broad back. Nick folded into him, his own hands slipping to Eli's waist. Eli took the invitation for what it was, pressing into Nick's hot mouth. It was a bad idea, but it felt too good to be wrong.

It lasted for what seemed like forever and also not long enough. When Nick straightened, his lips were wet. Eli watched them part, like Nick was about to say something.

Then came the groan.

"Did you hear that?" Nick got his flashlight out again, sweeping the light through the dark.

Eli was too busy trying to compose himself to really register what was happening. He blinked, his hands falling away from Nick. "What?"

"Listen."

Eli froze, hearing the sound again, but closer this time. Like there was someone in the room with them making a pained moaning sound that morphed into a screech.

"It's coming down," Eli whispered. Then, louder: "Nick, the building's coming down!"

"Go, run!"

They raced for the door, lights bouncing, the grind of steel and concrete loud in Eli's ears. He slipped on something wet and went down on one knee. Nick hauled him up by the arm.

Eli couldn't stop chanting, "We're going to die, we're going to die." And in the most pointless way possible. Fuck, the head-line would haunt his family for generations. *Florida Men Destroy Abandoned Building, Themselves.*

"Get *up*, we're not dying," Nick said, and then immediately tripped over a broken chair that was in their path.

Now Eli was the one pulling him toward safety. The ground under his feet seemed to go all liquidy for a moment, like the earth had given up on being solid. There had been an earthquake on the eastern seaboard about a decade ago, with the tremors reaching New York, and all Eli could think was it was happening again. Except Florida didn't get earthquakes, did it?

"We have to move!" He yanked at Nick's wrist until he was upright, and together they stumbled out of the library's gaping maw. Eli looked around wildly with his phone clutched in one hand. Everything was shaking, tilting slightly to the left: trees, fences, the surrounding buildings. Holy shit, what were you sup-posed to do in an earthquake? "Do we stand in a doorway?" he shouted over the sound of support beams collapsing.

He still had Nick's arm in a tight grip, so he felt rather than saw Nick twist around to look behind them. "Oh my god," he whispered.

Eli turned too and saw that the library they'd just escaped was—falling. It was sinking down into the ground, slowly at first, and then faster, faster, walls and windows and everything within turning into a cacophony of destruction.

"Sinkhole." Nick said it in a weirdly calm way, like he was comforted now that he understood what was going on.

Eli wasn't quite there yet, comfort-wise. He practically tore Nick's arm from its socket as he wrenched him away from the giant fucking hole opening up in the ground. "Get to the fence!"

A few days prior, a light jog at the beach had been more than enough of a challenge, but now Eli's arms and legs were pumping like he was trying out for the track team. He'd never moved that fast in his entire life, including the time he'd fought his way onto the field at Central Park to watch Lewis Black do a set for Summer Series. Nick was right next to him, sprinting just as quickly. Eli could hear his labored breathing and the pounding of his feet on the ground. He tried not to listen to the sounds of the sinkhole widening right behind them, sucking everything in its path down into the earth.

Finally, after what felt like an eternity of vaulting over felled palm trees, they reached the fence. It was not the section of the fence they had slipped through, though. Eli groped for the break in the chains but found nothing but solid links.

"Fuck it, we're going over the top." Nick tucked away his phone and grabbed Eli by the waist.

"Whoa," he yelped. "Hold on, wait a—" But there was nothing he could do about being tossed bodily onto the fence. He clung to the chain link and scrambled up until he could swing first one leg, then the other over the top. Nick was doing the same beside him.

They both hit the ground at the same time. Nick went down harder, sprawling in a heap. He groaned and rolled onto his back. "Is it still going?" he asked.

Eli stared into the blackness of the campus beyond the fence. It was so quiet, he couldn't hear a single bird or bug, nothing except for Nick's heaving breaths and his own. He approached the fence once more and hooked two fingers into a link. "It stopped." Half of their old high school was gone. The library and the orchestra room and the basketball courts, the courtyard with the cabbage palms: it was all swallowed up. Eli could see a few hundred yards in the distance, where half of the gym was gone, its innards exposed like an open dollhouse. The massive sinkhole sat still and ominous, a gash of absence on the world.

Eli grimaced. "Do you think anyone will notice?"

Before Nick could weigh in, the rest of the gym tipped over and fell into the void with a boom.

CHAPTER 15

December 22

Eli sat at his parents' kitchen table, slowly and methodically shoving Cheerios into his mouth while Cora and Wendall lamented over the morning newspaper. Because they were the kind of people who still subscribed to an actual newspaper. *Sinkhole Destroys Port Stephen Prep*, the headline read. *No Chance of Rebuilding Now, Sources Say*, said the smaller one right underneath.

"It's such a shame," Eli's mom said through tears. "Think about all the kids who were hoping to finish up the year at their own school."

Wendall sighed, pouring everyone more coffee. "Looks like Max will have to graduate from Southern instead. Poor kid."

Cora dabbed at her eyes with her wrist. "I don't understand how this could have happened. There was never any sign of instability in that area before."

Eli choked on his Cheerios.

"Well, what with all that storm damage, I'm sure things got shaken up," Wendall said reasonably. "And some of the buildings on that campus are pretty old. They opened that in, what, the early eighties?"

"Sixties, actually," Eli said while trying to clear his throat. He picked up his glass of orange juice and drank it all in three painful gulps.

"Hey, easy, kiddo." Wendall tipped his chin at the juice glass. "Try to taste it as it goes down, huh?"

"Sorry." Eli put his empty glass down, keeping his gaze on his bowl of mostly milk.

Cora pushed away from the table. "I've got to see your aunt Honey. She'll be devastated by all this. She was really hoping Max would graduate from Prep."

"And I've got some last-minute errands to attend to." Wendall gave Eli a wink for some reason—was he supposed to pretend like he still didn't know where Christmas presents came from?—and left as well.

Eli sat there and stared at the headline on the abandoned copy of the *Saint Stephen County News & Report* that was folded next to his dad's plate of toast crusts. They'd gotten a drone photo of the sinkhole from above. Another column under the main story wondered if it would break some kind of record for diameter.

Nausea roiled in his stomach. Before he could think too hard about it, he pulled out his phone and called Nick.

He picked up on the second ring. "Hey." He sounded just as rough as Eli felt.

"Hey." Eli licked his dry lips, chasing the taste of orange. "Want to go for a run?"

In no time at all, they were back on their beach, although running didn't actually seem to be in the cards. Eli plodded along the sand slowly with his arms wrapped around his trembling middle. Beside him, Nick looked equally queasy and disheveled. Probably hadn't gotten much sleep either. Even though Eli had gone straight to bed after being dropped off the night before, he hadn't slept a wink. He kept staring at the ceiling and wondering if he should expect a state trooper to come knocking on his parents' door anytime soon.

"We need to talk," he made himself say once they were far enough away from any other beachgoers.

Nick nodded. "Yeah. We do. That kiss . . ."

"What? No." Eli frowned. "The kiss was—nothing. An accident. I mean, we need to talk about the fact that we destroyed the school."

"Oh." Nick stared ahead, his back and shoulders rigid. "Sure. Of course."

Eli felt like an asshole, but what else was he supposed to say? *Sorry I went back on the pact that I said we should make?* After all, none of that mattered if he went to jail. "Do you think there were any security cameras?"

"If I did, I wouldn't have broken in with you in the first place," Nick pointed out. "Besides, it wasn't our fault."

"Wasn't it, though?" Eli was sure his eyes were bugging out of his head. "The hole only started sinking once we messed around with those bookcases."

"A couple bookcases falling over won't trigger a sinkhole. I think. I'm pretty certain." Nick frowned down at his bare feet as they walked. "It was a textbook act of god thing."

Eli kicked a lump of brown seaweed, scattering it across the sand. "Doesn't feel like a god thing. Felt very much like an Eli Ward thing."

"Okay, I was there too. If anyone's going to claim responsibility for burying our old school underground, it's going to be both of us."

A groan broke free from Eli's throat. "Can we not joke about this right now? I feel really, really bad."

"Why? You hated that place. You told me so right before—" Nick tucked his bottom lip between his teeth, politely cutting himself off.

Eli tried to rally. "Yes, okay, the school was a shithole. That doesn't mean I wanted to erase it from the face of the earth!" Eli flailed his arms around like a deranged Muppet. "There's a huge difference between working through my shit in a healthy way that doesn't hurt anything in the real world and *actively burning the motherfucker down.*"

"Again, you didn't really do anything. You were just kind of . . . present. And besides—" Nick worried at his lip some more as he slouched along the shore. It was really distracting. "Sometimes it's better for the past to stay buried."

Eli stopped, ankle deep in the warm sand. Nick didn't notice and kept going ahead. The shape of his shoulders was stark against the bluer-than-blue sky, his hands stuffed in his pockets like he didn't have a care in the world. And maybe he didn't. Maybe he had decided to forget the kiss they'd shared. He'd been eager to get into it a moment ago. But now Nick was saying, what? That they needed to let the past go?

Nick had kissed him first, damn it. Eli looked out over the water, like he was trying to find the spot where the crime had been committed. It was impossible to tell if they were close to where they'd been before; everything looked different in the daylight.

Eli shuffled his foot through sand, disturbing bits of shell and the remnants of paper that someone had littered along the ground. Straw wrappers and cigarette butts. Okay, so Nick had changed tack—so what? Eli had told him they weren't going to be anything more than friends anymore, and he had obviously taken that to heart.

So why was Eli feeling like a sinkhole of disappointment had opened up in his own stomach?

"E?"

Only Margo called him that. Seemed fitting that now Nick

did too. Eli lifted his head to find Nick in the distance, watching him right back with a look of concern on his face.

"You okay?"

Eli shook off the feeling of despair and pasted on a smile. He trudged forward to catch up. "Yeah, I'm fine." The vibe was heavy, too heavy for a morning stroll along the water. "Thanks for, uh, talking me down from confessing to the sinkhole situation. If it wasn't for you, I might have let the guilt eat away at me until I called up Channel 12 News and told them everything."

"The good people at Channel 12 would have informed you that even the most pissed-off person can't will a sinkhole into existence," Nick said.

Eli sighed. "Yeah. Good ol' Channel 12. The one—two—turn—two." He did the old hand thing they used to do on the local news program back in the nineties, sticking up one finger, then two, flipping his hand around, then back. Nick did it as well, and in perfect unison.

They shared a look that turned into a laugh. Nick actually giggled, the asshole. "That was some ancient knowledge we just displayed right there."

"We belong in a museum," Eli agreed.

They walked in silence for a few minutes. Eli was content to let the conversation lie where they'd left it, but Nick spoke up again.

"I know you're not the biggest fan of New Port Stephen," he said. "And I know you have a lot of reasons for feeling ambivalent about being here—"

"Ambivalent? It's more like distaste with a side order of outright hatred."

The joke didn't land like he intended. Nick's face shuttered before he looked away.

Eli grimaced. "No, sorry, go ahead. I'm just shooting my mouth off."

Nick sighed through his nose. "I was going to say: pretty much everyone in this town is here because we have something keeping us here. Like with me, I've got Zoe, my dad, the restaurant . . . I'm trying to make the best life I can. You can have your feelings about this place, but I hope you get why I'm still here and not—somewhere else."

Eli looked over at him, horrified. "Oh my god, of course I do. I mean, dude, if I was coming off like some sort of snob, ranting about how much this town sucks—"

"Not a snob. Borderline East Coast liberal elite, maybe." Nick gave him a lopsided smile.

That got a laugh out of Eli. "Well, please know that any disparaging remarks I might share about NPS are not a reflection on you. There's no shame in living in your hometown. It's different for me. I couldn't survive without at least one gay bar in a fifty-mile radius."

Nick stopped walking and turned to Eli. "Is that so?"

Eli paused, ruffling a hand through his windswept hair. "I mean, I'm a little old to be clubbing, but once in a blue moon? I need to be in a room full of queer people."

"But you don't drink," Nick said.

"There are lots of other things to do at a gay bar." Eli waggled his brows suggestively. "Like judge people's outfits."

Nick ducked his head, but not before Eli caught the edges of his smile. "Then you will be pleased to know," he said, "that New Port Stephen currently boasts one of the best gay bars in the tri-county area."

"Wait, seriously?" Eli blinked. Several times.

"Well, it's the only gay bar in the tri-county area, but yeah. It opened like, three years ago?"

"And how would you know this?"

"It was all over the news. They tried to get a license to serve food, but the city wouldn't issue the permit for some weird reason."

"The reason was homophobia," Eli deadpanned.

Nick didn't even acknowledge the very good joke, too wrapped up in trying to remember the boring details. "I think they said it was some old law that restricted establishments with dance floors. It was the talk of the restaurateur community for months."

"Wow. The restaurateur community sounds like it needs to get a fucking life."

Nick rolled his eyes. "Look, do you want to go check it out or not?"

"Check out—? The gay bar? With you?"

A shrug. "Why not? Could be fun."

Okay. Nick Wu was apparently in the running for the chillest straight person of the year. Or maybe the most supportive friend in the state. Eli got the feeling that they were playing some kind of game, but as long as it wasn't gay chicken, he didn't see the harm. Besides, a New Port Stephen gay club sounded like it might be rife with material. Train wrecks usually were.

"Where even is this place, allegedly?" he asked. He wouldn't put it past Nick to pull a very elaborate prank to get him out of his funk.

"In a shopping plaza on Route 1." Like that narrowed it down at all. "It's a Friday. Should be hopping tonight."

Eli gave a confused hum. "Won't you have to work?" Fridays were one of the busiest nights of the week at restaurants; he remembered that much from his ill-fated stints as a waiter while trying to break into comedy.

Nick licked his lips. "I worked so many hours this week, I actually have the night off."

"And you want to spend your rare Friday off . . . by going to a gay bar?" Eli shook his head in disbelief. "You're sure?"

Nick adopted a hurt expression. "Look, if you don't want me to come—"

"No, no." Eli held up his hands. The straightest man he knew at the only gay place in town? This was beyond a train wreck. This was getting into sinkhole territory, and he liked it. "By all means. You can pick me up at eleven."

"Why so late?"

"Eleven isn't late for a club. Why, what time were you thinking?"

"I was thinking more like nine?"

"What are you, an octogenarian?" Eli huffed.

"Well, I'm not twenty anymore! Do you have any idea how hard it is to get a sleep schedule back on track after one late night? My insomnia's already a nightmare."

"Jesus god. Fine! Ten o'clock. Split the difference."

"Deal." Nick had the nerve to wear a smug little smile on his face, like he'd gotten away with something. "Wear something decent. I don't want people to think I'm going to gay clubs with a slob."

Eli let out a high, offended gasp, then another when Nick turned around and kept walking down the beach. "I am not a slob!" he called after him. "This is *athleisure*."

"It's sweatpants," Nick said without turning around.

Eli ran to catch up. "Athleisure," he repeated.

CHAPTER 16

The Anvil, New Port Stephen's hottest (and only) spot for gay nightlife, was sandwiched between a ceiling fan outlet and a tattoo parlor. But now, a little past ten, everything in the Southern Breeze Shopping Plaza was shuttered and dark except for the Anvil and the freestanding Denny's that took up the middle of the parking lot.

Nick parked next to a pickup truck that boasted two bumper stickers on the rear fender: I'D RATHER BE FISHING and a rainbow pride COEXIST logo. It occurred to him, not for the first time, that being gay in Florida must be a real trip. He knew queer people were everywhere, but sitting in the parking lot out back of the Denny's, surveying the dozen or so cars clustered around the Anvil, he realized he didn't know any of them personally. Except for Eli, of course.

Eli had actually dressed up for the occasion: black jeans, sharp Chelsea boots (Eli had to inform him of that term, and then proceeded to mock him for not knowing it), a collared shirt with a violet floral print, freshly ironed. His hair was styled with some kind of nice-smelling pomade, and his mustache looked like he'd given it a trim. Next to him, Nick felt woefully under-dressed in his slacks and polo. He should never have made that crack about fashion.

"Before we go in," Eli said, "if anyone gets racist with you, give me the signal and we'll leave, okay? White gays are the worst. I can say that because I am one."

Nick made a face. "What's the signal?"

"I don't know. Wave your arms around? Or whatever works in awkward small-town situations," Eli said as they approached the nondescript front door. Nick couldn't see a pride flag any-where on the exterior. The only thing that denoted the purpose of the business was the thump of music that could be felt even on the sidewalk out front.

Well, that and the two guys who were milling around out-side, sharing a cigarette. They looked very young, too young to be at a bar, but then again, everyone looked young to Nick. He'd noticed somewhere around his midthirties that every movie star seemed to be an absolute child. The first time he'd gotten an ap-plication at the Manatee from a potential employee who'd been born after 9/11, he'd had to put his head between his knees and take five deep breaths.

Nick reached the door first and held it open for Eli. "Just try to contain your big city snobbery, okay? Gentle ribbing is fine, but let the good people of the Anvil enjoy their evening unscathed, hm?"

Eli mock-gasped. "I would never scathe," he said, sweeping through the doorway with a tiny smirk.

Once inside, they were asked to present ID to the doorman, which delighted Eli to no end, as it had apparently been years since he'd last been carded. "Can you believe it?" he said to Nick over the loud music. "We lucked out. It must be a theme night." He pointed upward to indicate the song that was playing, bobbing his head along with the beat. Nick listened for a moment, picking out the familiar lyrics of Nelly's classic hit "Hot in Herre." "Early aughts realness!"

The doorman, a bald white guy sitting on a high stool, gave Eli a strange look as he took Nick's ID. "What's a theme night?" he said.

Nick let his eyes close. "Oh god."

Even unseen, Eli was practically vibrating with excitement; it was palpable. "You're telling me this is just a normal night? Just a regular Friday night playing Nelly?"

"Yeah?" The doorman passed the ID back to Nick's out-stretched hand.

Nick took Eli by the arm, steering him toward the bar before he could piss off the guy who probably doubled as the bouncer. "Come on, let's get something to drink. You want a seltzer?"

"Sure, sounds good."

Now that they were inside the club proper, Nick took a look at their surroundings, although it was so dimly lit he had a hard time making out any details. He had an impression of a small but lively crowd, with couples and bigger groups of friends talking loudly to each other over the pounding bass. An attempt had been made to decorate for the holidays; strings of Christmas lights and gaudy tinsel bunting were draped along the black walls, then petered out halfway around the room. A few dollar-store cartoon Rudolphs and Santas were taped to the mirror behind the bar. A plastic blue-and-white menorah sat next to the cash register, which felt like a paltry gesture to New Port Stephen's Jewish population; by Nick's calculations, Hanukkah had wrapped up a week ago.

There was a dance floor to the right bathed in a rainbow of colors. There was no DJ, just speakers mounted along the walls that pumped out the music. No seating to speak of, only a handful of tiny high-top tables that people clustered around to lean on. They joined the pack at the end of the bar.

Nick made the mistake of resting his elbows on the bar's worn surface, which turned out to be a sticky mess. A quick reshuffle, and he stuck his hands into his pockets instead. Fuck, it was impossible to look cool. Why had he worn khakis? And why was it so hot in this place? He was already sweating.

As far as the clientele went, Nick was surprised to see it ran the gamut. There were men and women and probably people in between. Some were as young as the guys outside had been, and some looked closer to Nick's dad's age. Plenty of folks in the middle. White, Black, brown, one Asian woman who gave Nick a nod of recognition even though he'd never seen her before in his life . . . it was like looking at a cross section of the south Florida census.

Eli must have noticed it too. "Now *this* fucking rules, actually. Bars in New York tend to attract only one kind of queer, you know? There's a bar for leather daddies, a bar for Dominican guys, a bar for college students. Like, super specific gays. But this place is the only game in town. You'd never see this kind of melting pot in the city unless you went to a Beyoncé concert, and even then, it's only the ones with the—" He made a rubbing fingers gesture that meant *money*.

"It is pretty cool." Nick could count the number of times on one hand he'd been in a bar where white people made up less than 90 percent of the attendance. Here, it was more like 60/40, which, for Florida, was pretty good.

The Nelly song ended, and something else that Nick didn't recognize right off the bat replaced it. LeAnn Rimes, possibly? Some girl singing her heart out. What a random playlist.

Eli leaned close to hiss into his ear. "This. Is. Amazing! It's like we stumbled upon some lost civilization that never moved past 2009. Why is Florida so behind the rest of the world? It's ten to fifteen years out of date, consistently. It's giving monoculture." A group of four or five guys received their drinks and started making their way to the neon-lit dance floor, giving Eli plenty of time to stare at their outfits. "Nick, are you seeing this? That *actual* man is wearing a white belt. With Vans!"

"You said you weren't going to scathe," Nick reminded him.

"I'm not being scathing! I'm just reporting on what is right in front of my eyes. I mean, that guy put on that belt and those shoes of his own free will before leaving his house tonight. No one was twisting his arm."

More barflies cleared out, clutching their plastic cups of cocktails. Nick saw one of the guys was wearing a strappy leather harness thing over his shirt, but his companions were all dressed like they'd just come from church. He tried not to stare.

Eli apparently had no such compunctions. "Loving this look," he said, loud enough for the harness guy to raise his bottle of beer in a salute of thanks.

The bartender, an older white guy with a head of silver hair topped by reindeer antlers, finally turned to them after depositing about a million shot glasses into a bus tray. "What'll you have?" he asked, pointing at Nick.

Eli sidled in front of him and pulled out some bills. "A club soda with lime for me—put that in the usual cup, would you? Not a kiddie cup. And—Nick, what are you drinking?"

"I can get this." He reached for his wallet. It felt weird making the sober guy pay for his drink. Not to mention, Eli was currently unemployed. He didn't need to waste his money like that.

"Buying one round is the least I can do. You've been driving me around this town all week. Come on, beer? Wine?"

"I would not order the wine," the bartender said, already dispensing club soda into a cup.

"Bud Light, please." Nick had seen Leather Guy carrying a blue-labeled bottle, and it was easier to order something he knew was on offer than go through the rigamarole of asking what was on tap. He doubted this was the kind of place that carried local craft brews.

The bartender uncapped a bottle and placed it in front of Nick in less than an eyeblink. "Four dollars," he told Eli.

"Seriously?" Eli left a five and a single on the bar top. "I keep forgetting how cheap alcohol is down here. At these prices, I might take up drinking again."

"Ha ha. Very funny." Nick took a swig of his beer. It tasted like almost nothing.

"Let the addict have his fun, okay? It's the only buzz I get anymore." Eli lifted his plastic cup of soda water, lime jauntily plopped among the ice. "Thanks for bringing me here, friend-o. It was just what I need."

Nick tapped the neck of his bottle to Eli's cup. "No problem." He was not going to call Eli friend-o, not for a million dollars. Maybe if he played his cards right, they could move out of friend territory and get somewhere less restrictive. All Nick needed to do was show Eli how chill and comfortable he was in an environment like this, and then Eli would see that it was possible to pursue . . . whatever it was they had between them.

He was certain there was something between them. Right? That moment in the library, before everything went to hell—that had been real.

The pop-country song ended and "Party Rock Anthem" started playing. Nick hadn't thought about that song since he'd dated Laurie. It had been playing everywhere then, and it seemed the Anvil had not moved on from it.

"Holy shit." Eli turned to him with a gleam in his eye. "They're playing the song from the hamster commercial? Unironically?"

"Uh." Nick didn't know what he was talking about, but then again, he probably hadn't seen an honest-to-god television commercial since the last time the Marlins were in the playoffs.

Eli grabbed him by the wrist and pulled him away from the sticky bar. "Come on. I have got to dance to this."

Nick had guessed that dancing might make an appearance at some point in their outing, so he wasn't shocked to find himself on the dance floor. He was determined not to be like one of those straight guys who were such fuddy-duddies about it. Sure, he wasn't the world's best dancer, but looking around the Anvil, he could confidently say he wasn't the worst. A middle-aged woman in the center of the floor was currently having the time of her life miming an electric shock treatment, and one of the younger patrons was trying to grind on his partner with offbeat, robotic hip snaps. One extremely buff dude stood near motionless over by the wall, naked from the waist up save for a strand of blinking Christmas lights draped around his neck and a jaunty Santa hat on his bobbing head.

Nick at least had rhythm. His strategy was to keep it casually low-key. A little swaying, a little bopping, and he could get himself into Eli's orbit. They'd danced together at parties and winter formals; why couldn't they dance here, tonight? He glanced back at Eli to gauge the distance between them.

And realized that Eli had somehow grown into a worse dancer, which didn't seem possible.

When they were kids, Eli would throw himself into a song double-time, his hips and arms flailing twice as fast as was necessary. Nick distinctly remembered a middle-school dance where he'd suggested Eli take it down a notch during TLC's "Waterfalls." He'd gotten a butterfly hair clip chucked straight at his forehead for his troubles. That was the moment he'd decided to let Eli dance as badly as he wanted. For as long as he wanted.

He just hadn't thought that would extend all the way into the next quarter century.

"I love this song! It was playing around the clock when I first moved to New York," Eli shouted over the pounding bass. Nick didn't think it was the best time to share what he'd been doing when the song was big—embarking on the relationship that would become his failed marriage—so he nodded pleasantly. Eli sipped at his cup of water and turned to survey the crowd.

Nick saw movement across the room. A tall, skinny guy of indeterminate age wearing a ton of glitter makeup on his cheeks perked up at the sight of Eli. He made his way over without taking his eyes off him. Nick wasn't sure what to do; it wasn't a crime to approach someone at a club, but he'd secretly hoped any interested parties might see them together and assume they were a couple.

"Can I buy you a drink?" the skinny guy shouted in Eli's ear, loud enough for Nick to hear him.

"Thanks, but I already have one." Eli held up his faux cocktail as evidence.

"Your next one, then?" the guy asked.

Nick's stomach knotted up. He tried to look disinterested in the conversation, but he was certain his face was giving him away.

"That's sweet of you, but I'm good." Eli gave him a consoling pat on his arm. "Have a nice night." He sipped at his drink and meandered deeper into the dance floor.

A little tension slipped out of Nick's body, letting him breathe again. He gave the skinny guy a sympathetic shrug as he followed Eli. He knew better than most what it felt like to get the Ward Brush-Off.

"Why'd you turn that guy down?" he asked as they worked their way around some dancers. Nick racked his brain for some of the lingo he'd come across recently. "Was he too much of a . . . bottom for you?"

Eli stopped and whirled around, a shocked laugh bursting out of him. "Who taught you that word?"

"No one! I live in a society, okay? I pick things up." No way was he going to admit he'd spent several hours that afternoon trying to google his way through queer culture in addition to his research on demisexuality.

"Wow. Okay. A society." Eli shook his head with a smile on his lips. "And for your information, I'm actually a true vers these days." He winked and resumed his study of the crowd while he sipped at his drink.

Nick stood there frozen, flipping through his mental notes. He knew what a vers was, but *these days*? Was that in reference to the kind of sex they'd had as teenagers? It sounded flirtatious, but maybe it was just Eli being smug. Delighting in yet another way to make Nick squirm. Referencing their past sex life was certainly one way to do that.

Happy screeches rose from the dance floor as a particularly bendy person began to vogue. Nick couldn't clap because of the beer in his hand, so he joined in the hooting and hollering. It was a relief to see someone with actual skills, and as a bonus, most of the bad dancers stopped whatever they were doing to watch. Including Eli, who molded himself up against Nick's side so he could say in his ear, "Can you believe this is happening in the Neeps!?"

Nick smiled. "They're good."

Then "Party Rock" slowly faded out and was replaced with . . . Nick couldn't fucking believe it.

"Waterfalls."

Eli laughed, his head tilted back so the colored dance floor lights illuminated his throat. "I was just thinking about this song."

Nick licked his suddenly dry lips. "Weird. Me too." He took

a long pull from his Bud Light so he wouldn't have to say anything else. Definitely shouldn't mention out loud his childish plan
to dance closer and closer until they were dancing together.

As it turned out, he didn't have to say anything at all. Because
Eli made it all a reality on his own.

He grabbed Nick by the hand and slapped it in place at his
waist. "Come on. Like back in eighth grade." Eli took both their
drinks and set them down on a cocktail table, put his own hands
on Nick's hips, and held him awkwardly at arm's length. "Remember? 'There should be room for one more student between
you,'" he parroted in a scratchy voice.

"Mrs. Petinski." Nick hadn't remembered her name or even
thought of her in two decades. "She'd always chaperone the dances."

"Room for one more student? No wonder so many of our
generation have turned to polyamory. You planted the seed, Mrs.
Petinski, so cheers."

Nick mirrored Eli's hip-holding stance as they both re-created
the worst of their childhood dancing: shuffling from one foot to
the other as TLC crooned about—how you shouldn't follow your
dreams? Nick was never sure what the lyrics were trying to say.
He just knew he couldn't stop smiling.

Eli hammed it up, staring down at his shoes in an exaggerated flustered-preteen manner. "Um, gosh, Nicholas, you look so
nice dressed up. Maybe after this we can go to, um, Denny's? If
you want? My mom can drive us."

Nick clicked his tongue. "I don't know if my dad will let me.
I have to be home by curfew." He pretended to think hard. "But
maybe we could go to Skate World this weekend? I could buy
you a hot dog and try to win you a pencil topper in the arcade."

Eli looked up. He was a pretty good comedic actor, his eyes
overly wide. "Really? A whole top of a pencil?" He shimmied
closer, looking over his shoulder as if the ghost of Mrs. Petinski

might be watching. "Nick Wu," he murmured seriously, "you truly are all that and a bag of chips."

Nick laughed, shaking his head. Yet another phrase that hadn't crossed his mind in forever.

A dancer brushed by, barely making contact with Nick's elbow, but Nick took the opportunity to draw closer to Eli on the pretense of getting out of their way. He glanced down into the slice of space between their bodies. They were almost flush together.

The best he could hope for was to keep things fun and light so that Eli didn't pull away. "What kind of chips? And don't say something racist like sriracha."

"Hey, I don't go for low-hanging fruit like that." Eli gave the dance floor a pointed look. They weren't the only people who had coupled up for the slow-ish song. "Though if you ask me, the clientele here is all about the low-hanging fruits."

"And here I thought you were strictly anti–dick joke." They had moved into an area next to one of the huge speakers, so Nick got closer to be heard.

"I'm anti–*small*-dick joke. This one works on multiple levels." Eli moved closer too. The points of their hips met every other beat as they swayed. Nearer and nearer, but out of sync. "It could also be a ball joke. See? Levels."

Nick was already nodding. "You really are a poet."

"Sarcasm is what we in the business call the bottom of the comedy barrel, you know."

"Wow," Nick said sarcastically. "I'm learning so much."

Eli tipped his chin to his chest to laugh, giving Nick an opening to shift even closer. Then Eli looked up, and he seemed to realize how close they had gotten. Their hips were flush, no room at all between their bellies. Their chests met with every breath. And Nick was breathing fast.

Eli's eyes shone under the green and pink lights. Nick

swallowed. If they were going to kiss again, this would be the right moment. But he had to let Eli be the one to make a move. All Nick could do was be there, slowing their silly dance to a standstill and hoping that his eyes were saying everything he couldn't say aloud. *Come on, Elijah. Please, just do it.*

TLC stopped playing. Nick couldn't even begin to care about whatever started playing next. The only thing he could hear was the rush of blood in his ears.

Eli's throat bobbed. "Nick. . . ."

He willed it to happen. It seemed impossible for something he wanted so badly to not happen. Perhaps it was wishful thinking, or a trick of the light, but Nick could swear he detected a slight tilt to Eli's head. Like he was preparing to line up their lips.

Then a loud voice cut through the music and the furious pounding of Nick's heart. "Nick Wu? Is that you?"

Nick's stomach dropped. He watched as Eli's gaze left his face and fastened on someone over his shoulder. The light of recognition and an air of surprise passed over his features.

Well, he couldn't ignore whoever it was and hope they'd go away. Nick turned, reluctantly dropping his hands from Eli's waist. He squinted at the man standing behind him with a wide, familiar smile that showed perfect teeth.

"Jamar?" Nick almost swallowed his tongue. "What are you doing here?"

It was undoubtedly Jamar Winstead, the most popular guy from high school. He was less trim these days—who wasn't?—and his hair was worn shorn to the scalp instead of the signature hi-top fade of their youth, but the friendly twinkle in his eyes and the one dimple in his cheek hadn't changed. Normally, a kid like Nick wouldn't have gotten within three feet of Jamar's orbit back in the day; Jamar had been a year ahead, Nick was not nearly as cool, and besides, the school had discouraged Black students from taking the accelerated classes that Nick was in, because of course they did. But through a quirk of electives and alphabetical order, Nick and Jamar had ended up sharing a music stand in jazz band, and so became, if not close friends, at least nodding acquaintances.

Jamar had been one of those popular kids that everyone could agree was genuinely great. He wasn't snobby or a bully. He was sometimes a class clown, but all his pranks were at the teachers' expense. He'd been the student body president, yearbook editor, and prom king. The day after his sixteenth birthday, he'd pulled into the student parking lot in a souped-up Ford Focus with neon lights installed on the undercarriage—the pinnacle of cool. Every girl at PSP could claim to have had at least a passing crush on him. He dated the most beautiful ones and wore Air Jordans. In short, he'd been perfect.

"I'm gay now!" Jamar shouted, spreading his arms wide. "That's what I'm doing here, man. Well, I was gay before, too, but now I get to be *really* gay, you feel me?" He play-boxed at Nick's shoulder with a hearty laugh. "Looks like I'm not the only one! Good ol' Port Stephen Prep was churning 'em out, huh?"

"You can say that again," Eli said. He'd reclaimed his cup of club soda and maneuvered to Nick's side. "Good to see you, Jamar. You look fantastic."

"Awwww, too kind, too kind. Hey, did you go to PSP too?" Jamar snapped his fingers a few times. "Sorry, man, the name's on the tip of my tongue."

Nick made a strangled sound in the back of his throat.

Eli stuck out his hand. "It's Eli."

"Right! Eli. My bad." Jamar pumped his hand up and down. "Yeah, it's all coming back to me now. Eli."

It was a small lie, Nick knew, but what made it infinitely more bizarre was that Eli seemed perfectly content to let it go unchallenged. Maybe it was too much of a hassle to do the whole explanation if you didn't plan on ever seeing the person again. Then Nick remembered that Eli had explained it very clearly to him when they ran into each other at the Wine Barn, and it made something warm flicker in his chest to think that Eli might have wanted to see him again right off the bat.

But then Eli opened his mouth.

"And I'm sorry to have to correct you, but Nick here is still straight as an arrow. He just thought it might be fun to check this place out with me," Eli said.

Nick pursed his lips. Not an arrow, he wanted to say. More like . . . something flexible. Under the right circumstances. Maybe. Like one of those little hard pellets that bloom into sponge dinosaurs when you soak them in water. Did they still make those?

But the conversation was already moving forward without his input.

"Oh, that's cool." Jamar nodded at them both. "You in town for the holidays too?"

"I am," Eli offered. "Nick still lives here year-round."

"Ohhhhhhhh." The way Jamar said it—pity covered by overdone interest—made Nick want to sink through the sticky dance floor. "Hey, let me introduce y'all to my husband. Where's he at? Ernesto!" he called above the heads on the dance floor, which was no problem given his six-foot-plus height.

Out of the corner of his eye, Nick saw Eli mouth the word "husband" to himself.

A short, chubby man floated out of the crowd of dancers and moved toward them. He was—Nick couldn't think of any other word—cute. He had one of those cherub faces that seemed impossibly serene. Or maybe that was just the way he always looked at Jamar. "Yes, love?"

"Check it out, I went to high school with these guys. This is Eli"—he pointed at Eli, who waved—"and Nick." He pointed at Nick. "He's the straight friend."

"I'm—I do other things," Nick said in an attempt to defend his potential queerness, but no one heard him over the music.

"So nice to meet you! Merry Christmas, Merry Christmas." Ernesto swooped in for a quick press of a hug for both of them, then eyed Eli up and down. "Want to dance? Jamar does not like to dance with me." He passed a flat hand over his head. "The height. It makes it hard. But you are just my size!"

"I'm telling you, baby, one wrong move and I could crush you out there," Jamar said with a laugh. Ernesto gave him an unimpressed pout.

"I'd love to dance," Eli said. He gave Nick a questioning glance. At first Nick hoped that it meant Eli wanted to make sure Nick was okay with him dancing with another man. Maybe they had been about to kiss again after all. "You won't get too uncomfortable being on your own for a few minutes, right? If any guys try to hit on you, just yell 'straight!' and flash a picture of your kid."

Nick wanted to scream. But like every other time in his life when he wanted to scream, he just said, "I'll be fine. Thanks."

Eli gave him a thumbs-up and disappeared into the throng of bodies alongside Ernesto.

Nick might have stared after him for a long time, but Jamar nudged Nick in his side, capturing his attention. "You've got a kid? That's wild."

"Yeah." Nick shook his head. "Time sure flies."

"Should we grab another beer while the boys are shaking their behinds?" He held up his empty Coors bottle.

Nick's own drink was still half full, but the bar seemed a safer proposition than the edge of the dance floor, where he could watch Eli and Ernesto indeed shaking. Ernesto looked bewildered by Eli's lack of skill, but he was trying valiantly to keep up with the jerky motions.

"Sure," Nick said. "Another beer sounds good."

They ended up in the same spot at the bar Nick had been in before. There were a lot more people dancing and fewer trying to get served, so the bartender produced their fresh beers in no time. Jamar asked with great sincerity if Nick really had a picture of his kid to share, and Nick obliged by showing him the endless reel of Zoe photos on his phone. Jamar exclaimed over each one. "Looks just like you, man. Check those ears. Those are Wu ears."

Nick lifted a hand to his own ear. He'd never thought of himself as having super recognizable ears. "Thanks?" He sipped at his new, colder beer. "How about you? What have you been up to these days?"

"Besides the obvious?" Jamar handed Nick his phone back with a chuckle. "Ernie and I've got a place in Orlando. He works in hospitality, manages one of the big hotels. After college, I went into public relations. Sports teams, cartoon characters, museums, you name it, I've repped it."

"Oh." Nick couldn't help but feel a little disappointed. "I always thought you'd go into politics." They'd called Jamar the mayor of PSP, after all. He was the kind of person who could get anyone on his side, nerds to jocks, band geeks to drama kids.

Jamar laughed. "First of all, if I'd've gone into politics, you would've heard about it. And second: a Black gay man running for office in Florida? They'd get the FBI involved before I could get one damn lawn sign in the ground." He shook his head. "No, I decided it was a big enough challenge to just live a comfortable, quiet life after I came out. So that's what I'm doing."

Nick picked at the edge of the wet beer label on his Bud

Light. "Yeah, can I ask—? Like, how did that all happen? Did you always know, even back in high school, or . . . ?"

"Man, back then I was so worried about being everything to everybody that I couldn't even tell you who I was. I didn't *matter* to myself." He looked out over the dance floor, the blue and purple lights highlighting his handsome face. "I was obsessed with making other people happy, making other people laugh, getting every trophy and blue ribbon and certificate I could so other people would be proud of me. So nah, I didn't know in high school." Jamar lifted his beer in a salute. "You know, for every gayby who jumps out of the womb knowing all the lyrics to 'We Are Family,' there's someone like me."

Nick felt a thrill of recognition deep in his gut. *This* was what he needed to hear. He needed someone to tell him that whatever he might be going through, he wasn't the first, and he certainly wouldn't be the last. "If this is too nosy, ignore me," he said, "but—how did you figure it out?"

Jamar sighed through his nose. "Sometimes stuff doesn't make sense until you're in your thirties, and you realize, shit, someday soon I'll be in my forties, and after that I'll be in my fifties, so when exactly am I supposed to start clicking with a woman? And then you're like, well, fuck, I don't think it's going to take. I should probably work through my shit." He grinned. "Next thing you know, you're at Gay Days wearing rainbow mouse ears and getting pictures with Mickey."

Nick gave a small, impressed nod. He tried to envision himself wearing rainbow anything at Disney World; he couldn't quite get there. "Wow, so you've only been out for—"

"About seven or eight years, yeah," Jamar said. "Those first couple were a little wild. I had no idea what I was doing, so I dove into the deep end and flailed around. Then I met Ernesto, and we just . . . made sense." He looked back at the dance floor, where Ernesto was still bopping around with Eli. Ernie caught his eye and waved. The look of deep love in his eyes as Jamar waved back was unmistakable.

"Yeah." Nick watched as Eli—dear god—started doing the lawn sprinkler move with his arms. Somehow, Nick still found him achingly attractive. "I think I get that." He stared at Eli for one more moment, then another, and when he finally turned back to Jamar, he was met with a knowing raised-eyebrow look.

"You, uh, going through something, man?"

Nick wasn't sure how to answer—wasn't sure there even *was* an answer. Some things Jamar said had resonated with him, but not everything. He'd enjoyed dating women, back when he'd done it. He'd wanted to be married to Laurie—until he didn't. But that preoccupation with making everyone but himself happy? That struck a big-ass chord.

He opened his mouth, unsure of what was about to tumble out. "I—"

A short, sweaty shape slammed into the bar beside him. Nick stared at Eli, who was sweat-dappled and panting, plucking at the front of his shirt to try to generate some breeze.

"Jesus," he said, "I guess I haven't danced since this fucking playlist was actually in rotation on the radio. I'm like a dehydrated jack-in-the-box out there."

Nick signaled to the bartender without being asked. "Can we get a water? Slice of lime like last time?"

Eli accepted the cup with a grateful groan, using both hands. "Thanks, Nicky." He started gulping down the ice water. Nick pointedly did not watch his throat bob with every swallow.

Ernesto joined them with a beaming smile. He didn't seem to have one hair out of place. "Love, can you get me a drink, please?" he asked Jamar. "You know what I like." He produced a folding fan from his back pocket, snapped it open, and began fanning down Eli while his husband ordered a rum and coke.

"Oh shit, that feels heavenly." Eli leaned into the breeze produced by the fan, his eyes closed. Sweat ran down the length of his neck.

Nick looked away and drank more of his beer.

Jamar cleared his throat and said over the top of Nick's head, "So, Eli, where are you living these days?"

Eli swallowed down the last gulp of water. "New York."

Ernie lit up. "No way! I'm from Queens! I mean, I lived there for years and years before I came down here. But I don't mind Orlando. Yes, it's Florida, but at least there's *some* culture, you know?"

Nick tried not to let the flippant remark get to him, pursing his lips inward to keep from responding. It was true, but still.

Ernesto caught his look and gave a tiny cry of dismay. "Ah, I did not mean to insult you, Nick. Staying in your hometown is fine if that is what ends up happening."

Ends up happening. Nick felt the phrase dig deep into his bones. Every step of the way, his life had just . . . ended up happening. Like he'd had no control. Like it was the weather.

Eli jumped in. "Well, also, it's easier on someone like Nick. Living in New Port Stephen while straight isn't too bad."

Okay, now Nick was getting pissed off. Here he was, trying to find a good way to tell his oldest friend that he was dipping his toe into the Questioning waters, and he couldn't get a word in edgewise without being reminded how fucking heterosexual he supposedly was. It was getting to the point where he was ready to shout it out for the whole club to hear.

Probably a bad idea.

Nick set his beer down on the bar with a thunk. "I'm going to get some air." He left without a single glance at Eli.

Outside was downright crisp and cool compared to the stifling atmosphere inside. Nick stood on the sidewalk that ran down the length of the strip mall and put his hands on his hips, breathing it in. A pair of smokers stood a few yards away, but not the same ones that had been there before. Nick could feel their eyes on his back as he stared out across the parking lot at the traffic passing by on Route 1.

This night was not going the way he had hoped. There never seemed to be a good time to talk to Eli about how he felt. Maybe there would never be a good time. Maybe the whole thing was a bad idea.

Nick spun to face the smokers, who immediately averted their eyes like they could pretend they hadn't been caught staring. "Can I bum one from you?" he asked.

He'd taken up smoking back in college because almost everyone in the Asian Society had smoked. Then he'd gone to work at the Manatee, and since cigarette breaks were the only breaks they got in the restaurant business, he'd kept it up. Snatches of time out in the parking lot by the dumpster, sitting on milk crates with the line cooks, shooting the shit—he'd loved that. Of course, he'd quit when Laurie got pregnant.

Tonight, though, who cared if he had one cigarette?

"Yeah, no problem." One of the smokers, the one with long hair dyed neon green and a stud at the corner of their mouth, shook a Marlboro Light from the box and held it out.

"Thanks. Seriously." Nick leaned in, letting the other smoker light it for him.

It didn't exactly feel good, inhaling until the tip glowed orange, but it felt familiar, and Nick needed that after an evening of being so unmoored. It seemed like every time he was making some progress with Eli, he got shoved into uncharted territory. For every slow dance, there was a protracted reminder that he was only a straight friend in Eli's eyes, and a loser who still lived in the Neeps to boot.

The smokers finished up and headed back inside, leaving Nick alone in the night air. His only company was the regular buzz of cars on the road and the insects singing in the swale next to the parking lot. He smoked about half the cigarette, trying to think of nothing at all.

The door of the club opened, releasing loud music for a few seconds before it shut again. Eli came to stand next to him. Nick could tell it was him without even looking. He knew what it felt like to share a space with him, could tell just by the way the air moved.

"Didn't know you smoked," Eli said.

"I don't mean to shock you," Nick said, ashing onto the sidewalk, "but there are some things you don't know about me."

"Yeah, I'm—I think I'm starting to see that," Eli said.

Nick couldn't help the not-laugh that huffed from his lips at that. "Are you?" He rounded on Eli. "Because it seems like you're incapable of believing anyone but you can change."

"Wha—?" His mouth flapped open and shut again. "I don't even know what that means."

Nick sighed. Tossed the cigarette on the ground and put it out under the sole of his shoe. He couldn't even stay angry. Not at Eli. It wasn't his fault Nick's head was a mess. "I want you to stop introducing me as your straight friend. Please."

He glanced over to see Eli's eyes go wide. "Okay. How come?"

Suddenly what had seemed like such a complicated thing requiring a long and difficult explanation felt very simple. Nick took a deep breath.

"I don't know if I'm straight," he said. "I'm not freaked out about it. I just . . . thought you should know."

"Oh." Eli's gaze went all distant, like he was trying to figure out a complex math problem in his head, all the variables re-arranging themselves before his eyes. "Well, I—okay."

"That's it?" Nick said flatly. "Just 'okay'?"

"Hey, I'm trying to wrap my head around this," Eli snapped back. "Fifteen minutes ago, I thought the earth is round, water is wet, and Nick Wu is heterosexual. Give me a second to readjust my worldview." He stood there for a second, then said, "So when you say 'not straight' do you mean, like, bi?"

"I don't know," Nick said. "If I knew, I would tell you."

Eli nudged the toe of his Chelsea boot against the cigarette butt on the ground, hands stuffed into his pockets. "Thank you. For, uh, updating me."

Nick rolled his eyes. He made it sound like Nick had texted him with a new address for his contact list. "This doesn't have to change anything, you know," he said. "That's not why I told you. It's—the way you described me felt wrong, and I didn't like it."

Eli opened his mouth to reply, but the door opened again, spilling out Jamar and Ernesto. They both wore wide smiles, oblivious to the tension they'd stumbled into.

"You boys hungry?" Ernie asked. He pointed to the Denny's in the distance. "I want Moons Over My Hammy."

"Yeah, come get some greasy food with us," Jamar said, his arm wrapped around Ernie's waist.

"Oh, actually . . ." Eli looked to Nick in question.

Nick waved him off. They both could use some distance. Maybe that would give Eli some time to let it all sink in. "Why don't you go? It's late for me. I think I'll head home."

"If you're sure," Eli said. There was a tightness around his eyes.

"Yeah." Nick mustered a smile for him. "I'm sure. Go ahead."

"Aw, really?" Ernesto pouted. "Well, it was nice to meet you, Nick. Come on, Eli, we'll give you a ride home after we get some eggs." He looped his arm through Eli's and led him across the parking lot, chattering away about the legendary My Hammy.

Nick watched him go with a sinking feeling in his stomach. That could have gone worse, but it also could have gone better. He wasn't sure what he'd wanted Eli's reaction to be, but poleaxed shock wasn't it.

"Hey," Jamar said, pulling his attention back. "You all right?"

"Oh, yeah. Just tired." Nick ran a hand through his hair. "It was nice running into you like this, though."

"Same, bro. And listen—" Jamar reached into his pocket and extracted a business card. "If you're ever in Orlando, let me know. We can get brunch or something. Hell, even if you just need someone to talk to, I'm a text away. Won't magically make things easier, I know, but if I can help at all, I will."

"Oh, that's really kind of you, but—" Nick began. A lifetime of turning down offers of support was on the tip of his tongue.

"Nick." Jamar looked at him. Really looked. Nick felt a spark of something in his chest, something new and familiar at the same time. "No bullshit. Take the card. Whatever you're going through, you're not the only one who's been there."

Nick took the card. The thick paper felt buttery between his fingertips. "Thank you," he said. And he meant it.

Jamar grinned, gave him a little salute, and took off in pursuit of Ernie and Eli.

CHAPTER 17

December 24, Christmas Eve

Nick drove over the bridge that spanned the intracoastal waterway and headed down the causeway, a narrow two-lane road that was flanked by water on either side. It was the same route Nick took to reach the Thirsty Manatee, and he knew it like the back of his hand. In the past, there had been nothing of real interest on the stretch of road, just strips of sand on either side where people could pull over and fish if they liked. Families with small children would go there to swim even though the real beach, the one facing the actual ocean, was only three minutes away. Nick had never understood it until he had Zoe. Now, the thought of her being swept out into the Atlantic on a riptide made him reconsider the more enclosed, murkier waters.

These days, however, only the causeway's south side had any beach to speak of. The north side had been redeveloped into New Port Stephen's downtown waterfront. Brick walkways wound past the water's edge with tall cabbage palms placed every twenty yards. Concrete benches offered a view of the boats tooling around the water. There was even a little visitor center next to the paved parking lot with public bathrooms and a wooden manatee standee where you could stick your head through a hole where the manatee's face should be and have someone take your picture.

And, of course, this was the spot where the town put up the municipal Christmas tree every December with a ceremonial "lighting" on Christmas Eve. (It was technically lit as soon as it was erected after Thanksgiving, but the town council turned it off and then back on for the annual gathering.) The tree was more an idea of a tree: an upside-down cone covered in lights and shiny balls. Nondenominational oversized snowflakes were bolted to the nearby light poles. An oversized menorah was also there off to the side, but as with the one at the Anvil, it felt like an afterthought. Nick always felt bad for that menorah—the Christmas Eve festivities, the music, the boat parade were all clearly in honor of the tree.

He pulled into the parking lot next to the visitor center with what he had assumed was plenty of time to spare, but the causeway was already packed. He was fortunate to snag one of the few remaining spots. Up and down the waterfront, people milled about, many of them with kids in tow. Nick watched one such family stroll by with a surly goth teen bringing up the rear, playing with a lip ring. He felt a stab of sympathy, both for the kid and the parents. On the one hand, he understood the urge to wrap himself in all-black everything and take himself out of the running for normalcy. On the other, he thought about what he might do if Zoe came home with a facial piercing in ten years. Probably burst into tears. Fuck, when had he gotten so uncool?

"Dad?"

His eyes flicked to the rearview mirror to see Zoe sitting in her booster seat, craning her neck to try to see what was happening. "Yes, sweetheart?"

"Can we go watch the boats now?" she asked.

Nick unbuckled his seatbelt. "Yep, Dad spaced out a little there. Let's go see the boats."

Zoe beamed as Nick went through the motions of opening the back door and unclipping her harness. She had been looking forward to the boat parade for weeks. Every few days, she asked Nick or Laurie to confirm the facts: Yes, there was going to be a parade. Yes, she could go with her dad. No, they weren't sure what would happen if it was raining, but it would probably be rescheduled. "Reschedule" was what people did when things didn't work out as planned. That last one, Nick had taken great pains to explain, wondering privately if his life needed to be rescheduled since that really hadn't . . . worked out as planned.

In years past, Laurie and Nick would come to watch the local boats slowly chug along the causeway, decorated in increasingly elaborate Christmas light displays. Once Zoe was born, they'd bring her bundled up like a little hot dog against the—admittedly mild—night air. But now that they were divorced, Laurie had magnanimously given up the boat parade, telling Nick that he should be allowed to have Zoe for Christmas Eve since she'd spend Christmas Day with Laurie after an early dinner at Grammy Kay's house.

Nick led Zoe by the hand as they joined the crowds jockeying for a good spot to watch the boats. The handful of benches had long since been claimed, but many people had brought their own nylon camping chairs and were unfolding them near the low coquina wall that ran along the waterline. Zoe watched these preparations with interest.

"Look, there's Eli." Zoe pointed up ahead. "Can we watch the parade with him?"

Nick's head snapped up. Eli was, indeed, standing there with his hands in his jean pockets, wearing a plaid green shirt with the sleeves rolled up. He was chatting with his parents; Mr. and Mrs. Ward were wearing matching festive sweaters with what looked like blobby reindeer appliqued on the front. Tiny bells were sewn onto the reindeer's collars, and Mrs. Ward wore bell earrings in her ears.

"Eli's here with his family, honey," Nick said, keeping his voice down. After the night at the club, he and Eli had been keeping their distance. "He probably wants to watch the parade with them, okay?"

That was apparently not okay, because Zoe hollered as loud as her four-year-old lungs would allow: "Eli! Eli, watch the parade with me!" She waved the hand not held by Nick high above her head.

Nick groaned as Eli twisted around and caught sight of them. "Oh! Hey! You're here." There was a tiny edge of anxiety in his voice, but when he approached, his smile held nothing but warmth for Zoe. "I didn't know you were coming. You looking forward to the lights, Zo?" He crouched down so they were eye level.

She nodded her head so hard, Nick worried for her neck. "It's going to be pretty! Dad brings me every year because Christmas Eve is *our* day, and then tomorrow I have to go see Grammy." Her lips twisted into a pout.

Nick jiggled her hand in his. "But there will be lots of presents to open at Grammy's. And I'll be there to eat a big Christmas dinner with you, and we'll have pie. That'll be fun."

Zoe turned her head away and looked out over the water. Her silence seemed to indicate that she did not agree.

Eli grimaced and stood. "Well, I don't want to interrupt your father-daughter time, since this is your special day."

That changed Zoe's tune. Her head whipped back around, sending some strands of her dark hair into her mouth. "No, watch the boat parade with us, Eli. Please?" she whined. Her whole little body went into a ragdoll sag so that Nick had to bend his knees if he wanted to keep holding her hand.

"You really don't have to," he said to Eli at the same time Eli said, "I don't want to horn in."

Then Mrs. Ward's high, thin voice cut through the chatter of the crowds. "Is that Nick Wu? Eli, tell him they can come watch with us! We've got this great spot." She gestured to the enviable piece of real estate she and her husband had claimed with their camping chairs. Not only did it have a great view of the water-way, but it was close enough to the seawall that no one would be in front of them. Zoe could see everything, even if she wasn't perched on Nick's shoulders.

Nick looked at Eli, his eyebrows raised in question. Eli returned the look with a nibble to his lower lip.

"You're totally welcome to join us. But only if you want," he said.

"As long as you're fine with us barging in on—whoa, okay." Nick nearly toppled over as Zoe tugged him toward the Wards. She was so much stronger than she looked. "I guess that settles it."

They were greeted by Eli's parents with all the trappings of an overly prepared older couple. Mr. Ward offered a bottle of bug spray, which Nick thought was a little much considering the breeze would keep any mosquitos at bay, but he dutifully spritzed down Zoe's arms and legs. Mrs. Ward had brought a cooler filled with bottled water and snacks, so within minutes of enduring the smell of Off, Zoe was happily munching on baby carrots with ranch dip. She sat crisscross applesauce on the crabgrass next to Eli's folks and chattered away about her visit with the mall Santa between mouthfuls.

Nick stood awkwardly over her, hemmed in by the encroaching crowd. Eli was stuck on his other side.

"Nice night," he said. Like they had nothing to discuss but the weather.

"Yeah," Nick agreed. "It is."

They stood for a long minute in the pocket of quiet they'd created amid the buzz of the festivities. The sun had dipped down behind the mainland, and the sunset colors were slowly fading into midnight blue. A children's choir over by the tree finished up a slightly off-key rendition of "The Twelve Days of Christmas" to a smattering of applause. Soon it would be dark, and the boat parade could begin. Easy anticipation was in the air. Somewhere over by the parking lot, a dog started yapping. In the opposite direction, a man laughed so loud it made Nick jump.

"Hey, I'm sorry about the other night," Eli said all in a rush, like he wanted to get it out in one fell swoop.

"Oh?" What Nick really wanted to ask was, *Which part?* If Eli meant the dancing and flirting, Nick was going to dive straight into the freezing water.

"What you told me? Before I went to Denny's with the guys?" He glanced over at his parents, but they were enthralled by Zoe and not listening in at all. "I probably could have taken that news better. Been more supportive. I just—I'm sorry."

Nick sighed. "It's not your fault." He looked out over the water. "I probably could have picked a better time and place to talk about it."

"No," Eli said quickly. "That's not the point. There is no bad time to—" He stopped, screwing his mouth to one side. "Come out? Is that how you'd describe it?"

"I don't know. Do people come out as questioning?" Nick asked.

"If you want." Eli shrugged. "The point is, you told me something big, and I fumbled the ball. That's on me, not you."

"Oh, look at you. A sports metaphor."

"I can be butch."

Nick smiled to himself, then looked back at Eli. He was look-

ing right back with that terrible fondness that made Nick feel
floaty. "Look, it's not actually a big deal. At least, I don't think so.
Don't get me wrong, I don't want you to get the impression that
this is some sort of—" He struggled for the word.

"Phase?" Eli broke into a grin. "Yeah, I would never think
that. I know you. The fact that we're even talking about this
means you've thought about it. A lot." He jostled Nick's shoulder
with his own. "Probably googled everything you could about it."

"Hey! That is . . . entirely accurate," Nick said with faux in-
dignation.

They shared a laugh, and for the first time since they'd been
on the dance floor together, Nick felt the light of hope. This
wasn't insurmountable. He and Eli, they were okay.

Eli pulled himself back to a serious expression. "Whatever
you land on, I'm proud of you, Nicky. If you ever need to talk to
someone, I'm kind of an expert in coming to terms with identi-
ties."

"Thanks, seriously," Nick said. "I've got support, though. Just
so you know." He'd been texting with Jamar off and on yesterday;
mostly normal stuff, but also some of the more personal stuff.
Laurie, too, had kept up a supply of links to various articles she
thought might be helpful. Some of them actually were.

"Look at you!" Eli gave him a friendly slap on the arm.
"You're way ahead of the game. Damn, I don't think I was half
as chill as you when I was in the middle of my own Journey
of Self-Discovery." Nick knew he was speaking with capitalized
words because he was doing jazz hands. "And all while being here
in New Port Stephen? You're some kind of questioning miracle."

"Shut up." Nick let his eyes flick up and down Eli before
holding his gaze. "You know, as weird and awful as New Port
Stephen can be, the people around you can make it worthwhile."

He held his breath. It was the closest he'd come since the kiss at the beach to saying what he really wanted to say. He prayed Eli could read between the lines. *Would it be so bad if you stayed here? Could you see yourself staying with me?*

Eli gave a series of slow, bobbing nods. "Yeah. Okay. I see what you're saying." He glanced over to where Zoe was playing with two baby carrots, marching them along the ground. "Like how Zoe being here makes it worthwhile for you."

Nick's heart sank. Of all the guys in all of Florida, why did he have to fall for the biggest himbo of them all? Eli clearly needed it spelled out for him. His throat clicked as he swallowed. "Sure. That's . . . one example. But—"

A tinny version of "Jingle Bell Rock" started to play from the speakers arranged around the Christmas tree.

"Dad!" Zoe's screech rocketed along the causeway. "It's starting, come on!" She wriggled her way between them and took them both by the hand, leading them to the low seawall. "Eli, watch it with me."

Eli cast Nick an apologetic look, like he needed to apologize for his inability to say no to the cutest kid in the world. "I will, Zo. Careful, now." Without being told, he helped Zoe clamber up onto the seawall.

Nick took a seat with his arm around her so that, even if she bounced and wiggled, she wouldn't fall into the water. Eli sat on her other side. Zoe, predictably, would not let go of his hand. A stranger looking at them might think they were a family, two dads and their daughter.

Nick was absurdly pleased with the idea.

"Look." Zoe pointed out at the water.

As the instrumental version of "Jingle Bell Rock" continued to play, a sailboat came into view from beneath the bridge. Christmas lights were strung along the rigging, and a giant inflatable snowman swayed in place on the bow. The tiny figure at the tiller lifted a Santa hat from his head and waved in greeting. Behind that boat came a string of others, all decorated with various lights. One trawler had a huge blinking sign that had the words MERRY CHRISTMAS scrolling over it again and again in red and green. People oohed and ahhed as each vessel made its appearance.

Nick turned his head. In the dark, the lights from the boats and the town Christmas tree illuminated Zoe's and Eli's faces in splashes of bright color. They were both smiling. Eli pointed out an exceptional dinghy draped in rope lights captained by someone dressed like an elf, and Zoe laughed herself silly. Then Eli looked over and caught Nick staring.

For once, Nick didn't look away. He couldn't if he'd tried. Maybe it was the holidays making him maudlin, but this felt like one of those moments he didn't want to forget. And Eli seemed to understand. They held each other's gazes over the top of Zoe's head for a long minute.

It took a while for the faint rumble of the crowd to penetrate Nick's thoughts. The general buzz of confusion culminated in Mrs. Ward saying, quite calmly, "Well, that doesn't seem right."

Nick looked back to the parade he'd been ignoring, irritated that the moment was interrupted. That was when he realized one of the speedboats was veering out of the slow-moving lineup.

"Daddy?" Zoe released Eli's hand to curl up against Nick's side. "Why is that one going the wrong way?"

"I don't know, sweetie," he said, although he had some ideas.

"The guy's drunk!" someone in the crowd exclaimed.

Yeah, that had been Nick's leading theory too. If he squinted, he could see the person at the wheel had a bottle of something in hand. He watched in horror as the boat wobbled, almost clipping the stern of a slower sailboat, before turning sharply, chugging toward the pier where transport barges still docked sometimes.

"Uh, should we . . . do . . . something?" Eli sounded like he was on the verge of panicking. "Or is this pretty normal?"

"No, it's not normal. It's a parade. They're all supposed to be in a straight line," Nick snapped.

"Well, excuse me. I don't know what new traditions have sprung up around here."

Nick wasn't a sailor by any means, but he estimated this wayward vessel was moving about fifteen miles an hour, if that. Which is all to say, when it careened sideways into the pier, it did so in slow motion, giving the crowd of onlookers plenty of time to start screaming. The hull hit at precisely the wrong angle, scraping against the pilings before coming to rest with a thud.

"Oh, for god's sake," Mr. Ward said from somewhere behind Nick. He sounded annoyed, which was kind of funny considering a boat had just crashed. "Can't we have a nice, normal Christmas for once?"

"Dad?" Zoe's little voice was almost drowned out by the roar of the crowd, the eerie rendition of the Christmas carol that was still playing, and the grinding sound of fiberglass against wood that echoed across the water.

"It's, um—it's okay, sweetie. Look, he's fine." Nick pointed to where the captain was stumbling onto the dock, still clutching his bottle, Santa hat askew.

It was at that point that the boat caught fire, which really put a damper on all the festivities.

CHAPTER 18

Eli sat in the back seat of Nick's car so that Zoe could continue to clutch someone's hand while Nick drove. She was inconsolable, not that Eli could blame her. Seeing a boat parade effectively end with emergency services being called had disconcerted *him*, and he was an adult. He hadn't even thought twice; he'd hopped into Nick's car before Nick had even finished saying, "Would you mind—?" His parents hadn't needed an explanation, just waved at him through the rolled-down window with stern directives at Nick to drive safe. Good thing, too, because Eli's explanation would have been a little too close to "I'm starting to feel responsible for a kid that isn't even mine."

Zoe sniffled tearfully and held his hand so tight, Eli was sure he was losing circulation. "But what if—?" she began to ask.

"For the last time, sweetheart," Nick said from up front at the wheel, "no one was hurt. Not even dolphins."

"But how do you *know*?" Zoe wailed.

"Because dolphins can swim very fast. If there were any dolphins near the pier, they would have moved out of the way before the boat even came close."

Nick sounded so certain, even Eli was starting to believe him. No dolphins had been harmed in the making of this shitshow.

"What about manatees?" Zoe insisted. "They can't swim fast at all. That's why they get hit by boats all the time!" Tears welled up in her eyes again; she'd been crying off and on since they'd gotten her in the car.

Eli caught Nick's gaze in the rearview mirror. Based on his tense brow alone, he looked like he was at the end of his rope. On top of Zoe's extended breakdown, traffic was a nightmare as everyone tried to flee the causeway at the same time. Most of Nick's concentration was rightly on the road as he drove them out of the mess. Seeing no alternative, Eli took a shot at handling at least one part of the crisis.

"That's a good point," he said as he squeezed Zoe's hand. "Manatees aren't fast, but there definitely weren't any around tonight. We would have heard them. When they get hit by a boat, they sound like this." He tipped his head back and made a weird whiny groan that was a cross between Chewbacca and a hissing radiator.

The act didn't exactly get Zoe to stop crying, but the tears did slow down. She stared at him from her booster seat, an incredulous look twisting her lips. It was the exact look Nick always gave Eli when he did something unbelievably foolish.

"No, they don't," Zoe said.

"Yes, they do. You've just never been around when one gets hurt, thank goodness. Trust me, once you hear them make that noise, you never forget it."

Zoe craned her neck to peer at the driver's seat. "Dad? Is that true?"

"Yes, honey. Eli's right. We can be sure that no manatees were there tonight."

"Oh." Zoe subsided, slumping back in her seat. Her tiny hand still didn't leave Eli's. "What about mermaids?" she asked.

"Great question. Love that follow-up," Eli said. "You see, mermaids only come to the surface in the morning, super early, when no one's around. At this time of night? Oh, they're way underwater."

"I guess that makes sense," Zoe said slowly.

He wasn't sure if lying to a small child made him an irredeemable villain, but he caught Nick's face in the rearview mirror and saw how he mouthed *thank you*. That was good enough.

"You know," Eli said, thinking fast, "your Ah Ma used to call your dad and me mermaids when we were kids."

Nick's eyes met his again in the mirror. He looked impossibly fond and sad at the same time, but his imperceptible nod let Eli know he wasn't overstepping by mentioning his mom.

Zoe's eyes went wide. "She did?"

This, at least, wasn't a lie. "Yep. We could swim so fast and for so long, she would swear we were going to sprout tails one day." He slid his hand over his thighs like they were covered in slippery scales. "Zoom! She made plans to leave us food on the beach to make sure we were getting enough to eat."

"But not at night," Zoe said. "Because by then, you'd be way underwater."

"Exactly." Eli launched into a fanciful retelling of Mrs. Wu's laments about their aquatic lifestyle, including the time she threatened to drain the local pool so Nick and Eli would come back to solid land. Zoe listened with rapt attention, her tears forgotten.

"Here we are, home sweet home," Nick announced as they pulled into a driveway about twenty minutes later. Eli had been so distracted with calming Zoe, he hadn't even noticed they were approaching Palmetto Drive, by the canal. He peered out the window at the small yellow house with a patch of grass for a front yard.

"Nice place," he said, because it seemed like the polite thing to do.

"I'm renting, it's temporary," Nick said a bit defensively.

Nick went through the rigamarole of getting Zoe freed from her seat while Eli dawdled on the driveway. He caught sight of a light in a window of the house next door. The curtain twitched like someone had been watching them and then got out of sight abruptly. Eli suppressed the shiver that tickled at his spine. Fucking suburbia.

Nick's voice cut through the cricket-laced night. "Do you want to come in?"

Eli turned. The words were on his tongue: He should get back to his parents' place. Nick had Zoe to deal with, and after all, Christmas Eve was their special night. He could call his dad to come pick him up or even walk. But—

Nick was standing in the circle of light cast by his front porch's bulb. Zoe was in his arms, her face smashed into the space between his neck and shoulder. Even though she must have been unwieldy with her gangly limbs, Nick didn't seem to be struggling under her weight. The only sign of his previous frazzlement was the unruly twist to his shirt collar, one point of it lifting toward the sky.

"It's almost Zoe's bedtime," he said. "You could hang out. If you wanted. It's too dark out for you to walk home, anyway. At least come in and wait for an Uber."

Eli was about to protest that his parents' house was, at most, a twenty-minute walk away, but then he remembered how Nick's mother had died and decided not to push the issue. "Yeah," Eli said instead. "Yeah, that sounds good. If you don't mind."

Nick's smile was—new. Nervous? Coy? Eli couldn't tell, and he'd thought he knew all of Nick's smiles. "I don't mind. But I'd really appreciate it if you got the door for me?" He shook his key ring in the hand that was occupied with holding Zoe against his hip.

"Shi— shoot. Of course." Eli rushed forward to take the keys and get the front door unlocked.

Once they were all inside, safe from prying eyes, shoes off, Eli expected to get out of the way while father and daughter went through their bedtime routine, but he ended up enmeshed in every step. Nick sat with Zoe in the bathroom, helping her brush her teeth while Eli picked out her pajamas. (He and Zoe agreed that the green plaid ones with the pinecone embroidered on the front pocket were understated and classy.) By then, Zoe's tears had dried, and she was the kid equivalent of a wrung-out dishrag, rubbing at her tired eyes and yawning hugely.

Christmas cookies and milk were set out for Santa, and Eli listened attentively to Zoe's sleepy mumbles as she explained how Santa stopped at Daddy's house to deliver one gift that she could open in the morning before going to Grammy's, where the rest of her presents would be waiting. Also, Santa apparently entered Florida houses by making himself paper-thin and sliding under the front door, since there wasn't a chimney. Eli agreed that this all checked out.

He left the final step—the tucking-in and bedtime story—in Nick's hands, and fell into the cozy embrace of the sectional sofa to catch his breath. There was a ceramic tabletop tree in the corner of the spartan living room, its lights blinking in a slow, soothing pattern. He could hear the low rumble of Nick's voice from down the hall as he read *'Twas the Night Before Christmas* to Zoe. In another lifetime, he thought with muzzy warmth, this might have been his living room, and his Nick, and his Christmas Eve traditions.

Which was a dangerous thing to think.

He was dozing off by the time Nick finished. Somewhere on

the edge of a dream, he heard Nick's socked feet on the tile floor, coming closer. His hand touched Eli's shoulder.

"Cocoa?" Nick asked.

"Mmm." Eli lifted his own hand to pat Nick's. He didn't even open his eyes. He didn't want to leave this little bubble of warmth. "D'you have marshmallows?"

"Of course I have marshmallows. What kind of father do you think I am?"

Eli stayed on the sofa, luxuriating in the sounds of Nick shuffling around in his kitchen. The kettle being filled with water, the click of two mugs on the countertop. He would fall asleep if he let himself, so he opened his eyes and sat up straighter. He shook his arms out, moved his head from side to side, got his jaw working.

When Nick returned, it was very slowly, so as not to disrupt the ridiculous mountain of mini marshmallows he'd heaped atop the twin mugs.

Eli reached out to take one, trying not to laugh out loud. He didn't want to wake Zoe. "This amount of marshmallows is dangerous," he said. "It's an aggressive number of marshmallows."

"I didn't want to give you any more reasons to doubt me." Nick passed off Eli's mug like they were handling nuclear material.

"I would never," Eli murmured as he finally took control of the handle. The topmost marshmallow wobbled dangerously. "Jesus, Mary, and Joseph, how am I even supposed to reach the cocoa?" He started lipping his way over the marshmallows, trying to eat them before they started falling like sugary snow on Nick's couch.

Nick sat down very carefully, and very close to Eli. "You look like a deer grazing in the clover."

"Fuck you," Eli said through a mouthful of marshmallow.

Nick laughed, but silently, his whole body shaking. Eli made a helpless warning sound in his throat and tipped his nose at Nick's cup, which was going to slosh over any second now.

"Okay, you're right." Nick set his own mug on the IKEA coffee table and then took Eli's to do the same. "That's going to end badly."

Eli watched his cocoa go with a baleful look. "But I haven't even—"

And then they were kissing.

It wasn't a shock, not like it had been at the beach. Eli was almost prepared this time, or some version of expectant. All the little moments he'd spent with Nick over the last few days seemed like they were building up to this. So when he felt Nick's lips on his, and his eyes closed to match Nick's, he wasn't surprised.

The only thought in his head was: *finally.*

Nick tasted like marshmallow, proof that he'd snuck some in the kitchen while making the cocoa. Eli loved that. He tried to remember the last time he'd made out with someone on a couch. It had probably been back in high school. It had probably been Nick then too. Life was so fucking weird, Eli thought. He reached for Nick, threading his fingers through his hair. Nick moved closer, then closer still, until he was straddling Eli's lap and kissing him like it was necessary.

Thank god for weird.

Nick tore away from his mouth to kiss along his neck. Oh, that was playing dirty. Eli had always been sensitive there, right below his ear. Nick suckled at the exact spot that made his toes curl, which they did into the area rug. Was it a lucky guess or had he remembered?

Eli cleared his suddenly tight throat. "Should we—?" *Talk about this? Have a frank discussion about what this means? Stop kissing for a second so we can think clearly?*

Nick leaned back to look Eli in the eye. His hair was a mess. "Take this to the bedroom?"

"Uh." Eli goldfished for a second. That wasn't how he'd planned to finish his question, but now that the option was out there, his brain had turned into complete static.

"Or . . . not?" Nick's face pinched. "We don't have to—if this is too much, we can do something else." He shifted his weight in Eli's lap. "Zoe sometimes comes out of her room at night to get a glass of water, so . . ." He trailed off.

Right. This was not the kind of scene you'd want your small child to happen upon.

"I didn't think of that," Eli confessed.

Nick shrugged one shoulder. "Christmas Eve. She's more keyed up than usual. It'll be an early morning tomorrow."

Eli got the message loud and clear: he should hit the road before Zoe woke up to see if Santa had come. Not that he'd been expecting an invitation to stay the night. That implied something serious, and this wasn't serious. How could it be? Nick was still working through his stuff, still figuring out things. Eli felt like a lump of coal had lodged in his throat. This was simply all part of that process, right? Just an experiment for him.

He pushed all that into a corner of his mind. He could deal with that later. For right now, couldn't he enjoy what he had?

"Yeah, no, the bedroom. Let's go," Eli said quietly.

Nick's room gave the impression of a tidy, barren space. There was nothing on the walls except one photograph of Nick holding a tiny wrinkled infant, who Eli assumed was Zoe. The bed was covered with a plain gray duvet and made up with hotel-quality skill.

"You still make your bed every morning?" he blurted out. "Who *are* you?"

Nick laughed. His hands were doing that thing where they sought out Eli's just for fun, to push and pull and get their fingers all tangled up. "Sorry I'm not some troglodyte who rolls out of bed and leaves it looking like a bird's nest."

Eli kissed him on the underside of his jaw. "Sorry *I'm* going to mess up your perfect hospital corners." He pulled at the hem of Nick's sweater, shoving it up his torso. "Take this thing off, would you?"

He'd seen Nick naked a thousand times when they were dating as teens. But here, in the warm light of Nick's bedroom, it was all so new. There was softness around his middle these days, a softness Eli shared. There was that crisp trail of hair leading down from his navel to disappear into his jeans. His brown nipples. Ugh, his shoulders; Eli had always had a weakness for those shoulders. He went up on tiptoe, hands at Nick's waist, and pressed his mouth to the curve of one of them.

"Um, hey." Nick's voice in his ear was quiet. "Before this gets any further along, do you want to give me, like . . . rules?"

Eli was too blissed out on licking a line up to Nick's neck to translate all that into something that made sense. "What d'you mean?" he murmured.

"I mean it's been a while. Since the two of us last—got together like this. Are there things I should know? Dos and don'ts?"

Eli stopped his exploration of Nick's throat to rear back and look him in the eye. "Did you read a wikiHow article on how to have sex with a trans guy?"

"What? No." Nick's panicked face said otherwise. "I might have done some googling, sure, but—well, what was I supposed to do?"

Eli was trying very hard not to laugh, but it wasn't easy when Nick was standing right in front of him, shirtless and with a very obvious hard-on, looking more anxious than he had the time in ninth grade when Eli had convinced him to play lookout while he raided their geometry teacher's desk for her fancy breath mints.

"I'm trying to be respectful," Nick said. "Don't laugh at me."

"I'm not laughing at *you*." Schooling his face into a serious mask was impossible, so he hoped his smile was as fond as he felt in that moment. "I'm—it's not a CIA interview. And if you really want this to be fair . . ." He tipped his head and looked up at Nick. "I should get a chance to ask you the same questions. Get *your* rules."

Nick frowned. "But you know me. You know all about me already."

Eli's smile faltered. He did, was the thing. He knew that Nick always picked the top hat when playing Monopoly. He knew he liked his bacon just on the wrong side of burnt. And he knew, deep in his bones, that Nick was polite to a fault. Too polite to spell out things that were obvious. Like this was clearly a one-time thing.

Since his transition, Eli had hooked up with a few guys who were just curious, looking for a novel experience. He might have been angrier about being treated like that, but the truth was, horniness won out most of the time. (Thank you, testosterone.) As long as the guys were chill, he could get what he wanted.

This was Nick, though, not some random Grindr hookup. Eli wasn't sure he could pretend to be okay with one-and-done. But he'd have to be. For Nick's sake.

Eli must have taken too long thinking all this through because Nick broke the long silence. "You all right?"

"Yeah, I'm great." Eli hugged him tight so Nick wouldn't have a good view of his face. He was too practiced at parsing all of Eli's emotions from one look.

"Yeah?" One of Nick's hands moved from Eli's back to dig into his hair. He scratched at Eli's scalp in a way that made him tingle all the way down to his toes. "Also, I'm fine with anything. Really. Whatever you want to do, I'll try it. If you want to top, I don't mind."

Eli was very glad his face was hidden against Nick's neck because he was sure his eyes were boggling at this wild-ass offer. "Uh, that's very accommodating of you, but I didn't bring my strap. Doesn't exactly fit in my back pocket." He hadn't even packed it for his trip home, since he'd doubted he'd get a chance to use it.

Nick pulled back with a self-conscious shake of his head. "Right. Of course. I was just putting it out there. I am legitimately fine with whatever."

"Fine! Great. Get your dick out." Eli's hands went to Nick's belt.

Nick's hands met them there. "I'd like to know what I'm going to be doing with it first," he said.

"Really? You want to negotiate every detail before we get naked?" Eli rolled his eyes. "Why can't we just . . . see what happens? Like when we were teenagers."

"When we were teenagers, we fumbled through sex because we didn't know any fucking better." Nick frowned. "Did you even enjoy it?"

"Yes! Yeah." Eli looked into the middle distance, remembering bits and pieces. Everything he'd done at that age had a patina of wrongness hanging over it, but that hadn't been exclusive to Nick. "I think so."

Nick looked absolutely crushed, his brows folding downward. "You *think*?"

"I don't know! My memory isn't the most reliable, right? I remember liking parts of it." He liked feeling desired. He liked the way Nick had looked at him—kind of similar to how he was looking at him now, minus the grave concern. He gave up on Nick's belt and put his hands to Nick's hot cheeks instead, framing his face. "I liked you."

Loved. That was the word. He'd loved Nick. In that teenage

way he'd loved his cat and his Sony Discman and all the other simple pleasures of life. But also in the "I've known you forever and there's nothing more I want to do than make you laugh" kind of way. That feeling had never gone away; it had just lain dormant, waiting for Nick to come back into his life.

Probably shouldn't get into that right now.

He slipped his hands down to Nick's chest. His heart was beating so fast. His eyes were so dark.

"I don't want to mess this up," Nick said, quiet and slow. His hands came to Eli's waist.

"You won't." Eli pressed a kiss to his sad lips. "You can't."

Nick made a disbelieving huffing sound. "I absolutely can."

"No, false, incorrect." Eli shook his head. "Because we're going to make each other feel good." He reached for Nick's belt again, slow this time, with an eyebrow raised in question. When Nick didn't resist, he started unthreading the leather with patient movements. "We're going to kiss some more—a lot more, because you're really good at that—then we're going to mess up that super-neat bed of yours—"

"Making your bed in the morning is *normal*. I don't know why I'm under attack for this."

"Whatever, let's table that for now. We're going to get comfortable," Eli said, whooshing Nick's belt out of his belt loops, "and we're going to blow each other. Sound like a plan?" The belt hit the carpet with a thud.

Nick looked ready to vibrate out of his skin. "Yeah. Good— great plan."

He stepped closer and kissed Eli with all the confidence he'd earned. Eli smiled into it, letting himself be tipped back, nudged step by step over to the bed until he finally landed on it with a thump. There were clothes to be dealt with; not for the first time in their acquaintance, Eli was glad both he and Nick believed in not wearing shoes inside the house. One less thing to worry about.

In the interest of fairness, Eli started unbuttoning his shirt. He couldn't let Nick be the only bare-chested one in the room, clearly. For a brief moment, he considered tearing off his shirt so the last three or four buttons went skittering in all directions; it was a move he had perfected in recent years and it seemed to be a huge turn-on for most guys. (Most guys didn't realize how easy it was to sew a new button on a shirt, so in terms of ROI, it was a real winner.) But then Nick's hands batted his out of the way and took over the task of unbuttoning his flannel.

"Let me do it," he murmured. "I want to see you."

Eli smiled from his position sprawled under the cage of Nick's body. "You've seen it before. Both versions."

Nick's gaze flicked up to his and held. There was a soft promise in his eyes. "Not like this."

Eli swallowed. That was true.

When the last button was finally undone, Nick parted the panes of his shirt like he was unwrapping a gift. His stare was intense, sweeping over Eli from collarbones to hips, then finding its way back to his nipples. He licked his lips, not in a deliberate, wolflike way, but unconsciously, like he was remembering how Eli had loved having them sucked when they were younger.

"Can I?"

Eli had to clear his throat so he could speak like a normal human being. His voice still came out squeaky. "Be my guest."

Nick lowered his head, his black hair falling over his brow to tickle at Eli's sternum before his hot mouth closed over his left nipple. Eli let his eyes slide shut as his head fell back on the duvet. The sensation wasn't as intense as it used to be before he'd had surgery, but it still felt good. Each lick of Nick's tongue, each suckle of his mouth felt like lightning on Eli's skin. He threaded his fingers through the silky hair at the back of Nick's head and held him in place. The helpless, hopeful sound Nick made at that was enough to send him to some other plane of existence, where everything smelled like Nick and nothing hurt.

Nick switched to his other nipple, kissing along his skin as he moved. "Good?" he asked.

"Mmm." Eli nodded, his eyes mere slits. It occurred to him that maybe Nick wasn't personally aware of how good it actually felt. Had he ever done this for Nick back when they were horny teenagers? He didn't think so. That had been an era where men were men and their nipples were, for all intents and purposes, ignored completely for some reason. Probably rampant homophobia.

"Here." He sat up, dislodging Nick, who made a mournful whine at being interrupted. Eli laughed at that. "Your turn. Yeah?"

"Uh, yeah." Nick lay down with his hands palm up on either side of his head. Like this was a stickup or something. Or like he didn't know where he was allowed to put them.

Eli felt a wave of fondness wash over him. Even if this was only an experiment for Nick, he seemed determined to be on his best behavior. It was sweet. He settled atop him, straddling his waist. Without breaking eye contact, he put his thumb up to his mouth and licked the pad of it.

"Oh." The word left Nick on an exhale. His eyes sparkled in anticipation.

Eli brought the damp digit down to Nick's chest to rub slow, wet circles around the nub of his pebbled nipple. Nick made a sound like someone had punched the air out of him. Or had actually paid attention to an underserved erogenous zone.

Wow, Eli thought with a self-satisfied smirk. *It really* does *get better.*

"Good?" he asked.

Nick's eyes squeezed shut. "Do you have to be so fucking smug?"

"I'm not! You literally asked me the exact same thing a minute ago."

"Yeah, but I wasn't *smug* about it."

Eli pinched his nipple between his thumb and forefinger and gave it a quick twist. Nick practically arched off the bed. If Eli's balance had been even a smidge less masterful, he would have been thrown like a rider from a horse.

"Holy shit." Nick stared up at him, mouth hanging open. "Do that again."

Eli couldn't help the now-smug smile that took over his face. He did it again. And again. Each time Nick reacted like he was being shown some secret of the universe, if secrets of the universe could go straight to his dick. Eli could feel him against his backside, hard as a rock.

He had a whole checklist that needed to be dealt with, and top of the list was getting Nick naked. He removed Nick's jeans and boxer briefs with crisp efficiency. Nick's cock was, all joking aside, actually very big. He was uncut, which got him teased in the locker room back when they were kids, but Eli never understood what the big deal was. So what if his dick didn't match everyone else's dick? It wasn't the Rockettes; they weren't going to do some dance number together that required everything to look the same. Besides, Eli had read in some ancient *Cosmo* article that people with foreskins could feel more pleasure, so who was the real winner here?

He looked up from his affectionate reexamination of Nick's cock. "Did I ever ask you about an article in *Cosmo* back in the nineties? I must have."

Nick blinked down the length of his bare body several times. "Can we maybe discuss this later?"

"Right. Sorry." Eli gestured to his ear to indicate his wayward thoughts. "Went down memory lane, I guess."

"Anything I can do to maintain your interest in the present?" Nick sounded almost bitchy, which was one of Eli's most enduring turn-ons. Only Nick could manage imperious while flat on his back, buck naked with his dick in Eli's face.

Eli just gave him a smile before crawling up his body to kiss him some more. Nick opened to him readily, his mouth warm and wet, his arms winding around Eli like he meant to keep him there for a good long while. Eli settled atop him and basked in the sensation of Nick's hot skin against his.

This part wasn't so very different from their teenage make-out sessions. The only real change was they weren't working against the clock now. Half the challenge back then had been finding a private moment where they could get off with each other. Now, Eli didn't have to keep half an ear out for a car pulling into the driveway or a door opening. He remembered how fast Nick had pulled his clothes back on one afternoon when his dad came home early from work and almost caught them. Eli was certain Tian-yi hadn't been fooled when he'd walked into the living room: the both of them breathing hard, hair askew, the buttons on Eli's shirt not even done up right.

But other than that, kissing Nick still felt the same. Easy. Like neither of them had anything to prove, no power struggle to act out. It was like their mouths were saying *hello again. Come here. I've missed you.*

Eli pulled back, a string of saliva threading between their lips before snapping on an inhale. He needed to stop thinking such sappy shit; this was for fun. This was Nick just—working things out for himself. This was Eli looking for something familiar and nice, and it didn't have to be anything more.

Though that was all hard to remember when Nick was looking up at him with stars in his fucking eyes.

Checklist, Eli decided. Blowjob. Now.

He shimmied down the bed, pausing only to give Nick's nipple another sigh-inducing nibble before settling between his spread legs. The hair on Nick's thighs was soft under Eli's touch. He smelled like soap and a hint of sweat. It made Eli's mouth flood.

Nick made a small noise, something so faint it could have been the creak of a bedspring, but Eli knew better. He flicked his eyes upward to meet Nick's heavy gaze. His mouth was open, like he was surprised this was really happening. Eli could relate.

He gently smoothed Nick's foreskin down his hard shaft. His free hand cupped Nick's warm balls in his palm. His tongue lapped a single pearly bead of fluid from Nick's cockhead. He held that eye contact the entire time.

Nick was the one to finally break it, tossing his head back with a groan. "Eli, fuck."

Eli realized with a jolt that he was older now. Wiser, some might say. Definitely better at many things, given his wealth of experience. And tonight, he could suck Nick off better than he ever had before. An unexpected upside to aging.

He grinned against the silky skin of Nick's inner thigh as he gave his cock a few tugs.

"Oh, I'm going to have fun with you," he said, dark and low.

Eli took the head of Nick's cock in his mouth, savoring the sharp taste of him as he lowered down, down, nose tickling the crisp black hairs that Nick clearly kept as neat as his bed. His balls went tighter in Eli's palm. Nick lifted a hand and almost brought it to the back of Eli's head, but it hovered there without touching for a long moment.

Eli lifted off Nick's dick with an overly loud slurp. "Do you really need permission?" he said. "You know I like it." One time in bed, Nick had pulled a few strands of Eli's hair out by the roots. It had been an accident, but a hot one. Eli had been addicted ever since.

"I know you *used* to like it." Nick sounded like he'd jogged all the way down their beach. His breaths came hard and fast.

Eli took Nick's hesitating hand in his and pushed it into the hair at the back of his head. "I still do," he said. "Sorry it's so much shorter now, but you'll be able to get a good grip, right?"

Nick's mouth finally turned up at a corner. His fingers tightened in Eli's hair. "Yeah," he said, his eyes dancing like he couldn't believe his luck. Like it was Christmas morning, which, Eli realized, it was. "I can do that."

Eli barely succeeded at not smiling like a loon as Nick guided his head back down—not forcefully, not yet, but firm and assured. That move used to send a thrill up Eli's spine, and it seemed that twenty-five years had not dulled his reaction one bit. He moaned as he lapped at the ridge under Nick's cockhead before taking it in his mouth once more.

Nick was tall, but Eli was flexible; he stretched his arm up and caught Nick's left nipple between his fingers. He played with it while he sucked, letting Nick curse and buck into the dual sensations. His legs were doing that juddery shaky dance on either side of Eli's head. He knew exactly what that meant. Nick was close.

Eli tried not to be too disappointed; he was only getting started. He relaxed his jaw and took more of Nick into his mouth, jerking the sleeve of his foreskin around the part he couldn't reach. Nick's feet were scrabbling in the sheets out of sight, but Eli could hear the frantic movements. He closed his eyes and tried to savor the feeling of being the one who could do this to Nick, who knew exactly what he needed.

"Don't stop, don't stop," Nick pleaded. Like there was any chance of that happening. He held Eli's head down with a little more strength than before, forgetting himself, his hand pulling at Eli's hair.

Eli hummed, his eyes slipping closed. That was all it took. Nick came in three long, luxurious bursts in his mouth, tasting of bitter fluid. Eli sat back on his heels with a sense of satisfaction. Nick was staring at the ceiling, breathing hard.

"Oh my god," he kept saying. "Holy shit. Oh my *god*."

Eli grinned down at him. "So overall, Nicholas, would you say it's been a positive experience?" He dabbed his fingertips to the corner of his mouth to catch a tiny bit of come, then sucked them clean. "Any comments? Thoughts?"

"Yeah, I don't think I'm straight," Nick said breathlessly.

It had never been a personal goal of Eli's to quote-unquote "turn a guy gay." That kind of thinking was the provenance of guys who thought they were *so* magical, that one fuck with them could completely upend someone's life. Like, get a grip.

But for some reason, hearing Nick say that was music to Eli's ears. He felt proud, if not of his performance—which, honestly, had been pretty basic—than of being useful in some way. It was good to know this had solidified something for Nick. That clear-headed thinking of the well-fucked.

Also it was nice to know Nick wasn't one of those "a mouth is a mouth" kind of guys. Pretty validating, all told.

"You need a minute?" Eli shuffled around to rest against the neat pile of pillows that were stacked against the headboard. "Glass of water? A cold compress—? Oh, okay." Any further ribbing was cut off as Nick wobbled his way across the bed to crawl atop Eli. His mouth was red from biting at his lip in an attempt to keep quiet. Eli couldn't stop staring at it.

"Hey, Eli?" Nick was so close, his lips millimeters away.

Eli swallowed. "Yeah?"

"Shut up." He kissed him, filthier than Eli had ever been kissed. And he'd been to leather daddy street fairs.

Nick's fingers tore at the button on his jeans. Eli helped, since

Nick didn't seem to have the fine motor skills to handle it on his own. It was a team effort to get the jeans down his legs and on the floor, though. Then Eli was left in just his briefs. He thanked whatever deity was looking out for trans guys that these were his nice ones with the Y-front pocket built in.

He stopped kissing Nick long enough to say what needed saying. "Okay, so, that's my . . . ."

Nick traced the shape in his briefs with searching fingers. "Oh, nice packer. It suits you."

"Wait. You're—familiar?" He'd been gearing up for the whole speech.

His dark gaze flicked up to meet Eli's. "I read the wikiHow, remember?"

"Jesus. Fuck. You're such a nerd." Eli clamped his hands to either side of Nick's head and kissed him hard. "It's so hot," he said as they parted. In case Nick couldn't tell from how breathless Eli was.

Nick needed no further encouragement after that. He dove right in, settling between Eli's legs and pressing his face against the cloth-covered bulge, open-mouthed and panting. Eli felt his throat go dry. He was absurdly glad that he'd practiced some fucking self-restraint when he'd bought this model. Earlier in his transition, he'd stuffed his underwear with packers that would have looked more at home on an elephant. This one was proportional. Tasteful.

And Nick seemed to be into it. He nosed along the side of it, inhaling deeply. "Can I take these off?" His fingers hooked into the waistband of Eli's briefs.

"Great plan," Eli said. His voice was embarrassingly thready. He cleared his throat and tried again. "I mean, go ahead."

Nick flashed a look up at him. Now who was being smug? He peeled off the underwear, kissing along Eli's thigh as he went.

"Tell me what you want," he said, like it was simple. Eli wanted a lot of things, not all of them possible. Tonight, though—

"Don't put anything inside of me," he said with a hitch in his breathing. "That's, like, only for certain occasions. Got to be in the right mood. Stars have to align."

"But I can suck you off?" Nick made it sound like it would be an honor and a privilege. He was still kissing down Eli's leg, heedless of the crisp body hair, working the briefs off Eli's squirming feet.

"Yeah. That is . . . full speed ahead on that." Eli took a deep breath and tried to relax against the pillows. He put his hands above his head, but that felt a little too damsel-in-distress, so he lowered his arms to his sides. "Uh, actually, do you mind if I stand for this?" he asked. It was more comfortable, sometimes, not to be flat on his back, where he tended to feel too passive.

"That's fine. Here." Nick popped back up and held out his hand. Eli took the offered help.

Soon they were arranged to Eli's liking, with Eli leaning back against the bedroom wall and Nick on his knees in front of him. He looked like an absolute dream, naked and wet-mouthed and—

"Hold on," Eli said, because his fucking brain couldn't ever concentrate on the bigger picture. "The floor's going to be murder on your knees. One sec." He reached over to the nearby bed and plucked two pillows off of it.

Nick stared up at him with an incredulous look. "For shit's sake, E, I'll be fine."

"Your joints will thank me." Eli dropped down to stuff the pillows under Nick's knees. Nick huffed the whole time, muttering about how he wasn't a hundred years old yet, but Eli thought he detected a glimmer of warmth in his gaze. Like he appreciated the gesture for what it was.

"Now can I?" His hands were already finding a place on Eli's hips as Eli stood back up.

"Yeah." Eli took a shuddering breath. "Go for it."

Nick licked his lips—again, not trying to be anything but himself, which was hotter than it had any right to be—and focused on Eli's cock. His eyes went wide. "Oh," he said.

Eli's heart rate picked up. "Oh? Good oh? Bad oh?"

"Surprised oh." Nick touched him carefully, bringing his thumb under the shaft to lift the glistening tip out of the trimmed tangle of his pubic hair. "You said—I was expecting you to be small, but look. You're huge."

A startled laugh broke out of Eli's throat. "Come on, quit fucking around." He didn't need lies to stroke his ego—he preferred other things getting stroked instead.

"No, I mean it." Nick looked up at him, his expression full of wonder, no guile to be found. "I seriously didn't think you could look like this. It's . . . amazing." His face softened. "You're amazing."

"Well." Eli hoped he wasn't blushing. His face felt like it was Rudolph-nose red, though. "You can thank T for that. It's a miracle worker."

Nick didn't seem to be listening to him; he was too focused on touching Eli, soft at first, fingertips testing with a brush. Then, as Eli groaned and leaned into it, Nick got bolder, taking Eli's cock between his thumb and forefinger and jacking it to the rhythm of their harsh breathing.

"Nick—" Eli wasn't sure what he meant to say. Some kind of plea, but Nick didn't wait for him to form one.

He leaned forward and put his lips around Eli's cock, suckling like he had been looking forward to the taste for ages.

Eli threw his head back and hit the wall with a thunk. "Oh, fuck." He braced one hand on the wall, the other finding its way to Nick's strong shoulder. Nick's tongue drew a slow circle around him, then lapped at his tip. All very gentle, though. Not nearly enough. "Harder. You can go harder," Eli whispered.

Nick hummed—the bastard—and planted his hands on Eli's waist. Eli looked down, then bit his lip on a groan. Nick was staring back at him. That was a lot of eye contact. Had he always been so big on eye contact?

Had he always been this *good*? His mouth deserved some kind of award. Maybe a trophy. Eli looked back up at the ceiling, his shoulders shaking with suppressed laughter. Maybe a *parade*. One that wouldn't end in a minor disaster.

Nick lifted off Eli's cock with a parting swipe. "Something funny?" he asked. Not indignant, not even a little. The corners of his mouth were upturned like he was looking forward to being let in on the joke.

Fuck, Eli loved him.

Fuck. Eli *loved* him.

"Just thinking about how you're way better at this than you have any right to be," Eli babbled. He babbled when he was nervous. Or when he was on the brink of orgasm alongside the realization that he was in love—again? Still?—with this guy he definitely should not be in love with. Words could cover up a lot of stuff that didn't need to be seen. "Who allowed this? How dare you. I'm filing a report."

"Sounds official," Nick said, then bowed his head to take Eli between his lips again.

Eli couldn't help it. He wrapped a hand around the back of Nick's neck and pushed deeper into his mouth. Nick took the manhandling without complaint, his eyelashes fluttering. His moan zinged straight into every nerve ending Eli still possessed.

Don't say it, don't say it, he told himself sternly. He bit the inside of his cheek so hard, he tasted pennies. He came like that, silent and shaking, against Nick's face.

After, he felt drained in more ways than one. Nick was still licking at him, though he barely felt the tongue running along the insides of his shaking legs, chasing slick. He eased up on his death grip of Nick's neck and instead slid his fingers into that soft hair.

"Wow," he said. Casual. Keep things casual. "Thanks. For that."

Nick sat back and stared up at him with an incredulous raise of his eyebrow. "You're welcome?" He got to his feet with a series of groans and pops in his back. "Holy shit, okay, you were right about the pillows."

"See? I'm always right." Eli was very proud that he was able to say all that while his lungs were out of commission. Also his legs. He thanked Christ for the wall; without it, he'd be on the floor. Yep, he would probably stay here against the wall for, oh, the rest of time. He watched Nick's broad back as he turned around. Not a bad view for eternity.

Nick was pulling back the sheets on the bed. Eli watched him through slitted eyes, still too brain-scrambled to realize what was happening. Then Nick gave him an odd look and said, "Left side okay for you? I'm fine with either, really."

"Oh. Uh." Eli's addled mind caught up to the present. He finally pushed off the wall. His knees, miraculously, held him up. "I thought—I don't know if I should stay." Staying meant sleeping next to Nick. In his house. With Zoe right down the hall. While Eli's heart was trying to claw its way out of his chest.

Not to mention, what would it look like in the morning? Were they really going to explain to a four-year-old why Daddy's friend had a sleepover? What would Eli tell his parents when they asked where he'd been all night? What about the neighbors behind the curtains? Surely they'd see Eli leaving in the clothes he'd arrived wearing. Eli didn't want to make Nick's life any more complicated than he already had.

And if he was being honest with himself, he didn't want to make his own life any more complicated either. Falling back in love with his first boyfriend was one thing. Staying over? Acting like it had even a chance of going anywhere? That was a terrible idea.

Nick's arm lowered, puddling the bedclothes in the middle of the mattress. "You're leaving? Right now?"

Action. Move. Go. Eli started picking up his discarded bits of clothing from the floor. He found his phone in his jeans pocket and ordered an Uber with a few taps. "Well, not to make myself sound ancient, but I'm not primed to go multiple rounds in one night."

"That's not—I meant you can sleep here. If you want." Nick gestured to one of the pillows in invitation. "You'd just need to, uh, get going kind of early."

"Better to leave now," Eli said. "I don't want to make your Christmas morning awkward."

Nick made an apologetic nose scrunch. "I could set an alarm. You could be out of here hours before Zoe wakes up."

Eli tried to picture a pre-sunrise escape from Nick's house, tip-toeing in the dark away from the scene of the crime. The neighbors would have a field day.

"I'm calling an Uber. No big deal. But, like, seriously—" He paused in fishing his underwear from under the bed long enough to give Nick a peck on his motionless lips. "This was great. Amazing. Five stars. Welcome to not-straight land. Great to have you."

"Great to . . . be had," Nick said slowly.

He couldn't resist a bad pun. "Eh, that comes later, don't you think? This was just your intro." Eli winked, then slipped his briefs back on. Clammy and uncomfortable, but he didn't have another option.

Nick crossed the room and reached for a robe that hung

beside the door. Eli took a good, lingering look at the picture he made because he was A) weak and B) a bad person. "Well, maybe we can pick it up there next time," Nick said.

Eli could take a joke. He shrugged into his shirt. "Yeah, sure." Then, when he realized Nick was looking at him meaningfully, "Oh. Yeah. I mean, yes. A hundred percent. If you—yes."

Nick shrugged into the robe. "Thanks. I'm looking forward to getting educated," he said with half a smile.

Right. Because this was all in the name of education. Nothing else.

He finished getting dressed and let Nick see him to the door. Nick's robe was a little too short, showing a good mile of leg. Eli was so distracted by it, he didn't notice the sweatshirt until it was being pressed into his hands.

"It's cold out," Nick said in a whisper. "I know you're very tough and Florida winters are a joke to you, but . . . take it, okay?"

Any protest Eli might have made died on his tongue.

"Okay." Eli slipped the sweatshirt over his head and put up the hood. It was huge on him, the sleeves dangling off his fingertips. It smelled like Nick.

His phone pinged in his pocket. The Uber's headlights blazed through the windows as the car pulled into Nick's driveway. Their farewells were rushed, an awkward half hug, half peck on the lips.

Unseen in the shadows of the Uber's back seat, Eli buried his face in the warm fleece of his borrowed sweatshirt and inhaled. He was such a fool. He needed to get it together. Act like an adult. Communicate, or at least try.

He pulled out his phone and texted Nick, hoping it didn't come off as too desperate to reach out before he was even back home.

We should probably get that continuing education of yours on the calendar. The day after next?

That was fun. Sexy. Open-ended. Nick could respond with as much or as little flirtation as he liked. His phone pinged.

Can't. Going fishing. Then working.

Okay. A bit terse, especially for someone who had texted Eli multiple times in a row in quick succession previously, and in complete sentences. Still, Eli was determined to find out for sure where they stood.

The day after that? 😉

Yeah. Because a winky face was super adult. Eli tipped his head onto the Uber's headrest and groaned. He sounded so pathetic. At least this couldn't get any worse.

His phone lit up again with Nick's reply.

Can't. Working.

"I stand corrected," Eli muttered to himself. He could only get shot down so many times before his bruised ego couldn't take any more hits. He shoved his phone in the pocket of the borrowed hoodie.

"What'd you say?" the Uber driver said from the front seat.

"Nothing. Don't worry about it." Eli heard his phone chime again, fishing it out with dread in his stomach. It was from Nick, of course.

Some other time

Was that a question? A statement? This was why Eli hated texting. He couldn't see what Nick's face was doing, couldn't hear if his voice was filled with steady sincerity. He could only take the words at face value, and in his estimation, this was clearly Nick putting some distance between them. And why shouldn't he? No promises had been made, there were no expectations.

"Here we are," the driver said as the car pulled up in front of Eli's parents' house.

"Thanks, man. Have a safe night." His mom would be very proud; he was being polite to a service worker even though his heart was sinking somewhere into his sneakers. He sent one last text to Nick as he got out of the car, telling him he'd made it home okay.

He stared at the screen, willing the little "read" checkmark to appear. It didn't.

So this is Christmas, he thought bitterly.

What had he done?

CHAPTER 19

December 25, Christmas Day

Nick was living in a daze.

On the one hand, he was doing a pretty good job at the dad stuff. Zoe was up before dawn, bouncing on Nick's bed with excitement for Santa's visit. He made her a stack of mini chocolate chip pancakes, which she ate exactly one bite of before declaring, "I can open my first present now." Zoe tore the wrapping off the picture book about venerated journalist (and Nick's middle-school crush from Channel One News) Lisa Ling.

"She's a reporter too! Like Connie Chung!" she said, pointing at the face on the cover.

Nick took lots of pictures.

But while he was going through the Christmas morning motions, he couldn't shake the feeling that things with Eli had ended on a strange note the night before. Right after Eli's departure, Zoe had woken up with a bad dream about the boat parade, and Nick had spent over an hour soothing her back to sleep. Eli had texted him in the midst of it, which meant Nick had tried to handle both with divided attention until realizing he couldn't. He'd left Eli's last text unread as he coaxed Zoe to drink a cup of warm water and close her eyes. After everything that had happened, Nick had fallen into bed exhausted—and alone.

There'd been something so businesslike about the way Eli had gotten dressed and left. Like what they'd done wasn't a big deal. Maybe it wasn't. Maybe he was being too sensitive. He didn't exactly have a ton of experience with hookups, if that's what it had been.

"Dad?" Zoe's voice brought him back to the present. She tugged at his pajama pants leg, her other hand bristling with dinosaur finger puppets. (Nick and Laurie had agreed: one gift at Nick's, the rest at Kay's. But surely stocking stuffers didn't count as a real gift.) "What did Santa bring you for Christmas?"

"Oh, sweetie." Nick abandoned his coffee mug on the counter and bent to pick her up. She still fit on his hip, barely. "I'm a grown-up. I don't need toys or presents. I have everything I need because I have you." He made Donald Duck squawking noises against her cheek as she shrieked with laughter.

But when the giggles died down, Zoe said, "Being a grown-up isn't very fun, huh?"

Wow. Nick was going to think about that one all fucking day.

He bundled Zoe into her green-and-red-checked Christmas outfit and headed over to his ex-mother-in-law's.

Kay lived in a tacky McMansion situated on a prime lot that backed up onto the canal. Despite the canal being unsuitable for boating or even canoeing, and therefore home only to gators and discarded fast-food cups, Kay felt it gave her the right to call her house "waterfront property." The stucco facade was painted a dull taupe. The lawn was cut in perfect lines by a company who came by twice a month, though never on the day or time that Kay demanded they come. The only Christmas decor outside her house was a yard sign with a rendering of the Baby Jesus surrounded by a shimmering light with KEEP CHRIST IN CHRISTMAS in bold letters. A couple neighborhood kids were out on the street, already playing with a remote-control truck they'd no doubt unwrapped moments before.

Nick went up the walkway holding Zoe's hand. In his other hand was one of the bottles of mid-range sparkling wine he'd purchased in bulk from the Wine Barn. He'd forgotten to chill it, so it was room temperature. When Kay greeted them at the door and took it, she mentioned it specifically before bustling off to the kitchen. She was not what Nick would call a talented cook, but she insisted on making Christmas dinner every year, an arrangement which seemed to stress out everyone involved.

Laurie was sitting on the love seat in the family room right off the foyer. She caught his eye and grimaced in apology. Nick gave her a silent nod. This was just another day they'd have to bear Kay's unique brand of hospitality.

Nick took a seat in the armchair across from Laurie. Kay's tree was a Martha Stewart–perfect confection of silver and gold topped with a battery-powered angel that glowed. A video of a choir singing "Away in a Manger" played on the big-screen TV on the wall. The smell of overcooked turkey was in the air.

Laurie raised her large glass of white wine in his direction. "Want one?"

"Think I'll stay dry today," he said. He thought of Eli, no doubt surrounded by festive libations. He figured it might be nice to abstain in case—well, what if at some point he wanted to keep Eli company in his sobriety? This was good practice.

Laurie raised an eyebrow. Getting slightly tanked at Kay's was practically a Christmas tradition between them, so she had good reason to find his decision unusual. But when Nick thought about it, he wondered why he'd spent so many years doing such a clichéd thing. Kay was enough of a headache on her own; he didn't need to add a literal hangover to the experience.

Kay returned from the kitchen, clapping her hands like she was mustering troops. "I have about twenty minutes before I need to stir anything. Let's do presents, quick." She didn't even look at Laurie, Nick noticed. He wondered if their truce had crumbled since last week when they'd been perfectly civil at the mall.

Zoe attacked the frankly ludicrous mountain of beribboned gifts while the adults watched and snapped pictures. Most of the presents were from her grandmother, who couldn't ever pass up the chance to outdo everyone else. "Clothes," Zoe said, holding up a red velvet dress with a frilly lace collar. Where the hell was a four-year-old supposed to wear such a thing, Nick wondered. Zoe was a polite kid, and they'd taught her to be gracious any-time she received a gift, but even she was having a hard time not looking disappointed. "Pretty," was the best she could do before laying it aside to tackle a box that contained a tiny pair of roller skates that Nick and Laurie had bought on sale the previous sum-mer. "Yes!" Her enthusiasm bubbled over as she hugged the box. "I love them!"

"Santa put a helmet and knee pads in there too," Laurie said. "You have to promise to wear them when you skate so you stay safe."

Zoe nodded fiercely. "I promise."

Kay snorted and mumbled into her own wineglass, "Nanny state nonsense. A child can't even skin a knee these days?"

Nick considered telling Kay that letting kids crack their heads open on bare pavement was not the free-market utopia she pre-tended it was, but it was Christmas. He could pick his battles for Zoe's sake.

After presents came dinner. In years past, Kay's holiday dinners played host to dozens of guests, but then her husband, Peter, had passed away, and things changed. Nick had liked Peter; he'd been a quiet man, kind of reserved, but a grounding figure in Kay's life. After he died, she'd gotten isolated. Suddenly old friends weren't good enough to invite around because of this or that slight, imagined or not. There was also some dispute over Peter's will that Nick had never fully understood, and because of that, Kay stopped talking to most family members, including her son, Laurie's younger brother. Laurie reported that she'd started sharing lots of weird articles on Facebook about conspiracy theories and what was wrong with America, then got into awful fights with her few remaining friends in the comments. "I'm cutting toxic people out of my life," Kay had declared, though what she'd really done was alienate herself from everyone who'd ever cared for her. Instead of a table full of cousins and siblings and church friends, Christmas dinner was only the four of them.

Nick missed Linda from church and Cousin Carl, not because they'd been particularly fun people, but because they'd been warm bodies, buffers for Kay's nasty comments. Now the only cover Nick had was Laurie, and if she and her mother were in the midst of a cold war, that didn't bode well. The only neutral topic he could summon up was the food. He whistled at the array of dishes as he sat down at the table. "Wow, Kay, what an amazing spread. Thank you for cooking."

Like Zoe, Nick had been trained to be gracious, even when presented with five different kinds of under-seasoned starches.

Kay refilled her wineglass to the brim. "Well, it's not easy to do it all on my own," she said, shooting a look at Laurie like she blamed her for not helping. Nick knew that when Laurie had tried to assist in years past, Kay had had a meltdown and shooed her out of the kitchen, so . . . whatever.

He sipped his glass of water and made what he hoped was a sympathetic noise.

As usual, Kay made the dinner table her soapbox, making a tenuous connection between the fact that she got tired more easily these days and her opinion that people who didn't want to pay for health care were bums. From there it was a hop, skip, and a jump to abortion, which she referred to as "women troubles," presumably so that Zoe wouldn't be exposed to the idea of pregnancy at all. (Nick tried to tell her that Zoe knew where babies came from, but he couldn't get a word in edgewise.) Then, between bites of gummy yams and weird Jell-O salad, Kay declared that all of these problems, in her view, had a single root.

"Immigration in this country is out of control," she said, sawing through a piece of poultry that had all the tenderness of cardboard. "When those people flood in here, it gets worse for everyone. We're lucky our governor is doing something about it."

Nick was going to break a molar, he was grinding his teeth so hard. Kay must have registered the set of his jaw, because she added, "Oh, I don't mean *your* parents, obviously. They were good immigrants. They did it the right way. Plus, your father could contribute with all that education."

Christ on a cracker, as Eli would put it. Nick opened his mouth to say something—anything to get her to stop spewing such nonsense, but Laurie beat him to it.

"Hey, Mom? Why don't we cool it? It's Christmas. We can enjoy each other's company instead of talking politics." She ate some of her peas.

"Who said anything about politics?" Kay protested. "These are facts. But I guess if I say something you disagree with, you'll get up and leave, hm?" She pushed her potatoes around her plate.

Nick didn't roll his eyes, but it was a near thing. He hated how Kay always played the role of the hurt party no matter whose feelings *she* hurt in the process. "No one's leaving, Kay," he said.

"Oh, really?" Kay's head snapped up. She wore a triumphant look on her face. "What about how Laurie is moving across the country?" She stabbed her spoon across the table in Laurie's direction.

Laurie's fork and knife fell to her plate with a clatter. "*Mom*."

Nick screwed up his face in confusion. "What are you talking about?" Where was this coming from? Was Kay getting so paranoid that she was just making things up wholesale? He turned to Laurie, only to find her glaring daggers at her mother. "Laur? What's she talking about?"

"You may as well tell him," Kay said. "Tell him how this will be the last Christmas you and Zoe are going to spend here."

Nick's stomach, already heavy with potatoes and bread rolls, plummeted.

"What?" Zoe was looking around the table for answers. Nick was in the same boat and trying not to show it.

Laurie mustered up a smile for her. "Hey, honey, why don't you take a few of your cool new toys and go play in the fun room?" That was what they called the guest bedroom that Kay kept for Zoe whenever she stayed the night. It was clearly a misnomer, but it had been an attempt to get Zoe more excited for her visits with Grammy.

Nick took a shuddering breath. His entire life was being upended in front of his eyes, but that didn't mean he couldn't keep up the facade of a united co-parenting team. "Yeah, sweetheart, go ahead. Make sure those skates of yours fit, okay?"

Zoe looked around the table with deep suspicion, especially at Kay, who was downing her wine. "Okay," she said, and shuffled off.

Laurie stood as soon as she disappeared down the hall. "Thanks for airing all my dirty laundry, Mom. If you'll excuse us, Nick and I have some things to discuss."

"Well, what was I supposed to do?" Kay cried. "Let you get away with it?"

Nick stood as well, throwing his napkin beside his plate. He couldn't look at his ex-mother-in-law a second longer. If he did, he was going to end up flipping the table—all on his own, this time.

For someone who had just been complaining about being abandoned, Kay looked exceptionally pleased with herself as Nick and Laurie left the room. She was the lone figure presiding over a mediocre feast, smirking into her wine.

Nick and Laurie ended up outside on the screen porch next to Kay's kidney-shaped swimming pool. The hum of the pool pump and the sharp smell of chlorine permeated the air.

He turned to Laurie. She was looking down into the pool, worrying her necklace. "What the hell is going on? You and Zoe are moving away?"

"No! Maybe?" She scrunched her face up. "I don't know. I'm looking into some possibilities. It's only an idea at this point."

Nick's brain was still whirling. "Where?"

"Arizona." She still wasn't looking up. "There's a small clinic out there that's hiring. A nurse I used to work with is on staff. She basically said the job is mine if I want it. I'm still thinking it over, though."

Nick's breath left him in a whoosh. He felt like he'd been kicked in the stomach. "When were you planning on telling me?"

"After the holidays," she said. Her eyes flicked up to meet his. "I'm sorry, okay? I thought it would be better for you and Zoe to have a normal Christmas before we discussed it. I didn't want some pall hanging over everything." She sighed. "That didn't work. Obviously."

Nick couldn't even form words, he was so sideswiped. After the divorce, they had both wanted to keep things as amicable as possible. There was no court-recorded custody agreement, only an informal arrangement. With Laurie's weird hours at the hospital and Nick's changeable schedule at the restaurant, they'd agreed to be flexible, playing it by ear when it came to dividing up custody of Zoe. At the time, it had seemed better than coming up with a strict schedule. As long as Nick had Zoe for Lunar New Year, he never complained.

Was he going to have to travel to Arizona for Lunar New Year? What about the restaurant? What about his dad? He hated flying.

This was such a mess.

"You should have told me," Nick said. "Hell, you told your *mom* before you told me."

Laurie's nostrils flared. "I did not tell her, actually. She went through my phone and read my emails. That's how she knows." Her voice dropped to a hissed whisper. "And honestly? It's that kind of shit that makes me want to leave town." Her eyes went all red the way they did when she was trying not to cry. "She's impossible, Nick. The stuff she says? Out loud? It's grinding me down into nothing. I try to put up boundaries, and she keeps steamrolling right over them!"

Nick grimaced. He knew that Kay had gotten worse over the last few years, but he hadn't realized how bad it had gotten. Or how much it was weighing on Laurie. "I know you've put up with a lot. But Arizona? That's so . . . far."

She wiped at her face and lifted her head with a sigh. "I don't want Zoe to grow up around her. *I* don't want to be around her. This job, it's a good opportunity, and the schools there are nice, my brother and his wife would be nearby—"

"I thought you said it was just an idea." Nick crossed his arms over his chest, knowing it came off as a defensive gesture but not really caring. He was feeling defensive.

Laurie gestured helplessly. "I did some cursory research, okay? I wasn't going to come to you with zero facts!"

"We're supposed to be a *team*," Nick said. He saw a shadow pass by the sliding glass door out of the corner of his eye: Kay walking by on her way to the kitchen. Nick moved so that his back was to the glass and Laurie was blocked from view. "I don't like being left out of something as big as this," he said in a low whisper to her. "This is the kind of thing we're supposed to talk through together."

Laurie closed her eyes, took a deep breath, then opened them, all while Nick was left wondering what kind of therapeutic affirmations she was repeating to herself. "Look, maybe I should have gone about this differently. I acknowledge that," she said, "but are we really going to spend the rest of Christmas out here on the back porch arguing? Because that is exactly what would bring my mother the most joy, and I don't want to give her the satisfaction."

Frustration swamped Nick, hot and humid. He knew Kay was being manipulative, but at the same time, he had a right to be angry. He hated the idea of Zoe being taken far away, of not seeing her from one end of the week to the next. The mere thought of it made him feel like someone had opened his chest with a crowbar and rearranged everything inside.

"I don't know if I can slap on a smile just to spite Kay," Nick said. "How would you feel if I told you I was thinking of taking Zoe and moving three time zones away?"

Laurie's mouth thinned into a tight line. "I would ask if it was the best thing for Zoe. That's all that matters, right? You're a fantastic dad, don't get me wrong, but you're busier than ever with the restaurant, and I think growing up away from all this"— she made a window-washing motion with her palm in the direction of her mom's house—"might be for the best. But again, this is all up in the air!"

Nick opened his mouth to protest, but the words clogged his

throat. Maybe Laurie had a point about spending the rest of the holiday arguing; the discussion they needed to have was sure to be a long one, and they weren't going to come to any real decisions today.

"Okay." He pinched the bridge of his nose, trying to stave off the headache that was coming hot on the heels of a stomachache. And heartache. "Yeah. Let's schedule that long talk. I'll need some time to wrap my head around this idea, anyway."

"Exactly. After the holidays, we'll discuss it." Laurie nodded. "This sucks, Nick, I know. But please try to keep an open mind, okay?"

Nick swallowed. "Whatever's best for Zoe, like we always say." A small part of him was already leaping for solutions that would keep Zoe with him, but he told himself that he should at least be willing to hear Laurie out. Later. If he could get his head clear.

"Well." Laurie started toward the sliding door, awkward but resigned. "We should probably get back in there. There's pie."

Ugh. Nick could very much miss Kay's "famous" pumpkin pie and never once mourn it. It had *raisins*. "Why don't you go ahead?" he said, scratching at his brow with his thumbnail. "I'll be there in a minute. Just want to give myself some time to, you know, cool down."

Laurie paused with her hand on the door. "Are we good?"

Nick thought about his answer carefully. "We're not bad," he finally said. That was the best he could do at the moment.

Laurie seemed to understand. "For what it's worth, I wouldn't want to have a co-parenting fight with anyone else."

That got Nick to raise the corner of his mouth, at least. "Same," he said.

The door slid open with a whoosh, and she disappeared into the house. Nick stood there on the patio for a long moment, contemplating the little robot that was chugging along the bottom of the pool, sucking up debris. It would keep going around and around in circles until someone pulled it out of the water. Nick could relate.

He couldn't help but think about what he would do if Laurie and Zoe really did move to Arizona. Without his kid around, what was the point of staying in New Port Stephen? His dad was here, of course. And his job, though he could probably find work at any restaurant anywhere.

And maybe Eli. Probably not for long, though.

Nick paced along the pool's edge. He wanted to talk this through with someone he could trust. A friend that would listen, who he could be angry in front of. He hadn't planned on calling so soon after their—tryst? Momentary lapse of reason? Whatever it was, Eli was still his friend, right?

"Screw it," Nick muttered. He pulled out his phone.

CHAPTER 20

Eli woke up to the annoying vibration of his phone, audible even through the pillow he had over his head.

He felt like he'd been run over by a truck. He hadn't even done anything that physically adventurous the night before, so what the hell was that about? If his therapist were here, she would probably say something about how emotions tended to manifest in his body. Eli tossed the pillow off his face and picked up his phone, glancing at the time. Ugh, it was way later than it felt. The call was from Nick, but Eli couldn't fathom talking to anyone right now, least of all his oldest friend/one-night stand.

He sent the call to voicemail, flipped onto his stomach, and fell right back to sleep.

"Wake up, Eli," his mom whispered right in his ear maybe a minute or an hour later. "You can't sleep all day. It's Christmas."

He turned over onto his back. "Yippee," he croaked.

His mom beamed down at him. "And to make the occasion even more festive—" She placed a neatly folded stack of clothes directly on his stomach. They were dark green flannel, tied with a red ribbon on top. Eli tipped his chin to his chest to stare at them blearily. "Pajamas!" Cora pointed to her own torso, which was indeed covered by the same kind of pajamas. "I got us all matching sets. They're from the women's department—I hope that's okay with you. I wanted them to fit us."

Eli lifted the pajama stack. "Won't Dad—?"

"It's a tight squeeze," Wendall hollered from somewhere down the hall, "but I'm making it *work*."

"Jesus Christ." Eli rubbed the sleep out of his eyes, praying that his dad wasn't actually trying to channel Tim Gunn. He could only deal with one tragedy at a time.

"Hurry. We're doing gifts." Cora pressed a kiss to the top of his head and practically floated from the guest room on a cinnamon cloud of Christmas cheer.

Eli took a deep breath. He got out of bed. He took off Nick's hoodie and put on the pajamas. And he did not think about how he'd left Nick naked under a bathrobe after giving him his first officially queer orgasm. It was Christmas. He could get through Christmas. This was the big set piece, the whole reason he was visiting, ostensibly. His parents deserved a good show; he could give them that.

He shuffled out of the guest room wearing the pj's, with his hair askew. His dad took about a million long-armed selfies of the three of them in their matching finery. Thankfully it was all waist-up angles, because Wendall's pajama pants were way too clingy. Outside, Eli could hear some kids messing around on brand-new scooters.

Then it was time for presents. They gathered around the "family" tree, now divested of old photos and redecorated with new ones. Eli sat on the floor while his parents took the couch.

He tried not to feel embarrassed about the gifts he'd wrapped in his trademark half-assed way for his parents. They tended not to spend too much money on each other when it came to Christmas, picking out little things or silly joke gifts. One year, Eli had received a box of five thousand paper clips because he'd complained to his parents—once! Back in *August*—about never being able to find one when he needed it.

But this year Eli had really phoned it in. Buying books for librarians, albeit one retired, was like giving eggs to a chicken farmer. Still, his parents oohed and ahhed over them: a nonfiction book about the Florida Highwaymen for Wendall and a novel for Cora. *The Whatever's Wife. So-and-so's Daughter.* Eli hadn't really paid much attention; it had been on one of the big tables at the bookstore.

"Thanks so much, son," said his dad, already reading the copy on the back of his hardcover. "This is really neat."

"Okay, open yours, open yours." His mom handed him a big box expertly wrapped in shiny red-and-green-striped paper. The top was decorated with a gold bow and a sprig of pine that had been glued to a teeny-tiny pine cone. Cora had really gone all out.

Eli dutifully opened the present. Inside was a plethora of crumpled tissue paper. He dug the first layer out only to find another, slightly smaller box. "You guys . . ."

This was a gag from when he was about eleven. At the time, he'd thought it was the funniest thing in the world. Actually, he still kind of thought that. It was nice to know where he'd gotten his sense of humor, at least.

His dad chuckled. "Keep going!"

Eli opened three more boxes, each one nestled inside the other, until he finally opened a small elegant box that he prayed didn't hold a watch. That would make him feel even shittier about his gifts. But inside, he found an envelope. And inside the envelope: three hand-drawn tickets that said *Lion King* on them, along with the date of March 3 in his mom's handwriting, all curlicues and flourishes.

He stared at them for a moment, not understanding. Then his mom gushed, "We're going to take you to a Broadway show when we come up to visit you in March! I know it's silly, but that was your favorite movie when you were a kid."

He couldn't believe they remembered that. He and Nick had literally destroyed their old VHS tape, they'd watched it so many times. Any other year, he'd be happy to see an overpriced Broadway show with his folks and indulge in some shared nostalgia, but this year? What a mess.

"We wanted to make sure you were free around that date before we bought the tickets," Wendall added. "I know your new job must have you running ragged."

"Uh. Okay." This was not the way Eli had wanted to tell them. Ideally he would have told them the truth about his lack of employment when about forty members of his extended family were *not* headed their way for Christmas dinner. But they'd left him no choice. "So, the thing is, I may not be living in New York in March."

"What?" His mom gaped. "Why?"

"Because." *Like a Band-Aid. Just let it rip.* Maybe it wouldn't be so bad. His folks had been so understanding about the pictures; they could understand this, surely. "I lost my job, couldn't find another one, and I'm subletting my apartment until I figure out what's next."

"Jesus, Mary, and Joseph," his dad said under his breath. "Why didn't you say something?"

His mom reached down and put a hand on his knee. She didn't look angry; in fact, Eli noticed that she looked downright gleeful. "So you're moving back in with us?"

Eli closed his eyes. "Mom . . ."

"This is perfect! We can repaint the guest room. Make it yours again. Oh, Wen, do you think we can fix that closet door? Eli shouldn't have to deal with a sticky closet door."

"Mom!" Eli opened his eyes again in time to see his parents jump an inch off the couch. "Can we please just—not start cheerfully making plans for my possible incarceration?"

"Incarceration? That's a bit much," his dad said.

"Would it really be so bad? Staying here with us while you get back on your feet?" Cora asked, her face falling. Then she perked up again. "Ooh, you can come to my CrossFit classes with me."

"I don't want to go to CrossFit classes with you," Eli snapped. "I don't want to stay here at all. I'm almost forty! Moving back here will mean I've failed harder than I have ever failed at anything in my life, and trust me, that's saying a lot."

"Now, I'm sure that's not true," Wendall said.

"Yes, it is." Eli could feel his face getting red hot. Why weren't they listening to him? "Comedy is all I want to do, and I can't do it anymore because my career is fucked. Do you get that? Do you get why I might not want to start picking paint colors? I do that, it's over. I'm done. That's the worst-case scenario."

His words seemed to hang in the air once they'd left his mouth. Everything else was silent. Or would have been if his mom hadn't started crying. She put her face in her hands and sobbed quietly. Eli's dad put his arm around her and looked at Eli with all the disappointment that Eli had been trying to avoid by not having this conversation.

"You don't have to be so unkind," he said. "It's Christmas."

Cora sniffled into Wendall's too-tight pajamas as he folded her against his shoulder. "He hates it here."

Eli tried to tamp down his frustration. "It's not about you."

"We're your parents," she shot back. "How is it not about us?"

This was worse than the Christmas Eli had gotten food poisoning and threw up all over the dining room table. He'd been nine, so no one could really blame him for ruining the holidays. Now he had no excuse.

He left his parents consoling each other on the sofa and re-treated to the back porch. His phone buzzed in his pocket, and he checked the ID with a frazzled glance. Nick. Probably calling to say Merry Christmas like a person with manners. Eli couldn't deal with that right now. He declined the call and instead texted Margo. He needed her levelheaded advice. He needed to talk to someone who would understand.

Just ruined Xmas. Broke the news to my parents. Help?

Eli stared at the screen as long minutes ticked by. No response. Not even a "read" checkmark.

Even Margo was too busy for him. And why wouldn't she be? Amazing career, a hope, however slim, of breaking into primetime. She was probably eating Chinese food with the cool West Coast crowd.

Eli threw himself into one of the metal patio chairs and stared at the porch ceiling. A lone bug was making its way across the great, empty expanse. He wished he could tell it there was nothing on the other side. It was all wasted energy.

Eventually he heard cars arriving in the driveway, the creak of the front door and the voices of his aunts and uncles. Right. It was supposed to be an afternoon of cocktails and puff pastry appetizers before dinner. He could hear his mom, voice tight and strained, greeting everyone as they entered. The dutiful hostess. Eli was the biggest piece of shit on earth. Maybe in the whole universe. He gnawed on his thumbnail and tried to think of a way out of the mess he'd made. Was escaping to Key West to become a go-go dancer an option? Probably not; his dancing wasn't the best.

The slider opened and shut. Eli turned to see Max standing on the patio, dressed like a black smudge. "So this is where you're hiding. Everything okay? Aunt Cora's eyes looked a little red when we came in."

"Oh, that? Yeah, that's probably the heartbreak." Eli sighed and kicked his feet up on one of the empty patio chairs. "I kind of dropped a bomb. Don't worry about it." Max was still a kid; Eli didn't want to explain the whole tawdry situation to a kid, especially not on Christmas.

"Is this about how that *Beck's Call* guy got your show canceled?" Max asked. "And you've been letting your folks think you have a new job when you don't?"

Eli stared. "How do you know about that?"

Max spoke slowly with all the sarcasm of a teen. "Well, the cancelation was reported in *Variety*, *The Hollywood Reporter*, *Time* . . ."

"No, I mean how did you know I don't have a new job?"

"Uh, because if you had a new job you wouldn't be hanging out here for, like, weeks? You'd be sitting in an airless room with seven other white guys, one girl, and one person of color trying to come up with new ways to make some *famous* white guy sound funnier than he is."

"Okay." Eli pursed his lips. "Scathing indictment of the industry, but not untrue." He leaned back in his chair and put his fists to his eyes with a loud groan. "For the record, I never *lied* to my mom and dad. I . . . let them believe what they wanted to believe."

Max took a seat in one of the empty patio chairs, perching on it like a gargoyle. "Isn't that just a lie of omission?"

"Stop learning big words and using them against me," Eli said, letting his hands fall away. "Anyway, that's not even the part Mom's upset about. She wanted me to stay here with her indefinitely, and I—" He gave a full-body shiver. "It's like my worst nightmare, having to come back here with my tail between my legs."

"Hey," Max said mildly, "I get it. Some of us are living the nightmare on the daily."

"Yeah. Sorry. Didn't mean to rub it in your face." The survivor's guilt was real. Eli glanced over at Max. He didn't want to be pushy, but he knew he would have traded an arm and a leg for someone to confide in when he was Max's age. "You know, you can always talk to me. If you want. I know this place—it's hard. Sometimes. For certain people." Max's eyebrows rose one inch, and Eli started to babble. "Not that I'm saying you're certain people! But if you were, or if you think you might be—"

"Eli, I've been out since I was fifteen," Max said.

He sat up straight with a jolt. "What? Really? Fif—? What?"

"Yeah, I told my friends years ago I was genderqueer. Mom and Dad were later, but they're chill. They don't really get it, but . . ." Max shrugged. "Who does?"

Eli felt a million years old. At fifteen, he hadn't even known what gender was, let alone—well, anything useful. "Uh, and do you have pronouns? Fuck, of course you have pronouns. Unless you don't! That's also cool."

Max gave an amused tilt of the head. "Yeah, I've been feeling good about none lately. At first I tried out he/they but everyone picked one or the other and never used both, which pissed me off. None is better."

"And your friends, your parents, they're . . . good with that?" Eli asked carefully.

"Oh, no, they all mess up constantly, especially Dad. They try, though. A couple teachers, too, the ones who give a shit." Max picked off a flake of black nail polish.

"Wow." Eli slumped back in his seat. He could barely wrap his head around it. Even if he had known he was trans back in high school, there was no way he would have ever let his teachers know. "The world really has changed since I was your age."

"Let's not get ahead of ourselves," Max said. "It's still a fucking shitshow. Here especially."

"Ain't that the truth." Eli wished he could offer Max a couch to sleep on in his Brooklyn apartment, but he didn't even have that.

"But you know what?" Max changed positions, long gangly legs sticking out clad in ripped black denim. "This place can try to bury me all it wants. I'm not going to let it. Even if I end up here for my whole life, I'll still be me. Life's too short to be anyone else."

Eli reached out and put a hand on Max's knee, patting it in what he hoped came across as solidarity. He couldn't express in words how much he loved his cousin in that moment. He was proud and also jealous, but mostly proud.

"Yeah. Life's too short," he choked out. Before he could start tearing up and really embarrassing himself, he sat back and wiped surreptitiously at his eyes. "Damn, am I really learning a lesson from my little cousin on Christmas? What is this, an after-school special?"

"What's an after-school special?" Max asked.

Eli closed his eyes with a sigh. "Don't worry about it." As much as it sucked to be reminded of his age, it was also kind of comforting. Yeah, he was old, so what? Not everyone had the pleasure.

Life really was too short. So what if he wasn't sure what would come next? There was a kind of freedom in not knowing. He could choose to live in the moment.

He could, if he wanted to, choose Nick. Maybe it wouldn't be more than a few days or a few weeks, but Nick made him happy. He made him laugh. A little short-term happiness, even if it was in the guise of helping a friend out, was not nothing. Sure, it would all be one-sided—no way was Nick catching feelings the way Eli had—but that was fine. Lightning didn't strike twice and all that.

He pulled out his phone and toyed with it, thinking to re-turn Nick's call and get it all out in the open. Eli could tell him, *Hey, we're all adults here. You want to fool around some more? Be-cause I could definitely fool around some more.*

He pocketed the phone with a sigh. Nick deserved a better overture than that, surely. Eli would need some time to come up with something truly spectacular, something that would snag Nick hook, line, and sinker. In the meantime, he made a pact with himself not to contact Nick willy-nilly. That would come off as clingy, a fate worse than death.

In the meantime, there was Christmas dinner to get through, which was a close second.

"All right." He slapped his thighs and levered himself out of his chair. "Let's go slap on some smiles and eat some ham."

"Hallelujah," Max intoned.

CHAPTER 21

December 26

There was a weird liminal time between Christmas and New Year's where nothing felt real. Some shops and offices were closed for the remainder of the year, but the most random places remained open. Sure, there were fast-food restaurants and chain stores, but then there was also the year-round farm stand out on Midway and, of course, Jimmy's Bait and Tackle.

Nick pulled into the gravel lot outside the tiny outpost and looked over at his dad in the passenger seat. He was bundled up in preparation for a morning on the water, where temperatures might dip into the—gasp—high fifties. Eli would have a field day if he saw Tian-yi in his scarf and earflap hat, Nick thought, then felt a well of bitterness rise up in his gut. Nick had left him a voicemail asking him to call back when he could, but it was radio silence. The mature, charitable side of Nick wanted to believe that Eli was busy with family holiday stuff, but another, more vulnerable part wondered if he was being ghosted.

He'd never been ghosted before. He'd also never had a one-night stand—if that was indeed what Christmas Eve had been.

Could you have a one-night stand with an ex? Nick would have loved to ask, but since Eli wasn't returning his calls, he could only theorize.

"I will get the baitfish," his dad said, knocking him out of his reverie. He opened the passenger door. "I know how squeamish you get."

Nick sighed through his nose. His dad was referring to the time that Eli had thrown hermit crabs at Nick's head at summer camp. Somehow, Nick had gotten in trouble for screaming. Who wouldn't scream when they had a crustacean coming right at them with all those pointy spider legs? Thirty years later, and he was still getting roasted for it. "I am not squeam—"

But Tian-yi was already out of the car. A cheery bell rang as he opened the shop door. Nick slumped over the steering wheel. He would not look at his phone. If Eli had called or texted, he would have felt it vibrate. He didn't need to check it. Again.

His father returned with supplies for their fishing trip—a small Igloo filled with live shrimp and a couple cans of Coke—and Nick drove them to the spot on the intracoastal where they always fished together. The water was shallow there, more of a mudflat than anything, but Tian-yi swore it was the best spot for trout and redfish this time of year. They unloaded their gear, pulled on their waders, and went in with their poles until the water met their knees. Nick surveyed the causeway in both directions. They were the only people fishing, the only people there at all. If not for the occasional car motoring by and the handful of boats tooling across the water in the distance, they might have been the only people in the world.

Nick cast off and waited. Fishing was more of his dad's hobby than his, but he appreciated the quiet, meditative vibe, and it had become their own little tradition around the holidays. Especially now that his dad was retired, Nick wanted to make sure he was getting out of the house, doing things. He worried that unstructured swathes of time compounded with living alone would be bad for Tian-yi's mental health.

Which was why he didn't want to burden his dad with Laurie's news.

He had to tell someone, though, and since Eli wasn't picking up the phone, this was Nick's next-best option.

He cleared his throat and gave his reel a couple of idle turns. "I found out yesterday that Laurie's thinking of moving out to Arizona," he said in Hokkien. It felt like the right language to use for something this personal. It was so quiet out on the water, he didn't even have to raise his voice.

His dad whipped his head in Nick's direction, earflaps flapping. "Arizona?" His brow knotted. "That's so far."

"I know."

"That wouldn't be fair to you."

"I *know*. Thank you." Finally, someone who saw his side.

His dad shuffled closer, sending ripples out into the water. "What's in Arizona, anyway?"

Nick explained Laurie's reasoning, the potential job offer, Kay's increasingly scary rants. "I'm not happy about it," Nick finished, "but we agreed to talk it over soon."

Tian-yi hummed in thought. "I don't blame anyone for trying to get away from Kay." After Nick's divorce, his dad had said, *One good thing: I won't ever have to eat that woman's cooking again.* Kay still extended an invite every Christmas, and Nick always told her his dad had plans. Which was true: he went down to Fort Lauderdale to hang out with his fishing buddies. "Would you follow them to Arizona if they go?" his dad asked.

"What?" Nick hadn't seriously considered that option. "I can't leave, Dad."

"Why not?" Tian-yi reeled in, eyed his hook with its wriggling shrimp still affixed on the tip, and cast off again. "Lots of restaurants all over. You could get another job, easy. And you'll get your time with Zoe."

"But what about you? I can't leave you." His Taiwanese wasn't as good as his English, but he hoped it conveyed what he meant. He loved his dad. He couldn't abandon him.

"Chih-ming." His dad only called him that when they were being very serious. He turned to face Nick across the still water, his eyes soft. "You are my child, not the other way around. You shouldn't have to take care of me."

"Well, too bad." Nick reeled in. His hook was bare. Damn it. He trudged closer to the shoreline where their cooler was stuck in the wet sand, then got a new shrimp. "I worry about you, okay? Not just because Mom's gone, but because—you're getting older. I'm getting older. And I don't want you to be alone." Being alone was hard. Nick knew that better than most.

He stabbed his hook through the bait. His dad, he noticed, was facing away with a tense set to his shoulders.

"Ah. Now is probably as good a time as any to tell you," his dad said in what was clearly a tone meant to sound upbeat.

Nick tried to ignore the frisson of panic that ran through his veins. "Tell me what?"

Tian-yi turned and smiled gently at him. "I'm not alone." He looked . . . Nick had never seen his dad look like this. Almost bashful, with a hot flush on his cheeks. "I have a lady friend."

"A lady friend." Nick knew he was standing there with his mouth open like the fish he was never going to catch. "Who?"

"Her name is Mei-hua. She lives down in Coconut Grove," his dad said. "I wanted to make sure it was serious before I told you. And, well." He pursed his lips like he was trying to contain his joy. "It definitely is."

Nick closed his mouth with a click. "Well, that's—" It went

without saying that he was surprised, so instead he said, "Congratulations, Dad. Uh, what's she like?"

"Fantastic." His eyes twinkled. "She made those xiao mantou you were eating the other day."

So that's where the fussy baked goods had come from. Nick should have connected the dots. In his defense, he'd been distracted of late. He stared down into the water, trying to get used to all this new information. An overwhelming mixture of pride and awe warred in his chest. Here was his dad, who had gone through so much and lived so many years, taking another shot at love. *Good for him*, Nick thought. Truly, honestly, wholeheartedly: good for him. Tian-yi had always been the kind of father who taught by example, and Nick couldn't help but think maybe there was a lesson here for him.

His dad wasn't done, though. "What I am saying is: You don't need to worry about me. I am fine. Do I like having you close? Of course. But I am not so selfish as to keep you here if you have other places to be." He walked slowly toward Nick, water swirling around his legs. His face was a solemn promise. "When your mother died, I admit, I didn't see much point in life. But she would want me to be strong, and happy, and alive, so I am going to be." He regarded Nick with sharp eyes. "What about you? What do you want to be?"

Nick sat down heavily on the closed lid of the Igloo cooler. It sank a few inches into the sand but held his weight. Good thing, too, because Nick's legs weren't up to the task. "I don't know," he said with quiet honesty. He switched to English, not knowing the words for what he was trying to say otherwise. "I spend so much time worrying about other people—you, Zoe, work—I hardly ever have anything left over. I think I—might want things. For myself." He watched a minnow school flash by. "Sounds pathetic when I say it out loud, huh?"

Tian-yi splashed closer and held his hand out. Nick took it, letting himself be lifted back on his feet. "No," his dad said. "It sounds good. Live your life, whatever that is. Maybe you move. Maybe you don't. Maybe you find someone to love." His gaze darted away, his face pulling into a mask of innocence. "Maybe you already did?" He glanced back quickly to gauge Nick's reaction. It was so blatant, Nick had to laugh.

He slipped back into Hokkien. "Dad, come on."

"I'm just saying, I was there when you were falling in love for the first time. I saw how you looked at him then, and I see how you look at him now. It is the same look."

Nick opened his mouth to protest. It couldn't be the same; he was a different person now. Hell, Eli was a different person on multiple levels, some of them legally binding. And yet— "You really think so?"

Tian-yi nodded. "I do. And whatever it is you want, I want you to have it."

Nick hadn't realized until that moment that he'd harbored even a sliver of doubt about his dad's acceptance, but now it was like an elephant had been lifted off his back. Suddenly, a lot of things seemed possible. Things Nick hadn't allowed himself to even think of before.

He hugged his dad one-armed, his fishing pole dangling from his other hand. His dad wasn't the biggest hugger, but he returned it with a fierce slap of his own arm, squeezing Nick tight. "Thanks, Dad," Nick said into his scratchy scarf. "Whatever happens, I'm glad you're here."

His dad gave him an even bigger squeeze. He'd always been bigger on actions than words. Then, after a moment: "We're scaring away all the fish with our talking. I bet there isn't a trout for miles now."

Nick laughed, and they parted. They fished for hours, though Tian-yi was right: nothing was biting. Nick told his dad a little about Eli—not the really personal stuff, of course, but how much they'd been hanging out lately—and his dad told him about Mei-hua and how she had a chihuahua that she loved like a baby. Nick said he wanted to meet her sometime, and his dad said that could be arranged.

By the time Nick dropped his dad back at his house, he felt different. Lighter than he had that morning, more hopeful. Motivated to do something he'd never done before, just to see how it would go. While waiting at a red light, he realized he was close to the public pool where he and Eli had joined their first junior swim team back in the day. He hadn't thought about that pool in ages, even though he drove by all the time. He wondered—no, surely they'd be closed the day after Christmas. So many things were.

But some weren't.

When the light changed, he impulsively flicked on his turn signal. He had some time before the Manatee opened for lunch. Maybe the pool's schedule would be posted somewhere, even if it was closed.

The pool turned out to be very much open and in use. A lifeguard greeted him at the little window of the pool office, right inside the gate. "Checking out the Masters' swim today?"

Nick watched the lanes of swimmers stretching out ahead of him. He remembered vaguely that one of their old swim coaches, a hippie with only three toes on his right foot, had belonged to the Masters' team. As a kid, Nick would see the team coming to practice after the juniors' time was up and think, *Wow, they're so old*. They'd looked ancient to his child eyes, skin burnished brick red from the long hours spent swimming under the Florida sun, hair thinning and white. Now Nick looked at them in their Speedos and Swedes and thought, *Well, being old isn't so bad, is it?* His own gray hairs looked dashing in a certain light.

"Yeah," he told the lifeguard. "I'm thinking of joining."

He was given a couple of forms to fill out. For around sixty bucks, he could join the team, practice up to three times a week, and compete in meets if he was so inclined.

"I'm actually one of the Masters' coaches," the lifeguard told him. "Kind of a figurehead thing, but you know. You ever compete?"

"A long time ago," Nick said, "but I want to get back into it." Hearing it out loud was like hearing something come to life. He had barely formed the idea to himself, and here he was telling a stranger about it.

The lifeguard perked up. "What's your event?"

Nick hesitated. Back when he was younger, he was always pigeonholed in the fly or breaststroke. Big shoulders; his coaches thought he was naturally suited to those races. But personally, he always preferred— "The hundred back." When Nick kicked off the wall upside down for the backstroke, he would watch his air bubbles rising in a line along his body. Like silver jellyfish swimming to the surface, mirroring him. He'd always loved that.

"We could use more backstrokers." The lifeguard smiled. "The next practice is in two days. You could come try it out, no commitment. If you're really interested."

"I'd have to get a suit," Nick said. His baggy swim trunks wouldn't cut it with this crowd. Wow, was he really doing this? The smell of chlorine filled his nose. Every muscle in his body yearned to get in the water and—go.

"So get one," the lifeguard said, a tad aggressively.

Nick responded in kind. "Okay. I will."

He left the county pool feeling like, for the first time in a long time, he'd given himself something just for him. It gave him the courage to do what he might have otherwise put off for weeks. He sat in his car, engine off, and pulled out his phone. **We should talk about Arizona,** he texted Laurie. **What's a good time for you?**

CHAPTER 22

Eli slept late again, waking only for a few moments before rolling over and falling right back into a dream state. During one brief period of consciousness, he thought he heard the front door close and his parents' car rumble away. Then nothing but a stretch of dark. Until the doorbell rang. And rang. And would not stop ringing.

He pulled himself out of bed with a sour groan. His parents had to be out; they'd never ignore a doorbell and would never sleep as late as—he glanced at the old digital clock on the nightstand while he pulled on his pajama top—Jesus, well past noon. He shuffled to the door with all the enthusiasm of a dog being taken to a vet appointment. It occurred to him it might be Nick. He'd left Eli a voicemail during yesterday's interminable Christmas dinner, but Eli literally never checked his voicemail and wasn't even sure how to do it on his new phone. He figured if it was an emergency, a rational person would text.

He half hoped it was a Jehovah's Witness at the door; he still hadn't come up with a good way to woo Nick. Was it even possible to have that conversation about keeping up the fun, experimental sex (and nothing else, totally cool with just sex, nothing to see here) if he hadn't even brushed his teeth? Eli opened the door anyway.

"Holy shit." He scrubbed a hand through his hair and down his face. "Margo? What the hell?"

Margo—all six foot three of her—stood on the front porch. Her curly henna-red hair was pulled back in a headband. She wore a velour tracksuit. Her shoes were slip-ons. Everything about her screamed *hot off a transcontinental flight.* "Hey, stranger."

Eli didn't even consider playing it cool. He tipped forward and wrapped Margo up in a bear hug. She smelled like rental-car air freshener and cigarettes. He hadn't realized how much he'd missed her.

"Whoa. Okay." Margo returned the hug carefully. "You all right, buddy?"

"Yeah." Eli gave her one last squeeze before holding her at arm's length. "I'm just—it's good to see you. Unexpected, but good. What are you doing here?"

She scrunched her nose as she smiled. "What, I can't check in on my friend? Make sure he hasn't started wearing those oversized shirts with a deep-sea fishing mural on it while blasting Jimmy Buffett?"

Eli gave her an unimpressed look.

She sighed and took his hands in hers. "I wrapped up my last meetings in LA, went to some horrible Christmas party with the network people, then, like a good child, caved to the wishes of my elderly parents. I'm going to drive down to their place in Boca Raton later, but I thought while I was in the area . . ."

"Boca is, like, three hours in the other direction," Eli pointed out.

"Practically down the block." Margo's smile morphed into something more of a smirk. She gave Eli a glance up and down. "Nice pajamas."

"Thanks. It was a family thing."

"How've you been?"

Eli bit the inside of his cheek and looked to the side with a little laugh. His life and its problems all seemed so insignificant when Margo was around. "Doesn't matter. I want to hear about what you've been up to. Tell me about *Dorothy*."

"Oh, one hundred percent, you're not going to get me to shut up about it." Margo jutted her chin in the direction of the house's interior. "Should I come in for tea and cookies with your folks?"

"No, uh, Mom and Dad aren't here right now. But we can—" Eli licked his suddenly dry lips. "Do you want to go for a drive? You can tell me all about LA on the way." He glanced down at his pj's. "Give me one second to get dressed."

"Sure, nothing I love better than driving around suburbia." Margo flashed him a smile. "You know I passed two Applebee's between here and the highway?"

"Yeah, one is the good one. The other one is terrible."

In no time, they were tooling around the back roads in a rented compact, taking a route Eli sometimes took to school back in the day. He told Margo when to turn, when to slow down because there used to be speed traps set up, when to ignore the speed limit. Margo, for her part, filled him in on her adventures out west.

"So they love the concept; they love the names I've been tossing around," she said as they drove along the otherwise empty roads. The day after Christmas was quiet. "There's a lot of stuff still up for discussion, but, you know, I have a really good feeling. They said I should hear from them soon, whatever 'soon' means."

"That's great news," Eli said, trying his best to drum up the enthusiasm that Margo deserved. "It's a good sign they were willing to schedule time with you around the holidays, right?"

"I hope so." Margo glanced his way a few times. She wasn't subtle about it. "I want you to be involved. I'm serious."

He stared out the passenger window, gnawing on the edge of his thumbnail. "Well, I seriously hope you're not tossing around my name in front of the bigwigs when it comes to staffing the writers' room. I don't want to be responsible for getting *Dorothy* shit-canned."

"This may be difficult for you to hear"—she placed a hand consolingly on his knee—"but you're not so toxic a personality that the mere mention of you would torpedo five months of talks. I'm pretty sure most industry people out on the West Coast have never even heard of you."

"Wow. That is so uplifting," Eli grumbled. He shifted his knee away, curling into himself toward the passenger door in an exaggerated bid to get away from Margo's touch.

She laughed like he'd hoped she would. Then, sobering a little, she said with forced lightness, "And besides, who said anything about the writers' room?"

Eli watched his reflection in the side mirror as his brow scrunched up. "Where else would you put me?"

"In front of the camera," Margo said. She kept her eyes on the road and her voice bright. "I want you to play Felix."

"Felix." Eli stared at her. This was a bad joke, he was sure of it. It didn't even make sense. "But I'm not an actor," he said slowly.

"Lies. You performed every time you did stand-up. Plus," she said, "you basically created Felix all on your own. No one knows him like you do." That part was true, at least; Eli had spent many late nights with Margo, Chinese food containers scattered around, pencils behind their ears, the whole stereotypical bit while they crafted the character who would be the goofy but well-meaning foil on *Friends of Dorothy*.

Eli shook his head. "Telling jokes onstage isn't the same as acting."

"Why not? Acting isn't hard. It's just timing, and you've got that down. Gerald thinks it's a great idea, too, by the way."

"Of course he does. It's your agent's job to always agree with you."

"Not true! That's only half his job. The other half is telling me when I need to chill the fuck out, and he hasn't yet, not about this. Which means it's perfect."

"I've seen Gerald wear socks with sandals," Eli said. "Are you sure his instincts are good ones?"

But Margo wasn't budging. "Look, I don't want to share scenes with some shithead from Juilliard. I want to do this with you." She tapped her short nails against the wheel in a cheery drumbeat. "So? What do you think?"

It was already difficult to believe that Margo's dream might actually get off the ground; it was impossible to think Eli's life could go from zero to Hollywood happy ending practically overnight. "I don't know . . ."

She took her eyes off the road long enough to give Eli a look. "It's your role, E. It's got to be you."

"I'd have to move out to California."

"That is part of the deal, yeah." Margo shrugged, turning back to the road. "It's not so bad. It's like Florida but bluer. You'd fit right in. Are you allergic to avocado? How about smugness?"

Eli stared out his window. It was a lot to take in. This didn't change anything with Nick, did it? Eli had always thought— hoped—that his time in New Port Stephen would be limited. Besides, *Dorothy* wasn't a done deal. Nothing was certain, least of all Eli. "I'm going to need to think about it."

Margo's voice sounded strangely optimistic when she replied. "Of course. Take some time. It's a big decision. I just think you deserve a chance to reboot your career. Everyone else seems to get one." She muttered the last part almost to herself.

Eli turned back to her. "What does that cryptic little statement mean?"

"Hm? Oh. Nothing." She shrugged the way a liar might. Eli stared at her with narrowed eyes until she caved. "Okay, you obviously haven't heard, and I wasn't going to bring it up, but— Winston Beck announced a new special. It's airing next month."

"Are you fucking kidding me?" Eli's mouth hung open. Righteous anger flowed through him. "Not even one year after being caught with his pants down and he's getting specials handed to him on a silver platter? That's—"

"Ten kinds of messed up, yep," Margo said.

"He was crying in an interview not three months ago about being a victim of cancel culture and 'wah, wah, wah, everyone's so sensitive these days!' Yeah, you're so canceled you're getting a spread in *Variety*, and now this? Oh my god, I might throw up."

"Want me to pull over?"

"No." Eli took a deep breath to tamp down the nausea roiling in his stomach. "I'll be fine." There was truly no justice in the world. This was exactly why Eli had zero faith in *Dorothy* getting picked up. The assholes of the world kept getting handed everything they wanted; everyone else got screwed.

"Make a left at the intersection," Eli said, pointing at the main artery they were approaching. "Turn right after we pass the RJ Gator's, but before the Chili's."

"That sentence you just said? It's the worst one I've ever heard in my life."

Eli gave her a half smile. "Just do it."

Margo was laughing as they finally pulled into the parking lot. A real, deep-down laugh from her belly complete with snorting. It made Eli feel warm down to his toes to know he'd gotten to her. Or rather, the squat building in front of them had gotten to her: an old Pizza Hut, red roof still intact, with the windows blacked out and a neon sign that proclaimed: XXX ADULT.

"You took me on a scenic drive to your hometown porno store?" Margo wheezed as she bent over the steering wheel, parking nearly catty-corner in one of the many open spaces. She looked around wildly. "I can't believe this. Is that the Turnpike ramp? Are we actually going inside a skuzzy jizz-soaked gimp palace that caters almost exclusively to truckers?"

"Don't be so sex-negative," was all Eli said as he left the car.

Margo followed him up the cement ramp that led to the door. "Seriously. Why are we here?"

"Well." Eli paused with his hand on the door's handle. "Some of us did not pack certain accoutrements in our luggage for this trip that we . . . now . . . might . . . need."

Margo's mouth fell open. "You found someone in this town to dick down? Oh my god, congrats. Who?"

Eli let his raised eyebrows answer for him.

Margo's mouth fell open. "Don't tell me it's the DILF."

Eli made a series of faces at the sky.

"No." Margo hit him in the shoulder. "No way."

Eli shrugged helplessly. "It just happened, I swear."

"Okay. Wait." Margo held up both hands. "Is this wishful thinking? Or did he verbalize with his mouth and his words that he would, in fact, be interested in being on the receiving end of your strap?"

"Christ, Margo—" He wondered if it was possible to die from an overheated face. *Florida Man Spontaneously Combusts inside Smut Peddler's Paradise, Shames Family.*

"What?" Margo demanded. "I can't let you drop a couple hundred dollars on something that's going to stay in the box. Spill."

Eli allowed himself a quick cat-with-cream smile. "There was a discussion. He said he was very . . . flexible." Another, harder punch to his shoulder. "Ow!"

"Look at you! Making things happen. I know I told you not to get wrapped up in boys while you were down here, but I didn't know you actually had a shot."

"Thanks for that," Eli said. "And thank you for driving me to the sex shop to help me pick out a new dick. Can't exactly ask my mom to give me a ride for an errand like this, and Uber wanted to charge me fifty bucks for the privilege."

"Are you kidding? I'm going to be dining out on this anecdote for years. Let's get in there." Margo opened the other side of the double doors and rushed in, tugging Eli by the hand.

The store was exactly what he'd been expecting. It was brightly lit with shelves crammed full of lurid products, all of which seemed designed to titillate a specific brand of cishet man who had no attention span. Large-breasted women graced most of the boxes and plastic clamshell labels. In a far corner, a black curtain stood between the retail space and—whatever happened behind black curtains. Did people pay to watch porn? In this day and age, when every cell phone provided them with unlimited options for free? Maybe truckers didn't trust the internet, which, fair.

Besides Margo and himself, Eli saw only a lone bearded cashier at the back behind a counter, watching something explosion-heavy on a battered laptop.

Eli ducked down the dildo aisle. He could sense Margo following close behind, her airport-ready slip-on shoes shuffling along the cement floor.

"Keep your eyes peeled for something nonthreatening," he told her. "Beginner stuff. Something that says, 'My First Anal Experience.'" A lot of the silicone cocks on display sported names like the Punisher or Bareback Stallion, which was not the vibe Eli was going for. He picked up a box with a simple, smooth design that called itself the Rapture-Bringer, but on further inspection, this moniker seemed less about romance and more about evangelical imagery. Eli put that box back on the shelf with a heavy sigh.

"So. How excited are we?" Margo asked. She was on the other side of the aisle, poking at a pegboard bag filled with teeny-tiny plastic dicks suitable for a bachelorette party. "Hitting that hot dad. Getting some sweet ex sex. Claiming new territory." Her eyebrows did a Groucho Marx impression.

Eli groaned. "Stop making it sound gross."

"*You* stop daydreaming about taking this dude's backdoor virginity." Margo frowned and picked up a nearby dildo with a tie-dye design called Grateful Head. "Wait, is this the guy who took *your* virginity?"

Eli could feel the back of his neck getting hot. "Can we stop talking about virginity like it's a real thing?"

Margo's mouth fell open. "Oh my god, your therapist would be digging deep into this if you were still paying her. An eye for an eye. Except it's penetration." She gestured with the tie-dye model. Vigorously.

"This isn't—I'm not exacting *revenge*. Would you stop?" He grabbed the toy from her and put it back on the shelf. "At the risk of being dragged over the coals by your rapier wit for showing even a hint of real emotion, I like him. A lot." Understatement, but close enough. "I know this is just a fun interlude for the two of us, but—Marg, I really, really like him." It sounded so childish, but it was true.

Margo bit her lip and bobbed her head a few times. "And at the risk of sounding like the most self-serving bitch in the world: Do you like him enough to turn down LA?"

Eli rubbed the back of his burning neck. "I don't know. It's all so up in the air, right? I would need to talk to him about it. But first you need to tell me this offer is solid, that they really want me on the project, and that it's all going forward. I can't decide until I know where everyone else stands."

"That's fair. And hey." Margo stepped into his personal space. For a moment, Eli was convinced she was going to give him a hug, but she reached past his shoulder and retrieved one of the dildos from the shelf. She pressed the box with a picture of an iridescent blue dong into his hands. "Slim, compact, harness-compatible. And it matches your eyes."

"My eyes are brown," Eli said.

"My point is, if he's what's best for you," she said, "then that's what I want for you too. Sorry if I pile too much shit on you sometimes."

"Nah. Don't be sorry. It's what I need to hear."

Margo did hug him then, almost crushing the sleek cardboard packaging between them. She smelled like cigarettes, but Eli didn't mind. She smelled like backstage and late-night toil. She smelled of home.

"No bullshit," she said in his ear. "I love you, man."

He got an arm around her, too, and squeezed back. "Love you too." Then, after waiting a perfectly timed beat: "Want to help me pick out a harness?"

Margo laughed and pulled away. If her eyes were a little red, Eli was too much of a friend to mention it. "I want nothing more."

With her help, Eli selected a modestly sized and not-at-all intimidating model and its accessories. The cashier wrapped everything in nondescript brown paper before placing it in an unmarked shopping bag. Eli was going to give this place the best Yelp review ever.

When Margo dropped him off, Eli could see his parents still

hadn't returned. Great news for the bag of sex toys he was about to tote into his childhood bedroom.

"Hey. Amigo." Margo leaned out of the driver's-side window, cigarette smoldering in her fingers. Eli obligingly paced over to her side of the car. "I mean it. Whatever you decide, I'm still on your team. But I also selfishly really, really want you in LA."

"We'll see," Eli said. "One step at a time."

"Yeah, of course. California, baby." Margo sketched a "hang loose" gesture. "You and me. Mull it over. That's all I ask."

He nodded. "Tell your folks I said Happy Belated Hanukkah."

"Tell yours I said Merry Belated Christmas."

Eli stood on the driveway and waved as she pulled out and disappeared around the bend in the road.

CHAPTER 23

December 27

Nick got the text toward the end of a quiet dinner shift:
Want to meet me at the beach when you get off work?

He stared at the message for a long beat before responding.
How are you getting there?

Already here. I biked. Using my bike. That a very kind man gave to me.

Seriously? It was at least six miles from Pineapple Top Lane to
their beach. Or rather, the beach that Nick had started to think
of as theirs. Again.

Eli sent back an emoji with the angry puff of air coming out
of its nose. **Just come**, he said.

It wasn't a particularly busy day for the Manatee. Most people were still recovering from their overindulgent Christmas dinners and working through their leftovers. The last table left well
before the nine o'clock closing time, and with a little premature
tackling of the closing checklist, Nick had every staff member
out the door within minutes. He could admit he was nervous.
He and Eli hadn't spoken in a couple days, and he was beginning
to wonder if they ever would. But Eli wouldn't invite him to the

beach at night simply to deliver another "I think we should just be friends" speech. Right?

Nick rubbed his tired eyes as he locked up the restaurant for the night. He couldn't take another heavy conversation so soon after the one with Laurie. They had met at the Chili's near Laurie's work the day before and, over an untouched Triple Dipper platter, hashed out the thorny question of Arizona.

There had been evidence to sift through—Laurie's documentation of the now-concrete job offer, the spreadsheet she'd made that showed how much money she could start putting away for Zoe's college education with the higher salary, emails from her younger brother, a real estate agent who lived in the Tucson area and could help them get settled.

"But none of these facts mean a damn thing," Laurie had said, smoothing out the spread of papers on the table, "unless we answer the big question: Are you willing to give up regular access to Zoe?"

"According to you, I don't spend enough time with her as it is," Nick had said.

"We're not talking about my opinion right now. We're talking about you." Laurie had leveled a stare at him that made Nick feel pinned in place. "You've got to tell me how you feel."

The words had hesitated on Nick's tongue. "I feel like I should be fighting this as hard as I can. That's what everyone expects, right?"

"I don't care about other people's expectations," Laurie had said. "Don't tell me what you should do. Tell me what's going on in your head."

And Nick had. He'd spilled out everything, all his worries and emotions, while their Southwestern Eggrolls grew cold and congealed. He'd told Laurie how every cell of his body wanted to keep Zoe close, and how ashamed he would be if he demanded that if it meant denying her a better life elsewhere. He'd said she was right; he did work too much, and while he wanted to cut back on his hours, he couldn't promise a meaningful difference in the short term. He'd even told Laurie a little of what was going on with Eli, how close they were getting, and how terrified Nick was of being unable to spin one more plate on top of all his responsibilities. And the more he'd talked, the more it became clear why he'd been on the verge of tears ever since they'd put in the app order: because he knew. He knew what the answer should be, if only he could live with it.

Laurie had cried and thanked him. Said what they were doing was for the best. Yet Nick had never felt worse.

He was still raw from it all. Holding it together by the barest thread. The perfect time for another potentially emotional conversation, surely.

His was the only car in the beach's sandy parking lot that night. When his headlights dimmed away, he was left in almost total blackness. There was half a moon tonight, at least, and only a few clouds to obscure the starlight. He could see the vague shape of Eli's bicycle leaning up against the wooden post at the start of the short boardwalk.

Something caught Nick's ear: the tinny strains of music being pumped through a portable speaker. He walked down the steps, and the lyrics started to take shape. It was some early-aughts alt rock; he recognized the tune and probably could recite all the lyrics, but he couldn't have named the band for all the money in Palm Beach. It was some one-hit wonder that had played on the radio every hour for a few months before crumbling into obscurity. He remembered listening to this song, or ones like it, back when he and Eli were dating. God, he'd been so young. So foolish.

He reached the sand, and the entire picture came into view.

Eli was there, lounging on an oversized beach towel with blue and white stripes. The portable speaker sat atop a hard plastic cooler. There was also a tote bag on the corner of the towel, containing who knew what. Eli had not yet noticed his arrival, too absorbed with scrolling through what looked like a playlist on his phone.

Nick cleared his throat. "What's all this?"

"Hey!" Eli scrambled to his feet, phone still in hand. He was flushed, his hair damp and hanging in his eyes. He was wearing swim trunks, this time with pink flamingos patterned all over them, and a largely unbuttoned linen shirt that clung to his skin. "Nick, hi. I'm glad you could make it."

"Did you go swimming?" Nick asked.

"Yeah." Eli dragged a hand through his hair. "After that bike ride, I was kind of sweaty, so I thought—" He gave Nick that lopsided grin. "Doesn't matter. Come on, take a load off." He gestured at the expanse of the beach towel, then busied himself with juggling the speaker so he could open the cooler.

Nick approached slowly, his hands stuffed in his pockets. He felt justified in his wariness. The last time he and Eli had been alone together, on Christmas Eve, Eli had taken off without even waiting for the sweat to cool. Now it looked like he was trying to re-create one of their high school date nights. Anyone would feel the whiplash.

"Aha!" Eli brandished a bottle of Boone's Farm, the strawberry kind they used to share as unsophisticated teens. Bits of ice and rivulets of water sloughed off the bottle to patter into the sand. "Can I offer you a Solo cup of this vintage?"

"You brought wine?" Nick knew his eyebrows were rising, but he couldn't help it. "How's that work with you being sober?"

"Okay, first of all, it's barely wine. Second—" Eli bent over the cooler and fished out a can of Walmart-brand seltzer. "This will be my drink of choice tonight. I just thought the wine would be funny."

"Yeah." Nick crossed his arms over his chest. "Hilarious."

Eli slowly lowered the bottle back into the crunch of ice. The portable speaker tipped facedown on the edge of the towel, the song becoming slightly muffled. "You don't have to drink it. It was a joke."

Did he think their entire high school courtship had been a joke? Nick could remember paying a twentysomething lifeguard at the pool to buy Boone's Farm from the gas station so that he and Eli would feel wildly grown-up, sipping too-sweet wine straight from the bottle in between make-out sessions on this very beach. Eli probably found the whole thing very ironic in retrospect. And honestly, Nick was still pretty pissed about being ignored for days.

"Why did you ask me to come out here, Eli?" he asked, letting all the tiredness in his voice actually come through for once.

Eli looked a little wide-eyed, maybe guilty, at Nick's lack of enthusiasm. Good. He should be in apologetic mode, and so far, one bottle of bad booze wasn't cutting it. "Uh, I thought we could spend more time together?" He gestured again to the towel.

"That sounds like a question. Are you asking me?" Nick kept standing ankle deep in the still-warm sand.

"Well, yeah." Eli stood, too, apparently wanting to be at eye level for this conversation. "I want to be honest with you, all right? The other night was amazing. You were—come on, you were perfect. And if you're still interested, I'd like to keep it going."

Nick relaxed a hair. He let his arms fall to his sides. "So you enjoyed it." That crossed off about ten different anxieties from his mental list. "I wasn't sure. You never got back to me."

Eli hung his head. "Yeah, I know. Sorry. I had a whole dramatic thing at Christmas. I still need to smooth things over with my folks. You're, like, the first stop on the Eli Ward Apology Tour."

"Hm. There must have been some wild delays," Nick deadpanned, "considering how long it took you to get on the tour bus."

"Touch," Eli said, looking up at Nick with mischief dancing in his eyes. It was an old joke—their ninth-grade social studies teacher had always mispronounced touché.

It wasn't even a very good gag. Nick laughed anyway. Because Eli would always make him laugh.

Eli smiled at the sound and stepped around the beach towel. "Listen, I'm sorry, I am. But I needed some time to think things over—a lot of things, actually." He paused. "And I also needed time to amass this amazingly seductive setup," he said, gesturing to the items he'd brought.

Nick was trying not to smile. It was hard, though, when Eli knew where to find every one of his buttons. He stuck his tongue in his cheek. "Can I ask how the thinking went?"

A gusty sigh left Eli's lips. "I've concluded that I need to stop worrying so much about what the future holds. I want to be happy when I can be." He stepped forward and stopped right in front of Nick, their bare toes mere inches apart in the sand. "Does that—is that okay?" The wind coming off the water ruffled his hair like he was a goddamn cologne model. Nick was not immune.

He also felt, somewhere in his chest, a kinship with what Eli was saying. Seemed like Nick wasn't the only one doing some soul-searching lately. They were finally both on the same page. This could work. This could really, honestly work.

"Yeah," he said. His throat went dry. "It's okay."

"Yeah?" Eli swayed closer. His hands landed lightly on Nick's hips. His mouth was right there.

Nick held his face in his hands and kissed him.

Eli opened to him without a second's hesitation. He tasted like seawater, the salt burn of it pricking Nick's tongue. It must have been a vigorous swim because he was hot—literally everywhere: his mouth, the skin of his face, his neck where Nick's hands slid to cradle him, the whole line of his damp body where it pressed against Nick's. He could feel water soaking into his khakis from Eli's swim trunks. That, and the way Eli kissed him, like this was inevitable, made him shiver.

Eli pulled away, clearing his throat. "So. You like your late Christmas present?"

"An effort was made," Nick acknowledged as he surveyed the towel and the speaker and the cooler. "The whole 'just like old times' theme is . . . charming."

"Charming! You're charmed?" Eli slid his hands up Nick's chest.

"Thoroughly. You don't expect me to have sex with you on the beach, though, right?"

"Dear god, no. Couple of guys like us, pushing forty? Hard on the joints." Eli smiled with a flash of teeth. "And I can't imagine lube and sand are a good combination."

"Oh, you brought lube, huh?" Nick wrapped his arms around Eli's waist and pulled him closer. He could hear the faint strains of "One Headlight" coming from the speaker. "That's pretty optimistic of you."

"I figured we should have plenty of options available when we get back to your place." They swayed together. Like they were dancing the way they had at the Anvil, except this time it wasn't a gag. Eli snugged his face into the side of Nick's neck. "Besides," he said into his skin, "who knows how long we have. Might as well enjoy it while it lasts."

Nick made a confused hum in his throat. "I'm off work for the rest of the night, and Zoe is over at Laurie's, so we definitely have time."

Eli laughed at that. "No, I mean—you know what I mean." He pulled back, grinning, to look Nick in the eye. "It is what it is. You're still figuring things out; I might be moving to LA; we don't know how much time we have on the clock, but we know it's ticking."

A cold spear of ice went through Nick. He stepped back, feeling the wind pick up, freezing now that he was paying attention. "What do you mean, I'm still—? LA?" There was too much to dig through, and Nick didn't know where to start.

Eli looked at him like he was waiting for a punchline. "Yeah, I might move out there. Or back to New York. Who knows? But that's cool. I am cool with whatever." He patted his palms against Nick's chest like he was playing the bongos. Like this was too amusing. "We are adults doing adult things for a limited amount of . . . adult time."

Nick let go of Eli and took a big step back. "Okay, to be clear, then: this is not a long-term thing, the two of us." He kept his voice even, or tried to. If it wavered, it could be blamed on the night breeze.

Eli licked his lips. It was hard to make out every twitch of his facial expression in the moonlight, but Nick could see the broad strokes. He was still *smiling*. "Right. No, yeah. Exactly. We both know that."

Nick took another step back. Then another. If he hadn't known it before, at least he knew it now. This was nothing serious for Eli; it couldn't be. That was fine. But Nick didn't have to go along with it. He didn't have to pretend it didn't mean what it meant to him.

"Nick?" Eli's mouth fell out of his grin. "Are you okay?"

"Yeah. I'm great," Nick said, sarcasm bordering on a snarl. "I'm going to go home. Go to bed early. You get home safe." He turned and marched through the sand toward the stairs, ignoring the way Eli called after him.

"I thought you were charmed! Thoroughly!"

CHAPTER 24

Eli was going to get snatched by a serial killer, he just knew it. He struggled to pedal his secondhand bike over a bumpy series of potholes. This back road was in poor shape, but it didn't have the deluge of traffic that the main road did. No traffic meant that it was eerily dark and silent. Any moment now, a millennial Ted Bundy was going to jump out of the Brazilian pepper bushes that lined the roadside. The way his night was going, though, it would at least be an improvement.

How had he messed up with Nick so badly? Eli had done everything right: fun atmosphere, a little act of contrition, plenty of communication. . . .

He'd gone out of his way to make sure Nick knew that Eli knew that whatever they did would be a short-term thing, a group project but with orgasms. That was clearly what Nick wanted, so why had he stormed off?

The only logical explanation, as far as Eli could see, was that Nick had been replaced with some kind of clone. Like an alien abduction situation.

Because if extraterrestrials weren't to blame, then the only other option was that Nick wanted—something more. Which was ridiculous. Eli had managed to ensorcell Nick Wu once; no fucking way had he done it again. If Nick wanted a real commitment or whatever, how would that even work? What was Eli supposed to do, move into Nick's rental and drive down to Miami every weekend to get heckled by an audience populated by, he assumed, mostly street-racing enthusiasts? Work part time at some Orlando dinner theater with a four-hour round-trip commute? Play *cruise ships*? If they'd even let him onstage, what with all the fucking drag-show bans that basically tried to keep any trans person from being in public at all.

He'd rather be the ninth victim of the Bath Salts Slasher, please and thank you.

Eli threw himself into pedaling for all he was worth. His tote bag full of seduction supplies—including his well-chosen sex shop purchases—rattled loudly in the bike's basket. At least the cooler strapped above the back wheel was empty of ice, the Boone's Farm abandoned unopened on the beach for some lucky fisherman to find. If he concentrated on getting back to his parents' house in one piece, maybe he could outrun his annoying thoughts at the same time.

Because love wasn't enough, right? Even though he loved Nick, even though Nick was the funniest person he knew (and he wasn't even trying, the dipshit), even though he would be happy being with Nick until they were wrinkly and old and had no teeth—none of that changed the fact that if Eli stayed here for a guy, even one as amazing as Nick, he'd end up miserable and bitter and everything would be ruined anyway. So maybe it was better that he'd ruined it all now.

His phone vibrated in his pocket. Eli almost fell off his bike, he stopped so fast. Straddling the Huffy in the tall grass by the roadside, he fumbled to get his phone out.

His caller ID informed him it was Margo. He deflated, but answered.

"How's Boca?" he said between panting breaths.

"Shut up," Margo returned. Her voice held a giddy note Eli had never heard before. "Why do you sound like you just ran a marathon? Fuck it, doesn't matter. Are you sitting down?"

Eli looked both ways along the stretch of empty road. "Not really possible at the moment."

Margo wasn't listening. "*Dorothy*'s happening!" she yelled into the phone.

Eli had to hold it out, far away from his ear. "Seriously?" he shouted from a distance.

"Yes! They called me a few minutes ago. We're going to wait to announce after New Year's, obviously. Shooting starts at the end of summer. It's happening, Eli. It's finally happening." She squealed like a sea lion at an aquarium show.

"Wow. Congrats, Marg. That's so exciting." For a moment, Eli forgot all his petty problems. He leaned over the handlebars on one forearm, feeling pride for his friend well up in his chest. "You're a legend. I mean it. You're going to crush it."

"*We're* going to crush it," she said, "if you want to be my Felix, that is."

Eli stood up a little straighter. "So they're okay with me? It's not an issue?"

"Not only is it not an issue, when they heard I wanted to cast a comedian with no acting credits, they were thrilled. Dude, they're getting you cheap. Big names are expensive."

"That's . . . the most backhanded compliment I've ever received."

"You're missing the point: You're not an albatross. I showed them your stand-up. They know how hilarious you are. I told you, you're good."

Alone on a dark road in the middle of nowhere, Eli allowed the tears to well in his eyes. Hearing Margo say that—he realized it was something he'd needed to hear. For a long time. He dragged a hand through his hair, biting his lip. "You're sure?" He hated how his voice shook, but he got the words out. "They—they really want me?"

"You turnip, of course they want you. We all do."

Eli could feel the iron bands around his chest loosen. It was like he could breathe again after months of getting only sips of oxygen. He wasn't poison; he still had something to offer. If he had a mirror, he'd be doing his best Stuart Smalley impression. *And gosh darn it, people like me.* Sometimes it wasn't easy to believe that without proof, and this was proof.

Maybe it wasn't outside the realm of possibility that Nick wanted him too.

Oh. As soon as the thought came, so did reality. With a resounding crash.

"Eli? You still there? God damn it, did the call drop?" Margo sounded a million miles away instead of only a couple hundred.

He shook himself. "Yeah. I'm here."

"So? What are we thinking? Can I put your name in the press release or . . . ?"

Eli swallowed hard. "Can I think about it for a couple days?"

Margo made a blustery sound of acceptance. "Sure, absolutely. Big decision. Big move. I get it." There was a pause on the line, then: "Okay, I'm trying to get it, honest. But what the hell else is there to think about, E?"

"You're going to make fun of me."

"Well, now you *have* to tell me."

"It's just . . . LA is so far."

"Yes, geographically and culturally, it is quite some distance from New York," Margo conceded.

"No, I mean, it's far from here. Where Nick is."

"Ah." He could hear her eyebrows winging upward, they were that loud. "Okay! So things with Nick are getting serious?"

Eli sighed. "No, I'm pretty sure I destroyed every chance I had with him."

There was a long stretch of silence over the phone line before Margo said, "I'm going to need you to help connect the dots for me here. If you fumbled your ex-boyfriend, why is this a factor in deciding whether to take this job?"

"I don't know." Eli licked his lips. "It just—it is." He didn't know where to begin because the idea had only now occurred to him, but he knew he wanted to go for it. If he left New Port Stephen without telling Nick how much he cared for him, then he would always wonder.

Margo hummed. "Look, on the one hand, the showrunner side of me wants to tell you to get your head out of your ass and pack your suitcase, because this is the chance of a lifetime. The unselfish best friend side of me, though? Would probably say that if you like this guy more than you like the idea of becoming an Emmy contender"—Eli snorted at that, but Margo steamrolled over him—"then that might be a big clue about what your next move should be. Does he know you feel this way?"

"Not yet," Eli said. "But I think he should. Soon."

"That's the spirit. Says the half of me that isn't selfish." That got a laugh out of them both. "And you'd really consider staying in Florida for this guy?" Margo asked.

"I think I could be . . . flexible too," Eli said. "You've got to be willing to make sacrifices, right? For the big one?" Jesus, what a difference one conversation could make. He could go for it. He could tell Nick how he really felt. And if Nick felt the same, then maybe staying in the Neeps wouldn't be so bad. Plenty of queer people managed to live happy, fulfilled lives in towns like this.

Eli could learn how to do that if it meant he kept Nick in his life. He needed time to figure out how to approach this; he needed something better than the retro beach idea, something that said all the right things in the right way. He'd only have one shot at this, and that was if he was lucky.

"Keep me posted," Margo told him. "Either way, I love you, okay?"

"Thanks, Marg. Love you too. And seriously, congrats. You deserve this. If anyone deserves it, it's you."

"I know," she said. He could picture her tossing her hair in a pantomime of confidence. "Thanks for noticing."

He hung up and started biking down the road with renewed determination.

By the time he got home, it was well past midnight. His parents' car was back in the driveway, and a light had been left lit on the front porch. Eli stowed his bike and crept inside, willing the front door not to creak. The last thing he wanted was to wake up his folks. After their Christmas Day blowup, they'd been dancing around each other, not quite cold-shouldering but definitely avoidant.

He turned to the left to put his shoes on the rack and nearly had a heart attack. His mom and dad were sitting primly on the sofa with their hands folded in their laps, wide awake and clearly waiting for him to make an appearance.

"Well, well, well," his dad drawled, "if it isn't our only child, home at last."

"It's late," his mom said pointedly.

"Didn't know I still had a curfew." Eli scrunched his eyes closed. He hadn't meant to snap at them. "Sorry. It's been a day."

"We want to talk to you," Cora said.

"About that discussion we started over presents," Wendall added, like it could have been anything else.

"I want to talk to you, too, actually." Eli finished slotting his shoes in the rack and padded over to an armchair, then thought twice about sitting on the upholstery. "Uh, I'm very sweaty. I biked, like, ten miles today. Okay if I stand?"

His dad got to his feet. "We'll all stand."

"Dad, that's silly, you don't have to—"

"Hold on, I'm getting there." His mom struggled to leave the couch's cushy embrace. "Christ alive, I've been sitting so long my legs are asleep."

"Here, honey, let me." Wendall took her by the hands.

"No, I've got it!"

Eli tilted his head back to look at the ceiling. "We really don't all need to stand."

Cora got upright with a huff of triumph. She smoothed her gray-streaked hair from her face. "Nonsense. We're a family, and families stick together."

"What your mother is trying to say," his dad said, "is that we understand if you don't want to move back in with us. We support you, no matter what your decision is."

"Even if your decision is not financially sound," Cora put in.

"Even then," Wendall confirmed.

Eli could feel a headache forming, a real doozy too.

"We wouldn't ask you to pay any rent, at least for the first year."

"And if, after a year, you're still not back on your feet, we'd work something out."

"But again, if you'd rather not—"

"We totally support you."

"Thanks. I know I said some pretty shitty things about this place," Eli said, "and it hurt your feelings. I'm sorry. I love you guys, I do. I just hate this town sometimes."

His dad nodded absently. "Well, the whole state is kind of a write-off."

"Lord, I hope our governor doesn't run for president," Cora muttered. "What a disaster that would be."

"Don't worry," Eli said. "No one's going to vote for a short guy. People don't take us seriously." It was a joke, though he prayed it was true.

"If we could be closer to you in New York or wherever you end up, we would," Cora said. "How could we afford to move, though? Have you seen housing prices lately?"

"You get on that Zillow—on the web—and you'll see how right your mother is."

"It's madness."

"Completely untenable. When we moved into this house, do you know how much we paid?"

"Dad." Eli held up both hands. "As much as I'm loving the acknowledgment of your Boomer privilege, can I finish? Please?"

Wendall made a grand "after you" gesture.

"Thank you." Eli took a deep breath. "I have a tendency of going too far when I'm trying to get you to understand how I'm feeling. I want to be honest with you without making you cry. I'm not sure I'll always succeed, but I'll try my best."

"Oh, sweetie." Cora smiled, her eyes welling up with tears—happy ones. "That's all we could ever ask."

"We're trying our best, too, by the way," Wendall said. "I know it doesn't always seem like it, but we are."

"There's absolutely no rush," his mom said. "You can take your time figuring out what comes next."

"Yeah, about that." Eli looked down at his bare feet. "I kind of need to make a decision sooner rather than later." The whole story spilled out: Margo getting the show greenlit, the offer to take a lead role—

"But you're not an actor," his mom said. "You're a terrible liar too."

His dad put a hand on her arm. "Let him finish, Cora."

—how cool he thought Zoe was, the amount of time he'd been spending with Nick, everything. Well, except the part where they hooked up. His parents didn't need to know about that part.

"I think I love him," he said. "Or I still do. And maybe he feels similarly, I don't know. But I want to find out before I make any big moves."

Cora raised her hand in the air. "Sorry, I'm confused. I thought Nick Wu used to be married to a woman, no?"

"That doesn't mean anything. Some people fancy all sorts," his dad said.

"Oh! So he's a bi-SEX-ual."

"Why are you pronouncing it like that?" Eli asked. "And maybe. I don't know."

Wendall pulled his face into an elongated shape. "You should probably ask him before making any declarations."

Eli put his fingertips to his temples to try to rub some of the headache away. "What I mean is, he's not really hung up on labels right now? Or decided on one? But I do know he's interested. In me. At least, he was."

"Oh." His mom looked at his dad with wide eyes, and Eli watched them silently communicate for a good minute before Wendall spoke for them both.

"Well, we've always liked that Nick Wu."

CHAPTER 25

December 31

The Thirsty Manatee's New Year's Eve party was a tradition stretching back to the eighties. Reservations were normally booked solid by the summer, with the same old-timers attending year after year. A band played Jimmy Buffett and Tom Petty covers out on the patio, where a portion of the deck had been cleared as a dance floor. The buffet-style dinner was replenished all night long: steamed crab legs, peel-and-eats, cocktail meatballs, fried clams, thinly sliced roast beef, cheesy garlic bread, and the famous house-made key lime pie. The servers had only drink orders to fill, along with distributing the complimentary champagne (technically Asti Spumante) toast at midnight. After the ball drop and a rousing "Auld Lang Syne" sing-along led by the band, a continental breakfast replaced the dinner buffet, and all the guests had another hour to sober up with some bagels and lox before making their way home.

That was the plan, anyway. Nick checked his wristwatch. About twenty minutes to midnight. Sandra swooped by, a pair of novelty New Year's Eve glasses balanced atop her head.

"Smooth as a baby's butt, boss man," she said. "Quit worrying;

it's giving you wrinkles." She turned around and used her behind to shove open the door to the back of house, tossing Nick a saucy wink.

Nick touched his forehead gingerly. Sandra was a liar. He was *not* getting wrinkles. She was right about one thing, though: everything was going fine tonight. No one had gotten sick in the restrooms, no one was so blitzed that Nick needed to call them a taxi, no fights, no underaged kids trying to sneak a sip of Malibu. The restaurant was full of people dressed in their sequined finery, eating way too many crab legs and grooving to "Fins."

This should have left Nick with a sense of self-satisfaction for a job well done, but ever since he'd left Eli standing on their beach, he'd been feeling—dejected. Like there was a weight of sadness on his shoulders that he wasn't quite ready to shake off. Eli had called and texted, but Nick hadn't responded. The petty part of him was happy to give Eli a taste of his own medicine, but the sadder half thought that a clean break was best.

The only reprieve from his gloomy outlook had been his early-morning swim with the Masters' team last Thursday; for a few hours, his head felt clear. His body moved in patterns that had been drilled into it since he was seven, and his thoughts slipped into a near-meditative state. He knew he was going to be okay, but it still hurt knowing that Eli was not going to remain in his life in any meaningful way. Surely he was allowed to mourn that for a little while?

Not too much longer, though. He looked at the spangled clock above the bar while he helped one of the line cooks refill the meatball station. In a few minutes, the year would be over, along with the self-imposed time limit on wallowing over Eli. Once that clock struck twelve, Nick was resolved to pick himself up and get over this bump in the road. Already his brain was coming up with peppy kernels of wisdom, like "whatever the outcome, reconnecting with Eli gave you a better sense of yourself, and that's not nothing" and "it's completely valid if someone doesn't return your feelings; you're still a good person, regardless."

Penny clambered atop an upturned wine crate behind the bar, cupping her hands into a megaphone. "Ten-minute warning! Everyone, make sure you get some champagne for the toast!" Dozens of plastic flutes were already lined up along the bar, and servers zipped around delivering them to each table.

Sandra appeared at Nick's side and nudged him in the ribs. "Care for one, sir?" she asked, presenting her tray with one lone flute remaining.

Nick shook his head. "You take it. In fact, tell all the servers they can have one if they want. I'll bring some to the cooks too. We should all toast together."

"But not you?" Sandra's eyebrows—streaked in multicolored glitter for the occasion—lifted.

"No thanks. I'm okay." Nick didn't feel much like drinking tonight. No reason. Definitely not because he was pining for someone who also wouldn't be drinking if he were here.

"All right," Sandra said, and disappeared to spread the word to the other servers.

Nick grabbed a tray bristling with drinks and headed into the back. The cooks hailed the delivery like he was a conquering hero, except for Steph, a seasoned cook with a shaved head and two full sleeves of tattoos. She downed her portion before going right back to unwrapping a lox-and-red-onion platter. "I've got things to do," she said.

"Fair." Nick glanced out of the kitchen passway as he collected the empty flutes. The dining room looked like it was in good shape. Most people were trickling back from the dance floor to claim their champagne and wait for the ball drop on the bar's TV to start in earnest.

As the crowd thinned, Nick saw him standing by the front entrance—Eli, his hair combed neatly, wearing the same violet floral shirt he'd worn when they'd gone dancing.

He was up on his tiptoes, scanning the room. As Nick watched in frozen shock, Eli stopped Sandra with a touch to her elbow and said something that Nick couldn't hear over the noise of the party. Sandra answered him with a smile, turning to point toward the kitchen and Nick.

Eli looked in his direction. They locked eyes, Eli's warm and bright. Nick knew he had to do something.

Unfortunately, the "something" was to drop out of sight and crouch behind the fryers. What the hell was Eli thinking, showing up at Nick's workplace after the falling-out they'd had? Nick didn't have time for this. His fresh start was scheduled to begin in mere minutes. Maybe hiding like a kid playing peekaboo wasn't the best solution, but it was the only one Nick's frazzled mind could come up with at a moment's notice.

"Hey, boss?" Steph nudged him with the toe of her clog. "Can you, uh, get out of my kitchen before someone trips over you?"

"Yep! Sorry! Thought I saw a hazard. On the ground. That would be dangerous." Nick stood slowly, feeling his face heat. Thankfully, when he looked into the dining room, Eli was gone. Must have gotten the message loud and clear. Despite himself, Nick's heart dropped another inch in his chest.

He left the back as gracefully as he could after making such a huge ass of himself, then nearly collided with Eli as he stepped out front. Eli was standing right in front of the swinging door, a determined yet apologetic look on his face.

"Hey. Can we talk?"

"No," Nick said, the word slipping out more affronted than firm. "We can't. I'm a little busy right now."

Penny, dashing by with a case of extra plastic flutes, must have heard only the tail end of what Nick said, because she called out to him as she went, "We've got everything handled if you need a break, Nick!"

Nick couldn't argue with that. Looking around the restaurant, it was obvious even to someone outside the business that everything was on track. Servers were making their rounds like clockwork. The buffet's changeover was already in progress. Every patron had their champagne or preferred drink clutched in their hand, chattering away as midnight neared. Nick wasn't needed at all. It rankled, but it was true.

"Please," Eli said. He really had the biggest, saddest eyes in the world. Just like his namesake. "It'll only take a second."

Nick heaved a sigh. "Come on. It'll be quieter outside." He led the way out to the dock.

Eli was talking before Nick's foot hit the first plank of wood. "I'm sorry about showing up like this, but—I didn't know how else to get in touch. This was the only time and place where I could be sure to catch you."

"Well, you're here." Nick shoved his hands in his pockets and walked to the end of the dock, as far from the party as possible. It didn't feel right to be having a private conversation so close to all that revelry. "Go ahead and say what you want to say."

At best, Nick expected an apology. A very mature acknowledgment that they wanted different things, and Eli was flattered but yadda yadda yadda. At worst, Eli was here to read Nick the riot act, tell him off for getting in so deep when Eli had made it clear he was not interested in anything serious.

Eli stepped in front of Nick, drawing himself up to his full height, which wasn't a lot. "So, first of all—I love you, right? Obviously. And I want to say—"

"Wait. What?" Nick said.

Eli held up a hand. "Hold on, please let me finish. I want to say—"

Nick stared at him. "You don't love me."

"What? Yes I do." Eli face fell like a dive-bombing pelican.

"No you don't. And if you did, it would definitely not be obvious." Nick scoffed. "You practically ran out of my house after we slept together."

Eli gestured with both hands at an area of nothing in front of him, like he was pointing out evidence that didn't exist. "There was no running. I didn't run! It wasn't even a brisk jog."

But Nick was just starting to warm to his theme. "And then, the other night on the beach, you said there was no way we could be anything more than a one-night stand. Several-night stand. Whatever."

"Right, but I was only saying that because I thought that's what *you* were trying to say!"

"I never said anything like that!"

"Jesus Christ and all the saints." Eli buried his face in his hands, gave a muffled scream, and then resurfaced with his fingertips tented under his chin. "Okay. Let me start over."

Nick shrugged expansively. "Fine."

"Thank you. God." Eli took a deep breath. "You know me better than anyone else in the world, Nick. Getting to know you all over again these last few weeks, it's been amazing. I'm lighter with you. I laugh harder around you. You're so fucking funny and you're not even trying, which is annoying because I put so much goddamn effort into making you laugh."

Nick's lips parted. "You do?"

"Yeah. Tons. But only because you have the best laugh, and I want to hear it all the time." Nick could see his throat bob as he swallowed. "And I really thought I was wearing my heart on my sleeve here, but I guess not, so: I love you, I do. And I'm sorry it's taken all this"—he waved his hands back and forth between them—"to get that out in the open. You're important to me, and I don't want you to feel any pressure about anything. I just . . . wanted you to know, I guess."

Nick's heart was in his throat. He couldn't get a single word around it. Shouts rose from behind them. The countdown had begun. "Ten! Nine! Eight!"

Eli couldn't seem to let the silence between them stretch on, because he plowed ahead: "And in case it's not clear, I want serious. Because I can't imagine ever wanting anything but the whole shebang with you."

"Seven! Six! Five!"

"Foot rubs and weekends with Zoe and sick days in front of the TV. All of that. You're the person I want for everything," Eli said.

"Four! Three! Two!"

"Nick? Am I too late?"

"One! Happy New Year!" A roar of noisemakers and wordless shouts erupted from the restaurant. At the end of the dock, Nick stared at Eli in silence as the band struck up "Auld Lang Syne."

"I don't know what to say," Nick said.

He could see the light dim in Eli's eyes. "Yeah. No. I get that." He ducked his head and shuffled back a step, then thought better of it when it brought him perilously close to the edge of the dock. "This was kind of a dramatic long shot, right? I mean, New Year's, the ball drop—if this were a movie, I'd get to kiss you at midnight and everyone would cheer. Hooray." He shook a fist half-heartedly in the air. "Sometimes things don't work out the way you want. At least I got it all off my chest, huh?"

Nick felt like he was underwater in the way most people meant it: disoriented, breathless, senses muffled, no clue what to do next. But then he remembered: he was at his best underwater.

He reached for Eli's hand and pried it out of a fist. Their fingers threaded together.

"I love you too," he said. "Never stopped, actually."

Eli's mouth fell open. A sheen of happy tears formed in his eyes, colored by the fairy lights that hung along the patio. "And you couldn't have said that forty-five seconds ago?"

Nick shook his head, a smile already creeping across his face. "Too cliché."

"You rebel." Eli lifted their joined hands to his lips and kissed Nick's knuckles. His eyes squeezed shut as he did so. "Wow. Okay," he murmured into his skin. "You love me too."

Then he looked up and kissed Nick. Or Nick kissed him. It was impossible to say who leaned in first and who followed whose lead. It didn't matter. Nick had his arms full of warm, happy Eli, and that was all he cared about.

Actually. No. There was one thing he needed to make sure Eli knew.

He pulled back from the kiss and leaned his forehead against Eli's. "So we agree—boyfriends? It sounds so . . ."

"Like we're eighteen again?" Eli leaned in to peck him on the chin. "I don't hate it."

Nick wasn't sure why that made him smile, but it did. "Okay. Boyfriends. I am a man dating another man—and that man is fine with me being some currently undefined flavor of questioning?"

Eli stared at him like he was speaking Greek. "Dude. Yes. You're my favorite person. I am fine with everything you are or could ever be." He snugged his arms tighter around Nick's neck. "I don't need you to pick out a flag today, or ever, if you don't want to."

What could Nick do but kiss him again, thoroughly, with all the promise of the years behind them and ahead of them? Eli's fingers slid into his hair, pulling him down. The sounds of people cheering and tooting their noisemakers were a distant hum to Nick's ears. The only thing he wanted to listen to was the sound Eli's breath made when it hitched like that.

This time, Eli was the one to pull away, his mouth as red as fruit punch. "Awkward question, but when are you off the clock?"

"I can get everything shut down and cleared out by one," Nick said. His hands were kneading at Eli's waist like they couldn't wait to get under his layers of clothing. "Can you stick around that long?"

Eli cocked his head in mock disappointment. "Well, I took an Uber here, and I'm sure surge pricing is going to be wild now, so really, I don't have any choice except to go home with you."

The year was already looking up.

CHAPTER 26

This time, Eli didn't make fun of Nick's neatly made bed. He was too busy getting pressed facedown into it.

Nick covered his naked body like a weighted blanket, listening to Eli's downright sinful moans as all their bare skin made contact. When they were younger Eli would ask for this, for Nick to be heavy and hot against his back, even in the summer heat. He claimed it was better than visiting a chiropractor.

"Fuck, that's nice," Eli said into the cascade of pillows.

Nick grinned as he pressed kisses to the back of Eli's neck. "What can I do for you?" he asked. He was already on his way to fully hard, grinding against Eli's ass. Eli hissed in pleasure. God, he had a great ass. "I can fuck you, you can fuck me, anything."

Eli turned his head so he could speak more freely. "Okay. Pause."

Nick stopped grinding, stilling into marble above Eli. "What's wrong?"

"Nothing." Eli wriggled onto his back so he could look up at Nick. "But you know it's not either/or, right? Penetration, I mean. There are other things. Better things, arguably." He quirked his mouth to one side. "I will totally dick you down if you want. Just know there are options."

Nick licked his lips. He didn't mean to, but hearing Eli talk like that—it was exciting, and scary, and a million other things that made him want to do all the options under the sun if it was with Eli. "So you *did* bring a strap this time?"

Eli's brows drew together. "What? No. Why would I—? I was making a big dramatic gesture showing up at your place of business to confess my feelings. Bringing sex toys to that conversation is a tad presumptuous, don't you think?"

"I'm confused. How are you going to dick me down, potentially, without it?"

The look on Eli's face was pure sorrow. "I keep forgetting you're new to queer sex. What's it like to go through life with zero creativity?"

Nick pressed a pillow over Eli's face and pretended to smother him while Eli howled in laughter. "You don't have to be so judgmental about it," he said as Eli launched a tickling counterattack at his ribs. He jerked like a fish while Eli flailed. He flung the pillow aside and kissed Eli's ridiculous red face. They quieted somewhat, their faces so close Nick could see every fleck of gold in Eli's eyes. "But yeah. You might have to teach me some new things."

"Well, let me introduce my secret weapon," Eli whispered. He held up his hand and wiggled his fingers at Nick like he was saying a coy hello.

"Hands," Nick said flatly, and it sounded a little rude, so he tried again. "Yes, I can see how you might—use those. For many applications."

"You don't need a big dick to dick someone down," Eli said with a grin. "Not to mention, better maneuverability." He joined his middle three fingers in a sort of triangle and crooked them into a shape that had Nick's head spinning.

Saliva flooded into his mouth. The idea of Eli's fingers inside him made every nerve in his skin stand up and take notice. It seemed both impossible and intriguing. But if they got into fingering territory, Nick assumed that lube would—should, according to his intense googling—be involved, and the only thing he had on hand was the paltry tube of hand cream in his bedside table drawer that was on standby for masturbatory sessions. Embarrassing. And such a stereotypical straight-guy move that he couldn't be sure Eli wouldn't run screaming.

He was staring so hard at Eli's hands, he almost missed the amused smirk spreading across his face.

"Uh." He covered Eli's hand with his own, bringing it down to the sheets. "Let's try that sometime in the future." The near future, after Nick stopped at a pharmacy to pick up something suitably water-based. "Tonight, I want to . . . I don't know. Be close to you."

"Yeah?" Eli's eyes lit up, more brilliant than any light display. "I'd like that." He shifted under Nick's body to bring one lightly furred leg around Nick's waist. Their cocks aligned in a way that was so natural, Nick had only to rock his hips the tiniest bit to feel all of Eli. Eli returned the favor in spades, grinding up against him in a way that sent Nick's spine into sparks.

A flash of memory: being seventeen and doing this for the first time in his life in almost the same position with the same person. Back then, Nick had been sweaty and fumbling, eager and breathless, endlessly grateful that he was with Eli for this and no one else.

It was nothing like that now. It was better.

Nick lifted his head from where he'd buried it in the crook

of Eli's neck and took Eli's face in his hands. He wanted to make sure they could see each other; that seemed important. "I'm glad it's you," he said, still rolling his hips. "I'm glad you're here with me now."

Eli's smile broke across his face like dawn. No pretension, no jokes, for once. He slid his hands along the planes of Nick's back, slick with sweat. "No place I'd rather be," he said.

Nick groaned as his cock slipped into the humid crease of Eli's thigh. He was actually going to get off rutting like some teenager. He couldn't even be embarrassed about it; it was, after all, one of their greatest hits. Eli craned his neck up and kissed him through it, letting him stutter and shake and whimper as he came.

"That's it, sweetheart," he said between nips of Nick's lips. "You're so good. Fuck, Nick."

Nick had left a sticky mess between their stomachs, and he swiped his fingertips through it. Some old instinct urged him through his post-orgasmic daze; that was the only explanation for this level of motor control, which was to say, any. He reached down and rubbed at Eli's hard little cock, using his own come to ease the way.

Eli's eyes flew wide at that, his hips lifting in a bid to get more. "Oh," he said under his breath. "Oh—god."

"Yeah?" Nick couldn't help but smile down at him. He'd always liked it when Eli went from talking a mile a minute to forgetting every word he knew.

Eli's hands scrabbled at Nick's wrist, guiding him. "Right there, right—" His limbs trembled and his eyes shut tight. Nick soaked in the picture he made, greedy for it. The last time, he wasn't able to see much, being on his knees. Like this, he could drink in every twitch, every bitten-off groan, every jumping muscle. Damn, he was gorgeous.

After, a much-needed quiet enveloped the bedroom. Eli was as boneless as a house cat, going where Nick arranged him without much complaint. He made a pillow out of him, resting his head on Eli's chest, the rise and fall of it lulling him into a state of complete relaxation. They were still sticky, but Nick couldn't be bothered to get up yet. He twined his limbs around Eli and drifted for a long span of minutes.

"I—" Eli's voice croaked into the quiet eventually, "Really. Enjoyed that."

Nick hummed in agreement. "Want to go again?" He thought it polite to offer.

Eli, thankfully, scoffed at the idea. "Are you kidding? I'm not seventeen anymore."

"Thank god." Nick melted even more atop his—boyfriend. Yeah, boyfriend. "I think I pulled something in my back toward the end there."

"Oh, my joints will for sure complain about this tomorrow," Eli murmured. He turned his head enough to press a kiss into Nick's hair. "Want a rubdown?"

"I thought we agreed round two isn't going to happen," Nick teased.

"You know I meant a massage." Eli hit him on the arm and flipped their positions, propping himself on his elbows. "Now turn over."

Nick obligingly rolled onto his stomach, pillowing his chin on his folded hands. "You don't have to," he said.

"Shut up. I want to."

Eli's hands were surprisingly gentle on his back, sweeping over the planes of Nick's scapula, tracing along his spine. His fingers pressed into the sore muscles at Nick's lower back, and Nick groaned in relief. He hadn't been joking before; he really wasn't going to come again tonight, but a low hum of desire still pooled in his belly. It felt good just to be touched like this, like Eli was handling something precious.

"Ooh, that's a bad knot." Eli's voice sounded like it was coming from miles underwater. His thumbs dug in where Nick's neck met his shoulder. At first there was pain, but soon Nick felt the stubborn muscle unwind under Eli's hands.

"That feels so good," he mumbled into the sheets.

Eli left off the massage and draped himself over Nick's body, resting his cheek at the base of Nick's neck. "*You* feel good."

Nick could feel the heat of his skin, the damp of his sweat, the mess they were making of the sheets. The desire in his stomach expanded and sighed but didn't sharpen into anything urgent.

"We're so old," Nick said, his body shaking with silent laughter.

"Yeah." Eli let out a long breath along Nick's skin. "Isn't it great?"

It was, actually.

They eventually shifted positions, Eli on his back with Nick's head on his chest. Nick was on the cusp of drifting off—when was the last time he'd fallen asleep so easily?—when Eli spoke again. "We don't have to decide tonight, obviously, since my brain is oatmeal, but to be clear: I'll move back here if that's what you want."

Nick picked his head up with much effort and stared down at Eli. He was still flushed pink, but his mouth was set in a serious line. "But you hate it here."

"I . . . dislike some parts of it," Eli conceded. His hand sought out Nick's and curled it into his sternum. "But you're a big checkmark in the pro column."

That was sweet enough to make Nick's heart flutter, but he couldn't stop worrying. "It's not that simple. This is still Florida we're talking about. What would you do about health care?"

Eli's answer came so fast, Nick could tell he'd been thinking about it. "I'd stockpile my T. I already do, a little, just to be safe.

Worst comes to worst, I'll break the law. Get it from Canada or something."

Nick squeezed Eli's hand hard. He felt all kinds of protective and helpless, and wished they didn't have to talk about this in the first place. "How can you be so calm about that?"

"Oh, I'm not calm. I have an internal meltdown every time I think about it. But I'm not going to let some lump of gorgonzola in a bad suit dictate my whole life." Eli squeezed his hand in return. "I want to give this a real shot, and if that means staying here instead of moving to LA, then that's what I'll do."

"Wait, what's this about LA?" Nick shook his head. "I'm out of the loop."

"Oh, Margo wants me to be in the show she's making." Eli sighed like this was the biggest annoyance in his life. "It's a whole thing. I told her I'm not an actor. She keeps saying who cares, how can I give up this chance, blah blah blah."

Nick's heart sank. The tentative visions of Eli living here in New Port Stephen—with him? A few streets away at his parents'? Close enough to see every day, regardless—evaporated right before his eyes. He loved Eli too much to try to keep them.

"Eli," he said slowly, "you have to take it."

Eli looked at him funny. "No I don't."

"Yes. You do." Nick leaned down and kissed him. It was a soft admonishment, and a promise. "I've heard the way you talk about this show. You'd be amazing at it."

The pink of Eli's face deepened to red. "Big disagree. I could just as easily fuck it up. That's what I do, right?"

"Stop talking about my boyfriend that way. I get that the last year has been hard for you, but having setbacks doesn't make you a failure; it makes you human. If you don't take this shot, you'll always wonder what could have been."

Eli's eyes went round and a little wet. "But what about you?" His hand squeezed Nick's. "Don't you want to give this a chance too?"

"Of course I do." Nick hesitated, because this was a lot to bring up on Day One of their new thing, but he dove in anyway. "What if we try long distance, see how it goes?"

Eli groaned. "Long distance is so hard, though!"

"Is it harder than moving back to a town that gives you panic attacks?" Nick challenged. Eli adopted an appropriate look of chagrin at that. "Look, I know it's not ideal, but I'm willing to give it a try. Who knows? If things go well, we can think about something more permanent." He shrugged. "California is closer to Arizona, after all."

Now Eli was the one with the confused frown. "Wait, what's in Arizona?"

"Right, we haven't talked much since Christmas." Nick blew out a gust of air. "Laurie and Zoe are moving out there next year. We decided recently."

"Holy shit." Eli struggled to sit up, coming eye to eye with Nick. "Are you okay?" His stricken expression made Nick's heart grip the cage bars of his ribs all over again.

"Yeah," he said. Then, because he wanted to be honest with Eli if they were really going to do this, "No. I'm not. But it's not about me. Laurie and I talked it over—a lot—and this is where we ended up."

Eli nodded a few times. He licked his lips in thought. "So. Maybe California?" He looked at Nick with wild excitement dancing in his eyes.

"Maybe. Yeah." Nick let himself feel the bubble of hope in his belly, rising to the surface. He could picture himself on the West Coast. Maybe he'd even text his old college friend Ken in San Francisco, see what he was up to. For the first time—in months?

Years? A decade?—he could see a long stretch of fresh life ahead of him, something exciting and undiscovered and *his*. "Are we doing this?"

"We're doing this." Eli laughed, his head thrown back, his throat exposed. "It's a Christmas miracle!"

"It's New Year's," Nick reminded him, and kissed him to drive the point home.

EPILOGUE

One Year Later

Eli maneuvered the rented truck down his parents' street at approximately half a mile an hour. It wasn't his fault that his driving skills were still rusty. Nick had told him over their last FaceTime call that living in LA for nearly a year should have built up his confidence on the road by now, but clearly that had not happened and probably never would.

"Please, Lord Jesus," he muttered as he finally completed the slight turn, coming within a few inches of sideswiping a mailbox shaped like a marlin. The mailbox belonged to a house that was flying a MAGA flag so old and decrepit it was practically ribbons, so Eli wasn't too concerned about decapitating the fish. He didn't want to scrape the paint and lose his deposit on the U-Haul, however.

His parents were waiting for him at the end of the driveway in front of their overly decorated house. Along with Max. And Uncle Hank. And the dresser that Eli's mom had insisted that he and Nick would need when they finally moved in together.

"It's a great dresser! Solid mahogany, none of that particleboard. And look how deep these drawers go," she had said on their last FaceTime call, pointing her phone's camera into a black pit that could have been a coal mine for all Eli could tell.

He'd sighed. "I have a dresser already." It was fine. It was from one of those websites that was one step up from IKEA.

"Son." Wendall Ward's face had appeared on the screen. "Take the dresser."

So here he was, making a slight detour on the way to pick up his boyfriend so they could start their new life together because Cora really, really wanted him to have Great-Aunt Margery's dresser. But he hadn't known it was going to be a party.

"Why are you all here?" Eli asked as he dismounted from the truck.

His parents hugged him fiercely before his mom said, "To help you load up!"

"You didn't think we were going to let you fellas handle the move by yourself, did you?" Hank tightened the Velcro waist . . . cincher . . . thing that he wore around his middle; Eli didn't know what it was called, only that it conjured up images of dock-workers and the guys who stocked shelves at Costco.

Eli caught Max's eye. There was a silent communication the likes of which sometimes passes between the two queer cousins in a family. It said, in both directions, "Are you seeing this? Because I am seeing this."

They loaded the dresser into the U-Haul amid much debate about the best way to do so—Eli had no horse in the race so he did not enter the fray—along with the single piece of luggage that Eli had brought for his visit. He'd had a nice, relaxing Christmas with his folks and Nick, but he was more than ready to get back to the West Coast.

Cora insisted on riding with Eli while "the rest of the boys plus Max follow in the car." They made a slow parade toward

Nick's place, the five-minute drive taking more than twice that. It gave Eli's mom a chance to beam at him over the center console, her eyes sparkling.

"Mom, I'm driving," Eli said, negotiating the truck to a stop at a sign.

"I know. I'm so proud of you."

"For the driving? Because I'm not very good at it."

"No, for going on such an adventure. LA! Acting! Moving in with Nick," she said. "You look so happy."

Eli was certain he looked as frazzled as a bad driver could while in control of a rented vehicle, but he shot Cora a smile anyway. "Thanks, Mom."

He thought about how much his life had changed in one short year; there was no comparison between the Eli at the wheel and the Eli he had been last Christmas. *Friends of Dorothy* had wrapped its first season a few weeks ago, and the pilot episode would air in three months. Margo was already hearing good things about a possible renewal. "Our marketing department isn't fucking around. We'll be up for an Emmy for sure," she'd told Eli, and for once, he couldn't tell if she was joking. "We'll somehow lose to *Barry* even though it's been off the air for years, but you know what? I won't be bitter."

Finally, the caravan of two pulled up outside Nick's place. Nick came through the front door wearing a huge smile and the Dodgers sweatshirt Eli had shipped to him last month, when the temperature in Florida started dipping below eighty. For a gag gift, Nick was taking it very seriously.

Eli climbed out of the U-Haul and into Nick's arms. He smelled amazing. Eli squeezed him tighter.

Nick laughed against his cheek. "Happy to see me?" It'd been less than a day since they'd seen each other, but it was their sappy little inside joke every time they reunited.

"Yeah," Eli said. "And just plain happy."

"Can't wait to become a fellow Californian." Nick held him out at arm's length, his gaze traveling over Eli's bare arms and legs. "Perpetual tan and everything."

"Don't forget, I know three facts about wine. They give you a pamphlet when you move out there. You'll get yours in the mail." Eli listened to Nick laugh, soaking it in before clutching at Nick's bicep through the sweatshirt's cozy fabric. "With a body like this, you'll be on Muscle Beach in no time. Thank you, lap swim." A year of swimming had defined his arms, legs, and shoulders, though he remained somewhat soft around the middle. Eli was grateful for that; after all, at their age, the only path to abs was dehydration, and he liked his boyfriend well-watered.

Nick didn't preen, exactly—he was too well-mannered for that—but he did accept the compliment with a kiss to Eli's lips. "That's just a nice perk. I do it for the therapeutic benefits only."

Eli knew how important the Masters' swim team was to Nick. Over the last several months, he'd forged tight friendships with a lot of the members, becoming something like a surrogate son to the older ones. Besides moving away from his dad, leaving the team was going to be the hardest thing about the move for Nick. Eli bit his lip, thinking about how much this guy was willing to do for him. He was so lucky.

Well, no time like the present to show his gratitude. "Hey, I got you something." He pulled a slim envelope from the pocket of his basketball shorts.

Nick's eyes narrowed. "We already traded Christmas presents," he said slowly.

"This is a bonus gift. A moving gift." Eli pushed the envelope into his hands. "Come on, open it."

A printout of an online receipt wasn't the sexiest gift in the world, but Nick's eyes widened as he took it in. "You already signed me up for the local Masters' team in LA?"

"Well, there were, like, five to pick from, but I found the best one. The queer one, obvs." Nick had landed on "queer" as a good-enough descriptor for himself the previous summer. Wide enough to encompass everything. "And this team's pool happens to be the closest one to our condo." Eli did not mind preening. He was really good at it.

Nick smiled and wrapped him up in another hug. "Thanks, E." The last year of long-distance dating had been rough, but it was moments like this that made the trials all worth it. He let his eyes close and hugged Nick back.

Nick's dad's voice carried over the lawn. "Are you planning on staying in Florida forever, or can we get moving?"

Of course Tian-yi was also there. No dad could resist a chance to stack furniture and argue with other dads about what should go where. Eli would have pointed this out to Nick, but he soon realized Nick was also a father and therefore eager to join in. Things quickly became the most competitive game of cooperative Jenga Eli had ever seen.

"See, Wen, if we put the couch up on its end, we'll have more room."

"That's BS. The couch should go right there on its feet. More stable."

"Not for things stacked on top. They will fall. Anyway, this couch is ugly. Nick, why bring such an ugly couch across the country?"

"It's got good lumbar support!"

That earned a few impressed murmurs.

Eli watched from a distance, doing his part by moving things onto the lawn for the dad squad to handle. He was only a semi-stepdad, so he was staying out of it. Maybe the desire to lift heavy things and put them down in the optimal spot would come to him if he and Nick ever got married. The thought twigged something in his belly. He'd last seen Zoe in person for the Wu family's Lunar New Year celebration, but now that Nick was going to be out on the West Coast, they could all spend more time together.

Max broke through his reverie by tossing a box marked BED LINENS on the crispy winter grass with more force than was necessary. "Why is it that I always seem to get assigned chores related to you every time I have a winter break?" There was no animosity in Max's tone, only wry amusement.

Eli shrugged in apology. "In my defense, it's happened a grand total of twice." A change of conversational topic was in order. "How are your photography classes going?"

"Fine." Max had gotten a scholarship to a state school; the pros of saving money had outweighed the cons of staying in Florida, but just barely. Eli had been Max's sympathetic ear all through the spring when Max was agonizing about the decision, taking calls between scenes on set. "I can't wait to use my art to further the corporate advertising machine."

Eli patted Max's shoulder. "That's the spirit. Welcome to the club, sellout."

Nick's dad's girlfriend, Mei-hua, came out of the house bearing a stack of disposable cups and a huge thermos. Her dog, a shaky chihuahua named Noodle, followed close at her heels wearing a tiny pink hoodie. Mei-hua said something to Eli in Taiwanese that he couldn't parse, so Nick gave up his spot in the back of the truck to come over and translate.

"She says it's chilly out; we need to drink something warm." Nick literally had sweat on his brow, but Eli wasn't about to mention it.

He accepted his cup of what turned out to be hot water from Mei-hua with a smile. He was not going to get on the bad side of his semi-father-in-law's lady friend. Nick also took a cup and sipped politely at Eli's side. Together they surveyed the chaos of the lawn and the truck full of dads and the assorted pieces of their lives being packed away by their families. Over on the loading ramp, his dad and Hank were arguing about the safest place for a standing lamp. The lamp itself looked dangerously close to shattering on the ground.

"Regretting anything?" Eli asked, putting his arm around Nick's waist. "Wouldn't blame you if you did." He drank more hot water.

"Nah." Nick slung an arm around him. "I'd do it all over again." He pressed a kiss to the top of Eli's head. "I already kind of did, but you know what I mean."

Eli smiled to himself, privately pleased, then glanced up and saw the neighbor's curtain twitching. A memory flashed through his mind: that same neighbor spying last year around Christmas Eve. He wondered what sort of picture they presented now with their hot waters and their arms around each other and their chaotic family running around like manic ants.

Whatever it looked like, Eli loved it.

He lifted his cup in the neighbor's direction. "If I wasn't holding on to you and this water," he said out of the side of his mouth to Nick, "I'd be flipping the bird."

Nick toasted with his own cup. "I think the message is the same, honestly."

"Cheers to the snoop next door."

"And a happy New Year."

ACKNOWLEDGMENTS

Regarding my dedication: Tony, the best parts of Nick and Eli are pieces of you. You showed me that masculinity is big enough for beauty, kindness, humility, humor, and honesty. You'll always be my best man. I love you.

To my family, thank you for giving me a place to stay while I wrote the bulk of this book. Kara, thank you for your love and patience. Hadley, thank you for driving all the way from Orlando to have a drink with me. Xio, thank you for driving all the way from Jacksonville to watch a scary movie with me. Dana, thank you for reminding me this book shouldn't be a horror story. Da-ge, thank you for your generous help in shaping Nick and his family. Thanks to Crystal Shelley for the extremely helpful authenticity read. To my agent, Larissa Melo Pienkowski, thank you for your tenacious support and for letting me quadruple-text you. To my editor, Lara Jones, thank you for the gold star.

I owe everyone on the Atria team a huge debt for championing my books, especially Megan Rudloff and Zakiya Jamal. So many people touch a book, I couldn't possibly know you all, but to the unsung heroes from the art department through sales, I am singing for you. It's nineties ska, but I am singing.

Thank you to all the booksellers and librarians who have helped get my books into the hands of readers.

Lastly: the acknowledgments should be a place to acknowledge things, like what's going on in Florida as I write this. In the time it took to finish this book, the situation has worsened. Huge swaths of the population are being terrorized: teachers of Black history, queer and trans people, people who demand abortion rights, librarians, scientists, college students, people doing anti-racist work, environmental stewards, people who fight for accessibility and health protections, artists and writers, literal children. These hateful policies express a terrible fear of so many of us, it's kind of pathetic. And as my high school cohort used to say: they can't give us all detention.

(Well, they can, I guess. Fascism loves paperwork. But my point is, there are more of us than they want to admit. Don't let them forget it.)

Personally, I take comfort in the fact that our struggles, though distinct, are all connected. I couldn't articulate it when I was first writing this book, but Nick and Eli's story is about that connection at its core. So thank you, Nick-not-Nicholas, and thank you, Elijah. I feel like we're colleagues and not creator/creation. I will miss you when I hand you over to the world, but you two will continue to remind me that there is love, and there is laughter, and there is living despite it all. For that, I'm immensely grateful.

To the people who got out and the people who remain: thank you for existing. You deserve to live life joyously and without apology, whoever and wherever you are.